MEMORY'S CLAWS

The Barsian Job: Part Two

FJ Mitchell

Memory's Claws © FJ Mitchell 2024

The right of FJ Mitchell to be identified as the Author of the work has been asserted by her in accordance with the Copyright, Designs and Patents Act 1988.

All rights reserved in all media. No part of this publication may be reproduced, stored in a retrieval system, or transmitted in any form or by any means, electronic, mechanical, recording, photocopying, the Internet or otherwise, without prior written permission from the author.

All characters and events featured in this publication are purely fictitious and any resemblance to any person, place, organisation/company, living or dead, is entirely coincidental and unintentional.

Cover art and illustrations by Nataly Zhuk

ISBN 978-1-7392469-8-3
Printed and bound in Great Britain
by Clays Ltd, Elcograf S.p.A.

FJ Mitchell can be found on her website:
www.fjmitchell.co.uk
and
www.authorsreach.co.uk

to my family,
the hamsters of the apocalypse,
the real mvps,

they take the world
off my shoulders
and let me fly.

Contents

Prelude 1
Chapter One – Joy to the World 3
Chapter Two – Knife to Meet You 13
Chapter Three – Power to the Powerful 23
Chapter Four – Lettuce and Desolation 36
Chapter Five – Where Nobody Knows Your Name 42
Chapter Six – Kennedy Vs Science 52
Chapter Seven – Only Port in a Storm 67
Chapter Eight – Mine 82
Chapter Nine – Anywhere but Here 94
Chapter Ten – Familiar Faces 105
Chapter Eleven – You Can't Always See the Flames 118
Chapter Twelve – Unfamiliar Faces 127
Chapter Thirteen – Serendipity? 140
Chapter Fourteen – Long Distance Communication 152
Chapter Fifteen – Broad Shoulders 164
Chapter Sixteen – This Ship is on Fire 173
Chapter Seventeen – A Funny Thing Happened 185
Chapter Eighteen – Hold Firm 192
Chapter Nineteen – Adulting for Beginners 206
Chapter Twenty – Ghost Town 222
Chapter Twenty-One – Family Values 242
Chapter Twenty-Two – Soft Cell 260
Chapter Twenty-Three – Playing Chicken 268
Chapter Twenty-Four – It's Not the Fall that Kills You 287
Chapter Twenty-Five – Task Failed Successfully 301
Chapter Twenty-Six – Task Failed Spectacularly 312
Chapter Twenty-Seven – Bang! 331
Chapter Twenty-Eight – Bringing Smexy Back 345
Chapter Twenty-Nine – A Dress Too Far 362
Chapter Thirty – Smoke on the Water 371
Chapter Thirty-One – Memory's Claws 379
Chapter Thirty-Two – Safety is Relative 393
Chapter Thirty-Three – The Dangers of Exercise 404
Chapter Thirty-Four – Stand 417
Chapter Thirty-Five – Withstand 431
Chapter Thirty-Six – Understand 439
Glossary 457
Coming Soon 460
Acknowledgements 462

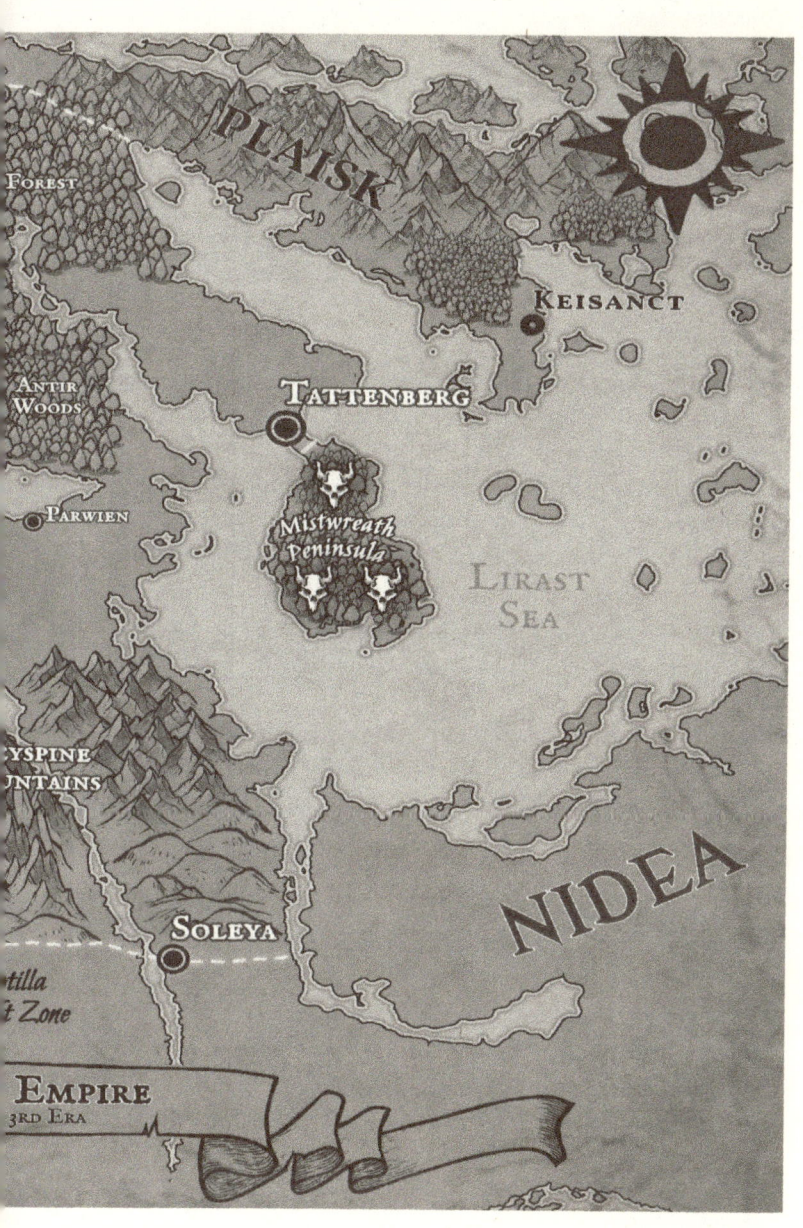

Introducing the crew of the *Warrior*...

Captain Philip Kennedy Jr Skilled pilot, talented swordsman, loyal friend. Utterly charming, but also as ruthless as a Labrador going through the kitchen bin.

Arke When your memories only start just after you sold your soul to a demon, you can pretend that's perfectly normal, and when that doesn't work... pretend harder. Arke is in Stage Two of denial.

Stabbington Bear The demon in question. He is endlessly supportive, waspishly wicked, and, according to him, emotionally available.

Dozer Arke's giant Rottweiler-shaped Hellhound. Utterly devoted to his mistress, food, and bedtime.

Ruby A seven foot tall, rainbow-coloured hawk Ornithol who was raised by cage fighting nuns. She bakes the very best cookies, and is definitely emotionally available.

Sparkz Ship's engineer, Kennedy's half-brother, purveyor of the finest snark.

Ellie The *Warrior's* halfling first mate, never afraid to speak her mind.

Urzish One armed orc, adorably savage and incredibly loyal to her friends.

Gurdi Ship's healer, ancient, wise, and wonderful. Only Arke has been aboard longer.

Porro Parrot Ornithol chef. In the battle of Porro vs food, food always loses.

Volk Great marksman, useful crew member, terrible mentor.

Gabbi Volk's long-suffering apprentice, scrawny and scruffy, but always in the right place at the right time.

Giro A snail-like Vonti, the slowest of the slow, but possessed of some useful weather related magic.

Klaus A soft-coated Tiax, hard-working, cheerful, and handy with a sword.

Prelude

"W‍E SERVE THE Autarch."

Dust carpeted the Faithful as thickly as the Faithful carpeted the floor at the end of the cavernous chamber. Their woven words of worship were the only sounds that broke the endless years of silence. They were dead, yet death could not claim them while He commanded their obeisance. Their leathered tongues rasped the ceaseless chant while their withered eyes stared unblinking towards His infinite magnificence.

"We serve the Autarch."

His bright darkness burned far above the Faithful as He watched and waited. He who was suspended in the hollow between always and never, the haze between reality and possibility, caged in the absence of the end.

He would be free. His will would be done.

He had laced His web meticulously. He had baited His lines and cast them wide.

He would be ready.

"We serve the Autarch."

And then it came. The briefest flare of energy from the world outside. The most sublime of signals. A challenge. A promise. That sweet taste on His lips.

The Autarch shuddered with a surge of memory. Rivers of static flowed from His bright darkness, crackling torrents of expectation that cascaded over the maelstrom of platforms suspended like stepping stones in the centre of the chamber.

"They are within Our grasp. Go now, learn more, prepare them. I await." His order resonated around His domain, yet He did not speak.

A grotesque creature slid out from behind His shattered throne. Finger-like tentacles clustered randomly on its obsidian skin, while arms that had once been legs hung limply at its sides, toes curling and uncurling in hesitant rhythm. Where a face should be, grey smoke shimmered over a shiny, featureless void. When it spoke, its voice was hollow, lipless words ripped from airless lungs. "I could send others and remain at your side, Your Majesty."

"YOU ALONE."

The retort smashed explosively into the creature's consciousness, and it reeled, gibbering backwards in instant submission.

A spectral hand loomed above the prostrated servant, one slender finger pinning it to the stone platform. "They must not be harmed. Stay unseen, seed their dreams. And bring – them – here."

The creature flickered as grey energy wreathed its form, twisting and warping it beyond comprehension before it disappeared in a hiss of heavy magic.

The throne room boomed with anticipation. Years of preparation were coming to fruition. On the wall in the antechamber, a lone clock began to tick once more.

Chapter One
Joy to the World

"You've surpassed yourself this time! Left as well-aged steak and came back as jerky." Gurdi's hand glowed with healing energy as she rested it on Arke's forehead, her touch gentle even if her tone was sharp.

"She's better than she was," Ruby protested, wings still quivering with the effort of her breakneck flight back to the *Warrior*.

"How, just HOW is this better?"

Moving with surprising speed for someone whose favourite topic of conversation was her ancient, aching bones, the dwarven healer threw open the doors of her potion cupboard. Grabbing vials from various shelves, she yanked their corks out with her teeth before mixing the brightly coloured liquids together like a cocktail waiter.

"Her pulse is weak, she's soaking wet, burning up, and by the feel of her veins, there's more juice in a month-old lemon!"

"Anything's an improvement on being dead," Ruby muttered.

"DEAD?" Clenching her jaw with an audible crunch, Gurdi glared up at the Ornithol's hawk-like face. "You could have led with that. You SHOULD have led with that." Then she poured one of the potions directly into Arke's ear, the next into her eye, and downed the last herself. "Stand in the doorway and tell me everything."

"IN the doorway?" Ruby tilted her head in obvious confusion.

"I don't need Kennedy messing up the juju in here."

"The what?"

"The restful healing environment. There aren't any books on the needs of the recently-dead, but I'm pretty sure a captain who's so worried about his nearly-mother that his voice has gone up an octave *isn't* one of them. So, when Kennedy barrels down the corridor like a squeaky sixteen-year-old, spread your wings to block his way. Then tell him to get the ship flying as close to the ground as he can and drink until he can't stand up." Gurdi pulled the curtain around Arke's bed before popping her head out to add special emphasis to her directive. "IN – THAT – ORDER."

She disappeared behind the screen, her tone softening as she talked to her patient.

"We both know I prefer treating you when you're out cold, but right now I'd feel better if you could peel yourself out of your fever dream and argue with me."

✕ ✕ ✕

After an hour of torrential rain, the track through the hills had turned into one big muddy puddle.

"Must be close," Arke muttered as she trudged through the mire.

"To pneumonia?" said the heavily accented voice in her head. "You should have taken shelter when the storm began. But no, you were too stubborn."

Her demon's role as mentor, protector, and pushy, opinionated bitch meant he was rarely silent, but after ten years as his host, Arke was skilled at tuning him out. She knew her passenger hated bad weather, although he wasn't able to feel the rain, the driving wind, or anything her body ever felt. However, embracing his self-appointed position as 'the exotically accented voice of caution', he viewed being cold and wet as inviting vulnerability, a state which he demanded she avoid whenever possible. Barsia was an unforgiving place for a woman on her own, even a Soulbound with powerful magic and an unbreakable demon blade.

"Yes, Stabbington, makes perfect sense to piss off the soggy and shivering person you live in," Arke replied.

"Remind me of the consequences…"

"Cupboards, compost heaps, toilets…"

The demon's response was a single phrase delivered at a volume that made her teeth hurt, and she smiled grimly. There wasn't much she could do to annoy a non-corporeal entity, but even the threat of leaving Stabbington locked in his blade form somewhere dark and lonely was enough to make her point.

"You know I need to get to the tavern while they're busy celebrating." Arke tugged her cloak more tightly

around her as the rain turned to hail. "And before they hear about the contract. The Full Deck have people everywhere and once they find out there's a bounty on their whole gang, things will be much, much trickier."

"But you do not have to kill this entire suit tonight," Stabbington muttered.

"You're right," she grinned wolfishly. "I'm really hoping there are more of them here than just the diamonds. Maybe a few hearts, a club, a couple of spades…"

"The Arke I first met was not nearly so cocky. <u>She</u> would have listened to her demon."

"But after ten years of your training, <u>this</u> Arke is far more capable and efficient."

"Ah yes, it is true, I am an incredibly good teacher."

"<u>This</u> Arke is also completely immune to your bullshit." She sighed as the hail intensified. "But not to the weather. Can't be much further to go."

She'd chosen the back route over the hills, knowing it was both the shortest and the least likely to be watched. However, after the storm had rolled in, she knew she could probably waltz up the main road accompanied by an entire marching band, and no-one would notice.

TWENTY RAIN-FILLED MINUTES *later, Arke quickened her pace as her destination finally came into sight – an old stone tavern covered with vines. It had once been a luxurious post house, built to cater to the needs of travellers on the primary route from Tattenberg to Volons, but since sky ships had come into the ascendancy, anyone with coin or sense travelled by air. Barsian innkeepers had needed to diversify or sell up, and The Rest Awhile, had done both – after a fashion.*

In an undeniably hostile takeover, the leader of the Full Deck gang had 'persuaded' the inn's owner to retire somewhere dark, peaty, and roughly six feet deep before adding the property to the gang's portfolio. It had remained in their possession ever since, for nobody in their right mind would cross one of the most notorious criminal organisations in Tattenberg. However, Arke wasn't worried. She wasn't going to cross them. She was going to kill them.

After vaulting over the rear fence, she headed into the stone outbuildings that stood behind the tavern. Slipping inside the only empty stable, she peeled off her soaking wet cloak and hung it on the hayrack before beginning to prepare herself for the task ahead.

She was in the middle of her warm-up when a glittering blade was launched towards her from the darkness at the back of the stall.

"Roll left!" Stabbington yelled. His warnings were one of the reasons Arke was still alive, and she dived away just in time to avoid the attack.

Another knife hurtled towards her as she rose to her feet.

"Flat!"

As she dropped to the floor again, the stiletto whizzed past her before slamming into a wall, its handle quivering with the impact.

"You don't stink like a Full Deck." The Soulbound kept her voice calm as she leapt back up. "So we don't need to do this."

A masked figure sprinted out of the darkness before launching into a flurry of acrobatics that whisked them across to where the first knife lay half-buried in the straw.

Arke stood perfectly still as her attacker grabbed it and sprang towards her in another series of rapid flips and tumbles.

"Left! LEFT!" Stabbington shouted, but his host didn't move.

As the stiletto slashed at her face, the Soulbound summoned her demon sword into existence, its hilt settling instantly into her grip, its black blade almost invisible in the low light. Deflecting the strike with a single movement, she watched the attacker retreat into the shadows.

"Look, I'm not interested in fighting you. Stop trying to stab me and I'll walk away."

Suddenly, a knife was hurled from the darkness towards Arke's face. As she sidestepped to avoid it, the masked figure leapt out of the gloom, spinning into what a surprised Stabbington referred to as 'an impressively athletic kick'. The impact would have been somewhere around the Soulbound's cheekbone had she not spotted the follow-up in time to duck the blow.

Before her opponent had even returned her foot to the floor, Arke charged, body slamming them into the nearest wall before stepping away.

"You're good, but I'm better," she commented. "What's your name?" The curse spat at the Soulbound by way of reply made her chuckle. "You must've been one ugly baby for your mother to call you that."

The almost unnaturally flexible attacker moved like lightning, delivering another high kick which caught Arke's wrist and broke her grip on Stabbington's hilt. Catching the black-bladed rapier just before it landed in the straw, the Soulbound's opponent quickly pointed the weapon back towards its owner.

Lips twitching with a quickly suppressed smile, Arke took a few steps backwards. "Nice shot. However, while it's great that this workout is warming me up, I really do have to get moving. Can I have my sword back, please?"

The masked figure began to whirl the rapier in intricate patterns, obviously wanting to demonstrate their skill. The Soulbound ignored them, paying more attention to her bruised wrist than the flashy display.

Her casual disregard clearly touched a nerve, and the blade was thrust so rapidly towards her it seemed as if the speed of the strike had made it invisible. However, as Arke well knew, the sword wasn't so much absent from view as absent from her opponent's hand. Sometimes, having a magical weapon that could be created and retracted at will was incredibly satisfying.

The attack stuttered to a halt and the Soulbound couldn't help chuckling at the masked figure's obvious confusion. Everyone knew weapons didn't just vanish. Object permanence was undeniable. Except, obviously, right now.

Before her opponent recovered from their existential crisis, Arke summoned the rapier back into existence and used its hilt as an impromptu knuckle-duster. One punch later, the attacker was on the floor in a crumpled heap and the Soulbound was sheathing her sword.

"Sweet dreams."

"You should not leave witnesses," Stabbington warned as his host swung both stable doors shut and bolted them from the outside.

"You're just salty because you had to play with someone else," she chuckled. "Now stop talking, we need to concentrate."

Memory's Claws

Peering into a window at the rear of The Rest Awhile, Arke saw a well-lit kitchen with a roaring fire in the grate and a weary-looking woman in a cook's apron scrubbing a mountain of dishes at the sink. She slid along the wall to the back door, wiping her boots carefully on the mat before walking in. Although the sound of her entrance had been masked by the raucous laughter and chatter coming from an adjoining room, the cook had noticed her arrival and turned to look at her with wide, anxious eyes.

Making sure to show the coins in her hand as she approached, the Soulbound placed them on the end of the draining board.

"Is that enough for dinner and a bed for the night?"

The woman nodded and shook her head simultaneously. Arke watched her carefully, noting the troubled look on her face as she glanced towards the door which seemed to lead through to the adjoining room.

"Too much," she whispered, "but lady, you don't want to stay here. The guys out there, they..."

"Don't worry about them." The Soulbound flashed a wicked grin. "They'll be very quiet."

Without another word, she tiptoed up to the well-worn serving hatch, opened it a crack and took a long look into the busy taproom beyond. Then, with a flick of her wrist, she tossed a glass vial through the gap and eased the battered door shut again. Suddenly, all the sounds of revelry were replaced by panicked shouting, followed by coughing and finally, silence.

HALF AN HOUR *later, Arke was sitting by the fire, a veritable feast laid out in front of her. It had been a profitable evening. Granted, the extra ventilation holes she had acquired from the men who'd been playing pool in the lounge – and were therefore not affected by her expensive enemy suppression elixir – had stung more than a little. However, Dozer, the most faithful of hellhounds, had been quick to respond to her urgent summons and although he was clearly aggrieved it wasn't yet bedtime, the Soulbound had persuaded him to take his irritation out on the gang members rather than her boots.*

Finishing her work with a warm sense of achievement and the warmer sense of a plentiful payday to come, Arke had dragged Dozer away before he started to help himself to snacks, and headed back to the kitchen. After almost fainting as a blood-covered giant dog with a furiously wagging tail charged towards her, the cook had grabbed a bottle of whisky and downed nearly a third of it. Once the liquor hit, nothing much seemed to worry her, not the hellhound, not the grisly mess on every surface of the taproom, and certainly not the bodies. She'd taken her time relieving the corpses of their valuables before sending messages to some nearby farms. Pigs weren't fussy about what, or who, they ate.

While the Soulbound ploughed her way through her far more traditional meal, she could hear the locals busily reclaiming The Rest Awhile from its recent, unfortunate career as a gang hideout. Her suggestion had been to burn the place down rather than clean everything, but if folks wanted to get on their hands and knees and scrub bloodstains out of the carpet, that was entirely their prerogative.

She was halfway through a hefty wedge of cheese that was pairing beautifully with some cold roast beef, when the back door opened, and a familiar masked figure appeared. They stood silently on the far side of the room, pointing the unmistakable blade of a stiletto knife directly at Arke.

"Come and eat," she offered, gesturing to the table. "Plenty here."

"Your ugly dog's useless." *The stranger's voice was deliberately muffled.* "I could've killed you while you filled your face."

The Soulbound reached down to stroke Dozer's head. He thumped his tail happily at her touch while continuing to chomp his way through a loaf of bread.

"Not so ugly he needs to wear a mask," *she remarked, before taking a sip of her wine.* "But just for reference, if I didn't want to offer you dinner, you'd never have made it inside."

The door slammed shut as the figure vanished into the night.

"You should have killed them when you had the chance," *Stabbington grumbled.* "I do not know why you are being so generous, but I do know it will come back to bite you."

Chapter Two
Knife to Meet You

ALTHOUGH TEMPTED BY Gurdi's directive, Captain Philip Kennedy didn't use alcohol to deal with his emotional response to Arke's full death experience. Instead, he used the *Warrior's* latest predicament to drive his thoughts into logical patterns rather than letting them wallow in sucking spirals of suffocating anxiety. He knew the 'what ifs' and vivid memories of the Soulbound's lifeless body in Ruby's arms had to stop. She was safe, and he needed to keep her that way. He needed a plan.

After he'd forced himself to concentrate on practical matters, he realised there was only one sensible choice: run, hide and heal. Without knowing who or what had attacked Arke in Theogenes, the safest course of action was to slam the engine controls to maximum and shoot the *Warrior* away from the city like a well-greased weasel.

He ordered the crew to remain at full readiness, watching for any sign of pursuit as they flew northwest on one of the main sky routes. However, as soon as night fell, he called for a ship-wide blackout. After every light was doused, he changed course to the northeast and brought them down to only a few hundred feet off the ground. It was a more vulnerable position than he was comfortable with, but Gurdi's instructions had been explicit – they had to go low and slow as Arke's body was struggling enough without altitude to thin the air.

He was confident that the *Warrior* could stay on its new heading as long as they needed it to. He'd chosen their direction specifically for its absence of anything bar rolling plains until you reached the edges of the swamps that surrounded the sprawling ruins of Great Barsia, the empire's ancient capital.

When the night paled into morning, the skies were clear. There was no sign of pursuit and no-one nearby. With a final check of the horizon, Kennedy headed below decks for breakfast and the crew-wide briefing that Gurdi had requested.

Down in the galley, bacon and eggs were served with a side of dwarven honesty. Gurdi's well-worn hands rested on the main table as she ran a serious gaze over the *Warrior's* crew. Rumours had been flooding the lower deck overnight and the ship's healer wasted no time introducing everyone to the plainest of truths.

"If you could shut up and listen, I won't have to repeat myself!" As the chatter in the room rapidly faded away, Gurdi continued. "All we really know about what happened in Theogenes is that Arke received a fatal wound and died – *but* is now alive. I didn't know such a thing was possible either. She's the gift that keeps on giving."

"Probably pissed off everyone in the afterlife and got kicked out," Ellie chuckled. Thankfully, being first mate of this particular pirate ship didn't require her to silence her inner bitch.

"I wouldn't be at all surprised," Gurdi agreed, and sipped her coffee until the crew had finished laughing.

"But this meeting isn't about what or who brought her back – it's about the now. Yes, she's alive, and that's a lot better than the alternative. However – and it pains me to have to point this out – being any sort of dead is, by its very nature, the antithesis of health. Arke is not going to recover in her usual speedy manner; this is going to be hard and it's going to take time."

Gurdi took another sip of coffee as a ripple of consternation ran around the table. Arke was a Soulbound which was as literal as a term could be. She'd sold her immortal soul to a demon in return for magical powers, longer life, and increased physical resilience. In short, she could stay young, cast spells, and take a punch better than someone twice her size, which was handy, given her natural ability to piss people off.

"Bodies are baffling machines that rely on many interdependent systems functioning in sync," Gurdi continued. "Arke died – her heart and everything inside her stopped. This isn't something that any sort of magical energy can hand-wave away. The good news is that she's a stubborn bitch and she's hanging in there. The bad news is that even now, ten hours after she got to sickbay, she's only slightly better than when she arrived. Every system in her body is struggling, her temperature is fluctuating and she's delirious."

⚔ ⚔ ⚔

"Another miserable night, another stinking tavern," Stabbington muttered.

Neither he nor his host were the biggest fans of Lower Tattenberg. Everywhere stank of smoke from the foundries and even if the sun was shining, its warmth never seemed to penetrate the smog, unlike the rain which always made it straight to the filthy streets and created viscous rivers that reeked of coal and rancid meat.

"Well, I'm not going to find Full Deckers in an art gallery," Arke snapped, peering at the faded name of the inn to her left before continuing down the road. "We're exterminating roaches, not the rich and famous. That was last month, and you didn't like that either."

"There are safer ways to make money than taking bounties and contracts."

"Of course there are," she retorted, crossing the street towards the next tavern. "Maybe if I'm really lucky I can find a job as a maid, work sixteen hours a day for a few pennies, and in twenty or thirty years I might even reach the heady heights of housekeeper! Or would you prefer I pursue <u>other</u> ways to sell my body?"

"I said MAKE money, not give refunds."

"Dead men don't need refunds."

The demon choked back what was definitely a chuckle. "Your business model needs a lot of work."

Arke stopped suddenly, her gaze fixed on a distinctly unexpected but undeniably anatomically correct sculpture that jutted boldly from the front of the next tavern. "Ah... Stabbington – I'm pretty sure we've found The Fighting Cock."

"And you said we were not visiting an art gallery," the demon replied, his tone dripping with wry amusement.

After dragging her eyes away from the strangely mesmerising carving, the Soulbound was about to head into the inn when she heard the sound of battle coming from inside. Listening for a moment, she slipped along the side of the building until she found a door marked 'Staff Only'.

Arriving behind the bar, Arke flicked a glance around the taproom, noting that it was empty of anything but furniture, blood, and bodies. From the ruckus on the floor above, she guessed all the action was currently upstairs.

"Someone has got here before us!" Stabbington growled.

"And? You did want me to play less dangerous games," she replied, running her eyes over the bottles below the counter and selecting one that looked to contain something that hadn't been made in someone's bathtub.

Sipping what proved to be a surprisingly fruity brandy, she took her time assessing the bloody scene in front of her. Bodies in all aspects of dead or nearly dead were scattered on every surface, with one unlucky fellow impaled with a lamp stand and stuck through the banisters of the main stairs.

Splayed on top of the bar to Arke's right was a man's bloodied body. As she poured herself another drink, he struggled back to consciousness, though it was obvious he would not survive his wounds. Putting the bottle down, she watched with detached interest as he turned his head towards her.

"He is not yet dead. So, technically you could take his mark..."

The Soulbound was already moving before Stabbington had finished his sentence, carefully cleaning the man's blood-covered neck with a napkin to reveal the tattoo of a playing card.

"Please..." he whispered.

Reaching a hand into her inner pocket, Arke brought out a notebook and flicked through it until she found a drawing that matched the design.

"Jack of clubs – you must be Urion?"

"Yes. Help me," he croaked.

She licked the end of her pencil and put a big cross through the entry in the book. Then, without hesitation, she plunged that same pencil into the man's eye socket and tapped it home with the bottom of her brandy bottle.

"More help than he deserved," Stabbington remarked. "I would say this gang were monsters, except they are far worse."

"Agreed. After what they did to those dwarves, I'd have done this job for free," Arke replied as she used her dagger to carve the tattooed flesh from the dead man's neck, "but gold is always welcome."

After finishing her grisly work, she stashed the skin carefully in between some bloodstained pages at the back of her notebook.

The fighting upstairs seemed to be intensifying, and she was just preparing to investigate when the masked figure from the countryside inn came sliding down the banisters. With a broad smile of recognition, the Soulbound saluted with the bottle in her hand before settling in to watch what she knew would be an excellent show.

"They tried to kill you," Stabbington growled.

His host shrugged and yanked her pencil out of Urion's eye. "By the looks of it they're also working this contract on the Full Deck, so the scrap we had back at The Rest Awhile makes more sense. Anyway, I'm just curious. The mask, the moves, it's all a little bit different."

"When this ends badly, I will say 'I told you so' and you will apologise for ignoring me."

"Now we both know that's never going to happen," she chuckled, wiping her pencil on the sleeve of her jacket.

As multiple gang members poured down the stairs, the Soulbound watched the masked assassin backflip off a wall to land on an opponent's shoulders before thrusting a stiletto into his ear.

"And this is why I have always told you not to stick things inside your ears," Stabbington remarked.

As the man collapsed to the floor, the masked figure rolled neatly away from his corpse and moved onto their next victim in a blur of flips and flashing blades.

"Or your eye socket. Or your... ohh... well you do not have one of those."

Ignoring her demon's running commentary, the Soulbound started to catalogue the bodies, putting a cross by each entry in her notebook before cutting off the tattoos and placing them in a pile on the bar.

A few minutes of grim secretarial work later, she was heading over to a man who had died in the middle of his dinner, when she saw two gang members working in tandem to tackle the assassin. After stepping neatly aside as the small group collapsed to the floor at her feet, Arke continued towards her destination, unbothered by the glare from the eyes behind the mask.

After removing a Four of Diamonds tattoo from the unlucky diner, the Soulbound was unable to resist sampling the bowl of mashed potato he'd never had a chance to taste. While she savoured the forkful of buttery goodness, she watched as the masked figure escaped from the hands that held them before spinning into a series of athletic counterattacks.

Outclassed by the assassin, both men scrambled away, but they weren't even close to being fast enough. The first was felled by a flying kick and kept down by the business end of a broken bottle while Arke moved to block the second man's escape routes.

As she spotted the masked figure sprinting across the room, she also saw a stiletto lodged in a body and ducked to yank it free.

"Sharp pointy thing incoming!"

Drawing her arm back, she launched the knife just as its owner leapt from a table towards the last living gang member. Arke watched as the assassin plucked it effortlessly out of the air, but then proceeded to miss the man-shaped landing pad by a painful margin.

After adding her latest tattoo to the pile, the Soulbound wiped her hands on a napkin and headed back to where the man and the masked figure were rolling around on the floor in a desperate struggle.

Tables and chairs were clattering in all directions, and Arke started dragging furniture out of the way as the weary combatants staggered to their feet.

"If you are not intending to kill them both, it is time for you to go," Stabbington commented. "You do not need another run in with the city guard."

"I want to see how this ends," she replied.

He sighed. "I can tell you how it will end – badly!"

"Probably." She grinned. "Ok, I'll leave when I've finished the mash."

Perching on a table, she munched her way through her delicious free dinner as she watched the grudge match creeping towards its conclusion. The assassin was oozing blood from several cuts and the man was wheezing heavily with every movement.

Finally, the masked figure broke through their opponent's defence and tackled him backwards, the pair of them crashing into Arke and knocking the bowl out of her hands.

Reacting instantly, she looped her right arm around the man's neck while her left hand carved his tattoo away. His hoarse screaming was a little distracting, but she wasn't about to let any amount of strangled yowling put her off her stroke. Once the job was done, she released him and watched them both fall to the floor, where the suddenly reinvigorated assassin ground their opponent's face into the fallen mashed potato.

Setting off towards the bar, Arke slid the last piece of skin onto the pile, grabbed her bottle of brandy, and left through the staff door just as the masked figure finally finished their job on the now tattoo-less bandit.

However, her evening was not yet over. The instant she stepped outside, Stabbington yelled a warning, and she threw herself to the side as an arrow flew straight towards her. The bottle smashed on the wall as she dived away from a second shot, and she looked down at it with an exasperated expression.

"THIS IS THE TATTENBERG MILITIA! SURRENDER OR DIE!"

A group of soldiers stepped from the shadows as the shouting of orders and clattering of horses' hooves heralded the arrival of yet more guardsmen. Arke sighed heavily and turned her attention to the five men striding towards her, swords raised.

She whistled once, then smiled as she heard an answering growl from an alleyway to her left. Dozer stepped into view, stopping only briefly for a big stretch before launching from a stiff-legged walk into a full gallop, his glowing eyes fixed on the soldiers.

Faced with an unnaturally large Rottweiler whose hot breath reeked of rancid takeaway, the men turned and sprinted for the safety of their colleagues. The Soulbound hurried in the opposite direction, wrinkling her nose as her hellhound rejoined her, his tongue lolling and his tail thrashing.

"You stink! Have you been in the bins again? How many times have we talked about this?"

Suddenly, a stiletto sliced through the air and carved a thin line across the back of her neck. One hand to the wound, she turned to face the masked assassin who was lurking in the shadows behind the tavern building. With a disappointed shake of her head, Arke picked up the knife and tucked it into her belt.

"Consider it confiscated."

Chapter Three
Power to the Powerful

THANKFULLY FOR KENNEDY'S stress levels and the completely unrelated hourly drills that had been testing his crew's ability to tolerate their captain, Gurdi's breakfast-time report on the third day was mostly good news. Arke's temperature was now holding steady, and when she'd been awake she'd been more or less lucid. The healer was feeling more confident about her patient's long-term recovery, but reminded everyone that her general instructions had not changed. The Soulbound must be constantly supervised, supplied with a diet of healthy food, and surrounded by positive energy.

"That last part will be easy with Arke's *radiant* disposition." Sparkz, the ship's engineer, the captain's brother, and the undisputed king of droll remarks, sat back in his chair with a satisfied grin as the room erupted in laughter.

Gurdi reached for her coffee with tired, shaky hands.

"You need some rest. I could sit with her while you sleep," Kennedy offered.

"So can I," Ruby added. "We could take turns?"

With a weary smile, the healer agreed, before informing them that Arke had to have frequent doses of what the dwarf described as 'vile-tasting gloop'. It would speed the healing process exponentially, but tasted, smelt, and tickled the back of the tongue like concentrated frog vomit. In her experience a good nurse/bad nurse situation often worked best, so one of them would need to shoulder that particular responsibility. Ruby's birdlike yellow eyes tracked expectantly to Kennedy, and he nodded, but remarked that if he was to be the patsy, he assumed they'd chip in for full body armour.

"She's very weak!" the healer chided, wagging a wrinkled finger at him.

Kennedy wasn't fooled. He'd known Gurdi all his life and would have seen through her mock innocence even if her deep-set brown eyes weren't almost being squeezed shut by the laughter lines around them. "You could do it yourself then. That's right, just smile and walk away!"

"You can take the day shift, captain," Ruby suggested. "I don't mind staying up."

"Is there a joke about a night owl in there?"

"Depends how brave you are," she replied.

It was never easy to read the Ornithol's expression and Kennedy wasn't sure if she was about to laugh or rap her beak on the top of his skull.

"Well, I am the one on potion duty."

"She said brave, not stupid," Sparkz grinned. "Thoughts and prayers, brother, thoughts and prayers."

Gurdi was already at the door, covering her mouth as she yawned. "I don't know why you're all so dramatic when she spends most of her time in dreamland."

✗ ✗ ✗

THE SOULBOUND WAS panting with exertion as she fled through the forest. The headquarters of the Full Deck gang was only a quarter of a mile behind her, but she felt like she'd been running for hours. However, she was painfully aware that her creeping exhaustion was more to do with the giant lizard-related gash in her sword arm than any lack of fitness. She'd tried to apply a wound closing ointment as she ran, but even when the bleeding finally stopped, the damage was so extensive that she couldn't hold on to Stabbington.

"I told you there were too many!" he roared. "If you had listened to me, you would not have been captured and thrown to their pet!"

Arke stumbled, then hauled herself back up on a tree trunk before looking around with a frown. "I swear I just heard something."

"We are being pursued, of course you are hearing things!"

"No, it's closer than that. Shut up and listen!"

After a long moment of utter silence, the unmistakable sound of excited hounds echoed amongst the trees, and she started running again.

"If they use dogs, then so can we." Stabbington moderated his tone to something more persuasive. "Should I call Dozer? I'm sure he misses you."

"<u>No</u> – <u>magic</u>." The Soulbound leapt over a ditch and grimaced as the landing jarred her injured arm.

The demon sighed. "There is no need to be so dramatic just because I made this joke or that joke."

"It wasn't a joke – you're a dick." She snapped her head to the left as she caught sight of movement in her peripheral vision, only to find nothing there. "Must've been an animal," she muttered.

"And if I apologise?"

"Go on then," she challenged.

"This is ridiculous! Use my magic or I will," the demon growled.

"Don't you dare! This contract has attracted too much attention already — the last thing I need is a Barsian mage-hunting squad coming after me," Arke panted, hurrying towards the sound of running water. A river was exactly what she needed to throw the hounds off her scent.

"Aha! You told me it was my fault, but now the truth comes out!"

"Doesn't matter. You should be nicer."

"I am a demon!"

"Being born in a stable doesn't make you a horse."

"A stable? There was no stable! I was hatched from an egg and had to fight through my siblings just to escape the nest, emerging onto a plain of ashes and..."

Ignoring Stabbington's far too familiar monologue about his life as a baby snake demon, the Soulbound slid down a bank and into the river below. Although the cold water numbed her wound, she was still unable to use her arm, so had to learn the hard way just why one-armed swimming was exceptionally ill-advised. Finally reaching the end of her endurance, she dragged herself onto the shore and lay there, coughing and spluttering.

With a sudden rustle of leaves, the masked assassin bounded out of the undergrowth and crouched down beside Arke, pressing the blade of their remaining stiletto against her neck.

"Gotcha! I'm Joy and I'm going to make you regret stealing my knife..."

Just to their left, a blast of magic whipped the air into a frenzy as a portal appeared. Joy's moment of triumph was utterly ruined as three ogres, bristling with every weapon that had a name, and many that didn't, charged through the shimmering event horizon and into her personal space.

WITH A GROAN, *the Soulbound forced her eyes open. Through a haze of pain and fever, she could see that she was lying on a filthy straw mattress and the wound in her arm was oozing some unsavoury coloured gunk. Lifting her head, she spotted the metal bars that surrounded her and, beyond those, the now maskless assassin sitting in an adjoining cell. She looked no more than twenty, her blonde hair cut in a short bob with a fringe that flopped over her left eye and a large scar in the shape of a number nine on her right cheek.*

"Arke, this is ridiculous. You are once again a prisoner of these disgusting Full Deck people and this time you are badly hurt." Stabbington paused, clearly intending to let his host take in her helpless position before he increased the volume of his self-righteous fury. "You will LISTEN to me now! Start tearing shit up – WITH MY MAGIC!"

"Shut up," she croaked.

"WHAT?" Joy leapt up and grabbed the cell bars. As she was unable to hear the voice that only existed in the Soulbound's head, she clearly thought Arke had woken up and chosen acrimony. "SHUT UP? ME? WHO DO YOU THINK YOU ARE?"

"You should have killed her the first time she attacked you," Stabbington muttered. "She is very irritating."

"Stop being such a grump. She's fun," the Soulbound replied. She was far too feverish to worry about strangers overhearing her one-sided conversations with the demon.

"Are you deranged?" Joy tried to shake the bars, but they were too firmly set to move.

"Yes, yes she is," Stabbington snapped. *"No sane person would have all these powers and not use any of them!"*

"She can't hear you." Arke croaked out a reply before attempting to get up and failing rather impressively.

"Who can't hear who?" Joy hissed. *"Are you hallucinating? Let me look at your arm."* Her sharp tone made the offer sound like a threat on the Soulbound's life.

"It's fine." Arke lay back, exhausted.

"It is not fine." Stabbington tried another tack, his voice softer and more sympathetic. *"Use my healing, at least you will not be in pain."*

"No magic," she muttered, welcoming the feverish sleep she could feel overtaking her. He could say whatever he wanted; she wouldn't be able to hear.

When she finally woke, Arke had to listen to both Stabbington and Joy moaning about the length of time she'd been snoring. After minutes of their complaints, she concluded that her noisy breathing had disrupted several hours' worth of the demon's attempts at meditating, and Joy was just being a bitch.

Unable to muster the strength to deal with any more of their whining, the Soulbound decided to go back to sleep, only to be returned to reality when a bucket of tepid water was poured over her head.

A heavily bearded gang member hauled her up by the collar. *"The boss wants to see you and your mate,"* he grinned, his face close enough to hers that she could almost taste his lunch. *"Reckon he'll kill you himself, after what you did to Ferret and Tawdry."*

In her current condition, it was easy for Arke to make sure her 'puddle on the floor' impression was on point. She had a plan, but she needed to reserve every scrap of energy she had left to pull it off. After trying and failing to drag her up some stairs, the bearded man simply carried her towards the main hall of the gang's stronghold, while Joy was forced to shuffle behind with a noose around her neck and her ankles manacled.

From his seat on a chair that had been painstakingly carved to resemble a house of cards, Ace, the unoriginally named leader of the Full Deck gang, assessed his prisoners with a disparaging glance. He shook his head slowly, the diamonds woven into his waist-long hair clinking together as he moved. "What a pathetic pair. There's no chance those pieces of trash murdered twenty-nine of my men in a week."

Bristling with ill-hidden fury, Joy immediately started reeling off a list of gang members and how she'd despatched them. The Soulbound looked at her in mute astonishment. While a power move like that was an excellent way to get them both killed, she couldn't help but respect the bravado.

As Joy was slapped into silence, Arke was carried across the room and thrown down almost on top of Ace's boots, which were covered in metal studs, each moulded into the shape of a heart. Wasting no time, he stood up and hauled her to her feet.

"After what you did to my bodyguards, I've got special plans for you," he hissed. "VERY special plans."

Normally Arke saved a pithy remark for this kind of situation, but today she was short on wit and long on fever. Her voice croaked a single word in response to his menaces.

"Goodbye."

Summoning Stabbington's blade to her right hand, she used every ounce of energy she'd been saving to stab Ace up through the stomach until the tip of the sword was just visible at his throat. He staggered backwards, making unintelligible noises and then dropped dead. She felt briefly disappointed with the anti-climax, as pest control really wasn't the same without dropping a killer line, but she could barely feel her own legs, let alone think of some witty repartee.

The instant Ace's lifeless body crumpled to the floor, Arke recalled her sword, just managing to toss it to Joy before a cluster of angry Full Deck members threw themselves on top of her.

⚔ ⚔ ⚔

*S*TABBINGTON'S OPINION OF *Joy underwent a sudden U-turn in the first few moments after she plucked him from the air. Spinning around, she swung him with power and confidence, decapitating the two guards directly behind her. Then, yanking the noose from her neck, she sidestepped the charge from another gang member and promptly fell over, since she'd forgotten she was manacled. Choosing success over failure, she swept the attacker's legs from under him, waiting until he hit the floor before plunging the demon blade into his ribcage and rolling away.*

"Use me to cut the manacle chain," Stabbington instructed. "Hurry, Arke needs your help."

As the heavily accented voice spoke in her head, Joy's eyes widened and she froze in a moment of shock so powerful that even the sight of a dagger landing inches from her face barely changed her expression.

"Yes, I am a talking sword, please save any personal crisis you may have from that revelation for later," Stabbington instructed. *"My blade is magical, so it will be the work of a second to set you free. Then you must get to Arke – they are taking her to the monster pit again."*

Another three gang members were coming her way, and their approach helped Joy past whatever issues she might have had with the voice in her head. She swiped the rapier through the chain, before charging towards the enemy and launching into a flurry of strikes. While the Soulbound was more skilful with the sword itself, Joy's strength lay in her mastery of movement. She tumbled like a gymnast while slicing and filleting with a brisk efficiency that not even Stabbington could deny.

As the last man fell, she turned and checked the room. Seeing no imminent threat, she sprinted over to Ace's body and removed his tattoo with four quick cuts before putting the bloody evidence in her pocket.

"This is NOT the time!" Stabbington's tone was murderously unimpressed. *"Arke needs our help!"*

"I'm sure it's what she'd want me to do," Joy replied and then turned, throwing herself through the nearest window as more gang members began to arrive.

※ ※ ※

THE SOULBOUND WOKE *briefly as she flew through the air, then passed out once more as she landed at the bottom of a pit, and was finally reinvigorated when a monstrously long, green tongue started taste-testing her.*

"You again," Arke groaned as she tried to sit up. *"If I had a florin for every time I'd been licked by a one-eyed, five-legged lizard with rotten teeth, I'd now be in possession of two florins."*

Memory's Claws

Apparently, the creature was a huge fan of suppurating injuries, but not so keen on the owner of said wounds, and growled malevolently as she spoke.

Struggling to her knees while trying to make herself concentrate on her exceptionally deadly lizard friend, rather than the exceptionally nauseating pain in her arm, the Soulbound hissed a reply towards its misshapen face.

"It was a draw last time, let's leave it at that."

The creature, who had obviously missed the module about 'the power of language' while at Monstrosity Elementary, swiped at its talking dinner. Unfortunately for the beast, its frustrated strike wasn't well aimed, totally missing Arke's head and slamming a single claw directly into her already injured arm. Having heard many of its meals cry out in agony, the monster's salivary glands reacted both stickily and vigorously to the guttural noise that burst from the Soulbound's throat.

As ribbons of acidic drool landed on her, Arke lost all ability to think rationally. Pain, fever, and exhaustion had eviscerated her self-control until all that was left was rage, vengeance... and magic. Stabbington didn't need to be in her hand for her to wield his power.

Seconds after its claw had slashed its way into her wound, the beast's body was immersed in caustic blue fire and it staggered away from her, making guttural noises of its own. She took the opportunity to use her magical painkillers while the monster was distracted.

The instant the flames died down, the lizard charged again, and the Soulbound raised a clenched right hand which sparked with static as she cast her spell. Bright blue light arced like a crown of lightning around the giant lizard's skull. It screamed in pain before scuttling backwards, trying to scramble for its den but, disoriented and battered, hit the wall and collapsed in a quivering heap.

⚁ ⚁ ⚁

"THERE IS NO *need to worry about Arke now,"* Stabbington's *voice reverberated with satisfaction.* "Only about the row we are going to have later."

"You — argue?" *Joy grunted as she fought her way through what seemed like never-ending gang members.*

"We do everything together; but yes, arguing is one of our specialties. That and killing. DUCK!"

Joy obeyed as a flail sliced through the air behind her. Without hesitation, she spun around and slashed Stabbington's blade towards her attacker, her strike neatly bisecting the man's arm before he'd even recovered from his swing.

"Thanks."

"You should probably move. If she is angry enough to break her vow about using magic, you may be collateral damage if she does not see you... yes. MOVE!"

Ahead of them, a leathery winged Rottweiler soared over the fence at the edge of the pit, Arke's collar firmly gripped between his teeth. Joy sprinted for cover as she saw the Soulbound's fingers turning blue with cold, frost gathering on her hand as she amassed her power.

"Faster!" *Stabbington urged.* "She always uses too much energy when she is angry. And she is incredibly angry right now."

Joy threw herself into the safety of a nearby hut before peeking back out of the door as Arke released a powerful spell over the mass of Full Deck members clustered near the lizard's pen.

"Together they stand," the demon chuckled, "and together they will fall."

Hearing some hollow cracking and splintering sounds, Joy watched, wide-eyed, as the entire mob froze in place, their skin turning white with frost, their expressions fixed in frigid horror. Any left untouched or just partly frozen lost their nerve and ran for their lives, sprinting out of the compound and into the forest beyond.

The Rottweiler lowered his mistress to the ground before licking her face with such loving force that she dropped to her knees.

"That idiot creature is far too pleased to see her, and she is too weak to push him away," Stabbington sighed. "Please take me to her before she drowns in his saliva."

Jogging past the flash-frozen gang members, Joy hesitated as Dozer levelled a warning gaze in her direction.

"Ahh... is he... friendly?"

"He probably remembers you called him ugly. Maybe apologise."

"Will he understand?"

"He is ugly, not stupid," Stabbington snorted.

Joy eyed the Rottweiler's meaty face and cleared her throat. "Sorry for... being mean to you."

It was at that exact moment that the exhausted and feverish Arke lost her battle to remain conscious. A second after he saw his mistress collapse, Dozer raised his snout to the sky and released a heart-rending howl that was so loud it could have broken windows.

Unfortunately for the frozen Full Deck gang members, as well as for Joy's hope of collecting their tattoos, the hellhound's song was also capable of cracking ice. With an ominous splintering sound, the entire mob fell apart, their bodies shattering into stalagmites which carpeted the ground like shimmering shards of glass.

Joy walked to Arke's inert body and poked her with a toe. "Is she dead?"

"Not even close," *Stabbington replied.* "Put me in her hand and I will shout at her until she wakes."

If the talking sword wasn't worried, neither was Joy. While Dozer lay protectively next to his mistress, Joy ran into the main building and finally re-emerged with her stilettos back in her belt and a bag stuffed with valuables. Digging out some medical-looking potions, Joy quickly bored of trying to decipher the labels and simply started to empty them over the Soulbound's face.

Spluttering into wakefulness, Arke tried to move, then groaned and croaked exactly three words, the second of which was 'off' and the last, 'Stabbington'.

"I thought he was kidding about the shouting," *Joy commented, pulling a bottle of cloudy looking alcohol from her bag and taking a swig before handing it to the Soulbound.* "Your sword is full on savage."

After downing almost a third of the bottle, a somewhat reinvigorated Arke handed it back. "Is there a word for angry-smug? There ought to be. That's what he is, and he needs to learn to shut up before I find a hole and bury him in it."

"Annnnyway..." *Joy interrupted the Soulbound's rapidly escalating rant.* "Let's get out of this shithole. I know a really terrible doctor. I'm sure he can save your leg."

"But it's my arm."

"Yeah," *she grinned,* "he's a really terrible doctor."

Chapter Four
Lettuce and Desolation

KENNEDY'S POTION ADMINISTRATION job had been easy when Arke was too tired to argue. However, it wasn't long before she started feeling a little better. She was still exhausted, but less to the point of compliance than the zone of irrational irritation. She didn't want healthy food, she didn't want to stay in bed, she didn't want to talk, she didn't want to be watched over and she did NOT want those disgusting potions. Things became somewhat tricky for Kennedy – she was too weak to get up, too headstrong to be left alone, and too bad tempered to inflict on anyone else.

Finally, he had a brainwave, offering to read to her from the only book he owned. Since she'd never read the tale of the last dragon in the whole world, his suggestion did the trick beautifully. The promise of being carried away into another reality one chapter at a time was enough to keep the *im*-patient as compliant as possible, given the circumstances. It didn't stop Kennedy learning never to leave anything that could be thrown at him within reaching distance of Arke's bed, but it did make her convalescence easier to bear.

※ ※ ※

ONE RAINY EVENING, around twelve days post Theogenes, Kennedy hurried into Arke's cabin with her dinner, his clothes already partly soaked just from running across the deck to her door.

"Everything's getting a good wash tonight," he smiled. "How are we doing?"

The Soulbound scowled. "Fantastic."

Gurdi didn't even look up from the table where she was writing notes in her treatment diary. "Patient's mood has not improved."

"Healer has the bedside manner of a necromancer." Arke folded her arms and glared.

"Don't threaten me with a good time."

"Annnnyway..." Kennedy slid the dinner tray onto the Soulbound's lap. "Grub's up."

Lifting the cover from the dish, she wrinkled her nose with disgust. "When can I have something that actually tastes of food rather than lettuce and desolation?"

"That's my great grandmother's recipe," Gurdi retorted, peering over the top of her wire-rimmed glasses.

"Was she a cast-iron bitch too?"

"Well, she wasn't quite in *your* league." The dwarf stood up, shut her book with a snap, and nodded to Kennedy. "Have a *lovely* evening."

The atmosphere in the room was somewhere north of glacial as Kennedy poured Arke a mug of herbal tea while she glared at her dinner.

"I could smell steak cooking earlier. Expect you had baked potatoes too." She sighed and swirled her spoon around the bowl of flaccid vegetables. "Even Porro can't mess that up."

"Actually, we had mash."

"Way to kick me when I'm down! You know that's my favourite."

"Ahh..." Kennedy hurried to extricate his foot from his mouth before things escalated. "We're out of butter so it wasn't that great."

"Still better than this." Digging out a misshapen lump from the yellowish stew, the Soulbound took a moment to examine it before taking a tiny bite. Face suddenly contorting with disgust, she dropped the spoon with a tepid splash and slammed the cover over the bowl.

"Go to the stores and dump every single vegetable you see over the side! And if it's fennel, *do it twice*!"

"I wish I could." Kennedy removed the tray and sat down in the chair next to her bed. "But I do have something to cheer you up – Ruby's been baking again." Easing a bag of biscuits from his inner pocket, he dangled the sugary-sweet mood enhancers in Arke's eyeline. "She told everyone that she needs extra energy before her moult, but I'm pretty sure she's making them for you. I can personally confirm their deliciousness – and that I'm willing to risk Gurdi's wrath by 'accidentally' dropping these in your lap."

"What's the catch?" Arke's eyes were fixed on the perfectly round, golden biscuits, each dusted with a light coating of sugar and marked with exactly two pricks from a fork.

"Maybe *you* can tell *me* a story tonight?"

"Once there was an evil courgette..."

He grinned. "As much as I want to know how that goes, no. How about my favourite one... Do you remember?"

She froze. Even if she hadn't remembered, she knew what tale he was going to request just by the awkwardly earnest expression on his face. He'd looked exactly the same ten years ago when he'd first asked to hear it. She couldn't deny that look then, when the last thing she'd wanted to do was explore happy memories, and she knew she wouldn't now.

Back then, he'd been a scrawny teenager, all head, hands, feet, and monosyllabic attitude. He'd barely looked her in the eye for months. Yet he'd been the purpose that had kept her going when she was desperate for everything to end. She'd promised her friends that she would take care of their son and nothing in the world, not even her own terrible grief, would make her break her word.

She'd had no idea that young Philip knew what had really happened to his parents. He'd never been involved in the hushed discussions – he'd never been told that a 'buy now, pay later' agreement that Joy and Philip Kennedy senior had made when he was a baby had come back to haunt them.

He hadn't heard them tell Arke that the payment was a job, but it was one they would never, ever do.

He hadn't heard her begging them to tell her what it was so she could do it in their place, no matter what blame or guilt was attached.

He hadn't heard them read the message reminding them the terms of the agreement were terminal – that if they didn't comply it wouldn't only be them who would forfeit; it would also be their teenaged son.

The Soulbound knew she'd been too wrapped in worry to think he might notice their attempts to evade the enforcer. They'd exhausted every avenue, every chance, and every location, but the threatening messages had kept coming. Young Philip hadn't heard the final argument because there hadn't been one. They all knew there was no other answer. There was only one way to break the contract. Two deaths were always going to be better than three, and they trusted no-one else to do it but Arke.

As young Philip had returned to the ship that terrible evening, she'd given him a letter from his parents that told him of their sudden decision to retire to a life of complete solitude. They'd written that he was under Arke's guardianship but explained that once he'd gained enough experience, their vessel, the *Warrior*, was all his. In the last sentence they'd sent all their love and promised they'd be watching from a distance as he stepped out from their shadows to become his own man.

Kennedy had been an adult before he'd told Arke his truth. On that dreadful night he'd finished his errands early and spotted her leaving his parents' house by a side door. He'd gone inside and seen it all; the last meal, the sleeping potions, the bodies of his mother and father clasping hands as they lay on blood-soaked sheets.

Back then, the Soulbound had been so consumed by her own pain that she assumed his dark moods and glowering silences were down to the letter which had changed his life. It had been months before young Philip had started to engage with her properly again.

She hadn't realised how much she'd missed his company until the moment he'd approached her with the same awkwardly earnest expression on his face that he wore as he dangled Ruby's butter cookies in her eyeline.

"Why have you asked me to tell you that story now?" she queried. "You haven't for years."

He shrugged "Just popped into my head, I guess."

"A coincidence, of course," Stabbington muttered as the Soulbound devoured the first cookie and held out her hand for the next. However, he didn't sound wholly convinced, and neither was his host, especially as she'd done nothing but dream about the past since Theogenes. "Perhaps it is because of the recent trauma that you all seek comfort in what once was? Ahh, let him have his story, at least it is fresh in your mind."

The demon made as much sense as anything else, and Arke nodded. Sugar still lingering on her lips, she sank back against her pillows and savoured the perfectly baked deliciousness of her rule-breaking snacks.

Finally, she turned to look at Kennedy, who was trying not to eye her with the anticipation he clearly felt. They both knew she was about to throw down one of the best stories, and his heady expectation was almost palpable.

"It was a long time ago. Your mother was wild. Like some sort of spitting kitten with these super sharp stiletto knives. When we first met she tried to murder me in a stable..."

Chapter Five
Where Nobody Knows Your Name

"Hey Sunshine, it's sunshine time!" The second after Kennedy opened Arke's door with a cheery greeting, a dagger thudded into the wall a few feet from his head. Without even flinching, he plucked the weapon from the timbers and slid it onto the nearby table.

He kept his tone light as he tried a more direct conversation starter. "And how are you feeling, say, for example, on a scale of zero to murder? Am I ok to come in after yesterday's... events?"

The only reply he received was a grunt from the direction of the Soulbound's armchair.

"I'm still sorry. I got carried away with the whole idea of an outdoor rest area. You said you wanted to sit in the sun, and I wanted you to be comfy and safe."

"It looked like a giant playpen!"

The unveiling had not gone to plan.

Kennedy had taken her displeasure on the chin, the nose and, well, his entire head, as Arke had thoroughly over-exerted herself smashing one of the newly painted fences over its architect.

Apologising profusely amid Sparkz's unhelpful puns about the Soulbound's use of of-fence-ive weapons, Kennedy had rushed to remove the nursery ambience while Ruby had calmed the patient with a bowl of forbidden ice cream.

"It doesn't anymore, and it's lovely out there now. The sun is out, the sky is blue."

"Fine."

Arke got to her feet with slow determination, her expression set as she forced herself to stand unaided. She ranted at least once a day about the inability of her body to heal itself on demand, about how she hated feeling weak and how she loathed having to be helped. Kennedy held her jacket ready, but the moment she straightened up, she snatched it from his hands.

"I don't need a coat!" She launched the unlucky garment away from her with a force that almost made her lose her footing.

Before Kennedy had a chance to reply, Ruby appeared in the doorway, her left wing protectively, if over-obviously, hiding something underneath it.

"It's a beautiful day, Arke! Praise Chromatia for blessing us with some more sunshine." She lowered her voice to a whisper. "And I totally didn't sneak you some of my special cookies from the galley." The Ornithol stepped forwards, slipping a warm and slightly feathery biscuit into her friend's hand. "So here you are, all the major food groups: sugar, butter and chocolate."

Over the past couple of weeks, everyone aboard had learnt that Ruby wasn't cut out to be a secret cookie dealer. The seven foot tall, rainbow-coloured Ornithol was not only easy to spot, but also a terribly untalented thief, and her crewmates had to run extremely active interference to prevent Gurdi seeing her filling her pockets with sugary treats.

Feathery or not, Kennedy was sure the Soulbound would relish the contraband. She'd had more than enough of all the wholesomely nourishing meals on Gurdi's list. He didn't blame her in the slightest, for when even Dozer, Arke's dustbin of a hellhound, refused a plateful of food, you knew it was disgusting.

Once the biscuits were finished, Ruby accompanied her friend out on deck and over to *The Warrior's Wrelaxation Wroom* (no running, no smoking, no dive-bombing, no heavy petting). It wasn't a room of any sort, but no-one else could think of a suitable word beginning with 'R' to use for an open-air comfort zone. Settling in the armchair next to Arke's, the Ornithol launched into an extended monologue about the beauty of the rainbow and the blessings of its god.

It was clear that the Soulbound had switched off after the first thirty seconds, her eyelids slowly lowering as Ruby droned on. By the time Kennedy approached, carrying a blanket, she was fast asleep.

"Perfectly executed." He smiled, patting the Ornithol on the back as they tiptoed away. "Maybe you can give her the medicine later?"

"I'm her happy place, you get to be the punchbag. Bye!"

Ruby scooted off below deck before he could try to persuade her otherwise. He sighed and shook his head. It was only another ten days before Gurdi said the course was finished. Ten days. If he survived.

"Hello? Help!"

Hearing an unfamiliar voice, Kennedy turned sharply around, trying to determine where it was coming from. He peered over the starboard side of the

Warrior and saw a man, suspended in mid-air by the wrist loops attached to a floating wand.

"Ahoy there, unidentified person!" he called back. "Are you in need of assistance?"

"Rewind... 'Hello? Help!' My ship had an unfortunate incident with the ground."

"He's got one of those fancy self-saving sticks we saw advertised in High Haven." Sparkz, the ship's engineer, appeared at Kennedy's elbow, his gaze resting on the magical lifesaver. "What was it they were called? Apart from expensive."

"The Drop Stopper?"

"That's it. This guy's clearly loaded, I'll go bring him in." The engineer grinned as he headed towards the storeroom where he kept his jetpack.

"Any excuse to burn a little fuel and look a little cool."

Sparkz fixed Kennedy with a disappointed stare. "Sometimes I question if we really are brothers."

Having strapped himself to his mechanical wings, the engineer zoomed away from the ship, making sure to put in a few extravagant moves before ferrying the unexpected passenger over to the *Warrior*.

After quickly securing his windswept hair with an orange ribbon, the man began greeting everyone he could see with a smile and a vigorous handshake. Dressed in turquoise shorts and a T-shirt that said *Another Fine Day Ruined by Responsibility*, he exuded nothing but warm congeniality.

"I love your shirt!" Kennedy beamed as his hand was clutched in an enthusiastic grip. "You must be in need of some refreshments."

"Only if it's not an imposition."

"Any excuse to eat cake is always welcome," Sparkz grinned.

As the first round of afternoon tea was served, the trio fell into an easy conversation. They discussed the weather, the ship, the way pre-packaged snacks were definitely smaller these days, and why cherry flavour tasted nothing like cherries. Other crew members gravitated over to join them and Porro, the ship's cook, had to enlist help to bring up more and more food. The only thing that stopped them breaking out the alcohol and barbeque kit to celebrate their successful rescue was that Arke was still asleep at the other end of the deck, and no-one wanted to wake her.

※ ※ ※

For his part, the Arbiter was enjoying his time away from the Gateway. Managing the Eternal Hall of Soul Allotment was as never-ending as its title proclaimed, but he viewed its infinite tedium as a bonus. Being a reliably boring cog in the divine infrastructure meant that the gods never bothered popping in. No-one cared if the Hall's manager was actually walking the floor or whether he was letting one of his two-dimensional facets take charge.

However, that was just a minor perk of his job – the major benefit was something both unique and incredible. In order to keep the Eternal Hall running smoothly, every soul ever born into the world was hard coded to trust him, but also to instantly forget him once he'd left. As a result, he was able to go anywhere he fancied, exactly as he pleased, causing exactly zero ripples.

This wasn't the Arbiter's first visit to the *Warrior*, and although he hadn't been aboard in a while, he knew he was going to enjoy every moment. He'd been told to keep tabs on the pirates ever since an unexpectedly dead Arke had ended up in Soul Allotment and had to be sent back with more than a little help from the gods themselves. It was imperative they stay safely on track, as her job, and the job of the entire crew, was becoming more important by the day. In theory, it would be easier to focus their efforts by telling them what the gods had planned, but everyone at the Gateway knew that mortals never thrived with such knowledge.

Watching over the *Warrior* meant he'd spotted the likelihood of things going sideways early enough for him to get onboard for refreshments before the show began. He sipped his drink and tried not to betray the anticipation that was wriggling inside him like an over-excited puppy.

The tea party was interrupted by the clanging of the ship's bell, Urzish's voice only just audible above it, her tone staccato with concern. "Sky Guard incoming! Captain, it's a BIG patrol! Never seen so many stinking griffins in one place!"

Kennedy, mouth full of flapjack, spat out a vicious curse before apologising to Klaus, the Tiax crewmember, who would probably be picking oats out of his fur for days.

Quickly downing the rest of his mug of tea, the *Warrior's* captain stood up, cleared his throat, and addressed the crew.

"Listen up folks, we've trained for this, so it'll be fine. Remember the drills, keep straight faces, cool heads, and they won't stay long." Kennedy turned towards the Arbiter. "Sorry about the buzzkill – we're about to be boarded and we need to make a few temporary changes to the ship to... accommodate their expectations."

"What can I do to help?"

The Arbiter was enjoying pretending not to know anything about the *Warrior's* unusual reaction to being pulled over by the sky police. Lots of pirates tried to outrun the law, others preferred to fight, but barely any chose the high risk, high reward strategy that this particular ship employed.

He knew that this modus operandi was the brainchild of Philip Kennedy senior. Like his son, Kennedy senior had been a pragmatic man with an easy charm and an innocent face. He'd been the first to run the bluff, much to the alarm of the rest of his crew – but they needn't have worried. No Barsian officer ever expected an illegal vessel to welcome them aboard with smiling faces and a plausible cover story. Over the years, the tradition had been added to, until the entire process had become as integral a part of the *Warrior* as larceny and alcohol.

As the Arbiter watched the crew manhandling flamethrowers down into the hatch like energetic ants, he knew *Stage One – Clear the Decks of Incriminating Evidence*, the first element of the Sky Guard drill, had swung into smooth and purposeful motion.

"Pretend you're one of us, it'll save awkward questions. Walk with me, I'll explain." Kennedy headed to his cabin and threw open a chest, hauling out armfuls of white coats. "We're a research vessel."

The Arbiter bit back the urge to chuckle and reminded himself to remain in clueless passenger guise as *Stage Two – Disguises* began. The pirates' sheer cheek of thinking they could slap lab coats on and pretend to be scientists had him doubled over with laughter the first time he'd seen it, but being in the middle of the scene was even more entertaining.

Before leaving his cabin, Kennedy removed the PROUD TO BE PIRATES sign by his desk and replaced it with a completely, totally, and utterly legitimate *Research Vessel Registration Form*. Then he slid the false back to his wardrobe across his cavernous weapon store before making sure his copy of *Skyjack Monthly* was safely stowed under his dirty underwear.

Finally, he returned to the main deck carrying a pair of signs and an armful of lab coats.

"Pop one of these on," he grinned. "We study meteorology."

"Meteorology?" the Arbiter queried, a frown nestling between his brows.

He'd been expecting the usual 'studies of migration routes', and the change of tack was worrisome. The ornithologist ruse had been wonderfully successful over the last year, with the *Warrior's* captain able to reel off countless species of birds, both real and imaginary, for as long as it took to bore his listener.

The Arbiter hoped Kennedy hadn't been browsing the non-fiction section of the library again. It wouldn't be so bad if he actually read the articles rather than just skimmed the titles. The last time he'd found some cool sounding words and stuck them together with smiles and lab coats, the *Warrior* had almost been impounded.

"Don't worry! All we need for the Sky Guard are costumes and technobabble. That's *Stage Five – Baffling the Police*. The plan's up here." Kennedy tapped the side of his head and winked conspiratorially. "We aren't actual researchers, you know."

The Arbiter felt nothing but relief that he'd decided to come aboard and make sure things went in the right direction. More specifically, that no-one got arrested and the unusually powerful mages in this patrol didn't find out anything important from a weakened Arke or the newly forged Irash. Events were in motion and their impetus must be maintained at all costs.

"Ellie, pop these on her bows." Kennedy handed the signs he was carrying to the first mate before turning to the Arbiter with a beaming grin. "She's the *Storm Warrior* now."

They headed towards the Soulbound who was standing, arms folded, while the outside relaxation area was packed away. With the main deck almost clear, the crew hurried below, passing Ruby who stood at the top of the stairs, handing out clipboards and protective goggles. *Stage Three – Lower Deck Preparation* was next – everything that hinted at their true identities had to be carefully hidden.

"Sky Guard? Really?" Arke's tone was heavy with a weary displeasure that only deepened as she turned her gaze to the Arbiter. "Who's this? Kennedy, how do you manage to recruit idiots all the way out here?"

"We rescued him; now put the lab coat on and try not to kill anyone," Kennedy instructed, clearly trying to walk the line between serious and pleading.

"Screw the Sky Guard and their disgusting feathered

ferrets, they always shit all over the deck and the bloody riders NEVER clean it up!"

It wasn't looking promising.

The Arbiter watched the approaching cloud of griffins, all immaculately turned out in Barsian livery, their patent leather harnesses effortlessly encapsulating the terrible aesthetic choices of the empire. Nothing said cheap and tacky more effectively than the sticky shine of the Sky Guard's mounts. Nothing except the uniforms of the officers which were the pastiest of blues and so dated they'd already come back into fashion twice.

Chapter Six
Kennedy Vs Science

"AHOY THERE, *STORM WARRIOR!*"

At the shout from the leading rider, Kennedy raised an arm and waved it in a friendly manner. The Sky Guard mounts, as with all the Barsian griffins he'd ever seen, were super impressive from a distance. Their iridescent bronze feathers wreathed them in their own halos, while their steel-tipped beaks shone with the promise of something far less beautiful. However, as they approached, the truth became disappointingly apparent. The creatures had become so rare after the destruction of the Grand Barsian Mews on the Night of Terrors, those left had been inbred for generations. As a result, what had once been a terrifying combination of eagle and lion now looked like a disgruntled chicken that had been rear-ended by a cheetah.

"SKY GUARD INSPECTION! STAND TO FOR BOARDING!"

"Standing to!" Kennedy called.

He pointed to Urzish, who stood at the helm, her lab coat straining across her broad back. She nodded and slowed the ship almost to a stop as the patrol encircled them. Three riders directed their mounts down onto the deck, where they were unnaturally quick to start availing themselves of the facilities. Kennedy had never understood why the Barsians trained their griffins to only relieve themselves once they had landed, until his father had told him the story of the Autarch who had his newest troops, the Sky Guards, form up for a fly past on his birthday. The entire court had been present for the marvellous sight; all of them gazing upwards as the griffin riders began their first, and as it happened, last, airborne parade. After that disastrously messy day, it had been decreed that any flying mount to release its biological weapons while in the air would be cut into strips and fed to its colleagues.

"My name is Sergeant Walden, and these are my associates."

Kennedy made sure his bright, friendly smile was on full view as he welcomed the Sky Guards on board. He knew he needed to be on top form, as, judging by the three who'd landed and the unexpected number of other riders flying warningly close to the *Warrior*, this wasn't an ordinary stop and search.

Sergeant Walden wasn't a run-of-the-mill Sky Guard. He was an older man, but not in a weak-looking way – his muscular physique suggested he bench-pressed his entire family before breakfast and his eyes had the predatory gleam of someone whose handcuffs wore out on a regular basis. However, he wasn't worrying Kennedy as much as the two figures still sitting silently on their mounts. He knew a Barsian truth mage when he saw one. To be fair, it wasn't difficult to spot them. They were always dressed in what could politely be described as overbearingly ominous beige robes, but those were never the first thing you noticed about them. Like all Barsian-controlled mages, they had shaved heads, but unlike the rest, any magic user capable of crawling into people's minds had their mouths sewn shut. Sure, there was a tiny space to poke pureed food in, but that was overshadowed by the hulking black wires that held their lips permanently closed.

As the sergeant clicked his fingers, the two mages, one male and one female, slipped off their griffins. "Hunt."

Kennedy tried to resist the urge to fold his arms, knowing that they'd immediately assume he was hiding something. Obviously he was, but the action would have been more about the instinctive revulsion he felt for the mages. He wanted to be empathetic, he really did, and his conscience twanged uncomfortably, as he knew he could not. Simply because of their innate abilities, Barsian law had given them a job for life but taken away everything that made them human.

As the inbred and overfed griffins pecked at each other's neck feathers, the woman began sniffing the air while the man stared at the deck below his feet, his bald head shining in the sunlight.

Kennedy couldn't think of a time where he'd seen a patrol with two mages, let alone well-seasoned ones. Normally the Sky Guard liked them younger, purely because they were more able to handle the physical exertion the job required.

That was perfect for the *Warrior*, as the more inexperienced the mage, the easier it was to disrupt their focus. The entire plan was built around distraction, diversion and, if necessary, giving the magic wielders literal headaches so they were unable to function effectively. However, Kennedy wasn't sure how effective those tactics would be against this particular boarding party, but he was also certain it was far too late to change anything.

"Welcome aboard the *Storm Warrior*," he beamed, as the sergeant approached him. "Tea, anyone?"

The Sky Guard was impassive as he swept a long glance across the main deck. "We'll try not to take up too much of your time; just spotted you a bit lower than we usually see ships and wondered if everything was alright."

Kennedy heard the female mage's footsteps as she moved behind him, sniffing the air close to his back with short, sharp sounds as if she were about to sneeze. He stood straighter still, making sure to concentrate on thoughts about charts, wind direction, and the mutton stew Porro had threatened to cook for dinner.

"Has she got the flu?" Sparkz asked as he strolled past, giving his mad scientist vibe the edge with the anarchy of formulae that he'd scrawled on his clipboard.

The sergeant's head snapped round. "She's just looking for corruption. In ANY guise. Who are you?"

"That's my chief engineer," Kennedy answered, as Sparkz walked away without replying. "Incredibly smart, but not great with social cues."

"I see. And what is the purpose of your current voyage?" Sergeant Walden slid a well-used notebook from his front pocket and started to write.

"We're a research vessel. Meteorology – studying the weather."

"I am aware of what that is, captain." Walden lifted his eyes from the page and looked hard at Kennedy.

"My apologies, sergeant. I'm so used to explaining it to people. They think the weather just – happens."

Memory's Claws

The Sky Guard's face was immobile as he wrote something else in his notebook before pointing his pencil towards Kennedy. "I need to inspect your entire crew. Every single person on this ship."

"Don't worry – we're all single." Kennedy chuckled at his own joke, even though he was the only one. "Sparkz," he called, "if you're heading below, please could you ask the others to assemble topside?"

The next part of his plan had various options, from mild to extra spicy, depending on the way things were going. *Stage Four – 'Topside'* was shoving the discombobulation levers to maximum, putting toilet roll in the freezer and holding on tight.

With a grunt and a nod, Sparkz disappeared below, and Kennedy knew he'd be passing on the escalation before heading to the engine room to flick the lever imaginatively marked 'Migraine Mode'. Put simply, it was a high frequency dog whistle – inaudible but guaranteed to give certain types of mage a headache.

"Is there anything I can get you while we wait?" Kennedy continued his charm assault, though it seemed to make little impact on Walden, who was looking around with narrowed eyes and writing rather too much in his notebook for comfort.

It wasn't long before Irash scuttled up the main stairs, a battered bugle firmly in one hand. With a show of taking what he clearly thought was the correct stance, he started puffing into the instrument, only managing a few horribly garbled notes before he just launched the thing overboard and stood by the hatchway.

"By the lllllleftt – MARCH! Left, right, left, right, left..." Ellie's voice echoed up from below.

In another life, the *Warrior's* first mate would have made an excellent drill instructor.

Then the stamping began, perfectly in time, perfectly loud and perfectly ready to disrupt the equilibrium of the mage as she stood by the hatch.

"We don't know, but we've been told,
On a petri dish grows mould."

One by one, the crew marched up the stairs and onto the top deck, lab coats swinging in rhythm with their steps as they belted out their marching song. As their show captured the sergeant's full attention, Kennedy was able to flick a surreptitious glance towards Arke and their recently acquired passenger. What he saw almost shocked him enough to make him lose every shred of composure he had. The Soulbound was actually smiling as she stood next to the friendly young man, who appeared to be plying her with sweets and engaging her in what must have been an incredibly amusing conversation.

"We don't know, but it's been said,
Scientists are great in bed."

The last person up the stairs was Gabbi, carrying a flag with a rather impressive painting of a tornado on it. Kennedy grinned with approval of the extra bit of flavour; the boy clearly had hidden talents.

"We don't know, but it's sure true,
We're the most efficient crew!"

"SOUND OFF ... 1 ... 2. SOUND OFF ... 3 ... 4. SCIENTISTS – HALT!"

Kennedy watched as the female mage started to walk behind the crew, sniffing at each of their backs without any hint she was struggling to concentrate.

"Everyone, this is Sergeant Walden of the Sky Guard. Please introduce yourselves."

At their captain's prompt, the crew took turns to stamp two steps forwards, yell their name, and stamp two steps back. More noise plus more vibration equalled more discombobulation for any mind readers. Sparkz joined the end of the line just in time, turning around instead of shouting to show that his name was scrawled on the back of his lab coat in what looked suspiciously like lipstick. Then the crew and the sergeant all turned towards the Soulbound and her companion. She was no longer smiling. There was a long, uncomfortable pause as a deck full of expectant eyes gazed at her, but she remained unmoved.

"That's Arke," Kennedy noted, "her field of study is ice. She's just recovering from being frozen, poor thing."

Normally by this point in any investigation that got past the offer of tea and biscuits, the mage's senses had been turned into porridge and the Soulbound could probably summon her hellhound without them noticing anything untoward. This time was different, and he was losing confidence with every minute that passed.

"Slowly, it seems," Walden commented. "And the other guy?"

"That's... Guy." Kennedy cleared his throat, before raising his voice a little louder than was strictly necessary. "Arke and Guy, can you form up please?"

With a nod, 'Guy' linked arms with the Soulbound and strolled across the deck with her anchored at his side. Kennedy wasn't sure he'd seen Arke arm in arm with anyone – ever. Whatever the visitor and his sweets were doing was nothing short of a miracle.

"Odd couple," observed the sergeant.

"Err…" Kennedy shrugged. "Opposites attract?"

The truth mage rubbed her temples before heading straight towards 'Guy' and the Soulbound who'd positioned themselves at the opposite end of the line.

"So, captain, what is your current field of research?"

"We… ahh." Kennedy cleared his throat as he forced himself to concentrate on the question rather than what he feared was about to happen when Arke came face to face with the Sky Guard's mage. "Weather. Yes. Some of our work is storm chasing – I suspect you saw our lightning rod at the front? My engineer is working on a new method of collecting energy to run the ship's systems."

"Lightning rod?" Walden tilted his head, eyebrows raised, with an expression that could only be described as triumphantly expectant. This was his 'gotcha' moment. "That's an aetheric lance, Captain Kennedy. Capable of slicing another ship clean in half – an exceptionally *piratical* tool."

"It looks terrifying, doesn't it? Thank goodness it was already disconnected when we bought her. Those sorts of weapons are illegal in Barsia, you know. Of course you do." He'd told the same tale so many times it was second nature.

"I see." The Sky Guard made some more notes.

"I'll be honest, Sergeant Walden, I was in LOVE with the *Storm Warrior* the moment I saw her. Smooth lines, sturdy build, and the hint of an indecent past – just like my ex-wife."

"Where did you get her from? And by 'her', I mean your ship."

Disappointed that the sergeant had expressed his disinterest in any ex-wife story, Kennedy told the truth. "Lucas Brothers in Tattenberg."

While the Sky Guard wrote that down, Kennedy had time to glance at the line-up, noticing Gabbi, the youngest of the crew, briefly distracting the sniffing mage from her route towards Arke by offering her a grubby handkerchief. His bravado suddenly disappeared when her head swivelled round and her dark-eyed glare seemed to scour his soul. Volk, who was standing next to the teenager, quickly apologised for the filthy offering and roundly berated his protégé, making sure that his voice boomed out at a far greater volume than was necessary.

The sergeant continued his questioning. "So, your field of study is weather, specifically storms and ice. Anything else?"

"Icy storms." Kennedy was trying to assess Arke's mood as she stood staring straight ahead while the mage stepped in close. He knew how the Soulbound felt about people invading her personal space and moved towards her, but Walden reached out to stop him.

"Hold it there, captain. You look a little worried about something."

"I am. Arke's been frozen recently and I'm not sure she'll ever be completely thawed. Blessings on her."

Ruby took her cue from Kennedy, quickly bringing her hands up as she trilled out a prayer, the movement making her bracelets of rainbow-coloured beads chime in discordant harmony.

The female mage held up one finger, her action capturing the sergeant's attention in an instant. She continued her investigation as she walked a tight circle around Arke, ducking as she attempted to look directly into the Soulbound's eyes. Kennedy noticed Walden's hand go to his sword belt and had to force himself to keep a friendly expression in place, all the while hoping something would happen to prevent the battle that was so close he could taste its tang on his lips.

Thankfully for the *Warrior*, they'd rescued the purveyor of the finest hope only half an hour before. Just as the two women's gazes were about to meet, 'Guy' cleared his throat.

"Being iced up really messes with everything. She's been struggling with her emotions since it happened, so I've been keeping her mellow with all the herbal tea I can get into her." He slid an arm around Arke's shoulders. "That might be confusing things for you. The herbs are VERY potent, if you know what I mean."

The mage looked at him briefly, her glassy eyes blinking a few times as she met his steady gaze, before dropping her hand and stepping away. As relief flooded over him, Kennedy felt his heartbeat start to slow and by the time Walden had finished making his notes, the *Warrior's* captain was back in control.

"So, to recap: ice, storms... icy storms..." The sergeant pointed skywards. "There aren't many of those around here, being as it's hot and sunny."

"Ah yes, after the unfortunate freezing incident we decided to come here for our secondary study." Kennedy's voice was as smooth as his lie.

Walden tapped his pencil on the pad, as if waiting for more detail. The pause lengthened until he cleared his throat expectantly. "Your secondary study?"

"Tectonic plates and their effect on weather patterns," Kennedy beamed.

"Tec-tonic plates? And the weather?" The sergeant echoed, speaking slowly as if dealing with a child.

He had an excellent point. Kennedy suddenly realised that although the line had sounded impressive when he'd practiced it in the mirror, it lacked a certain 'something' in real time. However, he was confident his tiny little oops could be fixed – just not by him.

"It's my chief engineer's pet project. Sparkz, would you like to take over? While he tells you all about it, I'll go and fetch our registration document."

Throwing his brother under the bus with a nod and a smile, Kennedy hurried off to get the framed certificate. It was typical of their recent luck that they'd been boarded by the smartest sergeant in existence; normally the Sky Guard would take any old crap as long as it sounded scientific. However, he wasn't worried, as the engineer could sell a warthog to a fisherman.

Nor was Kennedy wrong, for as he wandered back, cleaning the dust off the frame, he could see Sparkz holding court, using a pencil to point out the relevant parts of the complicated-looking computations on his clipboard.

"...in conclusion we have just finished our study of the correlation of wind patterns and volcanic activity under the seas to our south to ascertain if there is any possibility that those two effects could, in fact, act in a directly opposing manner to the currents. We found that it absolutely could not." Sparkz took a breath and looked the sergeant straight in the eyes as he added: "In layman's terms? You can't stop the motion of the ocean."

"Thank you, please step back." Walden had clearly bought into the engineer's earnest but deliberately convoluted explanations and just put a tick in his book before turning the page.

Kennedy could sense that they were so nearly into *Stage Six – Victory Dance* that he could taste the beer. Unfortunately, right at that moment of almost triumph, the female mage spotted Irash, who was sitting behind a barrel, eating a very strong garlic, cheese, and onion sandwich. She stalked over to him and sniffed. In mute response, he smiled and offered her a bite. She leant in closer, frowning as she concentrated, and the sergeant's hand flew back to his belt.

Arke snapped her gaze in the direction of the unfolding drama before taking a few steps forwards. Walden bellowed at her to stay in the line and she levelled a chilling stare towards him.

"Do you always let your crones molest young boys? He's just lost both his parents!"

As her words rang across the deck, Irash threw his sandwich on the floor and began to bawl like a baby. The crew stamped their feet and started shouting in support of their 'recently bereaved' crewmate. As the teenager's wailing grated the air far too close to her magically heightened senses, the truth mage stepped away and looked to her superior for direction.

Kennedy knew this was the chief operational weakness of the Barsian mage system; they were rigorously trained, but only for their one speciality. From an early age, any hint of independence was firmly quashed, and as a result, none of them could think for themselves. In so many ways they were barely more than magical automatons, blunted tools in the hands of people who didn't even understand how they worked.

"Obviously we'd like to make an official complaint." Sparkz glared at the Sky Guard sergeant, and as 'Guy' eased Arke back into the line, Walden jerked his head to call his mage away.

"I'm sure that won't be necessary; I'm sorry to hear about the boy's parents." The sergeant made another note while the woman returned to her griffin, shoulders hunched in discontent as Irash's wails seemed to follow her across the deck.

With all the activity, no-one had noticed that the second mage had disappeared until he climbed out of the main hatch and headed towards his sergeant. After one brief look at the man's notebook, Walden levelled an accusatory gaze at the *Warrior's* captain. Kennedy's smile did not falter for a single moment, even as he wondered who'd left their Pirates Union card on view this time. (*Give us your money and we'll give you this card. That's it, just the card. What did you expect? We're pirates.*)

"What's in the locked storeroom?"

"Oh! So sorry, completely forgot to mention the strange beast we rescued from an unstable situation recently. We believe it to be a crystal jaguar, non-native to this plane. It's highly illegal to possess such a creature, so as per regulations, we're taking it to Tattenberg's Central Institute for processing. Would you like a closer look?" If one could polish one's own fake halo, Kennedy would have the shiniest, twinkliest circlet in the history of counterfeit awards.

"That won't be necessary; but given the circumstances, we'll just take a quick dip of your surface thoughts." The sergeant's tone was light, but it was obviously not a request.

Kennedy kept his voice even as he replied, tapping the side of his head. "Absolutely, help yourself. Pretty empty up there though."

"Indeed."

There was no time to be offended by that, as the truth mage reached out to put a hand on Kennedy's arm, his thin fingers curling around the captain's sleeve like fleshy hooks. The instant the physical connection was made, Kennedy shuddered, revulsed by the uncomfortably intimate feeling of someone positioning themselves inside his mind. Being watched was a disconcerting experience, but being watched from inside your own head was a full-on violation.

"How did you come into possession of the beast?" the sergeant asked, one hand back on his sword hilt.

"It jumped aboard." Kennedy tried to picture the jaguar as it leapt onto the deck.

There was a brief pause before he felt words that he did not initiate being forced out of his lips. His voice was raw and oddly accented as the mage inside his head saw more of the memory than Kennedy had intended, forcing him to compromise himself with the fuller truth.

"During a battle."

"A battle?" Sergeant Walden cast a quick glance to his encircling riders as if checking their positions.

With an approach as silent as the big cat itself, Guy appeared alongside Kennedy and began to explain.

"The ship was attacked by pirates and the captain sustained life threatening injuries defending his crew.

During the fight, the beast leapt aboard and was subdued."

"Thank you." The Sky Guard replied in a warm, earnest tone, and the mage nodded solemnly, as if corroborating the story from inside Kennedy's head.

With a serene smile on his face that they hadn't seen before, Sergeant Walden motioned to his man to step away. "Everything seems to be in order, so you're free to go. Safe travels, Captain."

As the Sky Guards disappeared into the distance, the crew grew more and more animated. Once the lab coats came off, it was time for *Stage Six*. Beer. Lots of beer.

⚔ ⚔ ⚔

"They're still on track," the Arbiter remarked to the thin air around his cloud as he stood with a bottle in his hand, staring down at the *Warrior* as it flew on, *un*arrested and unconcerned. "It's almost time."

Chapter Seven
Only Port in a Storm

THE *WARRIOR* HAD only just reached the edge of the Granveldt mountain range when the entire sky, from horizon to horizon, turned an ominous black, and the wind started to howl.

Taking a horrified look at the apocalyptic scene, Kennedy made an instant decision. One that probably saved all their lives. He knew there was no evading or fighting the monstrous storm that bore down on them as if driven by the gods themselves. Striding across the deck to take the wheel, he swung the ship away from the rolling clouds and shouted down the tube to the engine room, demanding every ounce of power that Sparkz could coax from the aetheric crystal.

Kennedy and Urzish stayed at the helm as the *Warrior* took the wildest ride of its life. They'd flown through terrifying weather before, but this was something above and far, far beyond anything they'd ever experienced. There was no escape, there was no safe zone, there was no rest, there was nothing but the vortex of shrieking winds, the hammering of hail and the knowledge that death surged hungrily behind them.

For a full five days, the *Warrior* surfed the tempest's leading edge with the determination of a mouse clinging to a waving ear of wheat, its crew unable to do anything other than hold on and hope. Finally, after one terrifying moment where the ship hit an air pocket and dropped a hundred feet in a few seconds, the storm blew itself out. As Kennedy recovered from that sudden stomach-churning descent, he noticed the clouds were turning grey instead of black, and the raindrops felt a little less like bullets. The worst was over.

"Have you managed to work out where we are?" Sparkz called, stripping his oilskins as he stepped into the captain's cabin. "Just saying 'the hurricane's blown us west' doesn't inspire a huge amount of confidence."

"Similar to 'the aetheric crystal's loose in its moorings'," Kennedy replied, sitting on the edge of his bed and peeling his soaking wet socks away from his soaking wet skin. "Except my comment didn't convey the possibility of sudden death."

"It's all sorted now. Secondary circuits are back on, and Porro's cooking up some sort of food crime in the galley." Sparkz walked to the chart table and leant over the damp paper, spotting a large, blurred circle that had recently been drawn on the map. "What's that?"

Padding across the cabin in bare feet, Kennedy peered over his brother's shoulder.

"Somewhere in that circle is our position. Can't do much more than guess until I can see the sky." He yawned and rubbed a hand over his uncomfortably itchy stubble. "We've had terrible luck recently. Maybe we should make some offerings to the gods, just in case we've pissed them off somehow."

"Like they give a shit about grunts like us."

✗ ✗ ✗

UNLIKE THE REST of the crew, Arke hadn't been hugely busy during the hurricane. She'd offered to help out, but since they weren't attacking, defending, plotting, or scheming, there was nothing she could do that someone else couldn't do better. The *Warrior's* emergency protocols meant that all the energy from the aetheric crystal was channelled into propulsion, steering, and the most basic needs of its crew. As a result, her cabin was cold, damp and gloomy, so she'd spent most of her time in the galley where it was light and warm.

Peeling potatoes, pouring endless cups of coffee, and making sure the ship's violent lurches didn't launch Porro's 'Storm Porridge' all over the floor was better than shivering in the dark while her demon tried to out-sing the tempest. However, after the first night failing to sleep in what Klaus described as a 'crew cuddle puddle', while the air grew thick with the aftermath of oats, potatoes, onions, lentils, and the stringy brown meat that the Ornithol chef claimed was rabbit, the Soulbound was almost tempted to brave the cold and Stabbington's show tunes.

Five deeply unpleasant days later, her bed had never felt so good. Sure, it was chilly and a little damp, but she didn't have to share with anyone. Not even Dozer was invited during the first few hours back in her cabin as she tidied up everything the storm had thrown around, and changed into clothes which didn't smell of garlic, spilt coffee, and silent irritation.

Finally, she whistled her hellhound into existence before snuggling herself in blankets and letting sleep whisk her to a Joy-filled place.

She'd been reliving a memory of an adventure in Orbella where Joy had insisted it was a great idea to wrestle a ten-foot-tall troll, when Stabbington's voice disturbed the drama.

"Arke, you need to wake up – there is something strange going on. Wake up! And why are you dreaming about this anyway? Sure, Joy made a lot of money betting that you'd make it to the third round, but it took two months before you could even dress yourself after that over the shoulder suplex. I told you it was a bad idea, but you had to do it, because why? You could never say no to her? You were bored?"

"It was always fun," she murmured, hugging her pillow.

"ARKE – DO NOT GO BACK TO SLEEP!" Stabbington bellowed.

Blinking a few times, the Soulbound sat up. Her first realisation was that she'd kicked her blankets all over the floor. Her second was that her demon had been right. The ship's bows were angled downwards, not in an out-of-control manner, but more of a 'coming in to land' position. She hadn't been aware of any plans to set the *Warrior* down, but wondered if someone had spotted some storm damage in need of urgent repair.

Stepping out on deck, she shoved her hands in her coat pockets and looked around. The dark sky had finally given way to fluffy grey clouds which were in their turn being burnt off by a pleasantly warm sun. Patches of blue were appearing everywhere and as she ran a quick eye over the superstructure of the ship, she could see its timbers were already steaming in the slowly increasing temperature.

The *Warrior* seemed to have come through its ordeal with style. There had been enough time for the crew to lower her short masts and clear the decks of anything that could break free before the hurricane hit with full force, so there was no visible damage topside. The cabins appeared to be intact, and the engine sounded like it was running smoothly.

"Everything ok, Urzish?"

The orc stood stoically at the helm, her metal hand on the levers that controlled the pitch and the other on the wheel.

Arke's confusion grew as she couldn't see any obvious reason to land. There didn't appear to be anything wrong with the ship; Urzish seemed unconcerned, and Kennedy wasn't on deck. Normally, the instant there was even the hint of an issue with the *Warrior*, he was pacing up and down, fussing like a teenager on a first date.

She thumped a fist on his door. "Kennedy!"

There was no answer, and she yanked it open, immediately spotting that he was fully dressed and fast asleep on his bed. "Philip! Wake UP!"

She was just about to cross the room to shake him awake when her gaze fell on the chart pinned to his table and her eyes widened. There was something wrong. She brushed her fingers over the course marked in fresh pencil before turning and striding out of the cabin.

"URZISH!" Arke's shout echoed across the ship. "GET HER NOSE UP! WE ARE <u>NOT</u> LANDING HERE!"

The orc didn't move. She didn't react when Arke grabbed for the controls. She didn't turn her head or say a single word.

Nor did she let go.

"GET OUT OF THE WAY!"

Urzish's metal hand remained on the levers and as the Soulbound struggled to pull it away, she looked up into the orc's face. Her eyes were fixed on a point directly ahead of them, her expression blank, her posture rigid.

"I do not think she is in control of herself."

Stabbington's correspondence course in 'blindingly obvious remarks' had clearly been a success, and his host was about to unleash a torrent of frustrated abuse at him when the words stilled in her throat.

Silence was the only possible response to the reflection she could see in Urzish's wide eyes.

Arke turned around.

Directly ahead of the *Warrior*, and cauterised by a shaft of watery sunlight, was a single, dark structure. No Barsian needed to have seen it before to know exactly what it was. Before the Night of Terrors, the building had been blindingly white, the tallest in the world, and allegedly possessing five thousand windows through which the Autarch would spread his light over his beautiful capital city. However, it was hard to equate its majesty with the remains that squatted amid decaying threads of mist. Like a candle that had burnt too hot, the Grand Tower of Great Barsia was a hunched and blackened mass of twisted ripples. Its once perfect exterior was now a husk of puckered obsidian, its windows melted into stone, its magnificence cursed and pitted. Yet still it stood, a memorial of the cataclysm that turned a megalopolis into a graveyard and brought an empire to its knees.

After seeing the most recent plot on Kennedy's chart, Arke knew they were flying over the basin where

Great Barsia had once been. That was bad enough. To see the hideous tower directly ahead was something else entirely.

No-one had any business venturing into the magically tortured wilderness where the capital had once stood. Not only was it the resting place of thousands of people, but the area itself was poisoned – the heart of the old empire had become a mutated swamp of epic proportions. If the misshapen creatures who thrived in the wasteland didn't make you their dinner, the looters who risked their lives unearthing treasures from the remains of the city probably would.

Mutated swamp, ominous tower, hungry natives. The maths was simple. They needed to leave. And quickly.

Taking a step away from the helm, the Soulbound hit Urzish in the chest with the gentlest magical blast she could summon. Delicacy was not a skill she'd ever had to master, and the blow was enough to knock the orc clean off her feet, leaving her metal arm still clutching the lever. Arke made a mental note to fail to apologise later and grabbed the controls, spinning the wheel to yank the *Warrior* around while she cranked the metal hand back, setting the trim to bring the ship's nose up.

"What's going on?" Irash's voice sounded from the main hatch. "Everyone's asleep down there, I can't wake them up!"

"I don't know." The Soulbound looked over her shoulder as he appeared on deck, more than relieved that someone else was awake. "But we need to get out of here."

"WATCH OUT!" Irash's eyes went wide as Urzish suddenly leapt up and marched towards Arke, her bulk pinning the smaller woman against the wheel.

"He will see you now." Urzish's normally booming voice was no more than a croaky whisper as she crushed her crewmate against the helm, holding her there like a flower in a press.

"IRASH!" Arke shouted for help. The orc was a dead weight against her. She didn't want to use her teleport spell as the violence it left behind might kill her friend and would definitely break the controls.

Suddenly, Urzish's legs gave way and she slumped to the deck, revealing Irash holding a freshly shattered pulley on the end of a rope.

"Thanks." Arke slammed the lever back up and spun the wheel again, feeling the ship begin to respond. She glanced at the tower as it loomed closer. "We are NOT hanging around here anymore."

The aetheric crystal had just started to spool up to full power, the decks throbbing under her feet when, with a sudden jerk, the *Warrior's* engine fell silent. She jammed her finger on the restart button several times, but nothing responded.

"Arke." Irash tapped her on the arm. "Turn around slowly."

Doing as he suggested, she saw the crew had started to appear on deck, all walking like automatons, their faces expressionless and lips moving as if in prayer. Magic crackled on Irash's hands as he prepared to defend himself, but she shook her head.

"We can't hurt them."

"Ok, so what's the plan?"

Just as Arke opened her mouth to reply, she flinched, putting a hand to her temple and screwing her eyes shut as something tried to impose itself onto her psyche. It took a few seconds of effort before she threw off the heavy-handed attempt to climb into her brain, but as the spell failed, she squared her shoulders with renewed purpose. It was always easier to find the caster if you'd experienced their magic.

She swung her gaze slowly across the deck, focusing on enhancing her senses to try and locate the mage. However, although she managed to trace them to the rear starboard quarter of the ship, she wasn't able to zero in on their position. Whoever it was clearly had the power to keep themselves hidden.

"Plan?" She glanced at Irash.

It was obvious that even if he had one, he was too busy fighting off a personal hi-jacking to implement it. She watched him shaking his head as if a bug was trying to crawl into his ear before looking at the rest of the crew as they advanced with blank eyes and murmuring lips. It wasn't hard to guess they weren't going to be friendly when they finally shuffled close enough.

With increasing desperation, she began grasping at straws. Her methods of crowd control were too lethal to use on her friends, but she wasn't about to run away and leave them at the mercy of whatever was out there.

If in doubt, talk it out. That had been one of Philip Kennedy senior's favourite phrases and his voice popped into her memory just as she decided it was better to take a chance on negotiations rather than blasting the empty sections of the deck with ice and hoping to hit something.

"Can we help you?" She waited for an answer before continuing. "Sorry if we disturbed anyone, we were blown off course by a storm."

"He will see you now." The crew stopped in their tracks, expressionless eyes fixed on a single point, their murmurs perfectly synchronised.

She took a slow breath, deliberately blocking out the strange whispers from her crewmates as she addressed whatever was hidden on the starboard side of the ship.

"It's ok if you don't want to show yourself, but we're not here to hurt anyone."

"My master will see _you_ – now." An unfamiliar voice cut across the deck. The speaker remained invisible, but their words resonated with an echo that was not an echo, and a hissing static that interspersed the syllables like whispered lightning.

Suddenly, she felt the swirl of powerful locomotive magic, and everything went dark.

ARKE BLINKED AS her eyes struggled to accustom themselves to the dim lighting in her new location. The air around her smelt of dry decay and the only sound, bar her own breathing, was the slow ticking of a clock. As her vision adjusted, she began to see more details – the shapes of chairs and tables, paintings and tapestries – all contained in a long, thin chamber with walls of solid obsidian. Even if the Soulbound had any doubt as to where she was, the black stone confirmed it. She'd been teleported into the tower.

This room, with its unearthly glow that lit what should be dark, looked like a waiting area, similar to others she'd seen while 'visiting' the residences of kings and princes. She sighed as the irony of the situation suddenly hit her. In the past, the *Warrior* crew had performed elaborate charades to gain access to those places and their rich pickings. It was entirely on brand for her life that the only time she would rather have been anywhere else in the entire world, was exactly when she was teleported straight in.

One exasperated eye roll directed at fate later, Arke began to look around in more detail. Although everything was smothered in dust, the room was near-identical in form and function to every other antechamber she'd ever seen. She noted the extravagant décor and blatant displays of wealth, a standard tactic of the richest of rich to imprint their own magnificence on visitors. Shrouded under the dullness of time lay brocade, velvet, gold, jewels, artwork, statues, and under her continued scrutiny, not a single item looked to be missing. That surprised her, as she couldn't imagine why thieves wouldn't have ransacked the only building still standing in the entire swamp.

Lines of chairs flanked the walkway, their seats covered with the muddled bones of ancient petitioners, what was left of their clothes draped stiffly over the skeletal remains. She walked slowly past them, her attention drawn to the intricately carved doors at the end of the room. The blanket of dust which lay everywhere had threaded its way into every twist of the design, and without thinking, she traced a finger around the smooth channels chiselled into the wood. When the pictures finally started to show form under her gentle cleaning, she used her sleeve to polish the rest of the scene. First to appear was the delicate face of a wide-eyed fawn standing amid some summery trees, and she kept working until she'd uncovered both a wild-looking forest and a lake with a single island at its centre.

She was about to wipe off a coat of arms to the right of the deer when the door she was cleaning swung open, and a mutated creature shimmered into being directly in front of her.

As monsters went, it wasn't an overly horrifying specimen, greyish black in colour with vague purple tinges that suggested some sort of oily residue within it. Its cylindrical body was covered in a myriad of random tentacles, some woven into braids, some broken and ragged, even a pair that looked like the twisted remains of legs, the toes pulsating and twitching with every movement. The most disconcerting thing about it was what it lacked, or seemed to lack. Nowhere among all its fringed appendages was a face. No mouth, no eyes, nor any suggestion that its consciousness was focused on any one point.

Whatever it looked like on the outside, Arke recognised intelligence within, as she noted the obvious effort it had made to create its own grand entrance. However, if it was expecting a reaction from her, it was going to be disappointed. She'd had warning of impending activity from the moment the doors began to move, so instead of being taken aback by the reveal, she tilted her head to one side and assessed the mutant with calculated indifference.

The silence ticked away between them; time marked in gentle rhythm by the persistent clock. When the creature finally spoke, she knew for certain that it was the same entity which had controlled the crew of the *Warrior*. Not that it mattered, for nothing the monstrous thing said or did could do anything to increase her instinctive loathing. It wasn't that she hated mutants in general, but there was something about this particular one that she immediately despised.

"My master awaits. You will address yourself to me and I will relay His edicts. You will not speak out of turn, you will obey His every command…"

Without waiting for it to finish its list of demands, Arke walked through the doors and straight onto what she recognised as an extremely expensive elevator. When this was the hub of the empire, the font of innovation and the crucible of power, the Autarch's wealth and status had been flaunted at every opportunity.

She turned her gaze upwards into the skeletal tower, where thousands of shimmering lights ebbed and flowed, creating a kaleidoscope of colour and motion. Although the scattered ribs of rooms were still holding firm, the guts of the building had cascaded down, warping into twisted torrents of debris. Veins of the blackest obsidian wound their way through tarnished marble, as if liquid darkness had grasped the tumbling stone and crafted it into towering mosaics that loomed around the central platform.

Barsian society had grown stoic about the empire-shattering explosion that had happened two hundred years ago. The event had passed into legend and even become a generalism for disaster, no matter big or small. Lost your keys – Night of Terrors. Husband went out for milk and never came home – Night of Terrors. Wolves ate half the village – Night of Terrors.

That throwaway phrase couldn't have felt hollower as Arke stood in the heart of Great Barsia, the city destroyed by the magical explosion which had thrown the entire empire into chaos. As she looked around the ruined tower, the enormity of the devastation seemed disproportionately real.

The sudden movement of the platform as the mutant appeared alongside her shook her free of her melancholic thoughts. Blinking a few times as the musty air rushed past her face, the Soulbound squared her shoulders and set herself back on course. The city's inhabitants were long dead – she needed to stay focused on the living.

The elevator slowed smoothly, then stopped by an obsidian passage leading to a pair of ornate metal doors, their surfaces oddly unencumbered by dust. Arke took in the image of a triumphal scene – a conquering army in the foreground, Great Barsia behind and standing magnificently above it all, the tallest tower in Barsia. The same building that was now a twisted black lump in the middle of a fetid swamp.

"I am the Will of the Autarch!"

She looked at the creature with irritation. She knew she was supposed to be negotiating, but every time it spoke, she felt the urge to explode it with magic. Its words seemed to be stuck on variations on a theme, and nothing it was saying was getting her any closer to leaving.

She took a deep breath and marshalled her thoughts away from the tempting images of the tentacled monster shattering into tiny shards of ice. At least its ridiculous insistence on pomp and circumstance had given her an inkling of what she was about to face. Something arrogant enough to take the title of the old ruler of Barsia and use it to aggrandise itself.

"Doesn't he will you to open the doors then?"

The mutant seemed to hiss a little as it turned, but the metal doors swung inwards without a whisper.

A rush of tainted air poured from the room ahead, slithering over her face and through her hair, before whisking away into the darkness.

"My master, Cormydd the Fourth, Autarch of all Barsia, awaits."

He was not wrong.

Arke felt every instinct stutter, every inch of skin chill, and every breath struggle in her throat. Even the orange magic failed to ignite in the face of the overwhelming presence that was dust and time and longing, and cold, unadulterated power.

She knew this was not an upstart thief. This was not a mage who had happened upon this devastated tower and sought to become a false king.

This was Cormydd, the last Autarch of the Barsian Empire, the man who had been at the centre of the Night of Terrors. This was His domain, His throne, and His creation.

Chapter Eight
Mine

Faced with the unearthly crackle of power from the room beyond the doors, Arke fought a silent battle to control the only thing she could – herself. Instinct surged against intellect as she struggled to resist the urge to flee, fighting and clawing at anything in her path. Panic smashed its waves against her will, but she stood firm. If she was to save her friends, she must remain fully in the moment, not raging like a mindless beast.

As she fought to keep her focus, she felt a presence slide across her mind, carelessly brushing aside any defence she could muster. That idle violation was terrifying enough without it directing her attention to the cavernous humming coming from the room ahead of her – the chorus of dry, whispered chants. "We serve the Autarch."

The presence left her, and she gasped, forcing air into her lungs with frantic need. Her heart was hammering, cold beads of sweat trickled down her neck, and all her muscles burnt as if they were already running. She was losing the battle against whatever lay in this room before she'd even stepped inside. There was nothing in this place but everything.

"He will not be kept waiting."

She put her hand on Stabbington's hilt, desperate for some words of advice or comfort, but he was silent, and his terror radiated jarringly up her arm. She dismissed his blade instantly, feeling it disappear into her palm. If he wanted to hide, then she'd let him. She would have liked to do the same.

That acknowledgment of her own weakness finally galvanised her thoughts into a brittle semblance of control. Yes, she was frightened, but if the Autarch wished her dead, then she knew she'd already be a corpse. Clearly there was something he needed, and that might be how she could get the *Warrior* away from this terrible place.

She turned her attention to the mutant. "What does he want?"

"To see you."

"You're telling me he can't see me now?" She frowned as the creature waved its tentacles at her with what it probably thought was imperious command.

"He sees all."

"Then we can talk here. What does he want?" She held her position, concentrating on the only thing that mattered – the knowledge that the *Warrior* and its crew were just outside, and she must find an angle which would keep them safe.

"He is growing impatient."

"What does he want?" she repeated.

"You will accept His salvation."

It was such an innocuous sentence and yet it was entirely loaded with menace.

She paused for a moment, hoping the creature would continue with more practical demands. When it was apparent that nothing further was forthcoming, she answered in a tone that she hoped would not convey her attitude towards anyone who thought 'salvation' was a currency she dealt in.

"Fine. Thanks. Please free my crew and we'll..."

"COME FORWARDS."

"Look, I already said I'd accept it."

The mutant wrapped its icy tentacles around her wrist and launched a stronger attempt at magical mind control. Reacting instantly, Arke grabbed the twisted clusters of black skin and yanked them clear of her arm before shoving the monster away.

"Whatever rock you crawled out from is missing its ball of slime," she snarled, glaring at where she guessed its face might be.

The creature shimmered and disappeared into nothingness.

"Just tell me what you want." Her voice was quiet. "We're both aware I have no choice."

A giant spectral hand suddenly closed around her head, stifling and smothering her. This was not the mutant's ineffective touch – this was the master introducing himself. He flooded her mind with images of her crew in the agonies of death, skin being flayed from their bodies, blood pouring from every slash as they screamed and suffered. Then she was released, gasping for breath, and fighting the weakness in her legs that threatened to drop her to her knees. She would not give in. She would stand. She would endure.

"Do not question the Autarch. Do not speak out of turn." The creature reappeared, hovering to the right of the doorway. "He has shown you what will happen if you do not comply. It would have been better to let me control you."

"Never."

The monstrous hand slammed into her, launching her like a tumbled leaf through the doors and smashing her into the base of a statue. As the ancient sculpture toppled to the floor in a cloud of choking dust, the hand grabbed her again, this time dashing her body against a huge pillar.

The mutant appeared as she lay stunned, blood gushing from her nose and her mouth, the edges of her vision dimming as she struggled for life. It loomed over her, bobbing up and down as it spoke, pointing its tentacles towards a series of obsidian platforms in the centre of the room.

"He awaits. Climb."

The giant slabs of rock were suspended by nothing but magic – a set of impossible steps that led to the thrumming echoes of light at the end of the chamber.

The hand appeared again, yanking her out of the puddle of her own blood, its touch healing her wounds instantly. Arke cried out as pain was repaired by pain, the power forcing its way into her and smashing her body back together as brutally as it had been torn apart.

As she hauled herself to her feet, the Autarch's presence pushed against her temples. She reacted instinctively, refusing him entry, pushing the pressure away. His response was as immediate as it was overpowering. After a psychic impact that knocked her to her knees, she realised she was no longer in control of her body. Her head tipped back, and he forced her eyes wide open.

He wanted her to see it all.

He wanted her to know.

The grand throne room of Great Barsia had once been the place where the world bore witness to the glory of the Autarch. Now it bowed in crippled homage to the power of an unearthly light. The bright darkness that cascaded from the end of the chamber lit every corner, every edge, every angle, with the silken promise of damned eternity.

It crashed into Arke's senses like shattered glass, carving through the shreds of her composure and the tatters of her hope.

Her head was turned towards the slabbed staircase. The path to his presence.

"CLIMB!" the mutant hissed.

The Autarch forced another vision of the crew suffering his promised agonies into her mind before withdrawing his control.

"He would have you choose."

Arke stopped trying to calm her terror and used its energy to power every movement, forcing her body to clamber onto the first stone. He wanted her to climb, so she'd climb. She'd do whatever was needed to save her friends.

She jumped and scrabbled and hauled herself up each of the enormous steps, her fingertips bloody, her knees bruised. Her movements became automatic, her mind calming with the repeated exertion. And then she reached the fifth platform.

As she struggled to her feet, she looked up – and into an abyss at the end of the room. It burnt like a shadowed sun, blackness that was brightness capturing her gaze and stilling her body. Colours whirled and condensed in witless trails, pools of eternity sucked into cosmic comets which shattered inside an endless grey. And in the middle of it all, a figure, a silhouette, an essence, the presence. Cascading from himself and of himself. The Autarch.

She was lost. She was consumed by the shadows and patterns as they scored their way across her consciousness. Kaleidoscopes whirled behind her vision, the echoes of nothing blinding her as she struggled to comprehend the incomprehensible.

"If you wish your friends to live, you must climb." The mutant stabbed her lip with the tip of a tentacle until blood flowed into her mouth, the pain and the tang of iron hauling her back to agonised reality.

She fought with her eyes, making them move, making them pull away and refocus. She fought with her brain and her limbs and her lungs and her ears. She fastened her gaze on the stone, and she climbed.

The only thing that kept her body in motion and her thoughts from panic was the overwhelming need to save the others. Dogged determination drove her on, but even as she grew unbearably close to the top, she looked anywhere except where the infinite lay open, rippling and swirling with its terrifying power.

Breath burning in her chest, Arke finally hauled herself to her feet on the last platform when it disappeared from beneath her. She fell down and down, smashing to the floor with an explosion of pain as everything within her shattered and burst.

"Kneel in His presence!" The mutant's tentacles shuddered with furious emphasis.

The spectral hand smashed her back together once more, restoring her health but leaving her choking on the thick mixture of dust and blood that remained from her fall. It hovered nearby as she staggered to her feet, retching, and spitting out teeth that had already been replaced.

Taking a moment to reorient herself, Arke realised the origin of the whispered chanting was straight ahead of her. A sea of ancient robes clustered around the foot of the twisted throne, but as she looked closer, she saw not bones, but bodies. The shrunken lips of leathered skulls moved in perfect rhythm as the carpet of living corpses worshipped their Autarch. Time had claimed their flesh, but magic had bound them to their work. There were many things worse than death.

"CLIMB!"

With a stubborn set to her shoulders, Arke began again, walking back to the far end of the giant staircase and making her slow way upwards. Every part of her was ringing with agony from the brutal healing, but she was oddly grateful for it, since the pain prevented fear from overwhelming her.

As she rolled exhaustedly onto the final piece of obsidian, she tried to ignore the fact that she was lying on a slab of rock like a specimen ready for dissection. She'd been vulnerable many times before, but she'd always had a back-up plan, a clutch, a part of her no-one could touch. This time she had no way out, and nothing that could protect her.

She felt his attention slide across her skin and an instinctive revulsion galvanised her into action. Gathering her strength, she forced herself to her knees. She might have nothing, she might *be* nothing, but she wouldn't cower like a beaten animal.

The bright darkness was so close she could feel it lapping at her senses, but she refused its call and looked off the edge of the platform to the floor below. The nearest statue was one of the largest in the room, depicting a woman in stately robes, her figure oriented towards the throne. It was hard to make out much more than that as the entire sculpture had been hewed and mauled, her face half destroyed, bulging chunks ripped from the stone and smashed to dust.

"The Autarch must NOT be ignored. He and only He has..."

As the mutant's voice sounded close to her ear, Arke was jerked back into the moment with the sudden, awful realisation that she was alone.

Somewhere between the doorway and this platform, her demon had left her. He'd returned to his home plane before, but never without letting her know, and never when she was in danger. She'd been so overwhelmed by everything that was happening that she hadn't noticed he'd gone. She knew he'd been terrified, an emotion she'd never associated with him before, but she'd never even dreamt that he'd leave her when she needed him the most.

Rage hit her hard.

Rage without sense, without bounds, without the one presence she had always relied on.

She leapt to her feet, words tumbling from her lips. "I get it! He can kill me, he can kill my crew, he can do whatever he wants to in this place!"

And her ashes burst out from where she'd been standing, floating down to settle around her empty footprints.

Memory's Claws

Everything she was had been ripped into single cells, into dust, into nothingness, by one thought from the grey being suspended in his prism of power, alone in the bright darkness.

"I serve at the pleasure of the Autarch," the mutant hissed, backing away as, without a flicker of effort from the looming silhouette, Arke was returned to existence, her atoms slamming together as harshly as they had been torn apart.

She dropped to her knees in silent shock, planting her hands on the stone to keep her balance, trying to hold back the gut-twisting nausea as she shuddered with the pain of life and the horror of knowing that death was no longer an escape. He was inside her mind, her thoughts, her dreams. She felt him savouring every moment of her helplessness as he flexed his power, his incredible control of everything in this place. His silhouette pulsed with energy as his giant hand wrapped around her once more.

"Who – are – you?"

His question curled itself through her head. His voice twisted and turned, demanding, whispering, shouting, cajoling. She did not understand him asking something he had taken from her mind even before she came into his throne room.

She was Arke.

The hand slowly crushed that thought from her brain, and her brain from her body.

The Autarch renewed her life once more, only to take it again and again as he received the same answer to his question – the only one she could give.

She was Arke.

Finally, he was silent. She lay huddled on the platform, too weak to retch and too cold to shiver. She could feel him watching, could feel the static that crackled around his silhouette, and the single icy fingertip that stroked gently across her back.

"Please," she whispered hoarsely, lost in the depths of her own agony. Her eyes were raw with tears that had no time to fall between her lives and her deaths. She could not fight, and she could not die. "Tell me who you want me to be."

"Mine."

She nodded slowly, her cheek scouring against the obsidian slab. There was nothing but His will and she was nothing but His. He lifted her gently, wrapping her in the softest of breezes to bring her closer to Him, wreathing her in silence and calm as He brought Himself close to the shimmering rift between their worlds.

She hung in the air in front of the abyss, the horizon of bright darkness, and watched Him approach as blissful numbness settled through her. Nothing mattered, not the looming silhouette, not the past, nor the present. She didn't even realise she'd been pivoted away from Him until she felt the pressure of His touch on her back. Peace flowed through her as He slid His hands higher. Pain was just a memory as His fingers splayed to cup her face.

"Good." His voice was in her ear, His tone soft. She was ready.

The Autarch pushed through the surface of His abyssal realm and threw Himself into her. This was not possession, but an instant interrogation of every single moment of her life. She could feel His breath in her centre, His gaze through her memories, her self, her core. She felt His face form inside hers and saw the grey smoke leaking through her skin where He moved within her. He looked at her secrets and tossed them aside. He ripped through her shame and her fears.

And then He froze.

"Yes!" His voice was brittle with anticipation as His lips forced hers to smile.

The moment lingered.

Then it began. The ripping and tearing, the strangled scraping, the inescapable, unbearable agony in the deepest depths of her. And she did not know why or what or how to make it stop.

But something did, and it was not the Autarch. Without warning, Arke's body ripped itself apart with an intensity that made Him recoil into His domain, grey lightning triggering across the surface of the abyss in a shockwave of reaction.

He willed her back to existence in a torrent of rage. He threw her to the platform, then to the walls, the floor, the statues, burning, ripping, tearing, annihilating. He directed His fury into her destruction, caring not how many times He had to smash her together. He and only He had the power of life and death in this place.

His question rang out as Arke lay silent, barely breathing, as pale as the deaths she'd experienced.

"Who are you?"

She finally knew the answer. "Yours."

A ring spun through the air and landed with a clink beside her. The thin obsidian band bore no marking save a single unbroken line carved around its centre and it shone with an oily hue as it was illuminated by the bright darkness.

"Put – it – on."

Her obedience was instant, and she clawed a trembling hand towards it, fumbling with fervent desperation to slide it onto her finger. The moment she succeeded, the band smoked with grey-tinged magic and dug itself into her flesh, blood dripping around its edges as it activated a deeper connection.

As His cold fingertips stroked the hair at the base of her neck, she felt another ripple of His emotion wash over her. Something different, something that her broken mind could not or would not decipher.

"I'll be watching."

Chapter Nine
Anywhere but Here

THE AUTARCH'S NEW acquisition was teleported back onto the *Warrior* with a flash of grey-tinged magic. Irash felt the sudden termination of the spell that had held his crewmates in its thrall and rushed to Arke's side. Crouching down, he checked she was breathing before peering at the obsidian ring on her left hand with a darkening expression. Even if it hadn't been radiating unsettling power, he'd been a passenger in her body for long enough to know it wasn't hers.

"Battle stations!" Kennedy bellowed before looking at the Soulbound's limp figure. "Irash, what's happened to her? And don't just say magic, because I'm not a bloody idiot."

"I'm not sure..."

Without waiting to hear more, Kennedy scooped Arke off the deck and carried her towards the hatch. Picking up a piece of folded parchment that had been pinned under her body, Irash scurried after him and gestured to her cabin.

"That's where she needs to be. In there and away from this place."

"She needs Gurdi!" Ruby sprinted to Kennedy's side and slid a hand onto Arke's forehead. "She's burning up."

"Stop and let me show you something." Irash pointed to the obsidian band. "*This* is new. I don't know what it is, what it does, or anything other than that it's insanely powerful. She should be where she's the most comfortable – and where we can watch her. Bring the healer to her by all means, but we need to be careful."

"Is she possessed?" the Ornithol whispered, her bird-like eyes narrowed in concern.

"No," Irash replied. "It's only her in there."

Kennedy stared at the ring, his expression thunderous. "I assume we can't just take it off."

"Don't even try," Irash warned.

"Ellie, send word for Gurdi and get us underway!" Kennedy shouted.

"What course, captain?"

"Whatever way we're pointing! Anywhere but here!"

Ruby hurried ahead, opening the door to Arke's cabin so Kennedy could march straight in and lay the Soulbound on her bed. Quickly checking her scabbard and finding Stabbington wasn't in sword form, he turned to Irash, whose attention was captured by the contents of the parchment.

"Tell me what you know."

It took a moment for Irash to realise Kennedy's demand was levelled at him. "I don't really..."

"TELL ME WHAT YOU KNOW!"

The Ornithol busied herself cooling cloths for Arke's fever while a murderous-looking Kennedy stormed towards Irash, who put up his hands defensively, the parchment still clutched in his fingers.

"When I woke up the ship was descending, and everyone was asleep. Magical sleep. So, I headed up to the main deck, but Arke was already there, trying to get the ship's nose up. Then all of you started to show up, full on glassy-eyed automatons, and the engines cut out. Arke was talking to the thing that seemed to be controlling you when she was teleported away. It was only a few minutes before she came back, and the moment she did, you all came round. And this – this was underneath her."

Kennedy took the parchment that Irash held out to him. "What's the deal with the ring? What does it do?"

"I can sense its power, but as it's not actively doing anything, I can't tell you much more."

With an unexpected burst of dramatic light, Stabbington suddenly appeared in Arke's hand and with an even more unexpected burst of consciousness, she sat bolt upright before scrambling off the bed.

"Get out! All of you! Out! And take this useless coward with you, I never want to see him again!"

When no-one moved, she hurled the sword with such accuracy and force that it flew through the open door and dug into the deck outside. Without looking at any of them, she staggered into her tiny bathroom and kicked the door shut behind her.

There was a long moment of surprised silence in the cabin before Kennedy folded his arms. "I'm staying with Arke."

Ruby started tidying up. "Me too."

Irash looked out at the sword and sighed. "Fine, I'll talk to him and find out what happened."

⚹ ⚹ ⚹

SOMEWHERE HOT, SUNNY, and silent, the Arbiter was sitting by a fountain, the fingers of his right hand trailing in the water, a glass of fresh orange juice on the table by his side. His mind was elsewhere, his attention focused on the *Warrior* from a point far above her decks. None of the residents of the Gateway could see into the obsidian tower, and the wait to find out whether Arke had even survived had taxed his nerves. They had planned and predicted, but the pivotal moment was always going to happen inside the Autarch's sanctum.

The instant he'd seen her return, relief had flooded him. The years of preparation had worked. He'd fought for her when the others had doubted her ability, her strength, her character.

While he waited, he'd laced his orange juice with a little something special, something to celebrate with. The toast he'd intended to make was to their success, hopefully the first of many. However, his attention remained on Arke, and his drink remained untouched.

Suddenly his concentration was interrupted by voices, all speaking at once, all desperate for news.

"Is it done?"

"We've been looking for you!"

"Did he take the bait?"

"Is the plan working?"

"How did it go?"

He took a deep breath, trying to find the words he should say, not the ones he wanted to use. "She has his attention. And a ring."

The Arbiter reached for his glass and downed the heady liquid in one gulp while ignoring the babble of excited comments.

He knew it was all necessary, but could feel no triumph. He didn't know what had gone on inside the tower, but he could see the results.

✕ ✕ ✕

It was already late when Irash returned, slipping into Arke's cabin and closing the door behind him with a soft click. She was sitting at the table with her head in her hands and three empty bottles next to her but, judging by her posture, none of the alcohol had helped.

"Don't shout at me." He sat down and laid Stabbington's blade in front of them.

She looked at him, her eyes bloodshot and barely focused. When she'd been his host, he'd seen past the face she showed to the world, heard her thoughts, and shared her experiences. He'd also come to realise there wasn't always a need for words, so he simply slid a hand towards her and waited.

A few seconds passed before he felt her slip her fingers into his grasp.

"You're cold."

His only reply was her sudden onset of tears. He sat quietly while the trickle became a torrent, Arke's nails digging into his skin as she strained to stifle her sobs before they turned into screams. Irash said nothing. Even in his original form he wouldn't have been able to undo what had been done, and as a mortal all he could do was be present. Finally, her eyes watered themselves dry before fastening a furious gaze on the sword.

"What's he doing here?" she hissed. "Get him out of my room."

"We've been talking," Irash replied, his tone purely informative. "He told me what he saw, what he knows. If you can fill in a few gaps, then we might be able to put a plan together."

"A plan?" Arke stood up, yanking her hand free of his. "A PLAN? There's nothing... nothing I can do!" She grabbed the table and tipped it over before storming into her bathroom as Stabbington crashed onto the floor with the empty bottles.

"What do you know about the ring? What does it do?" Irash asked, picking everything back up again.

"It didn't come with an instruction manual!"

A bar of soap was launched at his head, and he ducked, letting it fall harmlessly away. A smile broke out from behind his frown and Irash knew the burst of warmth that flooded his body had nothing to do with his ability to avoid toiletries. Her reaction to what had happened in the tower had been worrying him, but after seeing that flash of temper, he knew she wasn't completely broken. She was tough and she was stubborn, and more importantly, she was still Arke. He took a deep breath.

"When I was four, I went into the woods, dressed extremely incongruously as a little girl, wearing a scarlet coat with an integral hood..." he began, pouring himself a shot from a half-empty bottle.

This time it was a nail brush, dangerously close to his eye.

"Don't!"

"Fine." He downed the silky rum with an appreciative smile. "When I was five, I grew tired of being a little boy and turned myself into a cat with a predilection for long leather boots..."

"I said don't!" She slammed the bathroom door.

He gave up with the glass and drank straight from the bottle before moving to lean against the wall, speaking loudly enough to make sure she could hear him. "When I was six, and a mighty fine young lady, I happened to choose a small mound of earth to sit on while I ate my disgusting slop. And what should happen but an arachnid, wondering what..."

Arke burst out of the bathroom and grabbed him by the shirt front. *"Shut – up!"*

Irash didn't even bother to smother his grin as a memory they both shared flashed into his mind. "I'm not going to kiss you, because I don't love you like he does. But I do have my balls covered, just in case."

She shoved him away before stalking over to Stabbington and staring down at the demon blade with glittering fury.

"You left me when I needed you! That's not love! YOU LEFT ME!"

"You should hear what he has to say." Irash picked up the bottle. "Much as I hate to give you two relationship advice."

"Shut up!" Arke snarled.

He gulped down a heady mouthful before not shutting up again. "I *could* tell you that the Autarch would have annihilated him if he'd got in the way. I'd have done the same back in the day. Oh wait, almost did, and I wasn't even a tiny bit as powerful." He took another slug. "Or I *could* tell you that you're still Arke, no matter what you went through, and that I know you really need your pathetic little demon right now."

The blade rattled warningly on the table and Irash pointed a finger at him. "Shut it, I'm doing your intro." He looked back at the Soulbound. "Pick him up. Ask him where he went, what he did to try and find someone powerful enough to help you. Go on, ask him."

※ ※ ※

Arke flexed the fingers of her sword hand and reached down, sliding Stabbington's grip into its rightful place. Images flooded into her head so fast that she had to lean on the table for support as her demon opened himself up completely. He had no time for words, so he showed her, bringing her into his memories with him. She saw him escape from the Autarch's first touch and dive away, desperately throwing himself into his viperous form. He had run to his home plane but not from self-preservation; he'd done it to find help.

She saw everything through his eyes. Everything he'd ever told her about his world was suddenly brought to life. The moment he arrived in the desolate rocky landscape, he was surrounded by his siblings, monstrous snakes with rippling scales and flickering tongues. He fled, using his smaller size to take paths they could not, and his desperation to take risks they would not.

He didn't stop until he threw himself off a ledge towards his mother. The gargantuan ruler of his world. The Brood Mother. She was the source of his power, his life, and the only entity he knew who might be able to help. The Soulbound knew how frightened he was of the behemoth who presided over the endless cycle of her children's lives. The strongest culled the weakest, growing bigger with each kill, until they were large enough for her to eat and begin the process again.

She saw through Stabbington's eyes as he crashed down in front of the Brood Mother's enormous fangs and blurted out his story. The colossal snake, whose eyeball was larger than his entire body, listened intently. She reacted with deep apprehension when he first mentioned the Autarch and flicked her tongue in and out as he offered himself to her as food in exchange for helping Arke.

Murmuring a strange chromatic melody, the gigantic snake touched her head to his. The Soulbound noticed the perspective change as Stabbington grew in size and listened to his mother's booming voice informing him that returning to her had been the right choice. The Autarch would have destroyed him, which would have been a waste of a perfectly good snack. Arke heard what she thought might be a peal of laughter before the giant eyeball levelled itself to Stabbington's face once more. Her son must return to his host, with the Brood Mother's blessing – and her aid.

The memory faded, and the Soulbound was in her cabin, leaning heavily on the table, the grip of the demon blade warm in her hand.

"Sorry will never be enough, my Arke." Stabbington spoke softly in her head, the way his accent wrapped around her name the most comforting sound she had ever known. "But if you will have me back, we will fight this together. You and I... and maybe them, but only if there is enough to go round."

She had never wanted anything so much. Swallowing dryly, she pulled his hilt to her chest, absorbing him into her. She heard her demon humming softly as he released his magical painkillers and shut her eyes as the familiarity of his presence began to soothe her. This wasn't the first time he'd helped put her back together – granted, there were more pieces now, but he was ready. There was a difference to him, a stronger essence, a more potent magic.

"Go outside. But put on a coat, for it is cold."

He was certainly more commanding. She'd have to consider that later, but for now, she'd go outside.

As she grabbed her jacket, an unashamedly tipsy Irash opened the door with a bow. Stepping out into the bright, cool moonlight, Arke was surprised to see that the deck was covered with people. Kennedy was at the wheel, rubbing a hand over his blotchy stubble. Next to him, Ruby was busy with one of her prayer meditations. A little distance away, Ellie snuggled under a blanket with Sparkz. They were all there, every member of the crew, right down to an exhausted-looking Gabbi who was pouring Volk a cup of coffee and buttering a scone all at once.

"You told everyone?" Arke frowned at Irash.

"I talked to Kennedy. He did the rest," Stabbington replied firmly. "Summon my sword."

"Now?"

"No, tomorrow. Of course now."

She held out her hand for her demon blade and as power cascaded down her arm, forming into the weapon, she could see exactly how Stabbington Bear had changed. His mother's blessing had not only made him a larger snake. He was no longer a delicate rapier but a wickedly sharp broadsword.

"Am I not THE most magnificent weapon you have EVER seen?" After that moment of personal pride, Stabbington's voice softened, his words so warm she could almost feel them. "So, you can see I am strong enough for us both, and if you should need anything else – look around, they are all here." He paused as Arke drew her eyes away from his blade and refocused them on her friends, who were trying to watch her without appearing to do so. "Ah, except Irash. From the retching noises over by your cabin, I think he is regretting his recent choice of beverage."

Chapter Ten
Familiar Faces

KENNEDY CALLED THE crew together the day following their flight from the obsidian ruin. It was understandable that everyone was on edge and rumours were running wild below decks. Nerves needed to be steadied, and purpose renewed before morale plummeted. Pretending things were fine was not an option, so he went straight for full disclosure.

Once he'd finished explaining what had happened in the obsidian tower, he asked for questions. There were absolutely none. Looking around the room, he noted a mixture of expressions ranging from horror to confusion. That was to be expected, as 'a powerful entity took over our bodies then kidnapped Arke only to repeatedly murder and reconstitute her and we have no idea why' would never be easy to hear. So, after dropping the truth bomb, he excused himself, hoping the crew's natural fellowship would help them ride out their shock. They'd probably be more comfortable expressing themselves without him there, and once they'd had time to process everything, he would return and explain their next move.

A few minutes later, he returned to the galley with a hand resting lightly on the Soulbound's shoulder. For obvious reasons, she'd refused to be a part of any re-telling, but had agreed to attend the second half of the meeting. He knew the sight of her red-rimmed eyes and trembling hands wouldn't settle anyone's nerves, as Arke's ironclad exterior was the stuff of onboard legend, but it was a reality that had to be faced.

Kennedy believed that keeping busy was the most powerful defence against negative thoughts, so after returning to his seat, he outlined his plan.

"I'll be honest with you all. My first instinct was to fly away – far, far, FAR away. But we do know that it doesn't want us dead…"

"*Yet*," Sparkz interrupted through a mouthful of noodles.

"Doesn't want us dead *yet*," Kennedy acknowledged. "If It did, we'd already be toast. And you'll note I'm not calling It anything but It – whatever title It gives itself or whatever identity It claims, in my books if you act like a monster, you're a monster." He took a moment to pour himself a cup of coffee before continuing. "So, this thing didn't only give Arke a ring, it gave us this."

Pulling the parchment from his pocket, Kennedy tossed it onto the table. At the top were three words written in heavy, old-fashioned script: *The Autarch requires*. Then came the picture of a pyramid-shaped object with the word *Capstone* underneath it, followed by the numbers one through four. The first number was annotated: *search southwest of the centre of Great Barsia*; while the others just had question marks.

Sparkz put his bowl aside and reached for the paper. "What sort of dumbass scavenger hunt wants four of the same things?"

"Four what?" Ellie asked.

The engineer shrugged and offered her the parchment. "Not a clue. Calls them capstones."

"Pass the paper round, everyone take a good look," Kennedy instructed. "All we have to go on is that drawing. I've never seen one before, but between us we've covered a lot of miles – so speak up if you have any idea what they are or might be. Now, before you say anything, I know we all want to tell that creature where to shove its capstones…"

He sat back and sipped his coffee as his crew launched into a debate about exactly what they'd like to do to the monster in the tower. He hid a smile behind his mug as he saw how quickly they were recovering from their initial shock. Although he knew Arke was nowhere near doing the same, he hoped it would do her good to hear them suggesting increasingly violent means of subduing her tormentor. Imagined retribution, even if utterly impossible, was always a morale booster.

"However," he continued when the general hubbub had died down, "since we're unaware of exactly what the ring does, or what might happen if we don't do what we've been asked, there's only one course of action that seems sensible: we start looking for the first capstone."

As the crew filed out, Kennedy turned to Arke, whose shoulders were slumped as she stared at the black band on her finger. He hated seeing her so broken, but was struggling to know what to say or do to help hold her together.

"Do you want a cuppa?" he asked, fighting the urge to cross his fingers in the hope she'd agree

She shook her head. "I'm going back to bed."

As the galley door swung shut behind her, Kennedy leant both hands on the table and exhaled slowly. During his conversation with Stabbington the previous evening, he'd learnt something oddly concerning. The demon had let slip that Arke had been having dreams about Joy ever since her full death experience in Theogenes. Shocked into sudden response, Kennedy had interrupted with the admission that she wasn't the only one dreaming about his mother. However, while he'd only dreamt of her occasionally, Stabbington informed him that every time the Soulbound closed her eyes she was flooded with happy memories, ones that had been previously locked away as too painful to recall.

That part of their discussion had been as fruitless as it was worrying, but Kennedy had agreed that the strange coincidence was hardly their priority. Right now, Arke needed as much comfort as she could find, no matter what the source.

※ ※ ※

"I TOLD YOU this would work!"

Joy chuckled as she leapfrogged Arke, landing only to immediately parry a double-handed sword strike with the pole of her glaive. She'd called dibs on the sailors sprinting to attack them from the ships at the end of the jetty so the Soulbound could deal with the patrol who'd chased them through the dockyard.

If Joy was to tell the truth, which was unlikely given her undiagnosed allergy to it, she would probably have admitted that the sheer number of shipyard guards was unexpected, unwelcome, and definitely not part of her plan. She might also have acknowledged that she never made plans. She'd seen the opportunity and persuaded a typically reluctant Arke that it was a good one before expertly lock-picking a side gate and inexpertly running into a guard patrol around the first corner.

The Soulbound didn't need Joy to admit any of her shortcomings, as they'd been working together long enough for all of them to be obvious. She was impetuous, impatient, impractical, and possessed of some incredible fortune – not all of it good. The bond between them had become unbreakable, and no matter what situation her friend threw herself into, Arke would be there, always ready to brawl, break or bail her out.

This evening's escapade was no exception. As the pair battled their way through the dockyard towards the shiniest of new ships that Joy had spent a good hour admiring earlier that week, they fought with their usual slick synchronicity.

"Multitasking would be a good idea right about now," Stabbington suggested. "They broke out the mages first so there is no reason you cannot use a spell or two."

The demon and his host had reached a permanent agreement about magic usage just after Joy joined them. Joined was the simplest way of describing the complicated beginning to their friendship. Following their escape from a gang hideout, Joy had decided that she and the Soulbound should team up. And after Arke's resounding 'hell no', came the weeks of stalking. When the answer became 'get away from me, I don't need your help', Joy had the Soulbound arrested so she could prove herself by breaking her out. Once Arke had escaped, gone back in to rescue Joy and punched her repeatedly in the face, she'd agreed that a partnership was the safer option. Thus, the duo had become a trio and while Stabbington never failed to remark that life had been simpler and less dangerous before, he always admitted, in the wryest of tones, that it had been a lot less joyful.

"Two, you say?" Arke grinned as she spun to face their pursuers and tossed her blade in the air to free up both of her hands. Their agreement had worked perfectly, keeping both her and her demon partner happy. She would never be the first to use magic, but the moment the opposition did, it was game on.

Casting multiple spells in the midst of battle was high risk, high reward, but then so was stealing a brand-new sky ship. The Soulbound grabbed a dagger from her belt and licked its edge, the touch of her tongue making the blade hum with power, while at the same time her other hand was gathering icy energy into its fingertips.

The patrol running down the dockside towards Arke became the unlucky recipients of a burst of cold so intense it froze every one of them. However, she barely registered her success as she concentrated on catching Stabbington before spinning to launch the dagger at a heavily bearded mage standing by a pile of crates while preparing a double handful of magical fire. She was still sizzling from the lightning bolt he'd hit them with a few minutes ago and wasn't keen to welcome another elemental attack.

"Switch!" she called.

They needed to keep moving or risk getting swarmed by the defenders.

"No! You deal with the mage!" Joy leapt in the air to avoid a pike that was thrust at her legs and landed neatly, pirouetting to dodge a slashing cutlass before swinging her glaive to remove the offending weapon as well as a couple of gnarly fingers from its owner.

"I just did!"

The Soulbound's spell-carrying dagger had flown true, taking the man in the chest and covering him with bright blue magic. The moment it finished surrounding him, the mage and his flames completely disappeared. He'd be back in a while, but she wasn't intending to hang around for a reunion.

"You said that last time and look what happened! Being a gnome was bloody terrible!" Joy shouted.

"You weren't a gnome, you were just teeny tiny. It was adorable."

"Have I told you how much I hate you?"

More angry-looking sailors were charging off the two ships as Arke started sprinting towards her friend.

"BOOST!"

Joy's glaive flashed even faster as she knocked her nearest attackers back before spinning around and holding the pole of her weapon out at thigh height. She positioned it just in time for the Soulbound to land her feet solidly on the shaft and heaved upwards, throwing her into the air.

"ON ME!" Arke bellowed out another instruction the instant before she landed in an even heavier populated part of the quay.

Muttering a curse at the late notice, Joy set the glaive windmilling in her hands, knocking her attackers away to make herself some room. Ahead of her, the Soulbound was almost invisible amid the mob of angry sailors.

Once Joy had given herself enough space, she accelerated into a sprint and used her glaive to pole vault over the wall of men. Arke kept fighting until the last possible moment before stretching up to meet Joy's fingertips and slamming Stabbington into the planks between her feet.

In an instant, both women disappeared, and a sonic boom sounded from the speed of their departure, the shockwave flattening everyone left behind.

As the pair reappeared on the sky ship docked on the right hand side of the jetty, Joy completed her descent. Unfortunately for the Soulbound and her collarbone, she was between her falling friend and the extremely solid deck.

"You're supposed to cripple the bloody enemy," Arke hissed as she cradled her arm across her chest.

"Oh, well why didn't you say?" Joy chuckled and patted her on the top of the head. "One day you'll learn how to catch me."

"Catch <u>you</u>? No healing spell in the world could fix that," the Soulbound growled, before nodding towards the mooring ropes. "Get us moving."

Since a cessation of mockery would let Arke know she was concerned, Joy sprinted across the deck to cast off while continuing to throw shade on 'anyone' who was careless enough to allow a friend to land on them.

As she untied the first knot, she noticed that some of the previously downed sailors were staggering towards the ship.

"Hey, Crash Pad! We've got incoming!"

Right on cue, a barrage of blue energy darts exploded against the gangplank, instantly preventing the men from charging on board.

"Fight smarter not..."

☆ ☆ ☆

When her friend's voice was cut off mid-sentence, Joy spun around to check on her. At first glance, it would have been charitable to say that the Soulbound was struggling with a burly opponent – but after a few seconds had passed, it was clear that there was no struggle whatsoever. The sailor gripping Arke's neck might have had the clean features and pointy ears of an elf, but he clearly identified as an orc. His biceps were the size of buckets, and he was using them to smash her head repeatedly into the top of a barrel.

Whipping a stiletto from her belt, Joy hurled it at the musclebound man. Expensive as the upgrade to her knives had been, the sleep enchantment had paid for itself many times over. As both the elf and a bloodied Arke slumped to the deck, Joy untied the final rope and sprinted to the ship's helm. Everything on board was so perfectly new that even the controls still had their labels attached. After jamming her finger on the 'Start Engine' button, she selected the lever marked 'Auxiliary Power' and shoved it to full before spinning the wheel hard over and heading towards the Soulbound.

"You really must learn to take your nanna naps at more appropriate times."

With a wicked grin, Joy upended the barrel that had been instrumental in Arke's concussion over her friend's head. Unsurprisingly, the sudden application of gallons of cold water proved more than enough to bring the Soulbound back to consciousness, as well as jumpstart some distinctly ungrateful cursing. There seemed to be a theme to the rant, something about Joy's personal habits and possibly her parentage, though it was hard to make out through the coughing and spluttering and the fact that she simply didn't care.

"It <u>was</u> water, right?" She crouched down and hauled on the front of the Soulbound's shirt to bring her to a sitting position.

"Don't you dare lick my face to find out!" Arke hissed. "I mean it!"

"It was one time!" Joy yanked her stiletto out of the elf and sprinted back to the helm. *"Anyway, you're fine... bags be the captain."*

Just as she got there, a magical ball of flame landed in the centre of the ship, covering the deck in a brief inferno before it receded and disappeared completely.

"You said you'd dealt with that prick! Stabbington, get her shit together!" Joy shouted, trying to alert the half of the partnership who was still capable of doing something useful.

The mage who'd hit them both with lightning earlier was standing on the quay, brewing up another handful of magical flame.

With a sudden splintering of planes, Dozer, the Soulbound's giant Rottweiler, bounced out of a black hole and onto the deck, barking what he probably believed was a cheerful tune, but was more like the rasping of a saw against rock.

As the mage hurled a second fiery sphere at the ship, the hellhound reacted, his wings snapping out with a resounding crack as he launched himself towards what he clearly thought was a particularly fizzy ball. Mouth wide open, the monstrous canine scooped up his new toy before chasing the man down the jetty, apparently unable to understand why this strange mortal didn't want to play fetch with him.

"WHAT A GOOD BOY!" Joy yelled before wiping tears of laughter from her eyes as the mage proved just how inflammable cheap robes were and Dozer's disappointed barking echoed around the sky.

As clumsy, calamitous hellhounds went, Arke's was pretty useful, as long as you didn't mind the snoring, gastronomic thievery, or strange anxiety that could liquidise his stomach in seconds if he wasn't told how clever he was several times a day.

When the distance between themselves and the dock increased, Joy hit the button marked 'Sails'. With a whirring of powerful servos and a hissing of ropes, the incredibly new white canvas rolled down from the yards, cracking as it tightened and the wind caught, powering the vessel through the air.

"Arke, wake up! I think we just stole a really expensive ship!"

Grabbing a vial from a pouch around her neck, Joy threw it onto the stern where it smashed and instantly filled the sky behind them with thick fog. Although anything magical was never cheap, they always kept a stock of that particular spell to cover any tricky escapes.

Then she headed back to the Soulbound who was lying face down on the deck and being stared at by a worried-looking Dozer. He whined at Joy before biffing Arke in the ribs with an indelicate paw.

"I agree. She needs to wake up! Let me have a go." Joy patted the dog on the top of his incredibly broad head before poking the Soulbound repeatedly with the toe of her boot. "Open your eyes, woman. This is a momentous occasion – our first sky-jack!"

Arke's expletive-ridden reply suggested she was distinctly underwhelmed by the entire situation as well as outlining where Joy's footwear would end up if she didn't stop kicking her.

"You're such a grump when you've got an ouchie." Joy grinned. "Stabbington, keep our lady of concussion awake while I search our new ship."

"No need." A tall, blond man in a perfectly tailored suit emerged from the main hatch and raised his hands. "I'm no threat."

Joy spun round, weapons at the ready. "Who are you?"

"The owner. This is my ship, I bought her last week."

"<u>Was</u> your ship."

"Is <u>our</u> ship?" He smiled warmly, dimples showing in his cheeks and more than a hint of a twinkle in his blue eyes. "If you put your knives down, I'll put my hands down."

Joy started laughing and tucked the stilettos safely in her belt. "Oddest surrender I've ever heard... if it was one, of course."

"Will it keep me alive if I say yes?"

Joy walked closer to the stranger, unashamedly sizing him up as she approached, her eyes tracking from his head to his feet and back up again, the smile never leaving her lips. "We respect the surrender... or she does, and she made me promise." She gestured towards the lump on the deck otherwise known as Arke. "Apparently without some sort of code I'm nothing more than a hot chick with a nasty attitude."

"You seem perfectly reasonable to this well-surrendered man. My name's Philip, by the way, Philip Kennedy." Tearing his eyes away from Joy's face, he peered over at the Soulbound's mostly inert form. "Does your friend need help?" Then, tracking his gaze past her, he pointed at the burly elf's body. "Is he dead? I mean, it <u>would</u> save on the wages bill."

Joy burst out laughing again, her amusement loud enough to haul Arke back to full consciousness, even if her vision appeared to have been stitched together by drunkards with an interest in modern art. She leant up on an elbow and managed to make out three copies of her friend, all of which seemed to be in an intimate pose with a tall man.

"She is searching him for weapons," Stabbington explained. "Though she is taking far too long, and they are very close together." His only reply was a groan as the Soulbound struggled to a sitting position. "It could be worse. It has been worse. This one has his own ship, teeth, and a very well-cut coat."

Joy noticed her friend's movement and turned her enthusiastic expression up several notches. "Hey, Arke, he's adorable, can we keep him?" She tapped a finger on Philip's chest. "You want to be a pirate, right?"

"'Pirate' always has such negative connotations." He looked down at her, his eyes twinkling with something that wasn't just merriment. "Philip Kennedy – Pirate, sounds much less entrepreneurial than..." His brow furrowed as he thought for a long moment, one hand slipping onto Joy's shoulder as he lost himself in ideas. Finally, he found the phrase he was looking for and beamed with the satisfaction of a job well renamed.

"Philip Kennedy, Wealth Transfer Enabler."

Chapter Eleven
You Can't Always See the Flames

STABBINGTON WAS READY as Arke woke from yet another bittersweet dream. It had been eight days since the obsidian tower, and while the demon was helping her claw her way back to some form of control of her daytime thoughts, they both knew that her dreams were sabotaging that progress. It wasn't even as if they were nightmares, but reliving her past, her best friend, and their life together every time she slept was bordering on emotional torture. The moment she opened her eyes, reality brought nothing but guilt and sadness, so any positive steps made the previous day were almost completely undone.

"Would you like to talk?" he whispered. "I am here to listen. And if you do not, sometimes it helps to cry."

"Talking makes it worse and I *don't* want to cry any more." Still fully clothed, the Soulbound stuck her feet in her boots and walked to the door. As she strode past the captain's cabin, she hammered her fist on the wall. "Kennedy! Send one out."

"It is dawn. You should..." Stabbington wasn't looking forward to yet another punishing round of sword play. It was his fault for suggesting his host needed to work on some new skills, since he was now a much different sort of blade. She'd taken it to heart and spent the last few days crashing him against anyone who would fight her.

She summoned her broadsword. "I should train more. You said it."

In obedience to her summons, Kennedy's alter, the other version of himself that he could magically bring into being, appeared on deck. It was fully battle ready, dressed in heavy armour, bearing a sword in each hand, but its posture was more than slightly reluctant. The instant it was within range, Arke started attacking.

The sound of metal crashing against metal rang out over the decks and filtered down, echoing around the swamps below them as the early morning sun glittered against the miasmic mist. A llama head poked up through the fog and kept rising as four scaly wings propelled it upwards, finally clearing the murk to show off its lizard-like body and eight spider legs.

"Another day in paradise," Kennedy yawned, walking onto the deck in his dressing gown and immediately having to duck as Stabbington's blade sliced through the air nearby. "Coffee? Tea? Decapitation?"

"Good idea." The Soulbound took his advice, briskly despatching the tired-looking alter which shimmered into nothingness before turning her bloodshot eyes to the captain. "Another."

"How about some breakfast to keep your strength up?" he suggested, but when she just glared at him, he sighed and summoned a second version of himself. Patting his cringing alter on the arm, Kennedy told it to do its best before muttering, "hopefully she'll wear herself out and be back asleep by nine."

As it happened, Arke overachieved massively, wrecking her shoulder by seven and being warned by Gurdi, who had clearly not been enjoying the rousing dawn chorus of metal on metal, that if she picked up any sword, sword-like object, or in fact non-sword-like object in that hand for at least three days, she herself would come out for a fight. The order was received in silence as no-one, not even the Soulbound, argued with the healer when she dropped her chin and glared over the top of her glasses.

However, it didn't stop Arke tugging the sling off the instant she stomped back onto the main deck. Kennedy hurried over to her as, eyes snapping with irritation, she balled up the fabric as if ready to launch it over the side.

"What?" she hissed. "I don't need it."

Naturally, it was at exactly that moment Gurdi appeared out of the hatch behind them, her expression hardening as she stared at Arke's sling-less back.

"I know she's there! Shut UP Stabbington!" Arke snapped. There had been very few moments in her life when the adjective 'unrepentant' hadn't been an appropriate descriptor, and this was definitely not one of them.

"I was helping her make it more comfortable." Kennedy smiled, easing the sling from the Soulbound's reluctant grip and trying, extremely ineffectively, to put it back on her.

"Captain, the sling of shame is better on the *injured* side." The healer covered the distance between them surprisingly quickly and took over from his inexpert hands. "Also, the sling of – maybe it's better to talk instead of hurt yourself. The sling of – just take up my offer of some alternative therapies. The sling of – I know you don't want to, but honestly it might help. The sling of – you can look at me like that for as long as you like, but you know I'm right."

If anyone else had said that to Arke, Kennedy would have already been breaking up a fight. But it was Gurdi. She'd been one of the first people they'd recruited to the crew of the *Warrior*, and she knew everything about everything.

"The sling of – screw you and your bullshit, I'm going back to bed. If I never wake up it'll be too soon!" The Soulbound strode into her cabin and slammed the door shut behind her.

"A rest will do her good. In the meantime, Philip, perhaps you need to talk?" The dwarf looked up at him, her deep brown eyes searching his face.

He was about to decline, but then changed his mind and nodded slowly. He absolutely needed to offload to someone. Gurdi wasn't so much a crew member as the heart of the ship; she could keep secrets, and she would understand.

"So where shall we go for our little chat?" she asked. "Your father liked to sit in his chair, but your mother always perched at the bow, bare feet dangling over the side and the wind battering her cheeks."

"I remember." He sighed. "I wish they were here now. All I have are questions without any answers, and I don't know what to do. How do I help her? How do I keep everyone safe? What if I can't do either?"

"Trust your instincts." Gurdi put her hand on his arm. "When I look at you, I see a little of all your parents. Your father's intelligence and charm, your mother's instincts, Stabbington's protectiveness, and Arke's sheer bloody-mindedness. You are exactly who you need to be. So try not to overthink – your best will always be enough."

"If it was, we wouldn't be stuck here, looking for capstones for that... thing."

Gurdi shook her head. "If it wasn't, we'd all have been dead years ago. Right now, we walk a rough path, but it's just one section of a far longer road. What is now will soon be then, and we will all move on." She looked out over the marsh and shook her head. "Unlike this poor place. It's still on fire, even if we can't see the flames."

He sighed and sat down on a barrel. "Everything started to go downhill when we took that bloody job from Gorki. And when I thought it was all over, we got hit by a monster storm that blew us right into the tower. It used to be so simple – we stole stuff, we sold stuff, we stole more stuff. Now it feels like the sky has fallen."

"Maybe it has. But I don't know any better crew to kick it back where it belongs."

※ ※ ※

ARKE OPENED THE door quickly before slipping into the small storeroom. The newly stolen ship hadn't seen port for ten days, a good few of which she'd been sleeping away her injuries.

When she finally got out of bed, she'd found the burly elf who had given her a concussion at the helm while Joy and Philip kept themselves 'occupied' in the captain's cabin. The Soulbound had been sure the novelty would soon wear off, but things began to look more serious when day merged into day without Joy throwing him over the side. And that was a problem.

So, in the most Arke-like way of dealing with troublesome emotions, she ignored them. To begin with, it had been easy, as being on a flying ship was both different and exciting, but it didn't take long for that to become mundane. Then she started exploring and found that one of the rooms was packed with treasure. Not the traditional sort of treasure – no gold or silver, but boxes and boxes of books. It had been ages since she'd had the opportunity to read in peace. Smiling almost fit to make her jaw ache, she selected her first book and felt the world melt away.

The next day she brought some blankets and cushions with her, making herself a comfier place to sit. Then came the snacks and the drinks. And after that, she didn't bother to go back to the cabin she'd been using. She and Stabbington read together. They devoured tales of magic and mayhem, comedies, tragedies, and everything in between. The disquiet she'd felt with the absence of her friend faded away and she was blissfully content as she lost herself in printed words.

"Knock knock."

Philip's voice interrupted her enjoyment of a particularly thrilling scene, and the Soulbound's reply was understandably terse.

"What?"

The door opened, and he popped his head inside. "Do you fancy some dinner? I've been cooking, don't know if you can smell it?"

"I'm not that hungry, but thanks."

At first, he seemed disappointed, but then his gaze fell on the book in her hand and his face lit up with enthusiasm.

"Isn't it a great story? I couldn't put it down either! Please come to dinner and bring it with you. I was never allowed to read at the dining table, but you know there really is no better place. Have you got to the bit where...? No, I won't spoil it in case you haven't. And then there's the sequel too. And the prequel. I think I've read them all several times!"

Stepping aside before she was bowled over, Arke watched as Philip moved around the boxes of books, selecting ones he recommended to add to an ever-increasing pile. His rapid-fire synopses were interspersed with comments about his own life. Over-sharing seemed to be one of his character traits as he told her about his rich family, how he'd been supposed to join the army like his father and his father's father but had refused. He wanted to see the world and choose his own path. He knew his parents had given him money to buy a ship, hoping that a dose of reality would send him running home. Instead, he'd met Joy, an amazing free-spirited woman, and he had no intention of going back to a place where a boy wasn't allowed to bring a novel to the dining table. Philip Kennedy, he asserted with a gravitas beyond his years, had found where he belonged.

To BEGIN WITH, *the Soulbound was irritated that she couldn't find anything to dislike about Joy's new man. In fact, he was everything she would have chosen for her friend if she'd ever been asked. For a start, he didn't smell of cheap cologne and lies. And it was obvious that he had fallen as hard for Joy as she had for him. Theirs wasn't a drab, draping love, it was ruddy-cheeked and bursting with life.*

Arke's anxiety about her friend's relationship drifted away as she watched the pair grow closer and closer. Philip was nothing short of perfect, he was the anchor that held Joy's feet to the floor and the warm and engaging man who accepted her just the way she was. That sunny summer, their first as sky pirates, was full of love and laughter as the trio became a quartet, and the world was as wonderful as a world could be.

⚔ ⚔ ⚔

A HAMMERING ON her door woke the Soulbound out of her happy dreams.

"You're needed on deck."

"Ok," she replied, her hand automatically stroking Dozer's solid head while she struggled to let go of the warm embrace of the past and the memories of her best friends. Everything was wrong without them, so empty, so useless, so cold. "What did they do that was so terrible? Why did they have to die?"

She sat up, clenching her jaw to choke the sobs that threatened to burst from her throat before striding into the bathroom and glaring at her tear-stained face in the mirror.

"Why wasn't it me? I'm the one with the body count. I'm the bitch, the bad apple, the one people cross the street to avoid. They deserved to live and see their son grow up." She swallowed another sudden sob. "Why couldn't it be me instead of them?"

Stabbington's voice was soft and sad in her head. "You are who you have needed to be to survive. But we both know that is not everything you are." He paused for a long moment. "Arke, if the stars themselves turned their backs, I would love you still."

Orange magic crackled in her hand as she snapped a brutal reply. "But you're only a voice in my head, and sometimes it's not enough."

She hated the truth, but not quite as much as she hated herself for what she'd said to the now silent voice in her head. She washed her tears away before slipping her arm into the sling and going out on deck.

Less than a minute later, she was back, kicking the door open to grab her jacket and dump the sling on the table. The present had just slapped her hard in the face – Ruby hadn't returned from her daily capstone search and it was about to get dark.

Chapter Twelve
Unfamiliar Faces

As the *Warrior* flew in a zig-zag pattern over what seemed like a never-ending swamp, Ruby felt as if she was locked into a zone of endless repetition. She'd wake up early, eat an energy-packed breakfast, and take to the air to scour her allotted search area. Swooping backwards and forwards on a bird's-eye tour of the wasteland and its mutant inhabitants was both mentally and physically taxing. The parchment had given no useful details about the capstones, such as size, material, or colour, so absolutely anything unusual had to be investigated. She'd lost count of the number of heaps of stone or sleeping creatures she'd hovered over, scanning for something even vaguely pyramidal.

This day was different. It wasn't the small, ruined settlement that piqued her interest, but the campfire with actual people sitting round it. Ruby flew towards them, hopeful they may have some information that would help the search. As she approached, she counted four figures and noted they were all oddly well-groomed for being in the middle of a fetid marsh. However, despite the strangest of silences that hung around the group, deadening their conversations as well as the crackling of their fire, the Ornithol thought that none of them looked particularly threatening and decided to land. Flaring her wings, she set down near their campsite and waved in their direction.

"Hello!"

The strangers reacted to her greeting with surprise, quickly motioning her to shush before beckoning her over. With complete disregard for the standard safety protocol Kennedy had repeatedly explained to her, Ruby walked towards them. As soon as she was within a few feet of the group, she could hear everything – the fire, the bubbling of a pan of boiling water, and the people talking to her.

"Are you quite mad?" A man sitting on a folding stool scowled up at her, but she barely noticed his displeasure since her eyes were drawn to his strikingly bushy moustache. "What are you doing here?"

Ruby watched his companions as they got to their feet, none of them bothering to hide their head-to-toe assessments of her. Although it was in her nature to be optimistic, she was starting to feel a little uncomfortable under their scrutiny and quickly decided to drop a white lie instead of the truth. "Patrolling."

"You don't look like a Barsian officer."

She wasn't quite sure how to reply. "Nor do you."

"It's illegal to be here." The only woman in the group moved closer, her eyes fixed on Ruby's hand. "That's a rather lovely magic ring. Can I have it?"

It was at this point, about two minutes too late, that the Ornithol decided landing here had been a terrible idea. She'd been wrong to assume these people might be friendly, but she wasn't going to compound her mistakes by losing the fire-producing ring that Sparkz had given her. "Sorry, it was a gift from a friend."

"Do we kill her now?" One of the men swept his cloak back, revealing a pair of well-used scimitars.

Two minutes and ten seconds too late. Ruby stepped away from the dark-haired man who was looking at her as if she would be wonderful served with chips in a basket.

"Does anyone know where you are?"

"Yes." She was just about to make her escape when the world went black.

※ ※ ※

ARKE STOOD IN a foot loop harness as Sparkz flew them across the marsh. They'd started on the far side of Ruby's search zone, intending to work backwards until they found her, but it was only a few minutes before they spotted a cluster of ruins looming out of the mire to the east. As they grew closer, the Soulbound could make out ramshackle houses, their stone walls still standing, their roof tiles valiantly clinging to what was left of the rafters. She guessed they'd held together for so long because they were dry, raised above the waterline by what might have been a hill, but was now just a tiny island in a sea of polluted slime.

There had been a stony silence in Arke's head ever since she'd snapped at Stabbington, but she was too worried about her Ornithol friend to try to fix things. So she concentrated on searching for Ruby. She could talk to her demon later.

"I see her!"

Despite the early evening gloom, the Ornithol wasn't hard to spot, for she lay in the middle of the main road that ran through the settlement, her feathers bright against the ancient paving slabs.

"Drop me off and keep watch overhead," Arke called.

Memory's Claws

As Sparkz started to descend, the Soulbound quickly made herself invisible and just as quickly had to hold back the nausea that was always her response to that particular spell. She could hear a lot of ominous noises around the ruins and tried to ignore her churning stomach. Although she hated being sick, it was far better to be reacquainted with her lunch than become dinner for something lurking in the shadows.

She jumped out of the harness when they were low enough and winced as she jarred her injured shoulder. Stabbington would normally have commented about the untouched bottle of Gurdi's herbal pain relief sitting by her bedside, but he remained silent. Sparkz flew off, circling as he watched for any sign of activity that the sound of his jet might have triggered, while Arke hurried over to the Ornithol and reached to check for a pulse.

To her immense surprise, her fingers felt absolutely nothing at all as her hand passed right through what she realised was only the illusion of her friend. Suddenly, the image of Ruby's body vanished, and a series of alarms sounded nearby, the clanging of bells echoing round the ruins far more noisily than Sparkz's jet. Arke looked up for her ride just as several hefty-looking mutant creatures tumbled out of the wrecked buildings and started sniffing the air. She bit back a particularly vehement curse. Invisibility was great unless you were up against some hungry tiger-oxen-monkey boys.

Some fast, hungry tiger-oxen-monkey boys. She sprinted towards a ruined house as the pack charged, but they already had her scent. A heavy head smashed into her back, launching her into the air, and she only just managed to curl into a ball before crashing down among the stripey beasts. Eyes closed, everything tucked in tight, she felt herself being kicked around by the melee of legs. The mutants could clearly smell the heady scent of dinner, but with the entire herd trying to claim it, none of them were getting any closer to their invisible meal.

Then, with a tremendous explosion of pain, a twin-toed foot slammed down onto her injured shoulder. She might not have been able to hear her collarbone break, but she definitely felt it snap under the weight of the stale-smelling shaggy leg. Bursts of agonising colour filled her mind, completely disrupting her ability to keep her invisibility spell active. As the mutants' legs continued to buffet her, Arke was now visible, and teetering on the edge of consciousness.

※ ※ ※

RUBY WAS BROUGHT back to her senses by a flash of lightning so powerful it made her feathers stand up. Although darkness was approaching fast, a hole in the roof of the room she was in allowed just enough light in to see, and she narrowed her eyes as she took stock of her situation. To her right, the woman who'd wanted her ring was now wearing it, and at the main window stood one of the men she'd seen by the campfire. The Ornithol's feathers were already raised, but now they started to bristle like hackles. When she was growing up under the care of the Sisters of No Mercy, everyone had to share, but there were no such rules out here.

Leaping to her feet, she charged at the ring-stealer, body slamming her against the wall and administering a heavy punch to the back of her neck. The dark-haired man reacted quickly, hurling a magical ball of caustic liquid which singed a line through the feathers on her side. As another bolt of lightning lit the sky, the Ornithol smashed her other fist into the woman in lieu of a goodbye and launched herself out of the large hole in the roof.

She knew Kennedy would have assumed her tactical retreat was due to his lecture on safe battle practices, however, the three M's (Multiple Mages is Madness) had completely passed her by – she'd always been a terrible student. Her strengths lay in different areas. For example, she'd instantly recognised the lightning spell as one of Sparkz's. If he was here, then so were the others, and she needed to help them rather than spend time in a risky situation just for the sake of some jewellery. Also, it was easier to take her possessions back when the thieves were dead. The Ornithol was a far more natural pirate than she had been a novice.

Ruby scanned the ruined settlement as she soared above the house. The fight, such as it was, did not appear to be going that well. Sparkz was struggling to keep in the air while being attacked by what looked like a cloud with multiple fists and a bad weather attitude. Below him was a milling horde of mutant beasts who seemed to be fixated on something under their feet, and in the near distance she could just make out the approach of the *Warrior*.

After seeing the cloud creature throw itself at the engineer with such force he almost dropped out of the sky, the Ornithol sped towards him. Calling up a little weather of her own, she hurled a magical blast of wind at the airborne attacker, pushing it away from her crewmate to give him a chance to regain some altitude.

"Sparkz! I'm over here!" she yelled, but only heard the beginning of his reply as a wave of magic suddenly surrounded her. In an instant, everything became very cold and very muffled. The spell was so intense that the top half of Ruby's torso was instantly sheathed in ice. Wings failing, she plummeted to the ground.

※ ※ ※

Struggling under the throng of mutant beasts, the Soulbound was curled in as tight a ball as she could manage. The blow to her shoulder had brought her to the edge of unconsciousness and, although that threat had passed, she couldn't concentrate on anything but trying to survive. The urge to vomit was even more intense than when she'd been invisible, as the air around her was so thick with the fetid stench of heated bodies she could almost chew it.

"Do you need me to take over?" Stabbington's tone was unusually terse, but clearly his host's inability to escape the milling mutants meant he couldn't stay silent anymore.

"Don't you DARE!" His question sent sudden fury through Arke. It had been years since she'd made him promise not to control her body, and she wasn't about to backslide now.

"Then USE me!"

The demon sword summoned itself to her right hand, nearly slicing through her foot as it hissed into existence. With the most painful of turns, she managed to get enough force behind the blade for its tip to hit the ground. A sonic boom tore itself through the mutant beasts as she teleported away, and unwholesome meaty chunks fell like rain as the animals who'd been standing over her suddenly became cheap pet food. The sword had not been the only thing made larger after the blessing from Stabbington's mother – the magic that came from him seemed more powerful too.

Reappearing in the roof space of a ruined house, the Soulbound was faced with the backs of two men who were busy watching the street below. She had no idea who they were, only that they reeked of magic. It didn't take a genius to work out they'd had something to do with the trap that had the illusion of Ruby as bait, and therefore must also be involved in her disappearance.

Multiple mages were only madness if you weren't angry, sore, and Arke. Energised from not being used as a football, as well as from a heavy dose of Stabbington's magical painkiller, there was no choice to be made. It was time to unleash some chaos.

Flicking a glance around the room, she spotted that what remained of the stairwell was blocked by the wreckage of ancient furniture and heard the rumbling and stamping of mutants below.

"They sound hungry," Stabbington remarked. "Maybe you should let them up for a little snack."

With a grim smile, she released a barrage of her magical darts to destroy the barricade. Both mages spun round, expressions radiating shock, and then fury. The first to step forwards was a black-coated man who had more hair on his top lip than his head and carried a wicked-looking staff that crackled with arcane energy.

"Surprise." The Soulbound waved a hand in what was undoubtedly an unduly confident greeting for someone who only had one working arm and was splattered in various unsavoury substances.

The moustachioed man's reply consisted of exactly thirty-two words, all of them relating to Arke's appearance, sexual habits, and likelihood of achieving a satisfactory end to her life. Just as he finished his rant, he stepped smoothly to one side, allowing his friend to launch a blast of green-tinged fire at her. However, she'd been using that particular type of distraction before the bald man grew his first facial hair, and sidestepped at the perfect moment. The gout of acrid-smelling flame flew harmlessly past before shooting into the night sky through the shattered roof behind her.

She was about to deliver a withering reply to the mage's tirade when he threw his staff towards her as if it was a javelin. Reacting swiftly, she smashed the projectile away just as he blasted a ray of scorching white light directly into her face. Her eyes lost focus, swimming with tears, and she staggered blindly backwards as he swung his fist at her head, the surprisingly heavy blow bringing her to her knees. Wasting no time, he grabbed her around the throat, his fingers digging into her flesh like metal talons as he squeezed.

From the instant Arke had teleported to escape the pointy hooved monsters, the orange magic inside her had been reacting – pressure was building with every hit she took as well as every spell she cast. It felt different to when it was boiling to critical mass, far more exhilarating than destructive, and although she had no idea what was going to happen, she knew something was on its way.

The cork finally popped out of the bottle the moment the moustachioed mage became her very own guide dog. She needed to know where he was before she could immolate him with the magical expression of her rage, and his hand on her neck provided the perfect locator beacon. As she released her spell, blue flame flung itself up his arm and spread across his entire body. And, with a sudden blast of burning orange light, she disappeared from both the house and the mortal plane entirely.

ALL ROUND HER was instantly silent and peaceful. This wasn't a dream, for she hadn't fallen asleep. Plus, everything hurt exactly as it had before the orange flash. This was real, but a weird kind of 'somewhere else' real. She was still on her knees and unable to see, but she knew this wasn't the ruined village. For a start, there were no sounds of mutants or angry mages, nor any attempts to redesign her skull.

Taking some slow, deep breaths, she turned her head, first to the left and then the right, curious as to why she could suddenly smell some of the nicest cologne Barsia had ever manufactured. She rubbed her face, trying to clear the tears from her eyes, before realising her demon blade, which had been in her grasp back in the derelict house, was no longer there.

With what felt like a careful touch, a hand took hers, and though her first instinct was to pull away, when her skin flared with strangely warming crackles of magic, the Soulbound allowed herself to be helped to her feet.

"Who are you? Where am I?" Her eyes watered painfully as they tried to recover from the blinding light that had seared itself onto her retinas.

"Well…"

That one word made everything curiously, astonishingly, and perfectly clear. Arke knew that voice, and she knew where her sword was. However it had happened, he was standing in front of her, and based on the hand that still held hers, he wasn't in snake form. "Well? Well, what?"

"Ah."

"<u>Now</u>? <u>Now</u> you have no words?" She kept blinking, suddenly desperate to have her sight back. "I've spent forty-three years listening to your constant chatter and <u>this</u> is the moment you forget how to talk?"

The reply came as a familiar irritated sigh, one she was accustomed to hearing inside her head. Except it wasn't in her head. It was out there, in front of her and although not being able to see him was incredibly frustrating, her smile grew and grew as Stabbington began to speak.

"You know that you are extremely annoying? I am trying to take in this moment, the first time I can look at you with eyes I do not have to share. There is no-one else in this body, so it must be mine. I want to remember how it feels to see you, even when you are covered in blood and excrement, but no, you must be disagreeable. And now you smile. Of course <u>you</u> smile. <u>I</u> am not smiling."

As her vision finally cleared, she found herself staring into the mostly human-looking face of Stabbington Bear. He had short, dark hair with elements of silver at his temples and a fake expression of exasperation as he gazed down at her, his lips trying and failing not to form into a grin. Everything about him appeared normal – except his eyes. They were bright blue, but their irises were vertical, which was the only suggestion that Stabbington wasn't your average man. Your average, very tall man, she realised, her neck starting to hurt as she looked up at him.

"You are definitely smiling. And also – you could be shorter."

"Forty-three years and you moan I am too tall! I am the perfect height. You will have to grow!" Despite his protestations, he dropped to one knee. "There, is that better?"

"Much." After a moment of hesitation, she reached her hand to his face, feeling the warmth of his skin under her fingertips. "You're real."

"And you stink." His eyes widened in mock horror. "Oh, was this not the 'blindingly obvious fact' game?"

She patted his cheek just a little harder than was necessary. "Good to know you're a prick no matter what body you're in."

He chuckled. "I hope there was never a doubt!"

She shook her head and turned to look at their surroundings. "Did you do this? This place?"

"If I could have, I would have done so a very long time ago. I believe this was your strange orange magic."

ARKE WAS SUDDENLY returned to the ruined house, Stabbington in his sword form back in her hand and a storm of curse-laden frustration in her head. Thankfully for her entirely distracted state of mind, the two mages in the attic were too busy fighting the ground floor tenants to notice her reappearance.

Forcing her thoughts towards self-preservation, the Soulbound stepped carefully away from the grisly scene. With a coldly amused smile, she noted the beasts who were pouring up the stairs appeared to be a large family of kitten-monkey-calf babies, chaperoned by their proud mother. Adorable as that was, it was time to leave. She'd been on the menu too many times for one evening and had far better things to do, starting with getting her collarbone fixed and ending with a discussion with her demon.

Sneaking out of the giant hole in the roof, she almost collided with Ruby and Sparkz.

"We saw some orange flashes and hoped it was you!" The Ornithol was the first to grab Arke, tapping her beak on the top of her friend's head with obvious relief.

"What a day to have a sense of smell." Sparkz wrinkled his nose with disgust. "Bags you carry the walking muckheap back to the ship, Rubes."

Chapter Thirteen
Serendipity?

As dawn broke the following morning, the *Warrior's* crew saw how effective Kennedy's rage-filled usage of the ship's aetheric lance had been. What had been a cluster of ruined buildings was now a collection of craters and scattered masonry. There was overkill, and then there was this.

After everything they'd been through recently, no-one judged him for venting so much fury that the weapon nearly overheated. They had, however, kept a wary eye on the area after their captain's cabin door had slammed shut. Mages were slippery things and until they'd seen the bodies, it was better to keep watch.

"Good morning, everyone." With a smile as bright as her tone, Arke strode out onto the deck. "Hope you're feeling energetic today."

"Look at their faces! They are baffled by your happiness!" Stabbington's voice was gleeful as the crew reacted to his host's unusually cheery behaviour. "Ha! Irash is casting a spell to find out if you have been mind controlled! Keep it up, I want to know if any of them are brave enough to ask why you are smiling."

She peered over the side to survey the destruction below the ship before looking at her crewmates. "It's awesome that you're all ready to head down to the ruins... or should I say rubble, to see if we can rustle up some loot from what's left of the mages." Her smile grew wider still. "Doesn't it feel good to get back to our pirate roots? We've done the smashing, now let's do the grabbing."

After a moment of silence, Ellie cleared her throat. "Yes... absolutely."

"Are you alright?" Ruby asked, head tilted to one side.

"A bit sore, so if it's ok with you guys, I'll pop to see Gurdi and grab a little something to help me through the day." The Soulbound eased the sling away from her neck. "Anyone need anything from the galley?"

No-one did, probably because they were all too busy trying to work out if someone had swapped their version of Arke with one from another reality.

The dwarven healer was grinding up herbs when the Soulbound breezed into the infirmary and slid a cup of coffee towards her.

"Zero milk, heaps of sugar, just how you like it. You said to pop by this morning for some more of that stuff that tasted of marmalade and pickled onions."

Gurdi had been on the *Warrior* for so long that she was used to life on board being several synonyms of strange. However, those years of calm acceptance did nothing to stop her eye twitching as she stared at the Soulbound's bright expression.

"She thinks you have lost your mind," Stabbington chuckled. "Last night you asked her to heal your broken collarbone when normally she has to wait for you to pass out; and you *never* ask for more of her disgusting potions. Look at her pinching her own arm to check she is not asleep. You are SUCH a terrible patient, I have always felt sorry for her."

Unaware of the demon's commentary inside Arke's head, the healer picked up a bottle and poured a measure of green and blue striped gloop into a small cup. "How's your shoulder?"

"It's a bit sore, but at least I can feel my fingers now." The Soulbound flexed her hand with a chuckle before downing the medicine without a single expression of complaint.

"Always a bonus." A warm smile spread across Gurdi's face. "It's been a long time since I heard your laugh, I'd almost forgotten what it sounded like, but I'm very glad that you reminded me." She leant back in her chair, cradling her mug with both hands. "So many years, you and me. Where do they go? I swear it was only yesterday that Philip was in short trousers, getting in trouble for leaving spiders in your bed."

Arke shuddered dramatically before patting the hilt of her sword with a grin. "I prefer to remember him wandering around with Stabbington in his chubby little fist, trying to shake us all down like a good baby pirate."

"Precious memories."

THE SUN WAS firmly in the sky by the time the *Warrior's* cargo platform lowered the working party to the ground. Keen to find her magical ring, Ruby suggested they split into two groups to cover the area more efficiently. She took one towards what was left of the house where she'd been held prisoner, while Arke directed the other to the site of her encounter with the black-coated mage and his friend.

As the teams sifted through the debris, the Soulbound kept watch. Not even their location and the ache in her shoulder could dent her good mood. The sun was warm and Stabbington was singing songs that didn't make her want to stab herself in the ear with a spoon. Whatever the orange magic had done to bring them together had changed everything.

It had been well past midnight the previous night when she'd finally returned to her cabin. She'd been high on magical healing and so battered she could barely undo her own boots when Dozer had arrived to take his usual place on her bed. The giant Rottweiler had obviously been waiting for her summons as the instant she'd whistled, he'd appeared with an extravagant crack of hellish thunder and a furiously wagging tail.

Arke had kept her back to the wall as the hellhound bounded over. She was already well over her quota of animal tramplings for the day.

"Paws on the floor!" she'd ordered as he readied himself to leap up and lick her face. "I'm walking wounded."

Dozer had skidded to a halt before licking her hand with such sympathetic force he'd opened up one of her cuts. Then, by way of apology, he'd helped pull her boots off, dropped into a ridiculously excited play bow and leapt onto her bed with them both in his cavernous mouth.

"If there is a positive here, it must be that the idiot creature does not shed," Stabbington had remarked as they'd watched the monstrous dog roll around on her blankets.

"Don't be mean, he's just warming it up for me." Arke had contemplated the logistical nightmare that undressing was going to be and given up before she'd even begun. Thankfully, since Gurdi had helped her out of her filthy clothes and into a shower before fixing her collarbone, sleeping fully dressed had been a much more acceptable course of action than it would have been otherwise.

"How? Friction?"

Stabbington had been about to launch into a lengthy monologue about the availability of body heat to a creature whose only claim to the ownership of a body was the magical adherence of skin and bones into a canine shape, when a question made him forget his entire argument.

"How do you think it happened? You said it was the orange magic."

"Yes." The demon had paused for a moment. "It is hard to understand what this is, even for me. This energy, power, whatever it is, I see it clearly, running like many rivers inside you. Right now, it is calm and slow moving, but back when you were fighting, it was turbulent. Every time you were hurt, every spell you cast, the current grew stronger, until – *poof* – we were in another place."

She sighed. "I wish I knew how to take us there again."

"I would suggest spellcasting and getting the shit kicked out of you, but my magic needs to recharge and Gurdi would be furious if you ruin her good work."

"Thanks for your deep concern for my wellbeing."

"Of course. Now get into bed before the stupid creature kicks all your blankets on the floor."

Having settled down beside the goofiest of hellhounds, sleep was already threatening to overtake her when she'd finally managed to frame the apology she knew she had to make.

"I'm sorry about what I said earlier, I didn't mean to upset you."

"Ahhh, my Arke." Stabbington's voice had been soft as he replied. "We always hurt the ones we love."

"In that case... all those people I've killed..."

There had been a pause, followed by a long sigh from the demon. "Well, at least one of us is emotionally available. Now go to sleep."

After a heavy morning's work searching the rubble of the village, the two teams finished their grisly tasks, having found everyone except the mage who'd stolen Ruby's ring.

"None of them are her," the Ornithol remarked with what was definitely a click of a very sharp, very irritated beak.

"We watched all night, no-one escaped."

"Then she's still here – somewhere," Ruby growled, the ferocity of her tone capturing the attention of everyone nearby.

Arke looked at her friend with raised eyebrows. "I mean, is seven feet of angry Ornithol ever wrong?" She grinned, holding up a warding hand as Ruby swivelled a gimlet glare in her direction. "And if they were would you tell them? Do you want me to summon Dozer so we can do the whole bloodhound act, or should I stop talking and start walking?" With the Ornithol's unblinking stare burning its way into her skull, she nodded quickly and pointed in the vaguest of directions. "You're right. I'll just get on with it."

Ten minutes later, Arke was still trawling the ruins, a headache building behind her eyes as she concentrated her senses on finding the missing mage. They'd found a few valuable items on the other bodies, but given the intense yellow gaze following her progress, she knew she had to find the one with Ruby's ring. Failure was simply not an option.

Finally she caught the scent of perceptive magic, the heady odour that always reminded her of sugar, and tracked it to its source. In the corner of what might once have been the village square, an old well had collapsed, the cover slipping to one side, and under its shelter was the illusion of some crippled buckets and barrels.

Arke waved the others over as she brushed the spell aside to reveal the mage who had stolen the Ornithol's ring huddled amongst some rubble. She was covered with a mixture of blood and dirt, and her face was heavily swollen around the unmistakable imprint of a two-toed hoof.

"Don't hurt me, please! I'm sorry!"

As Ruby surged forwards, full of righteous fury, the Soulbound summoned Stabbington and used the flat of his blade to hold her back.

"Hold up, Rubes. It's tricky to talk to folks if they have a beak buried in their eye-socket."

The injured mage cowered. "I swear I just did what I was told."

"Let's move swiftly past the 'They made me do it' defence. What's your name? Tell me what you were doing out here." Arke lowered the tip of her sword to the ground and waited.

"My name's Kilar. Ruberk, the guy with the moustache, paid us to find things here. Relics and arcane items from Grand Barsia make decent money on the black market. Plus, the authorities don't come out here, so if you're a mage it's a good place to be."

Flicking an anxious glance towards the looming Ornithol, Kilar tossed the ring it to its rightful owner. As Ruby placed it back on her finger, the Soulbound pointed her blade at the mage's throat.

"So what's your plan now?"

"I don't... know. To get out of here alive?" she replied, swallowing nervously.

"The odds are pretty stacked against you."

Kilar nodded her head in exhausted agreement. Arke took a moment to think before offering her a hand.

"Come with us."

Ruby stared at her friend with almost as much surprise as the mage. "What?"

"Always respect the surrender. So, what'll it be?"

"Are you sure?" Kilar stood up, wobbling unsteadily, barely able to hold herself upright.

Fingers still gripped tightly around her wrist, the Soulbound lowered her voice to a gritty whisper. "On one condition. If you ever – EVER – betray us, I will reduce your entire existence to a single horrific moment and have you repeat it for eternity."

One thing Arke had never struggled with was the ability to make completely unsubstantiated threats sound like legitimate promises, and as her dark eyes glittered meaningfully, there wasn't a soul present who didn't instantly believe her.

The mage nodded slowly. "I understand." She slipped a hand inside her coat and pulled out a leather pouch. "How about a show of faith? Everything we've found this trip is inside this endless bag. Take it, please."

AFTER DELIVERING KILAR to the infirmary, the Soulbound returned to her cabin. Her cheerful mood had been washed away the moment she'd seen the well-worn brown bag. There was a powerful tang to its presence that was unusual even for a magical safety deposit box, and she'd had little doubt about what lay within. Stabbington might deny it, but she was coming to believe that there was no such thing as coincidence.

She slid her hand inside the pouch the moment she was alone, the cool feeling of the lining giving way to an instant chill as she reached into the magical area beyond. Endless bags were expensive but still sold by the thousands, each granting access to a storage space with room for whatever you could squeeze past the opening. Closing her eyes to concentrate, Arke knew she wouldn't have to hunt around, that magic would go to magic, and as her fingers found a freezing cold, pyramid-shaped object which hummed with power, she hissed a single emphatic curse. There it was, almost exactly where the Autarch had said it would be. The first capstone.

"I heard it went well down there – you even scored us a new crew member." Kennedy opened her door with a smile that quickly faded as he saw the look on her face. "What's wrong?"

"We need to make a decision. I thought it would take longer to find it, but I guess luck really wants to shit in our eye today." With a slow shove, Arke pushed the bag over to her captain. "Think of the picture of the capstone and put your hand in this. Just don't... don't get it out. It's buzzing with magic and I'm not taking any risks."

He nodded and sat down, visibly steeling himself before reaching inside. The Soulbound watched his expression carefully, seeing it darken as he found what he was searching for.

"For some reason I thought it would be stone, but this is metal," he observed, his brow furrowing with concentration. "Feels like runes stamped into all the sides – except the base."

"Careful, it's sharp under there."

"Sure is. Maybe it's the broken ends of some sort of clamps or connections. Calling it a capstone suggests it goes on top of something, so I guess it would need to be secured somehow."

Arke frowned. "I don't know, and I don't care."

Kennedy sat back and shut the bag. "Well, it's pretty much where the note said it would be. Do you think 'It' knows we found it?"

"Maybe. Probably." The Soulbound's gaze fell on the obsidian ring that so innocuously encircled the smallest finger of her left hand. "But what do we do?"

"Give it the capstone in exchange for it removing that thing and forgetting it ever saw you?" he suggested.

"*'The Autarch requires...'*" Arke began. "His note said four. I doubt one will be enough." She looked up at Kennedy, her jaw clenching and unclenching as she marshalled her words. "Hear me out, ok? The more I think, the more I realise that this isn't just an evil bastard with some creepy fixation on me. When Stabbington showed me his memories, I saw his mother's reaction when he mentioned the Autarch. She's thousands of years old and rules an entire plane, so how does she know about him, and why does she even care? This is big, way bigger than us." She rubbed a hand over her forehead before looking at the ring again. "We've seen plenty of the darker side of this world, but that thing in the tower is different – more powerful, more vicious, more calculating than Irash ever was, and we were terrified of what he could do." She paused, easing her eyes back to Kennedy. "I wish I hadn't thought about things, I wish I could do what I was told and keep safe – but I've never done that and I'm not about to start now." She pointed at the pouch. "I don't know what that does or did or could do, but if something that vile wants it..."

"Then that's the last place it should go." Kennedy glared at the innocuous bag in front of him. "I hate this whole situation and most of all I hate that thing in the tower. I feel like we're tiny fish wriggling on the end of its line." He took a deep breath. "But that doesn't mean we can't escape." He pointed at her, his expression firm. "And just to clarify, because I know what you tried to do with Irash, you are not expendable. Not now, not ever." He placed his hand back on the table, tapping the pouch with an index finger. "So, what's our play?"

"There's a play?"

"You're Arke, so there's a play. That devious brain of yours has never let us down before."

Kennedy's confidence brought a weak smile to the Soulbound's lips, and she nodded.

"Well, we have an orbiculum... I was going to suggest asking Crimbles if he knows someone nearby who could work it. If we can use it to open a door to another plane, we could make the capstone doubly secure while we try and figure out what to do next."

There was a long moment of quiet acknowledgement between the two of them, Arke's dark eyes staring straight into Kennedy's blue ones. Their gaze communicated everything they did not wish to discuss – the risks, their fears, the uncertainty of not knowing how the man in the bright darkness would react and how much power he could wield outside his throne room.

Chapter Fourteen
Long Distance Communication

As usual when calling Mr Crimbles, Kennedy and Arke were put on hold for a good few minutes while an automated voice repeated: 'Your call isn't important to me at all, I have far more interesting things to do like sleep, push random items off shelves, and lick my balls.'

Despite being the overlord of the largest arcane smuggling operation in Barsia, Mr Crimbles was still a cat. A smooth-tongued, plush tabby cat with the shiniest fur that magic could produce.

"That stupid message has been the same for years!" the Soulbound muttered. "Why doesn't he change it?"

"He wants to tell everyone he can lick his balls," Kennedy chuckled. "If I could I'd want people to know too."

"Thanks for throwing that mental image into my already aching head." Arke rubbed at the back of her neck before trying to move the sling to a more comfortable position.

"You do know I just like listening in, right?" Crimbles' marmalade voice oozed out of the magical communication device which resembled a bell similar to one which might hang on a cat's collar. "You can learn a lot about folk while they're on hold."

The Soulbound put two fingers to her forehead in greeting as a real-time image of the tabby's broad face flashed into life in front of them.

"Catman."

"Bitchlady." Mr Crimbles scratched at his ear with more than a suggestion of a middle claw raised at the Soulbound as he did so.

"You're looking well." Kennedy threw on his best smile, leaning forwards and waving to bring the cat's attention his way before he lost focus on the meeting. The long-standing friendship between Arke and Mr Crimbles both enabled and predisposed them to lengthy bouts of verbal jousting that elevated Kennedy to the unwelcome roles of referee and grown-up unless he kept the discussions on track. "We're after some help."

"Darling, of course, what do you need this time? Legal, practical, or magical? Oh, please tell me you're in a Tattenberg prison, I've got some excellent new blackmail material that I absolutely can't wait to use. It's filth, my boy, pure, unadulterated filth." The tabby ran a paw over his face in a decidedly salacious fashion.

"Sorry, to ahh... disappoint you, but we're not in Tattenberg."

"Shame. Sure I couldn't tempt you to go there?"

"Any other time. But we have a sizeable 'issue' that we're hoping you can help us with. We need to use the orbiculum." Kennedy drove the conversation forwards with the focus of a sheepdog.

"I heard the Irash problem was... resolved?" Crimbles looked at him curiously.

"This is something else, we've had a run in with something that calls itself the Autarch and..."

"Rewind, dear boy. Re-wind. Autarch?" The cat's face loomed larger in the bubble, his whiskers so close you could see them quivering with every breath. "Speak slowly and precisely."

Arke leant back in her chair, scruffing her hair into peaks while Kennedy kept talking.

"The last Autarch isn't as dead as everyone thought. There's an obsidian tower still standing in the swamp where Great Barsia used to be and..." Kennedy glanced at the Soulbound before continuing. "The Autarch... ah... recruited us to do a job for him."

"He's alive?" Crimbles hissed. "I'd heard rumours but..."

Arke lurched forwards and stared at the tabby's face, her expression tense and her eyes narrowed. "Neither alive nor dead. Not mortal, nor ghost. He's just *there*, in this strange darkness that shines so brightly I could hardly bear to look at it. But whatever he is, he's powerful enough to murder and unmurder over and over again without even a twitch of effort." She sat back, her hand shaking as she reached for a glass of water.

"You went to see him?" Crimbles' fur had been fluffing up with every second of the explanation. "I know you're insane but ARE YOU INSANE?"

"I didn't have a choice!" Arke downed her drink as if it were alcohol and slammed the glass on the table. "And now he's got us searching for four pyramid shaped things that he calls capstones. We have no idea what they are or what they do."

The cat began to wash his face as if trying to rid his fur of the information he'd just been given. Finally, he stopped cleaning himself and looked from Arke to

Kennedy as he spoke. "History lesson for the educationally bereft. And by that, I mean both of you. Before the Night of Terrors, the Autarch summoned hundreds of mages from all over the empire to the palace and nobody knows why. Then one day 'Boom', no more capital, magical shockwave, shit got wild, Barsia nearly imploded." Crimbles let his gaze linger on the Soulbound as he continued. "Understandably enough, everyone assumed he died like all the others. However, if he was dicking about with such large amounts of magic that he needed all those mages, it could have done pretty much anything to him. The fact he's there but no-one has heard of him in over two hundred years suggests he's stuck in that place. And the one thing about people who get locked away that is always true? They want to escape. If it wasn't entirely as obvious as Arke's shaking hand, I would suggest you didn't help him."

"I'm not sure what other options we have," Kennedy replied as the Soulbound surged to her feet and started pacing, her fingers clenching and unclenching with every stride. "He made her wear a ring, we have no idea what it does, but apparently it's full of magic. Which is..." He took a deep breath and rubbed at his forehead. "Anyway, we found the first of the capstones roughly where he said it would be. His instructions didn't specify to bring each back individually, so maybe we have time to work out what to do while we find the rest."

The tabby glanced at Arke before returning his attention to Kennedy. "And you assume he can't get to the stone if it isn't on this plane, hence your orbiculum question. That's a bold move, my friends."

"Do you have any better ideas?"

Crimbles shook his head slowly. "I'm afraid I don't – but I do have a mage strong enough to work the orbiculum currently en route from Soleya to Theogenes. Would that be any good to you?"

Kennedy beamed. "Yes, yes it would."

"I'll set up a rendezvous. Don't stop for anything, do you understand?" The cat turned to look at Arke. "Show me the ring."

As she held her hand close to the image of Crimbles' face, a jeweller's eyepiece appeared over his right eye. After only a second of investigation, the tabby's fur stood on end and his lips curled back to reveal a set of gold-capped teeth. "That jerk has no style." He flicked the monocle off before continuing. "You probably already know this, but don't try to take it off."

"We worked that out. How screwed am I?"

"Arke, you've been screwed your entire life. What's one more bit?"

✕ ✕ ✕

The further the *Warrior* flew from the obsidian tower, the more obvious it became that the Autarch was aware of their intentions. The crew reported unusual things happening – items flying off shelves, ghostly faces appearing at portholes, food randomly spoiling and crockery shattering. Even before Kennedy ordered them to buddy up, no-one went anywhere alone.

Arke had barely slept since the conversation with Crimbles, as a constant sense of dread dogged her every moment. Her happy dreams of Joy had been replaced by nightmares. Each time she tried to sleep, she had to watch her crewmates being murdered, some of them exploding, some being ripped apart, some smothered, some burnt. The more she saw, the more she knew their decision had been the right one. They needed to put the capstone where he couldn't touch it.

They were only a few hours away from the rendezvous when Arke headed into the galley for lunch and was immediately attacked by every piece of cutlery on the table. Knives, forks, and spoons launched themselves at her as if she'd become magnetised, and she only avoided injury by sprinting for the exit.

Stubbornly stoic, she stood in the corridor to eat her meal, only to find that everything she put in her mouth suddenly became inedible. Giving up on food, she headed back to the top deck. On the way, a lantern landed on her head, and when she'd recovered from that, a rope snagged her ankles at the bottom of the stairs. Finally reaching her cabin, tired, hungry, battered and bruised, she shut the door which promptly fell off its hinges and smashed into her still painful shoulder.

Kennedy heard the crash and hurried over, looking through the empty doorway with raised eyebrows.

"I didn't do that." She sighed. "Nor did I throw cutlery at myself, pour a ton of salt in my food, drop a lantern on my head or trip up the stairs."

"The bastard in the tower's getting desperate, we just need to hold on."

"Yeah." She lay down on her bed, which promptly collapsed.

Kennedy sat next to her. "I'll stay with you."

The hours passed slowly as they looked out over the deck while trying to ignore the large red numbers that had suddenly materialised on the cabin wall. The highest was five, but that was already crossed out. Arke tried to reach out her senses and pinpoint the source of the magic that was creating the visual countdown, but she was so tired she couldn't concentrate long enough to make sense of anything. As the clock ticked on, an angry streak slashed through each digit, one by one.

Kennedy had been snoring gently for quite some time when the Soulbound gave up on trying to gain any sort of rest from her nightmare fuelled slumbers. She got up slowly, not wanting to wake him, and headed out on deck, feeling increasingly disconnected from everything around her. Stabbington was saying something, but she couldn't focus on his words – they were just so much background noise, buzzing in her head like distant waves.

As she leant against the wall of the captain's cabin, trying to anchor herself through the solidity of the timbers at her back and under her feet, Arke felt a sudden rush of cold shoot through her. She checked around but saw nothing. Exhaustion did odd things to people, so she assumed any strange sensations must be because of her physical state. She let her eyelids drift downwards while she focused on steadying her breathing and prayed they'd reach the rendezvous soon.

She didn't notice Porro, the ship's Ornithol cook, approaching until he was in front of her, carrying a plate of finger food. "Arke, I have had an idea! Hear me out – maybe if someone else tries to feed you then you will be able to eat..."

She opened her eyes.

It took her a second to focus on his familiar parrot-like face.

It took less than a second for him to explode.

Suddenly, she was covered in a fountain of blood and internal organs which drenched her with gore from head to foot. Red feathers fluttered in a cloud, hanging in the air before floating down to land in what remained of the kind-hearted, accordion-playing chef. The deck rang with the crew's horrified screams and shouts as Arke stood frozen to the spot. She could feel hot, wet pieces of Porro dripping off her eyelashes, rolling down her neck and covering her lips. Another cold blast shot through her, but she barely even noticed.

On the wall behind her was her silhouette outlined in blood and tissue, decorated with a few of the red and blue feathers from the dead Ornithol. She saw Kennedy running towards her, but lifted a shaking hand to keep him away. She had to hold it together, she had to force her legs to walk, she had to make it to her cabin. Everything was so distant, so muffled, so overwhelming. This was what she'd seen in her nightmares, this end for Porro, this terrible punishment meted out for a decision he'd never made.

She wanted to drop to her knees and scream, but she forced herself to keep moving. She struggled into her cabin, into her bathroom and finally into the shower, pressing her forehead to the wall as the floor of the cubicle turned red.

※ ※ ※

AFTER A QUICK discussion, Kennedy escorted the crew to their quarters. They'd watch each other's backs while Kilar, the mage they had picked up in the swamp, painted all the protective wards she knew on the walls and Ruby exhorted her god to extend some sort of divine shield around them. Irash headed to join Sparkz in the engine room to help guard the aetheric crystal.

Kennedy didn't know what else he could do to protect everyone. They were under an hour away from the co-ordinates that Crimbles had given them, and they were holding on by their fingertips. He squared his shoulders and locked the crew's door from the outside before heading back to the helm.

The tiny schooner waiting for them at the rendezvous was not quite what Kennedy had expected, but as he cut engines and drifted alongside, a cloaked figure appeared from the single cabin and glided over to the *Warrior*.

"Do I have permission to come aboard, Captain Kennedy?" The mage hovered between the ships, his cloak rippling in the breeze.

"You're from Crimbles?"

"Yes. Would you like to contact him to check my credentials?" The rumbling voice bore no hint of any irritation at Kennedy's question.

"No. There's no time – things have... gone wrong. We need to hurry."

The figure bowed its head as it flowed towards Kennedy. "I feel much negative energy here. Put this on – it will keep you safe while I prepare the ritual."

A bronze amulet floated out from beneath the mage's robes and pressed itself into Kennedy's hand.

"Thank you." He fastened the chain around his neck. "Do you need anything from me?"

"Only the orbiculum."

The robed figure turned away, and the deck came alive with a bevy of spectral brushes which started to paint sigils and runes in a ten-foot circle. Kennedy secured the helm before hurrying to fetch the unusually shaped artefact they'd stolen only a few weeks ago.

As he emerged from his cabin, magic frying pan in hand, the Soulbound walked out of hers. Kennedy stopped, lips pursed in a tight and anxious line as he watched her. She was even more deathly pale than usual, eyes red-rimmed and bloodshot. Her fingers were clutching the magical safety deposit bag as she strode across the deck, her step only faltering when the figure turned to her.

"Arke, it has been some time."

Kennedy had been inwardly panicking that the mage was some sort of agent for the creature in the obsidian tower. Hearing what sounded like a friendly greeting rumbling from inside the cloak made those particular worries fade away. He had plenty of others to replace it with, of course, but at least it was one burden less.

When the Soulbound finally replied, her voice was hoarse. "Why did it have to be you, Nox?"

"It wasn't personal, I was the nearest. Stand in the centre of the circle."

As Kennedy started to cross the deck, a barrel launched itself at his head, followed quickly by a coil of rope. As he flinched, both were slammed away from him by a sudden wave of energy from the amulet. He sprinted to Nox and held out the orbiculum, trying not to react as a grey and glistening appendage with octopus-like suckers emerged from the mage's sleeve. It wrapped itself around the pan's handle before retracting smoothly and placing the artefact next to Arke.

"We are ready."

Preparations complete, silver and black candles burst into flame at each intersecting line and Nox turned towards the Soulbound.

"Stabbington, please entreat your mother to allow swift passage to her realm. I feel energy building nearby – we must not delay."

"He's already spoken to her," Arke replied. "She will assist."

"Very well. Touch his blade to the orbiculum while holding tight to the object you wish to send. Concentrate on its destination."

The instant the sword connected with the metal of the pan, there was a sudden outburst of noise from below decks. Shouting, screaming, hysterical crying, and fists hammering on the doors and walls.

Kennedy gritted his teeth and gripped the wheel so tightly the skin over his knuckles paled to a skeletal white. With a glance to the main hatch, he summoned an alter and sent it down to investigate. They were committed, this had to be done and done now.

Nox began the ritual, his voice rumbling through otherworldly incantations. Words on words, rippling and chanting until the orbiculum suddenly flamed with bright blue light and floated upwards, dragging Stabbington's blade with it. Then the candles guttered, their flames turning black and shedding pure darkness into the circle. The mage never faltered, his words meaningless to all but the blackness which surrounded them.

The wheel lurched out of Kennedy's hands and started to spin wildly. Everything that wasn't lashed down threw itself towards the solid walls of darkness. He felt the amulet growing hotter as it protected him from the swirling debris. His face was a grim mask, for he'd seen through the eyes of his alter. It was too late to do anything but hope that the Autarch's rage would focus on the top deck instead of below.

Chapter Fifteen
Broad Shoulders

ARKE HEARD NOTHING but Nox's sonorous voice repeating his chant as she held Stabbington to the orbiculum. Everything was cloaked in darkness as a sudden change in pressure made her ears pop and her eyes water. The boards beneath her bare feet started to soften and warp under the thunderous waves of force that rolled around the centre of the circle. Suddenly the mage's words changed, and she was falling even while she stood. She sank and swirled into the blackness, struggling to breathe as the heat began to rise and a strange choking smell assaulted her nostrils with every gasp.

"We are here." Stabbington's voice sounded painfully loud in her head. "Take a look."

"Here? I wasn't supposed to go anywhere..." Arke opened her eyes, not even realising she'd shut them. "This isn't... the... oh, shit."

She knew where she was, for she'd seen it in his memories. Glaring grey rock was everywhere and the sky was a torrid red. Yellow fog clustered in patches, tiers of it rising hundreds of feet into the air, and all she could hear were scratchings, hissing, and muffled voices.

The demon sighed. "Yes, this was not quite the plan, but my mother wishes to meet you. It was she who helped open the portal so quickly."

"She wants to see me? Why?"

The Soulbound looked down at her hand. "And why are you still a sword? This is your home, right?"

"I wanted to make sure you were ok." He paused. "And I did not wish to frighten you."

"Well if I'm about to come face to face with your mother, better ease me in gently."

The demon blade shattered with a burst of pure blue energy so bright she had to avert her gaze. The subsequent cloud of choking dust as something huge took form beside her was equally disconcerting, but nothing compared to what she experienced when she could finally see and breathe at the same time. Viewing Stabbington's memories hadn't even slightly prepared her for seeing him in his true form. He was unbelievably immense and incredibly shiny. Just one of his glossy black scales was the size of her entire torso.

"Ah. You are far tinier than I thought."

As usual, Stabbington spoke inside her head, but she hardly heard him over the thundering of her pulse as the snake's gigantic nose swooped around and triggered all her primal instincts at once.

"Arke, it is me," he continued. "And no matter how much you irritate me, I would never hurt you."

"I know." The words had to be forced to her lips as he ducked lower, his blue eyes staring at her as his tongue flicked in and out. She concentrated on regulating her breathing. The monstrous creature was still Stabbington and if she didn't get herself back under control, he would spend the rest of her life teasing her. That horrifying thought was more than enough to return her to her normal self. "Unless you sneeze and launch me half a mile away."

"I will endeavour not to do so." He moved closer, his tongue tasting the air around her.

"You should probably stop that before it gets creepy."

"It is a snake thing! I do not throw shade on your natural habits."

"You absolutely do!"

He chuckled. "Yes, of course I do, you are all ridiculous creatures. However, now you are merely irritated rather than terrified, we must go to see my mother."

She took a deep breath. "Fine. Is there anything I should know? What do I call her?"

A deeper, more commanding voice hissed its way into her consciousness. "Mother."

The Soulbound's eyes widened, and she stepped forwards, poking Stabbington in the side of the head. "You could've said she could hear me!"

"Would it have helped you calm down? I do not believe so. Now hold still, I will carry you. It is a long journey for someone so miniscule."

Carefully coiling the tip of his tail around her waist, Stabbington lifted her a few feet off the ground and started to slither towards a distant ridge, carrying her behind him.

As the fog grew thinner, Arke caught sight of the Brood Mother's dark form. She was positioned in neat coils next to a circle exactly like the one on the *Warrior*, and her red eyes glowed in the darkness as Stabbington approached. She knew her demon's mother was far larger than him, but the closer they got, the more she realised his memories had just been of her head – they hadn't even started to convey how immense the rest of her was. The Brood Mother was the size of a literal mountain and then some.

Stabbington stopped and bowed low, his nose almost touching the floor as his tail moved round, placing the Soulbound next to him.

"Greetings, my son. It is about time you brought your partner to meet me. Arke, you are welcome in my realm." The Brood Mother rubbed her cheek on Stabbington's before moving towards the Soulbound, delicately using the very tip of her monstrous tongue to do the same.

The gigantic head pulled back and regarded Arke with unblinking red eyes before nodding slowly. "You would make a fine snake."

"Ahh... Thank you." It seemed the appropriate thing to say given the fact the largest living creature the Soulbound had ever seen was mere feet away, blocking out most of whatever light there was.

"So... where is this item you wish me to protect?"

⚔ ⚔ ⚔

AFTER LEAVING THE capstone with the Brood Mother, Arke endured the planar journey that returned her to the deck of the *Warrior*. The instant she reappeared in the circle, the mage's droning chant took on a different tone, and as the candles burnt away to nothing, the darkness around her dissipated.

"Is it done?" Kennedy asked.

She nodded, having to shade her eyes to see in the daylight, but as her vision cleared, she noticed the deck was strewn with wreckage as if the ship had been through a hurricane.

"Are you ok?"

"I am but..." He rubbed a hand over his face. "Did you hear the screaming from below?"

She shook her head. "But whatever happened, it's on me."

"No. We all agreed." He could barely hold back the hitch in his voice. "It's..." He looked away, clearly trying to compose himself before he could put words to what his alter had seen.

After listening to Kennedy's halting description, Arke told him exactly what was going to happen next. She would be taking whatever blame was required and he would be taking an entire bottle of whisky. Shutting his cabin door firmly behind her, she marched to the main hatch, ignoring Nox, who was busy carving protective wards into the *Warrior's* timbers, and disappeared below.

Jaw set and brow furrowed, she unlocked the crew quarters and headed inside. At one end of the room, she saw everyone huddled together, heads bowed.

She cleared her throat. "It's done. The deck is covered in debris."

No-one moved.

"Ellie, get a damage control party topside and clean up," Arke ordered, her voice pure gravel.

"What? LOOK!" The first mate lurched to her feet and pointed to where a bloodied sheet lay over a lump on the floor.

Having been warned by Kennedy, the Soulbound knew exactly what she was going to find and strode across the cabin to uncover Gurdi's body. All of the dwarf's insides were outside, and her corpse had been stretched and jointed like a slaughtered animal. The message was clear. Her friends were dying just as they had in the visions, in her nightmares. First Porro and now Gurdi.

Ellie slumped back down and started to cry, some of the others joining her, the sounds of their grief echoing around the cabin. However, their desolate sobbing stopped the instant Arke laid the sheet on the floor and began to shift Gurdi's mutilated body onto it.

"What are you doing?" Urzish stormed over, one hand scouring the tears from her cheeks. "You are NOT going to disrespect her. I don't care what you do to others, but I won't let you throw her overboard like so much rubbish."

The Soulbound ignored her, continuing her grisly task with deliberately sharp movements. Gurdi was long gone, safely in her afterlife, probably laughing and knocking back tankards of heady dwarven ale. The living could not afford to dive headfirst into grief, not having defied the Autarch, not being so close to his tower, not being so vulnerable that he had just murdered two of them. She needed to galvanise the crew into action, to give them someone they could blame. Anger was a dirty way out of sorrow, but it would keep them on their feet while time dulled the losses.

"We're going to bury her. With respect and love," growled Ellie.

"We all know what happens when you have corpses on the ship," Arke replied, using her boot to ease a reluctant part of Gurdi onto the sheet.

Urzish grabbed for her, but the Soulbound had been expecting her action and a burst of orange magic brushed the orc's hand aside as it surrounded its host in a shimmering field of protective energy that only enhanced the devilish aura of her grisly task.

"Interesting. It seems that spell works better if you are threatened. One day we might learn what else your strange power can do," Stabbington remarked, his tone reassuringly even. "Keep your concentration, I fear that you will need more of its protection before this is over."

The crew closed in, shouting angrily as she finished bundling up the dwarf's remains. Ellie blocked her way to the door as she tied knots in the bedsheet to contain its gory contents.

"What did you do to STOP this? We shouted but no-one came. It took minutes. MINUTES! We couldn't help her, but you could have."

"I was busy." Arke wiped her bloody hands on the sheet and then hoisted it onto her shoulder. "If you want to wave her off, you'd better get topside quickly."

"You aren't taking her!"

"Oh, ok then. Should I give you each a little bit as a keepsake?"

Urzish swung a fist, but the protective magic deflected her punch. The Soulbound swept a glance across the crowd before starting to speak, having to raise her voice to be heard above the curses being launched at her.

"I'm *not* having any corpses on this ship, I don't care who they are. If any of you have a problem with that then I will be available on the main deck as soon as I've dropped this off the side. One time deal. Fists only. No weapons or magic – for anyone. You each get a free shot and then you can get back to work."

The others left in a hurry, leaving Arke in the empty cabin with the bloodied bundle on her shoulder.

"Take a moment to breathe," her demon suggested. "We are both aware that it is not only their grief you wish to control. Will bruises make you miss her less? Is hurting on the outside easier than on the inside? When has that ever worked? I know, I know. 'Shut up Stabbington.'" He fell silent as she began to head up through the ship.

Sparkz was standing in the galley doorway holding out a mug of water as the Soulbound approached.

"Drink this now," he suggested, his tone brisk and businesslike. "Once it's done, I'll bring a bag of potions and rations up to your cabin."

"Thanks," she nodded and downed the mug in one.

She headed up the stairs and on past the crew as they stood at attention, creating a silent honour guard for Gurdi's last moments aboard. Ruby was already at the railing, offering Chromatia's blessings to the deceased as the Soulbound slid the heavy bundle from her shoulder and over the side.

Striding back amidships, she cleared a gap in the debris field and waited, the orange glow around her dissipating as she stood ready.

Urzish stepped forwards first, and Arke nodded in acknowledgement. A second later, the orc's enormous fist crashed into her cheek like a sledgehammer, and she staggered two steps backwards before collapsing. It took her a moment to recalculate the location of her limbs before she hauled herself up to see Urzish still standing in the same position.

"I said one each."

"I was nominated," the orc replied, her lips drawn back in a feral sneer. "The others think they couldn't do you justice, so gave me as many shots as I need to put you down properly."

"Except me," Ellie snarled. "After all Gurdi did for you..." She shook her head. "You're not worth the energy."

As the first mate turned and walked away, Urzish slammed another punch into the Soulbound's face, this time grabbing onto her shirt to stop her from falling so she could hit her again more quickly. After the fourth blow, Ruby stepped forwards and put a hand on the orc's arm.

"She's had enough!"

"No. I gave them my word." Arke spat out a mouthful of blood and tried not to sway.

The Ornithol glared around at the crew. "Does this feel right? Does it? Is this what Gurdi would want after her entire life was spent healing people? Is this honouring her memory?"

"Probably not," Urzish replied before punching the Soulbound under the jaw with a knockout blow which sent her flying to the deck several feet away. "But that one was for Porro."

Chapter Sixteen
This Ship is on Fire

*A*RKE COWERED AS *the Autarch's voice crashed into her. His fury was relentless, smashing into her senses over and over, his words the same, his wrath never-ending.*

"You are mine! You will obey ME!"

There was nowhere to hide as she floated in the giant nothingness of the bright darkness. She flinched with every word, waiting for the pain.

It didn't come.

His anger still flooded around her. Only around. Not through or inside her.

She realised he wasn't able to touch her. She wasn't back in the tower, not in his reach, not where he held ultimate power. All he could do was shout.

Only shout.

She began to tune him out, to calm herself, and finally, to utter a single, simple sentence.

"Leave them alone."

At first the words barely squeezed past her fear and tumbled out as whispers, but as she repeated and repeated, she felt her voice growing stronger, building in her chest until it surged out in a roar.

"Leave them ALONE!"

As the echoes of her shout died away, there was silence, and then he spoke, his tone coldly commanding.

"Bring me ALL the capstones."

"How do I find the rest?"

Her question was left unanswered as countless images of Porro and Gurdi at the instance of their deaths pressed in on her. "Your hands are drenched in their blood. How many more friends will you kill?"

ARKE RETURNED TO reality as a torrent of icy water shocked her body. She cranked her swollen eyes open to see Sparkz standing over her, bucket in hand, as she coughed and spluttered back to full consciousness.

"I've brought some wet cloths... oh. Well, the direct way works too." Ruby crouched by her friend, wiping some blood away with a handkerchief. "Can you walk?"

"Absolutely." The Soulbound's gritty reply was hoarsely convincing, and if power of personality was transferrable to power of locomotion, it would have been true. She tried to lift her head off the deck, only to realise that nothing seemed to be responding the way it should. "Not."

A pair of feathered arms swept her up into the air and she screwed her eyes shut as the world started to spin with the sudden movement.

"Let's get you to your cabin. You'll look better once you've had a few hours in bed," Ruby remarked in overly comforting tones.

"*Bed* is possibly overstating things." Sparkz looked at the wreck Arke's room had become and nodded to the Ornithol. "Get her in the shower while I fix the place up." He reached into a pocket and pulled out a bottle of *Just Say Go*. "Drink up, Punchbag."

The wave of familiar magical energy washed away the pain and exhaustion in seconds. Standing back on her own feet, the Soulbound watched as the engineer selected tools from his belt and began to repair her door.

"Ruby will probably be forgiven for helping me because she's as close to the god squad as we get round here. But you're going to be judged... Ellie isn't known for her ability to forgive."

"Most people would say thanks." Sparkz gestured for the Ornithol to hold the door in place. "Grab this, Rubes."

"I'm not most people," Arke replied.

He glanced at her. "Everyone out there is too stupid to figure out they just got played like the world's dumbest violins. That's on them. I'm a maestro, not an instrument."

⚹ ⚹ ⚹

WHETHER BY VIRTUE of the protective runes that Nox, the hooded mage, had carved on almost every surface, or Arke's conversation with the Autarch, there were no more 'incidents' on board as the *Warrior* flew south towards Soleya.

Their choice of destination was based purely on need. Their stores were nearly empty, and the sun-baked city that overlooked the Nidean border was the closest to their current position.

The ship was sombre, with morale at rock bottom. While the crew fully supported Kennedy's efforts to get as far away from the obsidian tower as quickly as possible, Arke remained public enemy number one. Her arrival could clear a room in seconds. The braver ones slammed doors in front of her or shoulder barged her in the narrow corridors, but mostly they treated her with silent contempt.

By the time they reached the northern bounds of the Granveldt Canyon, the *Warrior* was home to not only a morose, but also an increasingly discontented crew. Trying to mourn Gurdi and Porro without comfort food was bad. Trying to do it without food at all was far worse. As hungry days turned into hungrier days, Kennedy tried to improve what little morale there was by waxing lyrical about the culinary delights that lay ahead of them in Soleya.

However, until they got there, they had to choke down whatever Volk managed to cook. Kennedy called it 'experimental cuisine' but in reality, it was one step down from bin raiding, as everything left in the larder was disgusting, out of date or unrecognisable. They had dried anchovies on a bed of lemon blancmange, unidentified jerky with a bay leaf and pickle jus, and a grey and lumpy gruel the desperate chef called 'bits and pieces'. Only Volk knew what was in it and since they were so hungry, no-one wanted to ask. It was hot, filling, and if you swallowed it quickly, the furry bits didn't stick to your tongue.

Soleya couldn't come fast enough.

It seemed that the *Warrior* felt the same way, albeit in a far more dramatic fashion. The sun was just setting when the crew was roused from their discussions about what hellish concoction would be dished up and called dinner, by the ship's alarm bell rattling into life.

Gabbi came racing up the stairs looking for Kennedy and nearly collided with him at the main hatch. "Fire, sir, captain, sir! Fire in the engine room. Sparkz says for you to get us on the ground before we fall out of the sky."

"Ok. What else does he need?" Kennedy hurried to the controls, taking over from Ellie and putting the ship into a steep dive.

Gabbi's response was a direct, curse-laden quote delivered in exact mimicry of the engineer, and Kennedy nodded.

"I think that means he wants Arke's help. Either that or he's going into dog breeding."

"Already seen her sir, she was heading for the engine room." Gabbi left out the bit where the crew had pressed themselves to the walls of the corridor and glared daggers at the Soulbound as she strode past.

"Good. Now get below, tell everyone we're about to make an emergency landing. They know what to do."

Gabbi scuttled off, struggling against the tilted decks as Kennedy forced the *Warrior* to drop as quickly as it was able. He was concentrating on the canyon that yawned up towards them, knowing he was going to have to thread his ship through the cliffs before he could land on the water. It would be an incredibly tricky manoeuvre, but it was a far better option than crashing onto solid ground.

※ ※ ※

"Why doesn't this heap of junk work?" Sparkz was thumping buttons on the wall-mounted control panel by the engine room door when Arke arrived behind him.

"So we're on Plan B already?"

"Looks like it, since the automatic sprinklers have forgotten how to be automatic OR sprinklers," the engineer replied. "Got plenty of ice in your veins today?"

"As always." She looked around with a frown. "Where's Zeke?"

"In there, somewhere."

Sparkz grabbed a pair of extinguishers from a rack and opened the reinforced door. Raging inside was what would politely be called an inferno. Quickly opening the valves on the canisters, he started to spray suppressant over the conflagration. The Soulbound stood beside him, fingers blue with cold as she cast her ice spell over and over again. Despite the unbelievable heat which blasted them from within, neither of them moved until steam mixed with smoke and the booming roar of the fire finally sizzled away.

"Thanks for the assist."

The engineer took three steps forwards before suddenly backing up, shoving Arke out and slamming the door shut behind them both. The crystal itself, the primary power source of the ship, was burning, bubbling and twisting with magenta and turquoise flames which were quickly covering the entire engine room with magical hell.

"Aetheric's on fire." His tone was nothing but informative even as he reported the impending cataclysm.

She looked at him expectantly. "So how do we put it out?"

"By turning it off."

"Then we'd drop like a stone!"

"Well, you asked how to put it out." Sparkz picked up a pair of heavy-duty gauntlets. "See, I'd have asked how to slow the burn while Kennedy lands the ship. Then we can turn it off."

"And how do we do that?" she prompted.

He opened a locker to his left and pulled out a shovel. "Magic suppression sand. There are two barrels of it by the crystal. And if that runs out before we're down – normal fire trumps magical. A little fuel and a spark should do it. It's not ideal but it'll slow the aetheric burn."

"I'll do it." The Soulbound reached for the gloves.

Sparkz scowled and held on to them. "My engine room, my job!"

"And my magic can protect me from the flames. How about yours?"

By the time he'd finished explaining how to shut the crystal down once they'd landed, she'd persuaded her orange magic to do the one thing she knew it could, and her body was glowing with protective energy.

As Arke strode into the engine room, her nose and mouth were covered in a heavy-duty mask, and she was concentrating hard. Firstly, on her magical barrier and secondly, on keeping her bearings as clouds of colourful smoke swirled around her. The air was fogged with acrid residue, and every surface was sparking with wisps of super-heated aetheric, tendrils of twisting colour that pulsed and spun as if in the thrall of a wilful wind.

After fighting her way to the engine itself, her legs were crawling with magical flames. However, although the fire was trying to carve through her protective shield, she realised there was no heat involved. Whatever it was doing, it wasn't burning in a traditional sense. Raising the shovel high, she smashed it through the charred wood of the first barrel and dug into the pink sand as it flooded to the deck.

Arc after arc of magic suppression fizzed and sizzled over the aetheric crystal as she swung the spade in determined rhythm.

"Yes, it is working, the flames are dying back. Do not stop."

Stabbington's words of encouragement came as she was battering her shovel against the second barrel. This one had been far less damaged by the original blaze, and it took several heavy blows before its structure gave way and she could start shovelling once more. However, even in that short time, the fire had begun to flourish again.

The demon quickly changed his tack. "Keep going. We must be close to the ground by now."

The Soulbound barely heard him as she focused on the simple task of controlling the aetheric flames, as well as the far more complex one of keeping her protective spell active. Shovelling suppressive sand was great unless the only things keeping the fire away from your body was a magical barrier.

The ship began to level off when she'd almost finished the second barrel. Stabbington had already spotted the nearest oil cans, and after throwing the final shovelful, she headed in their direction. Outside the sand-laden area, multicoloured flames were writhing on every surface, and as she heaved the metal containers over to the base of the crystal, magical fire leapt up her arms and across her body.

"Burst them," Stabbington ordered.

Before she could, the *Warrior* landed with a punishing impact which threw her off her feet and into the console behind her.

"We are down. Cut the power!" The demon's voice was more urgent as his host struggled to reorient herself. "Turn around, count four sections up and one from the right."

Suddenly the Soulbound realised the ship was moving in a familiar pattern and knew they'd landed on water. She gathered her senses, tasting blood in her mouth where she'd bitten her tongue and feeling the flames eating through her defences. Every movement was an effort, and the more fire crept up her legs, the heavier they felt.

"Move your hand up. Up. More. Now right."

Stabbington's instructions were perfectly timed, as Arke was struggling to keep her focus. Her magical protection had saved her from serious injury in the crash landing, but keeping the shield active while under constant pressure from aetheric flames was increasingly exhausting. She was also aware that her orange magic was starting to react to the situation. She tried to slow its rising pulse, to control her breathing and calm her thoughts, as she couldn't afford anything to happen until the crystal was shut off.

"Keep your hands on the panels. The first two switches are together, here. They turn the auto-restart off."

She clicked them both and moved one section up to find the kill switch, which was well hidden behind a fake panel. The magical blaze raged over every inch of metal, bubbling the paint into geysers of brightly coloured energy as she plunged her hands through the maelstrom to unpin the security cover. She had to force herself to remain in the moment, to concentrate, as the aetheric fire seared its way across her body, her protective shield flickering almost as rapidly as the flames that covered it.

Stabbington's reassuring tone never wavered as she struggled to locate the catches by touch alone. Finally, the cover swung open, and she was able to slide the master switch to the OFF position.

The crystal's rasping hum fell silent.

Around the room, the fire stuttered and died away, disappearing from the walls and panels as the air filled with more and more choking smoke.

"Now we..."

Suddenly the *Warrior* collided with something solid, timbers giving way in spectacular fashion. A torrent of water erupted from a huge hole in the hull and launched Arke across the room. Helpless against its power, she was dashed into pipes and smashed against consoles, all the while struggling to find a moment to breathe. Concentration broken, her protective shield flickered and failed and, as she slammed painfully into the far wall, her unpredictable magic reacted. With a sudden flash of orange light, the Soulbound disappeared.

ARKE LIFTED HER head from where she appeared to be face-planting in some leaves and saw Stabbington in his human form sitting next to her.

"Is it ungrateful to wish your orange juice could choose better moments to throw us together like this?"

"I think it's trying to help."

She sat up awkwardly, wincing as she examined her hands. The aetheric flame had burnt her skin in multiple places, but although the marks looked more like craters than blisters, they hurt the same as traditional burns.

"We did well in there." Stabbington nudged her gently with his shoulder. "You will remember if things go right, it is always <u>our</u> success." When she didn't respond to his teasing, he nudged her again, his voice more serious this time. "I know it has been difficult recently with the crew treating you as the enemy, but they cannot keep it up forever." He paused as he looked down at her. "I would have hugged you already, but I learnt some hard lessons about consent once."

Her wicked chuckle was overtaken by a series of hacking coughs as her lungs tried to remove the acrid residue she'd inhaled. "And I make sure to replay that particular memory often. Just so you know how gross it is to be slobbered on by an enthusiastic ogre." She leant towards him and rested her head against his shoulder.

"My ego is crushed every time. So, do you want a hug?"

"I'm literally leaning on you. That's a yes."

"I was taking no chances." Stabbington eased his arms around her. "Perhaps the others will forgive you after this."

"I doubt it." She shrugged. "You know them as well as I do."

"And you did scrape Gurdi's face off the floor with your boot."

"Did the trick though, right? They got back to work with a vengeance."

"Against you," he commented.

"The ship's still in one piece and we're a long way from the tower. Could've gone very differently if they'd downed tools."

Chapter Seventeen
A Funny Thing Happened

THIS TIME, AS Arke flashed back into reality, she was chest deep in the rapidly flooding engine room and Stabbington wasn't shouting angry curses in her head. Instead, he was busy working out which way to go. The main door had to stay shut to protect the rest of the ship from the rising water, so they needed to find another exit.

"Turn to your left – there is a hole in the hull big enough to get through. One deep breath, dive down and out. Also, I have a request. Snacks. Keep them in your pockets at all times, just in case we should take an orange trip. I see no reason I cannot eat when I have my own body."

"You choose NOW to talk about food?" she hissed. "When I'm in a room that's filling with water and haven't eaten properly in days?"

Without waiting for her demon's reply, she took a breath and forced herself to duck under the murky water. Fighting her way down to the gash in the side of the ship, she finally slipped out into the river. Its current caught hold of her instantly, sweeping her away from the *Warrior* as she activated her teleportation spell.

Sparkz was peering down at the hull when Arke, soaking wet, appeared on the deck beside him. "No time for lying around, get up, get busy. I assume you managed to disconnect the crystal since we're still alive. What's the damage down there?"

Before she could reply to the engineer, Ruby rushed over and helped the Soulbound to her feet. "Looks like you need some *Go* juice and dry clothes."

"Thanks Rubes, but don't worry, I'll get sorted in a bit." Arke slicked the wet hair back from her face and turned to Sparkz. "Engine room has an unexpected window, maybe ten by six."

"I'll ask Kennedy to hem me some curtains." Sparkz pointed ahead of the ship. "He stacked it trying to get under this hulk of a bridge. Apparently he was aiming to land us on the other side of it, but gravity had other ideas."

Arke had to tilt her head back to appreciate the sheer size of the stone structure. It was immense, rising above the riverbed to carry a road that crossed the canyon far above their heads. It was so tall the *Warrior* could easily get underneath it, although her stabilising wings – or the one which hadn't been broken in the crash – would need to be raised to fit through the nearest arch. However, that was the only way forwards, as massive cliffs soared a good two hundred feet on either side of the river.

She frowned suddenly. "Where's Kennedy?"

"In his cabin." Ruby gestured towards the door. "He hit his head on the wheel as we landed. He was pretty groggy but said to tell you that you were in command. Then he laughed and passed out."

"Well, congratulations, being ancient just became useful." Sparkz grinned at Arke. Everyone knew she'd had years of experience as a pirate aboard traditional sea-going vessels and even though the *Warrior* was primarily rigged to fly, she was also capable of old-fashioned floating – when she wasn't holed and wedged in rocks. "Apparently you're as close to an expert with sailing ships as we've got. Get captaining."

Arke fought to stop her teeth chattering as she marshalled her thoughts. "We still have bilge pumps on board, send Volk to get them working. Ruby, tell Ellie to sort a rota as we'll need to keep them running full-time till we can beach up to make repairs. Mr Engineer without an Engine, get a sail and some rope. We'll drag the canvas over the hole and it'll slow the amount of water coming in."

"And what are *you* going to do, milady?" Sparkz muttered.

"I'm heading back into the river to check for other damage – unless you'd prefer to do that instead?"

※ ※ ※

IT WASN'T THE greatest time for the Soulbound to have to step into the captaincy, but after they'd eased the *Warrior* off the rocks and fothered the sail over the hole in her hull, there wasn't a huge amount to do. Away from the bridge, the river's current was strong, but its course wound so lazily that their rudder was able to keep the ship in the centre of the channel. Arke and Ruby took turns at the wheel, while the rest of the crew kept the pumps running and Sparkz was hard at work trying to repair Zeke, who'd been heavily damaged in the engine room fire.

Kennedy's concussion was serious enough that he was still in bed three days after the crash landing. After the second day, it was apparent that he was more or less back to normal when he was awake, but since that wasn't very often, he was left to rest. Even though she hated being in charge, Arke knew he needed time to recover – and the city of Soleya was only a little further downriver.

ONE FINE AFTERNOON, the Soulbound woke from an uneasy slumber when she heard Ruby's voice calling her name. The Ornithol sounded slightly alarmed but more confused than anything else, and Arke allowed herself a moment for a jaw-wrenching yawn before rolling a snoring Dozer out of the way so she could get up and head outside.

"Over there." Ruby pointed to a position just ahead of the ship.

As the Soulbound's bleary eyes peered, focused, refocused, and wished they'd never focused, she saw a naked man waving to them from the shallows. She sighed. It was a sunny day, they'd had freshly caught fish for lunch, and Soleya wasn't far away, but none of that meant it was a good time to see a hairy middle-aged stranger with his junk on display.

"Ahoy there!" The man waved a little more enthusiastically as she appeared on deck.

"The early bird really did catch the... worm," Arke commented, keeping her tone as steady as she was able.

She was managing to keep her composure until she noticed Ruby. The Ornithol was trying to avert her eyes from the stranger while simultaneously attempting to acknowledge him. That, combined with Stabbington's running commentary, meant the Soulbound was forced to turn away, shoulders shaking, as she struggled to hold back an unruly burst of laughter.

"Water a bit cold over there?" Sparkz grinned as he strolled across the deck, a cup of steaming coffee in one hand.

"If he's a powerful mage, you're going to get obliterated for saying that!" Ruby hissed, clearly still trying to find an angle at which she could appear friendly but also avoid looking at the man's nakedness.

"Ah, being a bird with super keen eyesight must be both a blessing and, on days like today, a *teeny tiny* curse." Stabbington had no need to control his mirth and Arke gritted her teeth harder as he roared with laughter in her head.

The man cleared his throat. "It is a trifle cold in the water, but the sun is glorious. Given you're heading towards Soleya, could you possibly give me a lift? I quite forgot the time and have an important appointment in the city that I mustn't miss."

The *Warrior* was already gliding past and would soon leave him behind. It wasn't good practice to deny aid to those in need, and Arke didn't want to tempt any more bad karma to head in their direction.

"Sure. Not like you're carrying any sort of weapon, concealed or otherwise."

"I'm not picking him up!" Ruby hissed.

"Why ever not?" Sparkz chuckled, before putting his coffee down and throwing a rope towards the stranger. "Grab on, buddy."

A few minutes of effort later, the still very naked man stood on the deck of the *Warrior* and shook himself like a dog.

"Thank you most kindly. My name is Jenkins."

"Welcome aboard. Can we offer you something to drink? Or to eat? Or to wear?"

Chuckling at Arke's talented impression of the most unwilling hostess in the world, Sparkz headed to the wheel to give Ruby some moral support. She was staring hard downriver, probably in case its perfectly straight, wide course might suddenly morph into rapids or a giant black hole similar to the one she clearly wished she'd fallen into.

"I am in no need of clothes. Let me explain why naturism is a life-enhancing pastime..."

THREE VERY BUTT-NAKED hours later, Jenkins disembarked at Soleya's northernmost jetty, waving as he strode away into the fishing district.

"That man can TALK!" the Ornithol exclaimed, once he was out of earshot.

"Think he swallowed a dic-tionary?" Sparkz chuckled.

"Would have given me less of a headache to kill him." Arke sighed, pinching the bridge of her nose. "Anyway, let's get busy. Ruby, could you fly ahead and find us a quiet place to beach for repairs? Sparkz, pass the word we're getting ready to bring her to ground."

The deck to herself, she leant a forearm on the wheel and bent her head forwards to try and stretch out her back. The sunshine was bliss on her weary body, and she held the position for a long time. Her job was nearly done, and she couldn't wait for it to be over.

"Of course you mustn't look around when you are at the helm, what could be in the way so close to a big city?" Urzish strode onto the deck and glared at Arke. "You'll crash the ship and kill the rest of us with your arrogance! You are stupid and dangerous." The orc was covered in grey slime and her hands were raw from the pump handles, but that was clearly not enough to stop her coming up to see Soleya and harangue the Soulbound.

Arke did not reply. She had a headache, she was tired, and most importantly, Urzish was right. There was nothing to say. She couldn't make any excuses, nor did she want to. What had happened to her crewmates was down to her, her choices, and her decisions. When she'd been able to lock her emotions away, it had all been so much easier, but now feelings bubbled unbidden and memories lurched uncalled for. Before her feral magic burst out and broke down her inner defences, she'd have ignored the orc's words. Now she felt every single one.

"It is ok," Stabbington remarked softly. "You have heard worse."

She had. But she had never felt so guilty before.

Chapter Eighteen
Hold Firm

THE FOLLOWING MORNING, just after the city gates opened, Soleya's westernmost park was blissfully quiet. Arke meandered down the maze of paths that led her past flower beds rich with brightly coloured blooms. As the sun began its work in earnest, delicate scents gave way to heady aromas. She stood by a fountain and dipped her hand in the crystal clear water, watching the ripples spread across the surface.

"Soleya has more colours than the rainbow," Stabbington remarked. "Every time we visit, I see new shades and patterns." He paused, as if waiting for his host to add a comment before continuing. "It makes no sense that they revere Thum over Chromatia."

"It does. The only weather they get here is sunshine." Arke's voice was dull as she replied. "They worship Thum, Mr Law and Order himself. Never been in a place with so many guards."

The demon cleared his imaginary throat as if he was about to address an audience. "Welcome to Soleya, the city of climate, colour and control."

"More like heatstroke, migraines and floggings," she muttered.

"Perhaps we should head to the lavender beds next?" Stabbington suggested, his tone unduly bright.

"This isn't working."

"You said you would try."

Arke scowled. "What do you THINK I've been doing? I'm not letting any more of them die because of me."

"I meant the gardens."

"Screw the gardens." She started walking, her strides sharp and decisive. "Screw the power of nature, meditation, inner peace, clarity, headspace, and the rest of your manipulative bullshit!"

He sighed. "Consider it very well screwed. Now, might I ask if you are intending to throw yourself into the bottom of a bottle?"

"No."

"Oh thank goodness." Stabbington sounded relieved. "I was worried you were going to get drunk and make some incredibly stupid decisions. So where are we heading?"

"The skyport. Tickets for the night flight to Keisanct always sell out early."

"Excellent." The demon sighed. "Nothing says 'smart choice' quite like running away to the other side of the world."

"I tried it your way, now I'm doing it mine."

⚹ ⚹ ⚹

In true survivor style, the crew had celebrated their safe arrival with a feast. They'd ordered so much food they needed several boats to row it over to their campsite, and enough alcohol that the number who'd passed out around the fire had been far greater than one. As a result, there were a lot of heavy heads and bloated stomachs the next morning, so it took a good while for anyone to notice the note pinned to the side of their beached ship.

Memory's Claws

Captain Kennedy etc., meet me at the Shattered Shin, room 302 – at your convenience.

Kennedy's still aching head meant he'd avoided the drinking on the previous evening. However, he had filled his stomach, and the energy from that, plus the mystery missive, had encouraged him to down a vial of *Just Say Go* and get dressed for the first time in days.

When he went to Arke's cabin to show her the note, there was no sign of her. Nor was she anywhere onboard, which was a little odd, but given the crew's attitude towards her recently, he guessed she'd gone ashore for some 'decompression' at one of the local bars.

So it was just Kennedy and Sparkz who headed to find the *Shattered Shin*, curious as to who'd sent the note. They spent some time checking out the quietly old-fashioned inn, complete with staging post and stables, before they ventured inside. Nothing seemed to be concerning, except perhaps the lurid neon décor which was utterly at odds with the countryside style vine-covered exterior. Everywhere they looked their eyes hurt, as everything that wasn't painted in retina-burning colours was a mirror, eager to reflect that 'toddlers stole my highlighters while I was in the bath' vibe from multiple angles.

The door to Room 302 had enjoyed most of a pot of neon pink paint topped off by a lime green hypnotic swirl, and its handle seemed to be covered in what looked like a giant fluffy ladybird.

Sparkz stepped forwards to knock and after a few moments, a muffled voice invited them to enter.

After braving the unusually plush handle, the brothers swung the door open and waited in the lurid hallway, half expecting some form of attack. However, the only reason they were surprised by what lurked in the room was that the walls weren't covered with neon paint, animal print wallpaper or any hideous mix of the two. Instead, they were a restful cream, and every piece of furniture was as bland as it was possible to be.

Sparkz gestured for his brother to go first. "A captain leads from the front."

As Kennedy stepped inside, he looked around warily. On his right was a small, neutrally decorated bathroom with tiny towels folded to make them look bigger. Over by the bed was a mini-bar with price list, and on top of that sat a kettle on a tray with a stack of cups and hand-twisted wraps of coffee.

"Hello?" he called.

A figure stepped into the room from the tiniest of balconies. Kennedy couldn't quite see the stranger's face as they stood in a shadow, though he could see enough to make out that they were male and smoking a pipe.

"Gentlemen." The man's accent was unusually bland for a Barsian, as if any regional inflections had been scrubbed from his speech patterns. "I doubt it's a surprise to hear that the *Warrior* and its crew have been of interest to the authorities for a very long time. Maybe you've had some incredibly good luck that has kept you out of their clutches, maybe Kennedy is as capable a captain as his father, or maybe you haven't been important enough for them to hunt you down. Whatever the reason, I believe things are on the turn for you all."

With measured tread, Sparkz stepped into the room and slid the door shut behind them.

Memory's Claws

"I'm not here to threaten you, if that's what you're thinking," the man added.

"Sounds quite a lot like it to me." Kennedy rested his hand on the hilt of his sword.

"Honestly, I'm here to help. Why else would I have made time to check you out, or set up this meeting?" The stranger stepped out of the shadows and inclined his head. "Hubert Von Jenkins."

"Well, well, well, if it isn't the manspreader." Sparkz frowned and looked at his brother as he explained. "This is the weird, nude guy who needed a lift downriver. At least this time he's dumped the stupid accent and gained some clothes."

Kennedy folded his arms. "Thank you for traumatising my crew. Are you offering to pay for therapy?"

"You can learn a lot about people from their treatment of an apparently helpless and naked stranger. I will admit that your crew were not how I imagined them." Jenkins drew on his pipe slowly.

"What did you think we'd do to you?" Kennedy asked. "I'm curious."

"Clearly reckoned we'd attack him," Sparkz cut in. "And if we had, how would you have defended yourself? Granted, you were in possession of an offensive weapon, but I doubt it could do anything other than emotional damage."

"I have my ways." Jenkins dismissed the engineer's question before looking at Kennedy. "Similar to the ones I used to find you."

"So, you're here to warn us about the authorities? Thanks, but it's a fact of life in our line of work."

Jenkins sat down in a chair and gestured for the brothers to do the same, but when neither moved, he shrugged, taking another slow draw on his pipe, and exhaling a very fancy smoke ring before replying. "My information says that you were in Theogenes recently. Visited the Apothecarium and then left very suddenly – before your resupply was complete."

"We were there, albeit briefly, a few weeks ago." Kennedy's tone was even, and his face betrayed absolutely nothing. "One of my crew was almost murdered by some criminals in the city, so we chose to avoid further issues by leaving the area."

"A noble effort to support law and order." Jenkins made no attempt to conceal the irony that dripped from his words.

"Not at all. My crewmember was unable to tell me who'd attacked them, so I decided the best thing to do was fly away. Live to pirate another day, as it were."

Jenkins pulled a notebook from his pocket and opened it. "I have a report here from a ship inspection of the *Storm Warrior*, also captained by a Kennedy. Your brother, perhaps?"

Kennedy settled a firm gaze on Jenkins. "Can you cut to the chase? I have places to be."

"Very well. Tell me about the Theogenes Apothecarium."

Kennedy shrugged. "Big white building, smells of bleach?"

"That was the swimming pool," Sparkz corrected, managing to keep a straight face until his brother failed to control a snort of laughter and nearly choked on his own mirth.

Memory's Claws

That was the moment where Jenkins looked from one to the other as if he was questioning his entire life's work, if not his entire life. He sighed. "If I'm honest, the report I read makes MUCH more sense having finally met you all." He knocked his pipe out with slow, rhythmic taps. "Gentlemen. Tell me what happened in the Apothecarium, and we can move towards a solution."

"A solution to what?" Sparkz frowned. "We just took someone there, neither of us went in."

"I'm sure you're more than capable of working out we're telling you the truth," Kennedy added. "We walked there, hung about outside, then left."

"I know. The same way as I know that your Ornithol crewmember, accompanied by what was probably Arke, went inside." Jenkins gestured as if rolling a script on and continued. "There was an outbreak of... 'something' just after they were seen in the Apothecarium. The centre of Theogenes is a waste ground right now, and as it stands, the Barsian authorities are actively searching for the *Warrior* in connection with this disaster."

"And your role in this search?" Kennedy asked.

"I work for the Firm. We are seeking to solve the problem as well as investigate some other – things – we've heard recently regarding your crew."

"Ah..." Kennedy looked at Sparkz with a swift shake of his head before moving to sit down. The Firm were not people you ever wanted to mess with. They were the original boogeymen, they worked in the shadows, part intelligence agency, part enforcers, part political power brokers – and they were above any law in Barsia. That his ship had come to their notice was potentially disastrous, however, he did know that if anyone could help them with their Autarch problem, it would be the Firm. It was time to talk.

⚔ ⚔ ⚔

THE ARBITER LOVED being able to escape the endless hall full of unclaimed souls seeking their afterlives, so he'd planned for a few extra hours of fun after the completion of his Arke-related errand in Soleya. However, things had not gone exactly as he'd envisaged. Instead of heading to the arena in keen anticipation of a night of martial entertainment, he was storming down a road in the opposite direction. His usual affable smile had been replaced by a frown as he cursed the god who'd invented free will. That was a genie that would not go back in its bottle, even though its creator had long disappeared from the Gateway.

For obvious reasons, he'd been watching the Soulbound carefully since the obsidian tower. It had been clear that she was drowning, consumed by the grinding trio of despair, guilt, and worry. He knew her solution was to leave in order to draw the Autarch's wrath away from her ship and her crewmates. That would be disastrous, and although he couldn't explain that to her, he was going to change her mind. This crisis was as inevitable as it was defining, so he'd prepared to deliver a message of purpose, hope and love to get her back on track.

Except his intervention hadn't worked. Arke hadn't even broken stride as the Tarot card he'd thrown had wafted its perfect path down in front of her. He knew she'd seen it, but instead of picking up the gently glowing card that he hoped would flood her with divine inspiration, she'd kicked it into the gutter and ground it into the dust with her heel. She was still marching towards the skyport, ready to catch her flight, and he was having to chase her down while trying to keep a handle on his own temper.

The Arbiter tried to stop himself picturing exactly how her face would look if he shoved the card in her mouth and made her eat the damned thing. He knew it wouldn't help in the slightest, but it was so incredibly tempting.

Ahead of him, the Soulbound stopped suddenly and turned her head towards the unmistakeable sound of Urzish's battle cry. A few of the *Warrior* crew were ashore, and it sounded as if things were well out of hand somewhere nearby. Soleyan law enforcement took a dim view of violence in their city and were always extremely prompt. He nodded slowly, his anger fading as Arke started to run towards the orc's terrible decision and away from her own.

"It seemed like a good shepherd/bad shepherd situation. You're welcome, by the way." The voice in his head was smug, but despite that he was relieved he wasn't the only resident of the Gateway who was paying attention to the *Warrior* and her crew. "Sometimes subtlety is overrated. You do get more flies with honey but if you want just one in particular, it's easier to hit it really hard."

The Arbiter released a deep breath, feeling the tension flood out of his body before smoothing a hand down his T-shirt with a slogan that read: 'May contain alcohol'. It was time to make the 'may' into a 'does' while he hung around to ensure things stayed on the right track. As he strolled along in the Soulbound's wake, he felt a pang of irritation at the hours he'd spent designing the Tarot card, before an idea flew into his head. His beautiful creation wouldn't go to waste – he could put an embossed copy in his office. It would look splendid on the wall, with its gold and silver tree branches winding round a cockerel and a snake. There was just one thing he needed. An office.

※ ※ ※

ARKE WAS RUNNING against a slow tide of battered and retreating people as she headed down an alley to a courtyard which was lightly littered with groaning bodies. At the far end was Urzish in a full drunken rage.

"This one is fine, he is breathing. That one not so much. And that skinny elf is going to take the bald guy with him. Do NOT let her kill the dwarf!" Stabbington was an invaluable battle tool when he wanted to be. And he was so relieved that his host hadn't left the city on her own that he was being incredibly useful.

Urzish seemed oblivious to everything as she prepared to throw one of her opponents into the side of the tavern. There was no time for pleasantries, so Arke just leapt up on her crewmate's back, cranking an arm round her neck and desperately trying to choke her out before she smashed the helpless dwarf into the stone wall from close range.

Being almost blind drunk meant Urzish was slow to drop the small, shouty thing and move to grab her new attacker. Too slow. Finally released from the orc's huge hands, the dwarf made his escape, just as Urzish's knees buckled and she lost consciousness. Arke rolled clear, taking a moment to rub her numbed arm before she started to get up.

She was completely unprepared for the heavy impact of a bottle that shattered against the side of her skull and flat-packed her back to the ground.

"Arke... Arke... wake up. You need to WAKE UP!" Stabbington's voice was anxious as it vied for attention in a head that seemed to be full of flashing lights and mangled noises. "I did not mention her arrival because it was Ellie, and she should not hurt you. But she has just drawn her dagger, and you need to move! NOW!"

The Soulbound blinked hard as she forced her eyes to focus on the *Warrior's* first mate, who was stalking towards her, blade in her hand, lips in a snarl. She'd seen that expression on the halfling's face many times and knew what was going to happen next.

"Ellie, what are you doing?" Kilar suddenly stepped out of her illusion of a pile of crates and leapt between them. She was sporting a blackened eye and a split lip but stood her ground with grim determination. "Arke just stopped Urzish killing that guy! We need to go before the guards come."

"What?"

The first mate looked round Kilar to where the Soulbound was getting to her feet, blood streaming down the side of her face. The whistles of the local law enforcement were already sounding and growing closer by the second.

"I couldn't stop Urzish – after some bald guy groped me, she went full on battle mode," Kilar explained. "I hit my head. It was a mess."

"I was gone TEN MINUTES! How did you manage to... never mind." Ellie scowled, sheathing her dagger as Arke crouched by one of the downed men. "Is he dead?"

"He'll be ok." The Soulbound poured *Just Say Go* into the man's mouth. This wasn't turning into a murder scene rather than the site of a brawl, there was enough trouble coming as it was. "Is there another way out of this courtyard?"

Ellie shook her head. "Nope. The doors are all locked."

Kilar crouched by Urzish, patting her cheeks harder and harder. "She's sparko. What do we do?"

"Keep her like that until the law's gone. She's got a thing about men in uniform," Arke replied, her lips twisting in a wry smile.

"She does?" Kilar frowned.

"Yeah, she likes to punch them." The Soulbound handed the rest of the bottle of *Go* juice to Kilar before dropping her backpack on top of the orc. "Make an illusion big enough for all of you. I'll distract the guards – once I've cleared the way, drop that in her mouth and get the hell out of here."

"Not a chance!" Ellie pointed at Arke. "Back off. She's MY friend and I'll do it."

The Soulbound reacted instantly, grabbing the halfling's wrist and yanking her sleeve up to show a line of brands puckering the skin. "S inside a circle. That's two strikes from Soleya." She gestured to Urzish. "She has the same."

Kilar tugged on Ellie's arm, pulling her backwards until she stood next to the orc's inert body. "It's the best plan we've got."

"Then go back to the ship and stay there. And do NOT tell the captain." Arke glared at the first mate, who finally nodded in curt agreement.

Memory's Claws

Kilar's magic shimmered into being and the three *Warrior* crewmates were suddenly disguised as a rather unpleasant looking set of dustbins.

Stabbington sighed as the Soulbound strode up the alley towards the approaching law enforcement officers. "This is VERY stupid. You also have two brands, and we both know what comes after that in the Barsian penal code."

"So I let them get arrested and hope they don't say where they're from while they're being interrogated? The Soleyans never need an excuse to run ships off, no matter what state they're in. That's too much of a risk while the *Warrior* needs serious repairs."

"But how do you intend to escape? Using magic would be an extremely bad idea."

"I don't. I'll keep my mouth shut, take my lashes and stagger straight to the nearest tavern."

The patrol appeared ahead of her, five or six officers completely blocking the alley.

"Hey you!" one of them shouted. "Come here, hands where we can see them!"

※ ※ ※

FROM THEIR VIEWPOINT inside the illusion, Ellie and Kilar watched as Arke walked up to the guards in a contrite manner before punching the tallest officer square in the balls. Understandably enough, that action resulted in her getting obliterated by his colleagues, and dragged off in shackles.

"How has she been a pirate so long and not got any brands?" Kilar asked, as she dripped the last of the *Just Say Go* into Urzish's mouth.

"Arke has all of them." Ellie shrugged as she looked

at her crewmate's shocked face. "Well, except Levenbrandt, but only because we've hardly ever been there. She knew exactly what she was doing."

Chapter Nineteen
Adulting for Beginners

Having been 'energised' by their conversation with Jenkins, Kennedy and Sparkz didn't throw themselves into the delights of Soleyan hospitality. Instead, they spent two long days getting the *Warrior* ready to fly. Since Sparkz still hadn't managed to get Zeke, his Bior assistant, doing more than making confused whirring noises, he deputised Volk and Gabbi to help him repair the engine room. Volk could do the simple tasks and Gabbi could do the fetching, carrying, and being shouted at when things didn't go to plan.

Kennedy hurried to a local shipyard to hire people to fix the damage to the hull as well as buy a new gig. It had turned out to be an extremely expensive shopping trip.

In his defence – the one he'd been practicing to give Arke when she returned – craftsmen and flying boats were never cheap. On the other hand, the beautiful sword that now hung at his side had been such a steal he felt guilty about paying so little for it. However, the man wearing a T-shirt with a funny slogan had been so happy for the weapon to find a good home that he couldn't resist. Kennedy had wanted the exquisitely crafted silver blade from the moment he saw it, a feeling that was only amplified when the grip nestled into his palm as if it belonged there. While he was well aware that the Soulbound might disapprove of the substantial dip in their coffers, he worked hard to convince himself that she couldn't fail to love the incredible sword.

The *Warrior* was bobbing at anchor in the river when a skiff rowed over, carrying not only Arke but also Ruby, Ellie, Urzish, Kilar, and a stranger. Kennedy, who was supervising the loading of provisions, scampered over to the tumblehome to welcome them aboard. He chose to ignore the fact they all looked incredibly unsober because he could clearly see that by some miracle, and with only a couple of days ashore, the Soulbound had managed to build bridges that he could have sworn would take months to even get planning permission for.

Flooded with joy, he greeted them with delirious jollity, shaking hands and slapping shoulders as they climbed onto the deck. Although he wanted to drag Arke into a huge hug, he knew not to try – warm and fuzzy was just not her style. True to form, she levelled a 'don't touch me' glare at him before staggering across to her cabin. Figuring whatever she'd done to fix her relationship with the crew must have involved gallons of alcohol, Kennedy made a mental note to be extra quiet around her when the hangover from hell set in. The newcomer boarded last, and he offered a hand to help her on board, since she was both short and carrying an enormous pack.

"Thank you."

"Welcome to the *Warrior*. I'm Captain Kennedy..."

"We found a new doc!" Ellie interrupted, wobbling as she pivoted to look in Kennedy's general direction. "We weren't just drinking and drinking and absolutely not fighting or anything."

"My name's Ibu – they said you had a vacancy on board? I'm not quite a doctor, but I am used to combat injuries after working in the arena for two years." The broad-shouldered gnome ran a hand through her unruly curls as she smiled up at Kennedy, her steady gaze indicative of the fact that she didn't stink of booze as badly as the others.

The idea of a different face in charge of the infirmary made Kennedy's insides twist painfully, but the ship needed a healer. "It's yours if you want it. I have complete confidence in the decisions of my crew."

Just as he finished his sentence, Kilar lost her balance and silently toppled down the main hatch. By the sound of the surprised voice below, she landed right on Irash, who was noticeably less than silent about the pain he felt. Kennedy turned quickly to see what was going on and noticed Ellie and Urzish also teetering on the top step, gleefully watching the scene below. Both he and Ibu hurried to usher them away from the stairs, almost bouncing off each other in the rush to stop any more alcohol-related injuries.

"I'm fine, I'm fine!" called Kilar. "I landed on something soft."

"Thanks," Irash groaned from the darkness.

Kennedy shrugged and smiled at Ibu. "Complete confidence in most of the decisions of my crew. Welcome aboard – let me show you around – if you like you can tell me an absolute pack of lies about your past and I won't care. As long as you're loyal to the *Warrior* and do your job then we're on your side, no questions asked."

They were ready to leave Soleya the following day. Despite misgivings about Jenkins' presence aboard, his promise to help them with the Theogenes situation seemed the best way to keep the *Warrior* from being top of the Barsian hit list. Kennedy had ushered the Firm's agent on board an hour before they were due to take off, suggesting that he kept his head down and his clothes firmly in place.

He'd informed the crew of the reason for their rushed departure as well as the fact that Jenkins would be travelling west with them, and their reactions to the two pieces of information had been wildly different. Learning about the Theogenes situation had barely provoked a single eyebrow raise, but the prospect of sharing air with a member of the Firm had almost started a riot. However, that had been preferable to Arke's reaction, as during their conversation, she'd simply left his cabin without a word. Kennedy was sure she'd emerge from her room at some point, and at some undetermined time after that, she'd probably talk to him again. He could wait, it was a long way back to Theogenes.

As the crew made their final pre-flight checks, Sparkz appeared on deck wearing his jetpack and announced that the repairs were finished. He added that he'd triple checked everything, so if they crashed this time, it wasn't anything to do with him.

After thanking his brother for his confidence boosting speech, Kennedy tried not to show any signs of engine-related anxiety as he prepared for take-off.

Thankfully, the *Warrior's* controls answered as they should, and she rose smoothly into the air before

Kennedy turned her west towards the city of Theogenes. As the crew celebrated their ship's return to duty with beer and snacks, Sparkz accepted the praise for his engine's perfect performance with absolutely no semblance of humility. Or the praise from most of the crew. Kennedy noticed that no matter the bridges that Arke had managed to build, Ellie was still exceptionally frosty towards his brother. However, as their working relationship seemed unaffected, Kennedy knew it was none of his business, and as he stood at the helm, feeling the sun on his shoulders and the wind in his face, a warm sense of wellbeing flooded over him. The *Warrior* was back in the air, and he was determined to live in the moment. Tomorrow and yesterday were out of his control, but he had now, and it felt good.

Unfortunately, his blissful bubble only lasted until supper time. His crew were great at many things, but keeping secrets was not one of them. Through the grapevine, he learnt Ellie had been writing the next chapter of the crew's adventure story. The protagonists of the completely 'fictional' book were Larka and Maddington Dare, a pair of smugglers who used a packet ship called the *Courier* as cover for their less than legal activities. The latest drama had the heroes sacrificing themselves to save their crewmates from a terrible punishment in the city of Oleyar.

After forcing himself not to jump to any conclusions, Kennedy headed over to the author's cabin for a casual conversation. Unsurprisingly, she refused to answer any of his questions, but she did show him the first draft and suggest that he might want to hang around the infirmary after midnight.

As a rule, Kennedy was firmly anti-eavesdropping. But after spending an hour watching through the half-open galley door, before finally seeing Arke slip into sickbay, he was determined to get his facts right before barging in. He tiptoed across the corridor until he was close enough to hear the voices inside.

"... terrifying. I've never flown before – so I've been doing inventory to take my mind off it. I found the treatment books and they've kept me busy too." Ibu sounded stressed, and Kennedy made a mental note to double check with future hires to find out if they'd ever been on a sky ship before.

"Gurdi was very thorough." The Soulbound's comment was hollow, as if she were forcing the words out.

"Bloody good at her job too. I can see why they said she was a tough act to follow."

Arke didn't reply, and Kennedy heard Ibu quickly change the energy in her voice as well as the subject.

"So, let's get you checked over. How's it been today?"

"I'm here to pick up some more painkilling stuff."

That was definitely the Soulbound's 'nonchalant' tone, and Kennedy knew she was trying to evade the question.

"You've used that whole bottle already?"

"No, I just felt like a midnight walk!"

Kennedy was keen to hear how the new healer would handle the worst patient, and keener still to find out what injury Arke hadn't told him about.

"I was making small talk. Hygiene isn't high on the prison's list of priorities so let's double down on everything in case of infection. So come on, get your shirt off and hop up on the bed."

"I can't keep coming here. Try and fix it this time."

Kennedy almost winced as Arke's attitude suddenly stepped up a gear.

"Oh, was that what I forgot to do yesterday?"

Ibu's tone was exactly as sarcastic as her words and when there was no reply from the Soulbound, Kennedy wished he had someone close enough to high five. It sounded as if the *Warrior's* new healer was entirely perfect for the job. He tiptoed back into the galley and made a fresh pot of coffee.

A little while later, Kennedy slipped into the infirmary carrying a hot drink in each hand. The curtains had been drawn around the corner bed and Ibu was sitting at the desk, making notes. She looked up, startled, and then pressed a finger to her lips, ushering him back out of the room.

"Before you think you have to make anything up about Arke, you should know that the crew absolutely can't keep secrets." Kennedy smiled reassuringly as he spoke. "Coffee? None of you are in trouble, in fact I'm just glad you're here to help. How bad is it?"

Ibu took the drink and checked the door was shut behind her before looking back at him. "Not great, not awful – her back's still a mess but I've cleaned out all the lash marks again and I think we're winning. I followed Gurdi's instructions and gave her a heavy dose of sleeping potion before I tried to do anything. I hope that was ok and she won't hate me too much for it."

"You handled the beast perfectly. How about I take the rap for the knockout while you get some rest?"

THE SHIP WAS coming alive with the sounds of movement and the smell of breakfast cooking by the time Arke woke, cursing as she rolled onto her side and tried to sit up.

"I'd like to say I was surprised that you didn't tell me you were flogged again." Kennedy was sitting in the chair beside her bed, holding out one of his old shirts, eyes carefully averted. "Put this on, it's looser than yours."

"And I'd like to say I was surprised that no-one could keep their damned mouths shut." The Soulbound ignored his offer and stopped trying to get up.

Kennedy threw the shirt at her head, sudden fury overtaking him. "You honestly think I'm THAT stupid? DO YOU?" When there was no reply, he kicked the leg of her bed angrily. "Fine. I'm stupid. I'm dumb as a bunch of rocks. I'm entirely comic value. I'm the LAST person that finds out that the closest thing to family I have left, and yes, right now you're a THING, the last thing I have doesn't trust me enough to tell me the truth! What did you have to lose? What was the point? Except to push me away again." He stood directly in her eye line. "I'm NOT leaving until you talk to me."

Neither of them spoke for a full three minutes.

Finally, and with what had to be an incredibly painful lurching movement, Arke sat up, grabbing the shirt, and pulling it on. She forced herself to her feet, lips pressed together so hard that they were almost as pale as her skin and walked towards the door, but Kennedy, arms folded, silently blocked her path. He was not going to back down.

"What do you want me to say? I'm the reason Porro died, the reason Gurdi died. They didn't just DIE either, they were slaughtered like animals!"

She turned away, moving unsteadily to the sink and splashing water on her face as Kennedy stood in silence.

"If I look behind me, all I see are tombstones – there's barely a single person I've cared about who's still alive. And that pattern's never changed so I know in front of me it's going to be the same. I'm so tired of being the last one standing – of not knowing how to make it stop."

She leant her hands on the basin, easing her back with a badly concealed grimace.

"I'd decided to leave. Thought if I were miles away, he couldn't punish you for what I fail to do – and I was so close to the skyport when I heard Urzish's ridiculous battle cry." She paused, shaking her head slowly. "I wasn't going to let her be flogged, nor Ellie, and Kilar shouldn't get branded – her arms are way too skinny for that. It was just a bar fight, but Soleya's all about order." Stretching a little too far, she flinched, holding her breath until the spasm passed. "Someone needed to take the rap and keep their mouth shut, which is exactly what I'm best at. I told the others to come straight back here, but they'd found Ibu and were waiting for me when I came out. I didn't tell you because I was worried you'd do something stupid. It was over, it was done, everyone walked away."

"Well – you staggered away," Kennedy said, smiling briefly before his expression turned serious again. "I'm hurt because I want you to talk to me, and hearing all of that, I know you need to. Lean on me, please Arke.

I'm not a kid anymore, I can take it." He sighed, putting his hands in his pockets. "None of this is your fault – what you endured, what's happening – it's all because you did what you had to do to keep the rest of us alive. I spoke to the crew before we left Soleya and all of them chose to stay with the *Warrior*. Every – single – person without a moment of hesitation." He took a deep breath before continuing. "Maybe this is unwinnable, maybe we're all screwed, but maybe, just maybe, if we're together, it'll be enough to tip the scales."

"If you start singing, I swear I'm going to end it now." The Soulbound straightened slowly. "Fine."

"So you'll pop in for a daily cuppa and chat?"

"Absolutely not." She walked to the door before turning back, her mouth quivering with a small smile. "However, in the interests of telling you things – better things. Back when we fought the tiger-cow mutants and again when we crashed into the river, my orange magic did something – weird. It sent Stabbington and I somewhere else, to a place where he has a human body. I have no idea how, but I'm not going to argue."

"No way!" Kennedy was instantly intrigued. "So come on, what does he look like?"

Arke just stared at him.

"Is he handsome or average? Young? Old? Does he have buck teeth, a grandad beard, love handles, chicken legs, a terrible hair cut? At least give me something!"

"He says he's gorgeous, why did you even have to check?"

"Ask him if he's interested in seeing my new sword, since no-one else seems to be." Kennedy sighed with a little added melodrama for effect.

"Bring me some breakfast and I'll take a look." She walked slowly away down the corridor.

Kennedy beamed and scurried to the galley. Bubbles might be fragile, but they were also easy to replace.

※ ※ ※

Despite the ship's distinctly unwanted passenger, the crew of the *Warrior* were in good spirits on the journey to Theogenes. The weather was glorious; Ibu was a great addition to the line dancing group and even seemed to be able to rival Sparkz at the poker table. The store cupboards were full again and Volk consistently dished up meals that no-one had any reason to complain about.

After their discussion in the infirmary, Kennedy had been relentless in his pursuit of a new level of communication between himself and the Soulbound. Jenkins' presence had actually helped the cause, as Kennedy had never realised just how much Arke loathed the Firm. Every time she started to withdraw, or got lost in her own head, he'd found a way of bringing Jenkins back into the conversation. That never failed to rouse her to eye-narrowing fury, to focus her emotions on something or someone she could hate in a more positive fashion than the vicious entity in the obsidian tower.

The only disappointment during the entire voyage was that Sparkz finally admitted defeat with Zeke's body. It had been so badly damaged by both the magical and the conventional fires in the engine room that he simply could not repair it. Every joint was melted, every connection dissolved. However, the sad news was quickly cancelled out. During what totally hadn't been a dissection of what he thought was his lifeless assistant, Sparkz had discovered that most of the Bior's consciousness remained intact. After he'd swigged half a bottle of strong alcohol to recover from the shock of hearing Zeke's reedy voice suddenly spark to life, the engineer had made a new plan.

It had taken him a full day to transplant what was left of Zeke into a set of armour he'd been adapting to carry his jet pack. Work of pure and perfect genius completed, Sparkz had slept for a handful of hours before suiting up and starting to teach his now very personal assistant how to fly. After making sure that Zeke was content with his new situation, a smiling Kennedy had rewritten the Bior's name in the crew roster and returned outside to be entertained by his brother's shouts of 'SLOWLY, YOU IDIOT!', 'YOU MIGHT NOT BE ABLE TO BREAK BUT I CAN!' and 'IS THIS BECAUSE I MELTED YOUR HEAD TO THE ENGINE THAT ONE TIME? I SAID I WAS SORRY!"

⚔ ⚔ ⚔

As their voyage neared its destination, Jenkins put a set of Barsian flags and beacons on the *Warrior*. The crew reacted as badly as expected, but Kennedy managed to settle the situation by pointing out the alternative was, at best, time consuming and, at worst, deadly. The skies around Theogenes were crowded with military vessels, and they needed to get to the city without being constantly or permanently stopped. Once the Apothecarium issue had been resolved, they'd leave both Jenkins and the flags behind.

A few minutes after first light, Arke found Ruby in her usual position of worship, praying atop the rearmost railing, wings outspread to welcome the sun.

"Morning Rubes, looks like we're almost there."

"Yeah. Captain wants Sparkz and I to do a fly-by of the Apothecarium this morning." The Ornithol hopped down and turned to peer more closely than was probably polite into Arke's face. "Are you ok with all this?"

"All this?" the Soulbound echoed, not quite sure what she might find wrong with a scouting mission.

"The whole... you know... murdery thing..." Ruby mimed a stab wound.

Arke chuckled. "If I held grudges against places where I've nearly died then I'd have to live on a rock in the middle of nowhere. Don't worry about me."

The Ornithol followed her friend towards the bow as the *Warrior* headed for the skyport. Normally, the floating quays would be populated by merchantmen of all shapes and sizes, but at the moment, the only vessels there belonged to the Barsian military.

Ahead of them, Theogenes was shining in the morning sun, but as they flew closer, Arke folded her arms and frowned as she saw the giant shimmering dome which seemed to loom over the entire city. She knew something that size had taken a small army of mages to set up. The structure was clearly some sort of containment field, and inside it the only thing she could see was a dense cloud of puke green fog.

"Guess that's not the drains," Ruby remarked dryly.

For the second time in a few minutes, Arke turned to her and grinned. "We'll have to ask."

Kennedy joined them at the bow and handed each a cup of coffee. "Good morning, two of my most favourite people in the entire world. I see we have some work ahead of us."

"Drain cleaning, according to Ruby," the Soulbound chuckled.

"Pirates, not plumbers," Kennedy grinned. "Shall I just send Jenkins down with a plunger?"

"Much as I would love to," Arke replied, "it might be counter-productive."

Sparkz, dressed in his new set of armour, complete with fully integrated jet pack, followed his brother to the bow and pointedly cleared his throat. "Paint job."

"Did you say something, bro?" Kennedy asked innocently, shading his eyes as he looked down at Theogenes.

"I think he coughed," Ruby suggested.

"That's what I thought," Arke agreed, keeping her eyes focused on the city.

Sparkz huffed and stepped in front of them, only to find they'd all turned away to scrutinise one of the vessels anchored nearby. "I swear I will burn the lot of you!"

Kennedy finally looked at his brother, pretending to shield his vision from the shiny new paint job. "Retina damage incoming."

"You missed a bit," Arke added.

"Where?" He frowned, quickly starting to check his armour.

She took a sip of her drink to hide the fact her lips were quivering with amusement. "Keep looking till you find it."

The instant before the engineer told her exactly where to stick her coffee, Kennedy patted him on the shoulder.

"Seriously bro, it rocks. We're just jealous."

While Kennedy started to brief Ruby and Sparkz, the Soulbound headed back to her cabin. As she crossed the main deck, she spotted Jenkins, and sped up in the hope of avoiding any interaction. However, he changed his course to intercept her as the two scouts soared away from the ship.

"I appreciate that you have deep-seated issues about men in positions of power..." he began.

There was nothing about Jenkins that didn't give Arke seriously murdery thoughts. His tone. His voice. His words. His smug attitude. His face. That perfectly punchable face with its stupid side whiskers and neatly trimmed grey beard that would look so much better if it were, for example, on fire.

"Oh? Then why do I hate you? Must just be because you're a..."

"Good morning, Jenkins." Kennedy arrived in time to interrupt her rising temper. "How did you sleep?"

"How do you think?" Jenkins snapped. "You were the one who gave me a cabin next to the forward head knowing your orc is both lactose intolerant and addicted to midnight milkshakes. Other captains would have moved someone ELSE to that room and put me somewhere better."

The Soulbound gasped theatrically. "I wasn't aware this was a cruise ship, Philip! Please tell me I didn't miss out on the shuffleboard tournaments or the harpsichord recitals?"

Jenkins scowled at her before quickly returning his expression and tone to something more neutral. "Captain Kennedy, are you intending to head straight down once we dock?"

"A little stroll sounds delightful, but we absolutely MUST be back in time to dress for dinner." Arke's accent was so tautly upper class it could probably have sliced through the finest crystal.

Jenkins ignored her and looked directly at Kennedy, whose cheek muscles were bulging with what might have been the stress of keeping the peace, or barely contained laughter.

"Kennedy, we should discuss the manner of your interactions with the Barsian commander. Behaviour like that will not be well received."

"I am sure we'll manage just fine. Now if you'll excuse us, we need to go and make ready. We're heading down to the surface as soon as my scouts return."

Kennedy put his hand on the Soulbound's shoulder, propelling her away from Jenkins and straight towards their cabins.

"I know he's an arrogant bastard, but you could at least try..."

"I did," she growled. "And then he opened his mouth."

Chapter Twenty
Ghost Town

THE DAY SEEMED to be populated by arrogant men with too much to say, Kennedy mused, as he waited in the antechamber of an enormous tent and listened to a Barsian commander holding court inside the main room. Arke had spent less than thirty seconds listening to the voice before walking out without a word. Granted, it was probably a good thing, as he didn't have to worry about her reaction to what was clearly an ego the size of the city itself, but it did knock him off balance not to have her at his side.

Finally, the morning briefings were over, and Jenkins, Kennedy, Sparkz and Ruby were ushered into the operations room. On the main table was a detailed map of Theogenes with markers that denoted troops, mages, and a large circle that showed the location of the magical containment field.

A grizzled captain with the badge of Theogenes on his uniform greeted Jenkins like an old friend while Kennedy's eyes were drawn to the commanding officer as he stood flicking through a bundle of messages. He was an imposing figure, tall and immaculately groomed, his physique still impressive despite the obvious clues that he was on the wrong side of forty, if not fifty. On his left shoulder he wore the Barsian crest, and on the right a red and green shield with a cockerel in the foreground – the symbol of Levenbrandt.

After a brief conversation with the grey-haired officer, Jenkins stepped back and gestured between the two captains. "Captain Serge, Theogenes Garrison – Captain Kennedy of the *Warrior*, and some of his crew."

The introductions immediately grabbed the Barsian commander's attention. He snapped his head round and raked an autocratic gaze across the group. Kennedy stood firm, returning the scrutiny with an even expression. He'd seen enough nobles to be unsurprised by the man's sharp cheekbones and haughty demeanour. Just like a stick of rock, this guy probably had 'Aristocrat' stamped all the way through him.

"Good work Jenkins," the Lord Commander nodded. "Now we can skip the chase and get straight to the executions."

"Excuse me?" Kennedy stepped forwards, trying to fight the urge to draw his sword.

"Lord Commander Kromm." Jenkins had moved too, keeping a half step ahead of Kennedy. "I have travelled here with the *Warrior*. They have agreed to help deal with the situation."

"Deal with it? Unlikely. They're probably so disappointed they failed to destroy the entire city that they've come back to finish the job." The Lord Commander strode towards them, sharp eyes busily assessing their reactions to his words.

"Whatever happened here was nothing to do with us," Kennedy replied.

"We have witnesses that place a pair of Chromatia's acolytes at the Apothecarium just before the catastrophe occurred. One of them was an Ornithol." Kromm looked hard at Ruby, who clearly had no idea how to respond other than to suddenly find something very interesting on the roof of the tent.

"With all due respect, the Apothecarium is a very busy place," Kennedy noted, trying to keep his cool.

"These two acolytes walked in alone and left with a healthy young orc who was, by all accounts, extremely *un*healthy before their visit. Moments after they exited the building, a patient who had been brought in at the *same* time as the now healthy orc, released a magical infection that caused the evacuation of the centre of Theogenes." The Lord Commander looked from Ruby to Kennedy to Sparkz as if he were already measuring them for coffins. "We *know* you were here. We *know* your ship flew away just after everything started happening. Do NOT try to tell me this is all circumstantial."

"But it *is*." Sparkz eyed Kromm with a defiant tilt to his head. "Yes, we were here. And we left in a łush because one of our crew members was nearly killed by thugs in the city – we didn't want any more trouble. Your Apothecarium *theory* is just that – pure conjecture. Some might even call us scapegoats."

"If we'd been the cause of it, would we be here to help?" Kennedy asked, hurrying to avert the argument he sensed brewing between his brother and the Lord Commander.

"*Three* of you," Kromm snorted.

"*Four* of us – we're specialists at dealing with unusual situations." Kennedy kept his expression and tone neutral.

The Lord Commander rolled his eyes. "You're pirates."

"Actually, we position ourselves as Wealth Transfer Enablers," Sparkz replied, tapping the logo he'd painstakingly stamped onto his armour.

"So let's 'position' this as *Life* Retaining Enablement." Kromm levelled a hard-eyed stare at Kennedy. "You fix the problem, and we'll forget who caused it. You die trying, that's one thing less for me to do. You try and leave without dealing with it and I'll hang you." With a single curt nod, he turned on his heel and walked away.

Captain Serge led them out of the tent and Kennedy looked around for a moment, before spotting Arke sitting quietly in the shade of a tree, polishing Stabbington with deft, sharp movements.

"We ready?" She got to her feet and sheathed her sword.

"Do you want to know what they think is going on?" Serge asked. "It might help."

"Yes, absolutely, book us a session with Barsian Intelligence," Sparkz remarked with clear amusement. "They're the ones who use joined up writing, aren't they?"

"Let's get moving." Kennedy hustled his brother away from the tent before he managed to cause any more trouble. "Walk and talk, captain."

As they headed down the empty streets, Serge described how the deadly green mist had spread outwards from the Apothecarium and added that the only reason so many had escaped was its slow-moving nature. He explained that he'd been on the front line of the evacuation, holding back the terrifying creatures that lived within the miasma until the emergency forces had arrived. Even then, it had not been easy. It had taken fifteen Barsian mages to erect the dome that had finally contained the fog, but no-one had worked out what it was or how to destroy it. The only thing that had been found effective against it had been fire, but he didn't recommend using that unless you were immune to significantly disproportionate explosions.

The *Warrior* crew listened, more because they didn't feel like talking rather than from any need to gather information. They already had their own ideas about the source of the disaster. Back on the ship, and well away from any Jenkins-sized ears, Kennedy and Sparkz had hauled Arke, Ruby and Irash into a meeting about what the Firm operative had told them was happening in Theogenes.

When they'd finished, Ruby and Arke had relayed everything they remembered from their experience in the Apothecarium. Just after the Soulbound gave her description of the dangerous bandaged humanoid she'd seen in the side room of the Palliative Care ward, Irash had interrupted with a snort of laughter.

"What?" Arke had snapped.

"What what?" Irash had shaken his head slowly. "Do you need crayons?"

"Only if I'm allowed to stick them in your eyes," she'd growled.

"Just spit it out," Kennedy had ordered.

"Fine. And since you're all looking at me with the vacant stares of ruminating cattle, I'll make it REALLY simple. You all know that before I gave up most of my power to fuse with this body, my magic was incredibly potent. What you have clearly not fully understood is that when I brought a corpse back to life, it stayed alive for a VERY – LONG – TIME." He'd paused and looked around. "Is anyone riding the brain train yet? Old me reanimated Paltos, and he ended up going overboard shortly after this masterpiece of an orc." He smoothed a hand down his chest before continuing. "This body and the huge, or should I say 'giant' guy were picked up together. Connected the dots? Just in case you haven't: the – bandaged – angry – guy – was – Paltos. The ruckus when we left was probably him reacting to my magic. Maybe he was cross because we didn't take him with us, or maybe he'd just run out of custard creams. Impossible to tell."

Struggling to control his frustration, Kennedy had asked if Irash knew how the reanimated corpse of Paltos, the affable giant who'd been the *Warrior's* first mate for years, his friend, the poster child for neatly trimmed beards and friendly oversized humanoids, could have caused a plague that had apparently infected a huge swathe of the city?

"Oh, that ward was so full of spirits it was like walking through dead person soup. Add a splash of ancient magic to that and anything could happen."

After Arke had uncalmly asked Irash why he hadn't bloody well mentioned that at the time, he'd shrugged and remarked that surely he wasn't supposed to know whether a city that wasn't even built when he was last out in the world could cope with a magical threat. And as for stopping the plague?

"Burn it all down," Irash suggested.

"You're sure?"

"I mean it's always a solid start. Rebuilding gives any survivors something to do."

They'd all agreed that they wouldn't be doing that. Well, not unless things got really out of hand.

✗ ✗ ✗

As every pane of glass in the Apothecarium shattered, and any doors which had been shut were thrown open by the torrent of super-heated air that preceded the eruption of flame that briefly turned the marble building into a devil's harmonica, Kennedy, Arke, Sparkz and Ruby were lightly poaching in the fountain that sat in the central atrium of the Palliative Care ward.

Things had most definitely got out of hand, and far more quickly than anticipated.

"It is a good thing you are not in the sea," Stabbington remarked, his tone calmer than the situation demanded. "This amount of blood would tempt any shark within a thousand miles."

"Shut up!" Arke hissed as she raised her head above the crimson-coloured water to check around the ruined ward. "There were hundreds of them! And since they were ALREADY DEAD most of YOUR magic couldn't do much against them."

"Arke, you can shout at him later." Kennedy scrambled to his feet, sword at the ready. Like the others, he was covered in wounds, slashes, bruises, scrapes and punctures. "Anyone see any of them?"

"No. But that green mist is coming back." Ruby stood up, shaking quickly as she tried to shed the water from her feathers.

"HOW?" Kennedy stepped out of the fountain and eyed the creeping miasma with a furious expression. "We just exploded half the hospital to get rid of it! How is it already reforming?"

"I guess our power play didn't take out the source," Sparkz replied from behind his twisted visor. His metal suit had taken an absolute beating, but it was still holding together, even if his jet was now making disappointing whooshing noises every time Zeke tried to get it to fire.

They stood back-to-back as the fetid smelling fog started to lick around their ankles. Swirling shapes formed in the darker corners of the room, rising from the mist, multiplying by the second.

"Here we go again," the Ornithol sighed. "If Paltos is at the heart of all this, he doesn't seem to want to talk to us. And if he won't, then what do we do?"

"Follow my lead," Kennedy whispered, before taking a deep breath. "PALTOS!" he yelled. "GET OUT HERE! I know it's you, and I know you're angry."

His only answer was a sudden thickening of the fog that surrounded them, the putrid-coloured waves now reaching to their knees. Wizened heads began to form from the pulsing miasma, green skulls covered with paper-thin skin and dotted with wisps of hair.

"It can't be Paltos." Arke made sure her voice was loud enough to ring around the room. "Letting someone else fight his battles? Never."

Kennedy swung his sword like a scythe, the glowing silver blade cleaving through head after head. Just as before, each time he cut one down, it would melt back out of existence, but another would take its place.

"Looks like he's being tactical," Sparkz suggested. "Wants to wear us down."

The Soulbound snorted with derision. "Paltos? Tactical? Are we talking about the same guy? The one who kicked his way through a metal door rather than look for a key?"

As the fog rose to their waists, Ruby was spinning her quarterstaff so rapidly that it was barely visible. "Honestly, I think you're just making him angrier."

"He probably sent these things because he's too busy conditioning his precious, tiny, little beard." Arke kicked away a tooth-filled face as it snapped its way towards her.

"Because that totally made up for the lack of hair on his head," Sparkz added as he sliced through two torsos with one swing.

The fog suddenly lurched upwards until it became a massive cylinder that towered over them, its sides populated by twisting legs, whirling arms, and grim faces that had no focus but the four living creatures at the heart of the maelstrom.

"Should we apologise?" the Ornithol whispered. "He was a really nice man and he's obviously upset."

"And how did that go for us earlier?" Arke hissed. "So badly that we had to find out what Serge meant by 'don't light a match near the green stuff'." She raised her voice to a shout. "He's probably busy having a facial and letting these pricks do the real fighting!"

The fog slowly started to rotate, more and more bodies populating the surface as it spun.

"You're just proving her right, Paltos!" Kennedy yelled.

A giant-sized fist suddenly coalesced from the miasma and punched the Soulbound so hard that she cannoned into Ruby, knocking them both to the ground.

"Cheap shot!" Kennedy roared as the fist disappeared back into the fog. "Come out where we can see you!"

Arke picked up her sword and scrambled back to her feet, ignoring the blood that ran down her face from the sizable split in her eyebrow.

"Are you *sure* this is what you wish to say?" Stabbington's tone was as close to horrified as his host had ever heard, but she'd already made up her mind.

She took a deep breath and shouted what she hoped would herald an end to this conflict – one way or another. "Who knew being dead would turn you into a coward!"

The tornado around them began to roar, all the mouths on all the heads opening wide in ghoulish screams that chilled the air and shook the ground. Paltos' axe, glowing with an unearthly green light, suddenly swung down towards her. She tried to parry the blow, but the power behind the unnatural weapon smashed Stabbington from her hands. However, hers was not the only sword that had intercepted the attack. Inches above her head was Kennedy's silver blade, holding back the giant's axe.

Quickly stepping away from their trial of strength, Arke kept up the pressure. "Is this what your loyalty REALLY looks like?"

"All – these – years," Kennedy ground out the words. "And – for – what?"

"And – for – what?" The deep voice that echoed his question was hoarse and broken, but still recognisable.

Suddenly, the axe withdrew and the cone of fog fell back, sliding away until the wall of bodies wreathed the edges of the room.

With a sudden ripple of movement, Paltos appeared in front of them. Apart from the fact that everything about him was green, he looked just as he had the day he'd died.

"You question MY loyalty? MINE? When you chose that *child*, that pathetic orc, over me? Why did I not have the opportunity to live again?"

"He does have a point," Stabbington remarked in the Soulbound's head. "I would definitely kill you for that."

"NOT helpful," she murmured, before raising her gaze to Paltos' face. "When I was here, I didn't know it was you and I didn't know it was Grimlet."

"How could you not? It was so OBVIOUS!" Paltos retorted, pointing his axe towards her.

"It's Arke. Seriously, what did you expect?" Sparkz shrugged. "Dumbest smart person ever."

"Oh – thanks," she hissed.

"I didn't work it out either," Ruby added quickly. "And you were well guarded, we weren't even allowed in your room."

"That job was a shitshow from start to finish." Kennedy eased his sword arm and changed hands briefly to allow him to flex his fingers. "But we didn't choose him over you – Irash picked a body to take over." He paused. "We can handle it being Grimlet's but I'm not sure how I'd cope if it had been yours. I think I prefer to miss you properly rather than see you around but know it's not really you."

Paltos looked at him, then at the others, his gaze finally landing on the Soulbound as she stepped towards him.

"Me too." She wiped away the blood that was trickling down her cheek. "I'm not sorry about that, but I am sorry, actually way, way more than sorry, that I couldn't save your life."

"We all are," Kennedy agreed. "Maybe things would have gone differently if we had, maybe we wouldn't be so screwed right now."

Paltos was silent for a moment and then he smiled slowly, pointing at Arke's face. "Is that a tear?"

"What, from my increasingly swollen eye under my incredibly painful eyebrow you bisected with your stupid fat fist?" she scowled.

The giant's smile turned into a grin, and he began to chuckle. "I made Arke cry. NOW I can die happy."

As he laughed, the ghouls started to howl, a keening note that reverberated around the ward.

"So, my friends, let us fight together one last time, We stand together, shoulder to shoulder against our foes!" Paltos bellowed, turning to face the miasma. "COME AND GET IT, UNDEAD BITCHES!"

"What?" Kennedy's eyes widened in shock. "Paltos – no. Just NO!"

"He can't... go in peace?" Ruby looked warily at the fog, which was thickening in several places.

"I am no longer angry, so they can be put to rest!" Paltos swung his axe a couple of times as if loosening up. "With a little persuasion."

The flat of Stabbington's blade slammed against the giant's back as the Soulbound glared at him. "Just tell them it's over! Walk towards the light, people!"

"That was their problem the first time," Paltos shrugged. "They didn't want to leave the party."

Kennedy sighed. "Good, because I'd really hate to fight completely unmotivated monsters."

Sparkz watched the ghouls mould and squelch together, forming into vaguely humanoid shapes covered with extra flapping limbs and far too many creepy eyes. "They're so motivated they just unionised."

The first conjoined creature started to lurch towards the small group by the fountain. The other huddles of undead were slower to create a single organism, but they were working hard to catch up.

"Paltos – can you throw me over the top of that thing?" Kennedy asked. "Aim for about ten feet above its head."

"My pleasure, captain."

The giant took hold of him like a javelin, drew back his arm and hurled him towards the hulking monstrosity. Somersaulting through the air, Kennedy straightened his body at the perfect moment and dived, holding his sword out ahead of him. The combination of gravity, accuracy, and the wicked sharpness of the blade meant his attack cleaved the creature in half before he tucked and rolled into a neat landing between its two twitching sides.

"Work smarter, not harder, brother," Sparkz muttered before turning his attention to the next shambling conglomeration and activating one of his most expensive tattoos.

With sudden flashes of magical energy, the conjoined form shrank from the size of an elephant to that of a donkey.

"MINE!" Paltos' voice boomed with enthusiasm. He sprang forwards, using the flat side of the axe head to strike the shortened monster so perfectly that it soared straight towards one of the others. With a splattering of shrieks, both abominations shattered into broken parts and fell to the marbled floor.

"To fog ye shall return..." Leaping across to the newest jumble of fallen ghouls, Kennedy's sword swung like a pendulum, its blade glowing as it administered some final blessings.

"Who's next?" Unfortunately for Sparkz, the answer to his question was himself, as an entire torso of angry green bodies suddenly landed directly on top of him.

"Sorry dude, my bad!" Paltos was spinning around the room, swinging his axe by its handle, and spraying puke-coloured body parts across the entire ward.

Arke dodged and dashed across to rescue the engineer. However, the monstrosity that had crushed him was ghoul-spreading quite some distance on either side of his last position. She wasn't sure how heavy it was, but after she'd put her shoulder against it and pushed, she knew the answer was 'far too much to move'.

"Ruby, I need help!"

Kicking a twisted and clawing hand away from her legs, the Soulbound started hacking into the torso with her demon blade as the Ornithol landed next to her.

"Just – like – the world's – biggest – marrow!" Ruby sliced her quarterstaff down with every word and twitching green body parts began dropping to the floor around her.

Arke levelled a confused gaze at her friend. "Marrow? What – the –hell?"

"INCOMING!"

A chunk of flying monster suddenly slammed the Soulbound into the V-shaped hole she'd been carving in what she knew was definitely not a marrow. Those vegetables had bland, squishy interiors. This creature was made of bones, anger, and the stench of death. As more than one set of unsanitary teeth sank themselves into her jacket and a myriad of hands tried to drag her further into the cavernous body, she reacted instinctively. Driving Stabbington to the ground, through bone, sinew, and gristle, she activated her emergency teleport.

From her new position on the other side of the room, Arke watched the Ornithol climb out of the fountain for the second time that day. Her feathers were plastered flat, and her beak was tapping together with staccato irritation.

"I do not believe Ruby is terribly pleased with you right now," Stabbington remarked. "That spell is not the best one to use when your friends are close by." The demon was indeed the smoothest purveyor of the finest obvious truths.

"Sorry!" the Soulbound called as she got back to her feet. "I owe you a beer... or seven." That offer, although honestly made, was not hugely effective in softening the glare of her friend's yellow eyes. "But look! There he is!" She gestured towards the newly revealed Sparkz, who lay among a smattering of ghoulish body parts.

Without a word, Ruby waded through the thick bank of torn green flesh in order to reach the engineer.

Stabbington cleared his non-existent throat. "I believe it would be safer for us to help the crazed, undead giant who is now surrounded by monsters than to return to her."

"Again with the obvious!" his host muttered as she dodged another random chunk of monster.

She scrambled across the battlefield towards where Paltos had been besieged by towering green creatures. Kennedy was already busy cutting one of them down to size, his silver sword swinging rapidly as he carved away at its base. It finally staggered back, beginning to topple as he made the final incision in its tree trunk of a leg and he quickly sprang his alter, merging with it just as the monstrosity landed where he'd been standing only seconds before.

"Behind you!" Arke yelled, as she noticed the creature next to Kennedy's new position react to his sudden appearance. A huge fist, faced with rows of ghoulish skulls, was flashing straight towards him.

"CAPTAIN!" Paltos' axe dropped from his hands as he tackled the conglomeration, thrusting it away before the attack could land.

"Only three to go! Let's get this DONE!" Kennedy's ability to count while rallying his crew had always been suspect. More than suspect. In fact, it lay somewhere between 'outright lie' and 'toddler maths'.

As he merged with his alter on top of the nearest conglomeration, the Soulbound began to hack at the second monstrosity while Ruby charged across the room to attack the third. Paltos punched the other third repeatedly while the final third one ripped off its own half severed arm and used it like a golf club. Arke never saw it coming, but she certainly felt it.

Disorientated, winded, and only partially aware that she was flying directly towards Kennedy's monster, the Soulbound was at the mercy of two things. One was the reaction time of a ghoul conglomeration, and the other was orange.

As she began to descend, Stabbington's shouts finally triggered her to ignite her magical protection. The barrier rippled into existence a millisecond before she was launched back into the air by a kick from a monstrous leg. And just as if her chaotic inner power had been waiting for that exact opportunity, in a flash of orange light, Arke disappeared.

"BREATHE. IT IS ok." Stabbington was immediately reassuring and then by degrees, more impatient. "You need to concentrate on my voice, gather your senses, such as they are. I know the bar is set indecently low, so it is not difficult. It cannot be difficult. ARKE! WHY ARE MORTALS SO FRAGILE? THIS IS RIDICULOUS! ARKE!"

"If you shut up then I can answer," she groaned.

"Ah, she is back in the room. Or the... demiplane?"

"Yeah, fabulous. Where are we this time?" The Soulbound opened her eyes to see nothing but blackness. She could feel she was lying on something soft and vaguely grassy, but since there was no source of light, they might have been just about anywhere.

"Some place with no stars. Hold still."

"Why? Hey, what are you doing?" Arke's hands moved to intercept his as they roamed around her torso.

"Aha! Got them!" There was a rustling noise as the demon pulled a bag from her jacket.

"You were going through my pockets... for snacks? When I'm... are you... you're incredible."

"Thank you. You are unpleasantly damp so I was concerned that the wrapping would be compromised. But no – this is a wonderful result." After a moment, there was the sound of crunching, followed by an ecstatic sigh. "Oh. Now I get it! Sugar. Chocolate. Butter. There are no words. I have no words! You were right all along!"

"We're fighting for our lives back there and you're in ecstasy over biscuits." She poked him in what she guessed was probably his chest. She was briefly satisfied by the yelp that resulted, even though that exclamation of discomfort was quickly muffled by what sounded like an entire mouthful of chocolate chip delights.

"They are not just ANY biscuits. They are MY biscuits."

Arke lay back, half exasperated, and half amused. "I mean it's certainly different. In the face of death – eat cookies."

"Ah, you will be fine. Are there any more?"

She felt his hands go searching again and quickly slapped one away from its investigations. "That's not a pocket!"

"My bad. But are there?"

With a flash of orange, the Soulbound completed her flying lesson by crashing down on top of monster number two, who was busy being filleted by an extremely worried looking Kennedy.

"Where'd you go?"

"No idea," she groaned, "but Stabbington ate all my snacks while we were there."

Memory's Claws

Most people would have questioned Arke's reply, but Kennedy took it in his stride as he hauled her away from the twitching creature. "You can put him in a cupboard later. Paltos thought something had happened to you and went into a bit of a frenzy. Well, a full frenzy. Actually, I'm not sure frenzy is a strong enough word."

As she blinked to accustom her eyes back to the light in the Apothecarium, the Soulbound saw that there was one monstrosity left upright, and that was probably only because Paltos had smashed a column and used it as a pin to fasten the creature to a wall. Every inch of the ward was strewn with puke green body parts which were slowly melting back into the miasma that had created them.

"Hey, Paltos! She's fine, look!" Kennedy called, but the giant appeared to be in a world of his own as he tore the pinioned monstrosity apart.

"He seems to be relieving some... frustrations." Sparkz hobbled over, using a crutch to help him walk. His armour was distinctly battered, bits that had been smooth and shiny now dull, bloody, and dented.

"It's getting brighter in here." Ruby sat down on the edge of the fountain and started to clean her feathers. "The fog's going from outside too."

Thin streaks of sunshine shone down on them from the shattered dome above, highlighting the lumps of ghoul as they withered away into nothing, their shrieks dissolving back to silence.

"Paltos, it's over..." Kennedy began, looking over to where the giant had been. As he realised their crewmate had vanished, his shoulders sagged. "Guess saying goodbye again would have sucked."

"Yeah." Arke eased herself down on an overturned bed. "Knowing Paltos, he wanted your last memory to be of him being awesome."

"Dammit! That's a power move." Kennedy forced a smile as he sat beside her. "Although now I think about it, every memory you guys have of me is awesome, right?"

Chapter Twenty-One
Family Values

A BEAMING CAPTAIN SERGE met them at the magical barrier and escorted the weary group along the empty streets towards the main encampment.

"Can we just head back to our ship?" Kennedy asked. "We need to clean up and... stuff. I promise we won't leave until the almighty lord of all medals agrees we're off the hook."

The four of them were battered and exhausted after the fight – their emergency supply of magical healing had got them this far, but they definitely needed more. The last thing any of them wanted to do was deal with the Barsian commander's attitude.

Serge frowned. "I'm not sure that you should go without seeing Lord Commander Kromm. He can be..."

"Rude? Unpleasant? Officious? Or just vindictive?" Sparkz scowled.

"Barsian." Kennedy nodded slowly. "Fine. We'll get signed off now then." He eyed the others warningly. "Don't say anything that'll cause a scene, OK?"

They were trudging towards the command tent when they heard a sudden ripple of applause echoing down a side street.

"I am here today to announce that Theogenes is safe once more." The unmistakable voice of the Lord

Commander carried easily to their ears. "We carved a path directly to the source of the infection and after a long and tiring battle, Barsia prevailed!"

Kennedy stopped. "What the...?"

Arke tugged on his arm. "We'll just go. It's all bullshit PR."

"He wanted to hang us and now he's taking all the credit?" he scowled. "Absolutely not."

"Do you even have half a clue who he is or what he can do?"

"No, and I don't care!" Kennedy snapped. "We were the ones who dealt with the problem!"

He tried to yank his arm away from her grasp, but she held firm, her eyes glittering darkly.

"Fine, I'll deal with it," she said. "You guys get back to the *Warrior*."

While he was trying to find the appropriate words to express his frustration at her foolhardy suggestion, Serge's voice cut across his thoughts.

"Look left, captain!"

Sparkz had limped off towards the sound of the Lord Commander and was just disappearing round the corner.

"Oh – SHIT! Ruby, get back to the ship. Tell Ellie we might need to leave in a hurry," Kennedy ordered, before sprinting to catch up with Arke as she ran after the engineer. "You distract and I'll extract."

Ahead of them, the street ended in a small park. Almost every inch of it was covered with people busy drinking what was undoubtedly free wine from Theogenes' cellars – the Barsians knew how to pack in a crowd. Soldiers and civilians stood, glasses in hand, as

Lord Commander Kromm addressed them from a central platform.

Arke quickly disappeared into the mass of bodies, pushing through the throng to find the optimal position to create chaos. Kennedy had no idea what she was going to do, and nor did he care, as long as it gave him a chance to grab his brother. He wasn't quite sure how worried to be about Sparkz's intentions, as while his loathing of the Barsian upper classes was no secret, he was also inherently rational. A park filled with soldiers under the command of a man who had already threatened to execute them was clearly not the place to cause any sort of scene. However, he had taken a heavy blow to the head in the fight, and concussion could do a lot of strange things. Kennedy needed to get to him, and fast.

Moving through the crowd as quickly as he could, apologising left and right as he pushed past people, Kennedy finally spotted his brother making his way towards the dais where Kromm was now answering questions from the audience with surprising charisma.

He was about twenty feet away when Sparkz hauled himself up on a park bench.

"So you're all just LAPPING up this man's absolute *bullshit*?"

The Lord Commander snapped his gaze to Sparkz's battered, bloodied face, his dark hair matted in clumps, his damaged helmet hanging over one shoulder.

"You have no..." Kromm's angry voice was suddenly cut off and he dropped to his knees, making choking noises. All around the platform, the crowd started to react with horror. Orders were being bellowed while people shouted and screamed in terror, panic driving them to push and shove each other in their efforts to get away from the dais.

Kennedy stopped trying to be polite and strong-armed his way towards the bench. Mages were clustering around the Lord Commander whose face was covered in bugs and beetles which seemed to pop out of his mouth only to disappear back up his nose.

However, Kennedy's amusement at what he recognised as Arke's timely and incredibly satisfying intervention was suddenly negated as Sparkz began to address the crowd, his voice almost as powerfully persuasive as Kromm's had been.

"That man did absolutely nothing to save Theogenes except stay here in safety and send others to risk their lives. Do you want to know the truth about who he sent to fight the monsters? Me and my friends! We're not 'his' soldiers, we're not even Barsian citizens! We went because he was threatening to execute us if we didn't do what he wanted! And you know what else? FOUR of us did what Barsian troops couldn't! Stop buying into their lies and start asking questions! Stand up and make your voices heard!"

Kennedy had never been prouder of his brother as in that instant when he stood, covered in dirt and drama, utterly and magnificently defiant. He glanced over to where Kromm was back on his feet, still spitting out the odd beetle as he glared at Sparkz. Soldiers were converging on the bench from every direction – extraction was going to be impossible.

He leapt up beside his brother. "And you say I'm the theatrical one."

Up on the dais, Kromm raised his voice as he tried to control the situation. "Ladies and gentlemen, there is no need for alarm. As a Barsian Lord Commander, I..."

Sparkz interrupted with mock applause. "Sounds like a position entirely won by merit. Have you ever even DONE anything in your life?"

"These men are pirates! The same ones who CAUSED this entire disaster and you can trust me when I say that they will be dealt with accordingly. I will sign the warrant for their executions tonight!"

The soldiers were joined by two mages as they closed in on the bench.

"Super convenient," Sparkz shouted. "See what he's doing? Making sure he gets to claim the victory by getting rid of the people who actually fixed the probl..."

※ ※ ※

ARKE WATCHED KENNEDY and Sparkz dragged away after being blindsided by a strong paralysis spell. She knew there was nothing she could do for them while they were unconscious and surrounded by so many soldiers. The instant they'd been subdued, she'd made herself invisible in order to escape. That in itself was incredibly risky, as she needed to battle against nausea and slip through the buffeting crowd while avoiding the Barsian mages who were trying to find the source of the magic that had made Kromm spit crickets. She smiled a little, unable to suppress the deep, personal satisfaction those bug-filled moments had given her.

However, before she slipped away, she couldn't resist another look at the platform where the Lord Commander was already charming his way back into the hearts of the people.

"But what did he mean?" one of the civilians asked. "He certainly looked like he'd been in a battle, unlike any of your men."

As she watched Kromm quickly pinch the bridge of his nose, her lips twisted into a far wider grin. That little movement was evidence of just how annoyed that particular topic of discussion was making him, even though his smile never wavered, and his well-practiced public performance didn't miss a beat. She dragged her eyes away and kept moving.

Almost an hour later, the Lord Commander made exactly the same movement of irritation when he walked into his tent and saw an expensive bottle of port half empty on the desk. However, when he read the note left underneath it, he exploded into silent rage, colour flooding his cheeks in a wave of fury.

You promised you'd never let power corrupt you.

He crumpled the paper in his hand and scanned the room with a single glance. Then, as he muttered an incantation, all the zips on the tent doors fastened themselves and the lanterns flickered, emitting a burst of smoke that briefly flooded the interior.

Only a few seconds passed before the anti-magic haze stripped away Arke's spell and she shimmered into visibility, snuggled into the cushions of his comfiest armchair.

"You know if I close my eyes while I'm invisible I don't feel nauseous? Makes it tricky breaking and entering though – so yeah, sorry about the mess outside. Anyway..." She took a deep breath, finally meeting Kromm's glittering gaze. "Hi Will."

With a furious flick of the wrist, he threw the crumpled paper in the air where it instantly disintegrated in purple flames.

"Do you do children's parties?" The innocent expression on the Soulbound's face did nothing to hide the wicked provocation of her words. She specialised in administering the finest jibes to the most deserving people and in her opinion there was no-one more deserving of a verbal slap to the side of the head.

Willem Kromm, Lord Commander of the Western Armies, member of one of the oldest noble families in Barsia, who probably hadn't been spoken to like that for thirty years, glared at Arke with what was easily recognisable as incandescent fury.

She yawned as she watched his eyes track to where her very filthy boots were very deliberately nestled against his very expensive-looking velvet cushions. Half a bottle of port combined with Stabbington's magical painkiller had been reasonably effective against the discomfort from all the cuts, gouges, dents and bruises that covered her, but being able to watch Will's temper rise and rise made her forget she'd been injured at all.

"I knew you were in Theogenes when it all started, and I knew it was you earlier. Did you think I wouldn't remember how your magic feels? Or was that part of your plan – you thought I'd go easy on them because you were on their side? It's not going to make ANY difference. In fact, it probably makes things worse, so your whole *'bargaining for your friends' lives'* ploy is pretty poor so far."

With a dismissive shake of his head, the Lord Commander stalked off into the rear section of the tent, yanking the well-polished buttons of his dress uniform jacket undone as he went.

"I'm not bargaining." She hauled herself out of the chair and followed him, picking up a hanger from his dresser as she passed.

"That's *utterly* apparent." Turning to face her, his eyes narrowed to match the force of his scowl, Kromm stripped off his jacket before holding out an expectant hand for the coat-hanger.

"You're not going to have them killed." Her even-toned reply was more informative than combative, her steady gaze meeting his angry one, her fingers still gripping the hanger.

"The order I'm about to sign says different, and now I can add your name."

She simply tilted her head to the side in reaction to his threat, and with a sharp movement, Kromm abandoned the battlefield, throwing his jacket at her face and striding away.

Arke caught it easily and slipped it onto the hangar, making sure to take her time smoothing out any creases and fastening the buttons.

"You don't need to, I'll add it myself." She smiled with sudden devilment. "*Then* I'll issue a press release – should do your reputation the world of good. Maybe even get a T-shirt with my name on, just for the execution."

"You're being ridiculous! I should call the guards to arrest you right now!" He slammed his highly polished boots onto the shoe rack so hard it fell over, spilling its contents haphazardly on the floor. "You humiliated me, and you think you can use the past to get away with it?"

"The past is the only reason I didn't kill you on sight." She looked over at the tumble of fallen footwear with a brazenly sardonic lift to her eyebrows.

He took in her expression immediately, a challenge suddenly sparking in his eyes as he started unbuttoning his shirt. "Oh – really? Arkz was never a match for me, even with her shitty little demon blade. I – won – every – time."

"I – let – you." The grin that interaction flung to her lips was unstoppable, and she turned away quickly, heading towards a wardrobe. "So... what colour shirt should the mighty Lord Commander wear to the execution of an ex-wife?"

He threw his dirty laundry into a wicker basket and shrugged. "I'm not sure. Something bright that screams celebration, similar to the one I wore when I had our divorce finalised."

"You never owned anything with any colour to it." She opened the cupboard doors to reveal an array of white, black, and grey. "And I see nothing changes."

"Exactly." Kromm reached round her to unhook a shirt, his voice no more than a whisper as he released his bombshell so close to her ear she could feel the warmth of his breath. "Nothing *has* changed. You're still my wife."

Arke froze, eyes widening in shock.

It was his turn to smile as he backed away, sliding the clean shirt over his shoulders. His satisfied expression only intensified with the loud crash as she slammed the wardrobe doors shut.

Silence reigned for what seemed like endless seconds as he started to do up the buttons and she fought to steady herself. She'd expected a lot of things from this confrontation, but never that, nor the emotions it unleashed within her. She knew she needed to think clearly to negotiate and save Kennedy and Sparkz. Concentrating on that one goal, she shut her eyes and breathed slowly, feeling her focus returning.

"The family never accepted our marriage anyway," he added, "so it seemed pointless to annul it. You were gone, I was busy."

His words, his voice, sounded so casual. So matter of fact. So inflammatory.

So much for her self-control.

"I was gone because of *your family*!" Arke spun to face him, her expression dark, the vicious tone of her accusation ensuring that he was only a few seconds behind in mirroring her rising fury.

The atmosphere between them had changed in an instant, from a teasing remembrance of what they'd been to the flare of brittle anger for what they'd lost. They'd never had chance to say goodbye, and even if there had been nothing else, that alone was more than enough to fester for thirty years and emerge as full-blown rage.

"Their threats had never worried you before. You left because I wouldn't renounce my position, because I wouldn't do what you wanted me to!" Kromm stepped forwards, hurling his words with venom, every muscle straining to keep himself from shouting.

Arke's expression flickered with brief confusion before she regathered her composure and slammed a hand against his chest to push him away. "That's *not* why I went!"

He shoved her arm aside. "That's what your letter said!"

"Letter? What letter? I didn't have time to write one! I escaped in the middle of the night with your mother's men trying to KILL me!" she shouted, feeling her orange magic lurch in reaction to the sudden memory that crashed through her head like lightning splintering the sky.

"Bullshit! There is no way you caused her to go to such lengths! No way at all. This is pure fantasy!" His self-control had vanished, his voice perilously close to full volume.

"Don't you DARE call me a liar!"

Obeying only the rage that thundered in her ears, she swung a fist at his face, but he intercepted the blow, twisting her arm as he thrust her away from him, a hand on the back of her neck as he shoved her against the wardrobe door. She reacted immediately, stamping her heel down onto his bare foot and using his pained reaction to yank herself free.

"So show me some PROOF!"

They watched each other warily, Arke's face burning with emotions, an orange glow lighting the scar on her left palm. Then she turned away, shoving her hands in her pockets, as clarity chilled her fury, as his words finally sank in, and she understood what had happened all those years ago. The only thing Will had been guilty of was believing his filthy bitch of a mother.

"It took me months to stop hoping you'd come and find me. I never knew why you didn't." She leant back against the wardrobe, eyes squeezed shut. "But now I do. And you know what? It makes everything so much worse. All these years, Will, all of them, all because of the 'marvellous' Martine Kromm."

"You're not making any sense. Yes, she hated you, but we were young, she was sure our relationship would run its course. She told me that all she had to do was wait."

Arke had known what she would have to do the moment Kennedy and Sparkz were arrested, the moment she heard Kromm announce their execution. But knowing what must be done and doing it were two very different sorts of pain, two very different sorts of action.

She heaved a ragged breath and fixed her gaze on his. She knew she had to look into his eyes when she told him. She knew he had to see the truth from hers.

"You used to call me your specialist subject. Remember?" She kept her hands in her pockets, her fists clenched tightly as he gave a single nod of affirmation. "You said you could read me like a book. You could then, and I'm pretty sure you can now. So do it. I'm not lying to protect my friends."

It took a moment to compose herself, mustering the strength to set three worlds on fire. Longer still to force the simplest of words to her lips, the sentence tripping over itself as she dragged the sounds to life.

"I'm here to stop you killing our son."

The truth landed like a sudden fall of snow, silencing and stilling, obscuring everything but them. She saw his shock, saw those familiar green eyes desperately searching her face, the pain in his expression so obvious that she dropped her gaze before she lost what little composure she had left.

"What do you mean? A son, what son?" He reached for her, settling his hands on her shoulders. "Arke, talk to me!"

She forced herself to answer, even though it meant digging through more painful memories. "You were away when I found out I was pregnant. I guess your mother had people watching me. She came to visit and said I could get rid of *'it'* or she would. She offered me money. When I refused she called me a low-born whore and summoned her guards." Suddenly, her voice strengthened in an echo of the past. "I told her I would die for my child and asked if she felt the same way. When her men tried to grab me, she learnt that I wasn't just a low-born whore. I was a low-born whore with demon magic and a baby to protect." Arke looked into Will's face, her expression raw and pure emotion. "I would never have left you, but I had no choice. So tell me I'm lying. Please, tell me, because I really, really, really wish I was."

He shook his head once, his voice hoarse. "You're not. I knew she hated you, but I never... I never thought she'd..."

"That wasn't all of it." Arke forced herself to keep talking, even though her next words would hurt him more. "She hired assassins and sent them after me. They were everywhere – so many of them and they never stopped coming. Joy helped me but we couldn't escape them, no matter where we went, they were there."

"What?" His grip on her shoulders grew painfully intense before he snatched his hands away, beginning to pace up and down. "I never knew. I promise I never knew. I'd have come, I swear, I'd have found you."

"I wish you had. I wish you'd have seen him. He was so tiny, but so full of life, with dark hair and perfect little fingers..." She covered her mouth with a brief shake of her head while she forced that memory away. "I kept running to keep the assassins' attention and Joy took the baby, gave him her family tattoo. She found him a new home and told the people he was hers. A few days later, I dug a fake grave, put a marker on it saying he'd died at birth – and they finally stopped chasing me." She blinked and rubbed her eyes, pressing the corners to stop the tears that threatened to appear. "But I could never risk going back for him."

Will stood still and stared at her, his expression flickering with conflicting emotions.

"So?" she asked. "Are you going to finish what your mother started?"

"Of course not!" he frowned. "Did you even have to ask me that?"

"It took you all of thirty seconds to threaten to execute me!"

He stepped forwards, smoothing his hands down her arms, and taking a long, slow breath as he flooded her body with healing magic.

"I know I've changed. All the responsibility, everyone wanting a piece of me, difficult decisions... It's not easy. There are no right answers, no wins, at best tactical draws. I must be seen to be strong..." He paused and shook his head quickly. "Sorry, that's the Lord Commander speaking. And you need to speak to Will, and he has missed you so *very* much." He took another long breath before he continued. "I can never make up for not being there when you needed me. I never knew what she'd done to you... to us..." He had to stop again, jaw clenching and eyes burning darkly before he forced his anger to one side. "The moment I get back to Levenbrandt, I'll be adding a couple of very important names to the family tree. *My* wife. *Our* son."

Arke almost flinched at his last two words and shook her head quickly, putting her palm on his chest as she spoke. "He doesn't know who he is. I never told him – about anything. He turned up one day believing he was Joy's and it was just easier to let that be the truth."

He nodded slowly, looking down firstly at her and then to where her hand rested on him. "What's his name?"

"Sparkz."

Breaking into a sudden broad chuckle, Will wrapped his arms around her, hugging her tightly to him and shaking them both with the power of his laughter.

"What? Don't tell me you had a dog called that. What's so funny?"

He released her just enough so he could see her baffled expression before ducking his head to brush his lips across hers. That tentative kiss suddenly became a far hungrier embrace as she responded with an instinctive passion that surprised them both. Finally, Will pulled away and rested his forehead on hers, his tone smoky and soft as he replied.

"*Arkz*, your son is called Sp-*arkz*. You're telling me no-one noticed? No-one thought that was a little bit – suggestive of something?"

"You're the only one who calls me Arkz. Oh..." She paused, frowning as the penny finally dropped. "But Joy knew you did, and she named him." She shook her head, smiling mistily as she realised what her best friend had tried to do for her before covering her face with a hand. "Well, that's unbelievably embarrassing."

He nudged her fingers with his nose, moving them over so he could kiss her again, and as he did, Arke started to unbutton the shirt he'd only just been buttoning up.

None of the scenarios she'd played out in her head had considered the effect that such close proximity to Will would have on her. How she still felt the same as she had thirty years ago, how every cell in her body felt like it was electrified, how each shared glance made her feel like she was blushing, how she absolutely needed him in every way possible. Her brain was busy trying to frame their discussion, but her body's physical response was increasingly distracting.

"It should be," he chuckled, kissing her again. "But it doesn't matter. *We* have a son."

"You can't just bludgeon your way into his life! He grew up on his own, no help from us, he's his own person," Arke protested, her words firm but her hands soft as she smoothed them over his chest, tracing lines that made him shiver. "Everything he has he's earned. He's as far removed from House Kromm as it's possible to be."

Will crouched, shrugging off his shirt as he quickly undid her laces, and she dropped a hand on his head, her fingers running through his hair, undoing its immaculate styling in seconds.

"Maybe, maybe not. He's the one who called me out on being a useless aristo, isn't he? He must get his balls from you and his dickhead charisma from me," he chuckled, lifting her straight up and out of her boots before carrying her towards the bed.

Arke leant to kiss him with such intensity that he had to stop walking, but as she pulled away, Stabbington's voice, laden with ennui, sounded softly in her head.

"If you are going to keep re-enacting the past, please remove me to a cupboard so I too can re-live my part in your relationship."

With a knowing look, Will stood her on the bed, kissing her between every few words as he started to undress her. "I recognise that expression. Demon blade getting twitchy? Pop him in the wardrobe."

She tried to concentrate on what she needed to say, tapping a finger on his cheek to get his attention. "Sparkz might never want to be part of your family."

"Oh, I'm sure he will when he finds out he's my only heir."

"What?" She was more shocked at that revelation than at the speed her jacket and shirt were peeled off and flung to the floor.

"Four other marriages. No children." He traced a gentle fingertip down one of her many scars before starting to undo her belt.

"He could not get the job done with his other wives, eh?" Stabbington had clearly recovered his good humour with that tasty snippet of information.

"What did you do? Execute them?" She raised her eyebrows as Will looked back up at her with an amused shake of his head.

"It was tempting for a couple of them, but no. Divorces. Proper ones that I actually wanted to happen. Why are you laughing?"

"Because if you were still married to me then all those other wives..." She wrapped her arms around him, unable to stop the devilish amusement that shook her body.

"Weren't my wives at all – which is exactly how I felt about them... because they weren't you."

"Really?" She eased away to look at him, stroking one hand through his hair as she ran her thumb gently across his lips.

"Really." He flicked his fingers, and all the lanterns blinked out. "Now why are you still half dressed? We have thirty years to make up for."

"Put me in the cupboard! Arke, if you ever loved me, put me in the cupboard."

Chapter Twenty-Two
Soft Cell

THE CELLS WERE not as awful a place as Kennedy might have imagined. They were simply cages covered in anti-magic glyphs that sat inside the main guard tent. Granted, that did make their occupants feel like they were exhibits at a zoo, especially with the whole bucket as a toilet thing, but since neither he nor Sparkz had any inhibitions about their bodily functions, it was probably a worse experience for the guards.

The Barsian Empire treated their prisoners humanely, no matter what their sentences. After a couple of hours with the camp doctors, Sparkz's leg was magically mended, Kennedy's cuts and bruises were all gone, and he no longer suffered that niggling ache in the small of his back he'd had for months. The medics had remarked that it was a shame all their good work would be for nothing, but at least the two men would have a comfortable final night alive. Kennedy had always thought it strange how the Barsians insisted on only punishing the healthiest of prisoners, but he knew the empire prided itself on its standards, double or otherwise.

On the less positive side, dinner was atrocious. The myth of the last meal was just that. The steak was overcooked, the peppercorn sauce was basically gravy, and the creamed vegetables were distinctly lumpy. Yes, it was stew and mash, or more correctly, unidentified meat and potato that was both soggy and crunchy at the same time. Not even Kennedy's descriptive talents could raise the bowl of slop to the status of slightly edible. But it was hot, and they were hungry, so what wasn't retch-inducing gristle was hoovered up in short order.

"We're having bacon for breakfast." The guard grinned as he sat down at his desk with a mug of tea. "Except you'll miss it, being hung at dawn and all."

"Surely we get to duel to the death?" Kennedy yawned, trying to make himself comfortable on the straw mattress.

"Yes. With a rope." The guard chuckled. "I know who I got my money on."

"Man's a comedian," Sparkz commented, putting his pillow over his face. "Do we at least get some dark to try and sleep?"

"Dark enough where you're going. Chess? Checkers?"

"Hangman?" Kennedy suggested with a wry smile.

"Don't rush it. C'mon fellas," the guard pleaded, "the nightshift is so boring."

After two hours of the most tedious game of chess with the guard who whistled tunelessly through his teeth while he tried to decide his next move, Kennedy and Sparkz had absolutely no trouble sleeping. They slept and slept, only waking when the enticing smell of food wafted to their nostrils. It was daylight outside, the lanterns were turned to low, and they were still breathing.

"Awake at last! Lucky for you I saved you some breakfast!" The guard carried two platefuls of badly cut bread and flaccid bacon over to the cells.

"I'd say being alive is also a bonus." Kennedy rubbed a hand over his face and yawned. "Did we sleep through our appointment?"

"Nah. We can't do nothing without orders, and the old man's still in his tent. Hasn't been on his normal morning run, hasn't been to status meetings, hasn't signed your death warrants. So yeah – bacon it is."

"Hopefully he's really sick," Sparkz commented, taking his plate from the guard.

"Not my place to care. Tea or coffee? Both taste the same, come out the same vat. If you want, I'll get you a hot chocolate."

"Let me guess, also from the same vat." Sparkz rolled his eyes.

"You catch on quick!"

After finishing their breakfast, they had nothing to do but wait, hope and worry. The fact that Arke wasn't in the cell next to them was encouraging, but Kennedy couldn't shake the growing concern that the Lord Commander's absence from duty was down to something more permanent than sickness. He knew they were in a tight spot and the Soulbound didn't have too many options open to her, but he really hoped she'd found a less apocalyptic way to rescue them than straight up murder.

⚹ ⚹ ⚹

AFTER WHAT COULD only be described as an energetic night, Arke was far too exhausted for any sort of apocalypse. Thirty years apart had left the still-married couple with plenty of catching up to do, so they'd done very little of that and spent most of their time finding every way possible to break the furniture.

In the end, it was the persistence of his valet which finally dragged Will away from Arke's side. The queue of officers outside the tent was growing ever longer and the servant was concerned enough about Kromm's wellbeing to start tugging on the zips that held the door shut.

"Tomas, if that's you, I told you I don't want to be disturbed!"

"But sir, I need to check you're alright. You've missed all your appointments for the morning."

Suddenly, the tent opened and a heavy-eyed Kromm strode out, wearing only a luxuriously silky dressing gown.

"I'm fine."

"Ah. Sir." The valet's expression on seeing the daytime use of perfectly good nighttime apparel was somewhat reminiscent of a cat being fired from a cannon while riding a cucumber. "Are – you – alright, sir? Shall – I – get – a – doctor?"

The Lord Commander tilted his head, eyebrows raised imperiously. "Stop talking to me like that or I might think it's you who needs a medic. I haven't had a day off in years, so now the threat is dealt with, I've decided to take a rest, some 'me' time, a holiday, call it what you will."

"A – holiday?" Tomas was still wide eyed with shock, unable to fully comprehend the notion. "You – sir?"

"Do any of you have anything important to tell me?" Kromm looked at the queue. "Life and death only." When there was a resounding silence, he raised a hand, pointing out a few people as he addressed them. "Captain Johannsen, I do NOT need to rule on the appropriate use of bullet points in minutes. It doesn't matter, I don't read them anyway. Major Orme – stop petitioning me to allow the magisters to get their choice of whore. As far as I'm concerned, it's first come, first served."

The officers goggled at him, uncertain how to react to what would have been a joke from almost anyone else. It was obvious that no-one had ever suspected that Lord Commander Kromm even knew what a sense of humour was.

"Rhodri, it's a no from me on another talent show. We found out the hard way that the men's talents lean more to bootleg alcohol and gambling, not to mention attempted murder when the voting doesn't suit them. Georg and Andreas. You again? I don't care that you hate each other. Go away and make it work before I put you on latrine duty."

As Kromm dismissed most of the queue, he spotted his valet was about to head inside the tent and quickly sidestepped to block his path. "You can take the day off too, Tomas. I don't need anything."

"But... sir... I..."

Captain Serge and Jenkins were the only petitioners left when Tomas finally gave up his efforts to be of service. Kromm waited for him to walk out of sight before he pointed an authoritative finger at Serge.

"Please take personal charge of our two friends from yesterday and escort them to the shower block. Then bring them here for lunch, I'm sure they'll be hungry so ask the chef to provide a decent spread."

"You aren't going to execute them, sir?" Jenkins asked, scratching at his beard.

"Officially? They died at dawn." Kromm directed a piercing look towards him. "You can take care of the paperwork."

Jenkins shrugged. "Not a problem."

"Just to be clear," Serge frowned, "the two sky pirates, collected from the cells, washed and brought here for lunch as... guests?"

"Yes, and send word to restock their ship with whatever is needed. Treat them as allies." Kromm nodded as the captain saluted him and hurried off, before turning his attention to Jenkins, who was unashamedly trying to look into the tent.

"Lord Commander, there is one member of their crew who is currently unaccounted for..."

Kromm strode back inside, waiting for Jenkins to follow before magically zipping the door shut. Then, with absolutely no warning, he turned and punched him hard enough to knock him off his feet before hauling him up again, fist poised for another blow.

"You worked for my mother for years, doing all her dirty jobs." Kromm's voice was barely above a hiss, but his eyes were narrowed with murderous intent, and he shook Jenkins with every moment of emphasis. "Don't you DARE try to lie about your part in this. I know you'd have been involved. My WIFE! My unborn CHILD! Think VERY carefully about your next words. They should be reasons why I don't just *kill* you where you stand and bury your body where no-one will *ever* find it. And you know I can."

"We were following orders." Jenkins rubbed a hand over his jaw, his composure unruffled.

"Why didn't anyone tell me?"

"The heir to House Kromm was young and in love with someone unacceptable. She had no family and an extremely undesirable... career. It wasn't, and still isn't, an unusual situation in certain parts of society. Granted, your mother was more determined in her pursuit than other matriarchs I've known." Jenkins kept talking in a neutral tone, ignoring the way Kromm was becoming more, rather than less, angry with every sentence. "I think the realisation that you had omitted to inform her about Arke's more magical attributes tipped her over the edge from protecting the family name to something... else."

"She had no RIGHT! The child was INNOCENT!" Kromm shoved Jenkins onto a chair and turned away, fists clenched.

"I knew there was a reason I didn't like you." The Soulbound's voice was ice cold as she stepped out of the bedroom. "You were one of the assassins?"

Jenkins seemed unsurprised at her sudden entrance and simply nodded. "It was a long time ago so I can't say I remember much except the relief when it was over. It wasn't until I saw you and Sparkz side by side that I asked a few of the crew some questions and developed a working theory. Anyway, congratulations, you were victorious over some of the best the Firm had to offer." He bowed his head towards Arke, who had stopped by Will, her hand on his arm, her knuckles white from the strength of her grip.

"Victorious?" she snapped. "You call that a victory?"

"You're both alive." Jenkins stood up. "Don't think we pulled our punches because you were a pregnant woman; that's not how the Firm operates."

Kromm broke the ringing silence as the Soulbound's dark eyes bored into the older man's face. "If you *ever* touch her again..."

"*She* will rip your body into so many pieces that not even flies will find enough to shit on," Arke interrupted with one last threatening glare before heading back into the bedroom.

Kromm watched her leave before leading Jenkins towards the exit and dropping his voice to a murmur. "My personal feelings about you aside, the Firm's orders remain. Find out everything you can about these capstones."

"Sir, before you... 'go' any further... That ring she wears. It's some form of conduit to the Autarch... You should..."

"What I do is none of your concern. Order your agent on board to keep them both safe – my wife *and* my son. You hear me?" He looked towards the back of the tent before returning his gaze to Jenkins, his expression inscrutable, his voice the dark essence of a heartfelt promise. "Because if you don't, I will kill you and then sell my soul to anything that will resurrect you just so I can do it again."

Chapter Twenty-Three
Playing Chicken

Kennedy's morning improved immeasurably after Serge's visit to the cells. Freedom was a tremendous relief and although their invitation to lunch had been a surprise, he guessed Arke had made some sort of deal with the Lord Commander, and that they were about to learn the price of liberty over the dining table.

He felt a flash of pride in her achievement, knowing she'd had to overcome her dislike of nobles in order to negotiate their release rather than just taking the easy way out and slitting Kromm's throat. As he walked through the camp in the glorious sunshine, he started to smile – everything seemed to be going right – even Sparkz had agreed to behave as long as there was plenty of food on offer.

Plenty was an understatement, for Willem Kromm and his... *wife* were wonderful hosts.

Kennedy had never experienced such emotional damage at a meal before.

He was speechless when Arke told him the truth about her relationship with the Lord Commander. There were so many questions he wanted to shout uncontrollably at her, so many things he wished he could scream into the void, and so many memories he needed to utterly re-evaluate. It was all far too much to cope with.

Sparkz, on the other hand, just looked from the Soulbound to her husband with a raised eyebrow, as if weighing up the value of the information, before shrugging and giving his complete attention to the plentiful feast in front of them.

"It feels wrong leaving her there," Kennedy muttered as he and Sparkz walked back to their gig.

"Why, are you jealous?" Sparkz chuckled. "She said she'll be back in a couple of days. Relax."

"But..." Kennedy sighed heavily, emotion, confusion and incredulity whirling round his head like a rat chasing a terrier chasing a rat. "He's actually quite... ok when he's not in uniform."

Sparkz jabbed him in the ribs with an elbow. "Everyone has their own brand of bullshit, public face, private persona. Mr Law and Order might be useful if we keep him sweet. And Arke is definitely keeping him sweet right now."

Kennedy felt distinctly queasy after that comment and tried to change the subject. Sparkz, who was more than devilish with a couple of bottles of the finest red inside him, spotted Kennedy's discomfort and spent the entire journey back to the *Warrior* suggesting spicier and spicier scenarios that could be happening in the Lord Commander's tent.

⚔ ⚔ ⚔

A bleary-eyed Arke returned to the ship just before noon on the third day after the Apothecarium. She was dressed in tailor-made clothes, all in the same style as her normal ones, but made from more expensive fabrics. The crew had already unloaded a few crates from the boatloads of stores which contained similar clothing – entire sets for both Kennedy and Sparkz, as well as general items for whoever fitted into them. Although Kennedy wanted to take offence at the Lord Commander's assumption that they needed some new threads, once he slipped his feet into the softest socks he'd ever worn, he couldn't wait to try on everything else.

Sparkz had made sure to be on deck for the Soulbound's return and his grin was nothing short of devilish as they locked eyes. "Been up all night?"

He had promised Kennedy that he wouldn't out Arke's marital status before she was ready to tell people herself, but that didn't mean he couldn't enjoy needling her about it every chance he got.

Her only reply to his question was a middle finger salute.

"No no, it's that one." Sparkz pointed to the fourth finger on his left hand and was rewarded by Arke deliberately smashing her shoulder into his as she stormed past.

She completely ignored his amusement and headed over to Kennedy, who stood expectantly by his cabin, and followed her inside without a word.

As he shut the door behind them, he gestured towards the table, his voice low. "Coffee. And so – many – questions."

In return, she pointed to the charts hanging on the wall before pouring herself a mug of the blackest brew and heaping sugar into it. "Plot a course to Levenbrandt."

"Haven't you had enough sex?" Kennedy snapped, instantly forgetting his carefully prepared list of far more polite queries the moment she told him to head for Kromm's hometown.

Without even appearing to have heard his outburst, the Soulbound sat down and started to sip her drink. He glared at her, moving closer so he could keep his voice low.

"You didn't ever think to mention that you were married to one of the Barsian elite? A Lord Commander no less! You could have said something at ANY time in my ENTIRE life! Did you even tell my mother?"

Arke remained unperturbed by his frustrations. "She knew." She took another sip. "Will was still a student when we met, but yeah, he's a Lord Commander now, and has access to a lot of things we don't. He's going to try and locate the other capstones, so we decided to meet in Levenbrandt in a couple of weeks." She raised her tired eyes to Kennedy's. "And I won't lie, I do want to see him again. Is that a problem?"

"Yes! No! Of course not. Just what DID you tell him? You don't look like you've slept for days! Can he be trusted? Because nearly being executed by him wasn't the most enjoyable experience of my life!" He glared at Arke as she sipped her drink.

"Are you done yet?"

"No! Not even close!"

"Ok." She leant back on her chair and gestured for him to continue.

Deflated by her calm acceptance, Kennedy shook his head slowly before unhooking a chart and beginning to plot a course to Levenbrandt.

"I honestly thought he'd divorced me years ago so there wasn't anything to tell, but since his family didn't recognise our marriage, he didn't get it annulled." She poured her second cup of coffee, cradling it in her hands as she spoke. "However, just because they didn't think it was valid, doesn't mean that it wasn't. So, am I extremely amused that his four high-born, 'perfect' wives weren't actually his wives? Hell yeah. To the very core of me."

Over at the chart, Kennedy was desperately trying to remain angry, but the sound of her laughter washed the last of his frustration away. He sat down next to her, poured himself a drink, and tapped her ankle with his boot.

"Well, you'll have to tell me the story now. How did you meet?"

She didn't hesitate, a warm smile flickering on her lips. "Wish this popped into my dreams as often as your mother does. Don't get me wrong, I loved Joy but I've dreamt of her every night since I was stabbed – so a change would be nice." Taking a deep breath, she settled herself more comfortably in the chair. "Anyway... we've been to Levenbrandt a couple of times. Did I ever take you to a tavern called The Beer Behind? Small place, mainly students, right up against the east wall."

"I don't think so, you always scooted us out of the city as soon as you could. And thinking about it, that makes much more sense now."

"Doesn't it?" She shrugged. "Didn't need any awkward situations. Of course, it was different back then, your mother and I spent a lot of time there when we were in between, 'other' things. The place is sleepyville compared to most of the other cities in Barsia but that suited us just fine."

⚔ ⚔ ⚔

Joy and Arke were busy absolutely not hiding out in Levenbrandt while the Soulbound recovered from an unexpected bloodletting. They'd had to spend all their money on a tumultuous escape from some irascible people, so they couldn't afford a magical repair of the bone-deep sword slash to Arke's thigh.

However, as time and alcohol healed all wounds, the pair had been more than happy to accept the offer of work for bed and board at their favourite hostelry, The Beer Behind. Joy served the customers, while Arke usually sat in a quiet corner with a book in her hands and her bandaged leg up on a stool. Lame or not, her intense air of indifference made her the most effective bouncer the pub had ever had.

It was a beautiful sunny afternoon in the northern city, and Joy was setting out tables on the cobblestones of the square in front of The Beer Behind. The inn had been unnaturally quiet while the students crammed for their finals, but today was the last day of exams. Terri, one of the orcish tavern owners, had been cooking since dawn and Wanda, her wife, had stocked the cellar high. Things were about to get busy, rowdy – and profitable.

Terri wiped the sweat from her forehead as she finally emerged from the kitchen to see Arke balancing on her right leg as she stacked plates ready by the serving hatch.

"How's it feeling today?"

"Fine." The Soulbound shrugged.

"Remember she doesn't want fussing!" Wanda clambered up the stairs from the cellar, a keg of beer over her shoulder.

"But when has that ever stopped us?" Joy breezed in with a grin. "And in completely unrelated news, I'm totally not going to mention that she didn't drink that herbal tea

you made her." She threw Arke's walking stick towards her. *"Use the bloody thing! Stop hopping everywhere, you know it only makes your leg worse."*

"The tea would have helped with the pain," Terri sighed.

"Not as much as alcohol." The Soulbound finished stacking plates and made exaggerated use of the walking stick to help her over to the sink.

"You're working, so stay sober," Joy warned, before leaving with an armful of clean tablecloths.

Terri winked at Arke as she reached into a cupboard and pulled out a bottle. "There's sober and then there's miserable. It's gonna be a long one, so take a nip of this. Just don't have so much you trip over and blow the place up."

With a brief smile, the Soulbound took a swig. "It was only a small explosion."

"And they deserved it — but we'll be too busy tonight to risk any magic. You know how people talk and there's always folk who'd happily take the bounty on a mage."

Arke eased her leg with a grimace. "I'm aware."

"You never did tell us what happened in Orbella." Terri grinned at the Soulbound's dour reaction to her questioning. *"Just lie if it's easier, I love a good story."*

"She was glassed by a dwarf." Joy strode back in, grabbed the bottle from Arke's hand, and took a long drink.

"Bitten by a hamster?" Wanda popped her head through the serving hatches.

Terri returned the bottle to the Soulbound and stood between her and Joy while she drank again. "It's gotta be good or you'd say."

"Don't believe her if she says it was my fault." As she talked, Joy wrapped cutlery in faded pink napkins, her hands moving at lightning speed. *"She picked a fight with the security detail at a jewellery shop. I was strolling innocently down the street when I turned to see her being shredded by an elf with a longsword."*

"That sounds exciting – and extremely unlikely. If you want the truth... I cut myself shaving." Arke grabbed her walking stick and limped away, Joy's high-pitched peal of laughter following her.

The customers were piling in through the doors as the Soulbound sat down in her usual corner. She opened her book and began reading while keeping half an eye on the group of regulars who had clearly sprinted straight to the bar after their exam had finished. They were all still wearing their dark green blazers but had already stuffed their college cravats in their pockets. Terri and Wanda were quick to serve them, encouraging the students to eat a hearty meal alongside their beers, their appetising descriptions of the available dishes backed up by their chief barmaid.

IT WAS ALL *going as expected for a few hours. The piano had been dragged outside and music was echoing around the square. Everyone bar the bouncer was working hard, and that was exactly how the staff of The Beer Behind liked it. Their usual customers came from Corffe College which was a hotbed for languages, the arts, and terrible poetry. None of the regulars were known for any real boundary-pushing issues and the worst Arke usually had to do was remove any sobbing poets after open mic night, mediate in board game arguments, and loiter meaningfully near any students from the other institutions in the city who thought they could be edgy by drinking at another college's tavern.*

The first sign of trouble was when the piano went silent. The Soulbound put her book down and stood, listening, as the chatter inside also stopped, allowing the sound of an approaching drum beat to be heard. Wanda looked over at her with a frown, quickly clearing the tills and heading down to the safe in the cellar to secure their take. The students downed their drinks and hurried outside as the drums got louder.

"Arturo College." Joy was busy gathering glasses as she saw her friend limping towards her through the crowd. "Apparently there's been a bit of bad blood. Something about a stolen turkey."

"Cockerel. We stole their magic cockerel." A nearby student finished his pint and handed the glass to Joy.

Arke blinked. "Their what now?"

"I'm guessing they're coming to get it back." Joy looked hard at the young man. "So where is it?"

"We put it behind the bar."

The Soulbound raised her eyes to the heavens. "Really? It's been pretty quiet then."

"Yeah, it died. Suffocated in the bag."

Neither Joy nor Arke had any adequately polite ways to express their feelings about the <u>dead</u> magical chicken behind the bar as multiple owners of said bird marched into view barely a hundred feet away.

"Are any of your friends sanctioned mages? And more importantly, if they are, can they make it alive again?" Joy's smile was becoming less natural and more forced as everything started to unravel.

"Maybe one of the seniors could but there's none here. Don't worry – we'll be fine. Quick fight, they'll run away." The student grinned and turned to join his fellows in what they clearly believed was a threatening version of the Corffe College song.

"Yeah, that'll be exactly how this goes down." Arke sighed before turning to Joy. *"I'll see what I can do, if nothing else I'll stall them while you get the place closed up."*

Joy hurried back inside as the Soulbound limped her way across the square to the new arrivals. The cobblestones made walking deeply uncomfortable, but she hoped that negotiating might calm things down. And by 'negotiating', she meant lying.

"Good evening. How can I help you?"

The drumbeat slowed as the opposing students halted and then timed itself mockingly to follow Arke's limping footsteps as she crossed the last few feet to the front of their ranks.

The leader stepped forwards, a flag with a cockerel embroidered on it draped over her shoulder. *"I don't know that you can. We didn't order your tavern's famous flat beer."*

"Then I assume you're not here for the tasteless stew either?" the Soulbound asked, keeping her tone as light as she could.

"We're here for Sebastiaan."

The Arturo students started chanting the name over and over. Arke eased her position slightly, putting both hands on the handle of her walking stick until the noise had died down enough for her to be heard again.

"Sebastiaan? Don't think I know him."

That was how the Soulbound, who knew exactly who Sebastiaan had to be, had to suffer the Arturo faithful shouting "Cock" at her in perfect unison before laughing uproariously at their amazing comedic timing.

The leader brought her flag down and waved it in Arke's face before pointing it over towards the Corffe students. "<u>They</u> took him and we're here to get him back. FOR THE HONOUR OF ARTURO!"

Once again, Arke had to wait several minutes for the echoing shouts to die down so that she could be heard, and she spent the time listening to Stabbington's recipes for making pies from their overused tongues.

Finally, she was able to put the 'lie' in replied. "There are absolutely <u>no</u> chickens, cockerels, turkeys, geese, peahens, pheasants, grouse, quail, pigeons or other fowl at The Beer Behind. Might I suggest you look elsewhere?"

"We know he's there and we will rip the place apart to find him!"

The Soulbound ran her dark gaze across the entire front rank of the mob as she drew the line in the proverbial sand as clearly and loudly as she possibly could. "You can do what you like in the street, that's for the city to sort out. HOWEVER, anyone performing any aggressive acts inside The Beer Behind will be removed with whatever force is deemed necessary. Do – you – understand?"

"My father's chief of the city guard. We'll be JUST fine." The leader stepped forwards and shoved the Soulbound out of the way before waving her flag in the air. "SEBASTIAAN!"

Arke leant on her cane, looking up at the sky with a world-weary expression as the student bodies crashed into each other, shouting and scrapping, green against blue.

"I have never seen a worse advert for higher education," Stabbington commented.

"Just one, little ice spell…" the Soulbound muttered.

"If you were able to run away afterwards, I would be encouraging you."

She walked back across the square, skirting the melee and working her way around until she was standing guard in front of the tavern's main doors. Joy opened a window to tell her that they were as ready as they'd ever be, before Terri suggested she stay out of any fighting because of her leg, and Wanda reminded her not to use any magic.

Minutes of noisy brawling later, there was still no sign of the city guard. Arke stood quietly, hands on her cane as she watched the students punch and kick each other with youthful vigour, bloodied noses and torn shirts rapidly becoming the new universal uniform. She was just beginning to hope the two sides would fight each other to a standstill when a group of reinforcements arrived from Arturo and bulldozed their way to victory.

The leader of the poultry-less college strode towards the tavern doors. "We won, now give us Sebastiaan."

"We do not have your magic chicken." *The Soulbound spoke slowly and loudly as the students started to close in.*

The top of the flag was pushed against her forehead. "Listen, cripple – this is your last chance to get out of our way before we squash you like a bug. So just step aside, we'll go in, get our property and leave."

"WE DO NOT HAVE YOUR CHICKEN." *She made sure to shout in case anyone was hard of hearing instead of simply stupid.*

Suddenly, one of Arturo's finest idiots lunged forwards and tried to grab her. He clearly wasn't expecting the tip of her cane to impact his balls with both speed and power, a choking cry squeaking from his astonished mouth as he crumpled in a heap.

The leader watched her sidekick's abortive attempts to do her dirty work, her eyes round with surprise as he writhed on the ground, and Arke used that distraction to yank the flag out of her hand and launch it away from the tavern.

"Go – home!"

As the student reacted to that infamy by swinging a wild and furious punch, the Soulbound dodged, then slapped her cane across the woman's face. The resounding impact staggered the Arturo leader backwards, hands pressed to the bright red welt on her left cheek.

"SEBASTIAAN!"

In retrospect, Arke wished she'd taken a deep breath before the tide of angry students charged. The sheer weight of numbers crushed the air out of her lungs and broke the locks and bars on the main doors, leaving her in a heap on the cobblestones as they rampaged their way into the tavern. She could hear battle being joined inside, the familiar sound of Joy swearing up a storm as she set about herself and Terri's disappointed tones as she castigated the intruders with both her words and her trusty yard broom.

Wanda was someone who was defined by her actions rather than her volume, and as quickly as the door area cleared, it began to get busy again with students getting some orc-induced airtime. Arke had only just peeled herself off the ground before a half-stunned student landed in that same spot. She pressed a hand to her aching ribs while easing in a few deep breaths as Stabbington threw some painkilling magic her way. His distinctly unhelpful comment, which he was happy to repeat in case she hadn't heard, was that if she'd have sliced holes in two or three it would have ended this 'ridiculous episode' instantly. However, since she wasn't keen to earn any of the punishments meted out for serious bodily harm, especially on the children of the city's elite, she ignored him and limped into the taproom.

Inside was mayhem. Wanda was launching anyone she could reach in the rough direction of the door while Terri manned the barricade of tables that prevented the students gaining access to the back rooms, and Joy hurled buckets of dirty mop water over the mob from the top of the bar. Arke grabbed a broken chair and got to work with practiced efficiency. A hit to the legs knocked them down and one to the head kept them there.

Her furniture-based weapon managed five victims before it shattered on the broad shoulders of the sixth, who reacted by spinning around and throwing a punch at the side of her face.

The Soulbound ducked and slammed her fist into the man's groin. As he doubled over, she was grabbed from behind and lifted off her feet. She sank her teeth into one of the arms that held her and was promptly dropped, just managing to land on her good leg. That escape was only temporary as someone snaked an arm around her neck and began to choke her out as the man she'd bitten punched her in the stomach. Moments before he let loose with a follow up, Wanda appeared. She fastened a hand round his wrist and yanked him towards her before delivering a headbutt that exploded his nose in a fountain of crimson. Then she turned to the student who was trying to throttle the Soulbound and slapped him so hard round the side of the head that his knees buckled. As he staggered, Arke struggled free and the tavern owner hauled him away by his hair.

"Terri is being swarmed!" Stabbington warned.

The Soulbound was shoving her way towards the barricade when the Arturo flag-bearer tackled her to the floor. A blast of red-hot agony shot through her injured leg as the woman landed directly on the wound, and she was only just recovering her senses when a fist smashed hard into her cheek.

"This is for my face!"

A finger tapped the student leader on the shoulder, and as she turned, Joy slammed the heel of her hand into the woman's nose. "No, this is." As she crumpled to the floor, Joy stood over her, tilting her head left and right with an assessing gaze. "And it's a definite improvement."

Little birds were singing merrily in Arke's ears as she watched her friend suddenly bulldozed away by a pair of students still chanting for Sebastiaan. She tried to get up and almost managed before her leg gave way. However, in a stroke of fortune, another Arturo student was close by to offer his own form of help.

"Ah look, he is carrying you to the window. He must know that fresh air is just what you need to clear your head." Stabbington was always triggered to the finest savagery when his host was not fully in control of her wits. "Oh really, is he trying to throw you out? If only this had been obvious from the start."

The Soulbound grabbed the sill with both hands, locking her elbows to stop herself from being forced through the window. She had no issues with defenestration – unless it was happening to her. Only temporarily thwarted, her assailant dragged her away, adjusted his grip and tried again, this time with a little more speed.

"I do believe he has a better grasp of what he has to do," Stabbington commented. "This may be..."

Suddenly, the meaty fists clutching her shirt let go. She twisted her body to avoid the window, took an elbow to the face and staggered back towards it. Just as her demon remarked she was about to accomplish a perfect auto-defenestration, someone hauled her upright and propped her against the nearest wall.

"Sorry, so sorry, hope I didn't grab you anywhere I shouldn't have."

Arke caught a quick glimpse of her rescuer as he strode away, her fuzzy brain noting only that he was tall and, as he showed the would-be defenestrator exactly how it should be done, appreciating his neat technique.

Suddenly Stabbington alerted her to the fact that Joy was unwillingly airborne, and coming into land nearby. As her friend skidded across the floor, the Soulbound saw a burly student chasing after her. Pushing off the wall to gain momentum, she stumbled into his path and the inevitable collision knocked them both to the ground. He was up on his knees quickly and had just raised a fist when one of Joy's spinning kicks connected with the side of his head and he landed next to her with a thud.

"I think you can stay down now," Stabbington suggested. "The cavalry has arrived."

From Arke's heroic position of 'spread-eagled on the floor', she watched as the bar was swept clean. A group of newcomers, led by the man who had helped her, took control of the fight, throwing punches with military precision and dragging every insensible body out of the tavern. Finally giving in to the pain in her leg, she shut her eyes and hoped unconsciousness would follow quickly.

"You're a mess!" Joy's bedside manner was never her strong suit. She poked the Soulbound with a foot. "Stop bleeding on the floor unless you're going to get the mop out."

"Excuse me, miss, but did they do that?"

The helpful stranger's voice was far more useful than Joy's boot at bringing Arke back to full consciousness. She blinked a few times to clear her vision enough to see the tall stranger looking down at her blood-soaked leg.

"She cut herself shaving." Joy hauled her to her feet before handing her a bottle of vodka. "Half for you then half for the bloody mess you made of your little ouchie."

"Might I assist?" the man asked.

"She'll be fine," Joy replied, letting her go. "See?"

As the Soulbound's good leg nearly buckled underneath her, the stranger swept in, lifting her up and sitting her on top of the bar.

"Thank you." Arke knew Joy would never let her forget the day she'd allowed a random man to tidy her onto the nearest work-surface. However, after the briefest moment of contemplation, she realised she didn't actually care. She was already tuning out Stabbington's voice as he remarked that she must have a serious concussion. According to him, that was the only possible explanation why she hadn't punched, kicked, bitten, stabbed, murdered or even cursed the dark-haired man who had not only picked her up but was still loitering in her personal space.

"You're welcome," the stranger replied. "Now, about your wound..."

"She's had worse. I'll restitch it later." Joy shrugged.

"Re-stitch?" He looked more than a little horrified.

"Can't afford much in the way of medical treatment right now," the Soulbound explained as she yanked the cork from the bottle. "It'll be ok."

"May I?"

As she locked gazes with the tall man, Arke suddenly noticed his beautiful green eyes, and realised she was already nodding without even asking what he was going to do.

With a sudden burst of pain, she felt his hand press against her injured leg, but after less than a second, a tide of warmth surged into the wound, a searing heat she instantly recognised as healing energy.

After a good minute of concentration on his spell, the magic receded, and the stranger smiled apologetically. "All done. There is going to be a scar though, I'm sorry."

"It's ok, I leave the swimsuit modelling to Joy. Who do I have to thank for my new leg?" She offered a hand, quickly wiping some of the blood and dirt off her palm.

"Will." He seemed amused about something as he took it, enacting the slowest shake she'd ever experienced before letting her fingers slide away. "You're not from Levenbrandt?"

"No. Only visiting."

"It's a beautiful city," he smiled. There was a long pause as they gazed at each other until he appeared to realise his hand was still resting on her thigh. "My bad, Miss..."

"Arke. Just... Arke. Umm... so which college are you with?" Small talk wasn't her forte, but she knew she didn't want him to turn and leave. Asking questions was a good strategy, even if her voice was a little hoarse.

"Ah, I suppose all of them, in a way. And speaking of colleges, would you happen to know anything about a missing chicken, Arke?"

There was no pressure, and she could absolutely have lied, but Will was obviously a decent guy — he'd helped them to clear the tavern, and he'd healed her. Oh, and he was the possessor of incredibly attractive green eyes that hadn't left her face since they'd shaken hands.

"Some of the students said they put him behind the bar. However, they also mentioned that he's a lot less perky than would be accepted by most people looking for a, you know, living bird." *She swigged from the bottle before offering it to him, suddenly hoping this wouldn't be the news that would make him leave.*

He took a long drink. "So, we have a dead magic cockerel situation."

"We do. Apparently it suffocated due to a bag/oxygen malfunction." The Soulbound was starting to realise that when Will talked to her, it felt like no-one else in the room existed.

"Is this a competition for long words? I can do longer and sciencier if you're breaking out the big guns. Sciencier isn't a word, before you say, but I was going for the laughs." As he spoke, Will lifted a hand to her face, stroking his fingers gently over the cuts and bruises, his touch healing them as he went. "How am I doing?"

It took Arke a couple of breaths to snap out of the moment, his beautiful eyes still locked on hers as they mirrored each other's smiles. "Pretty well so far."

With a slow, teasing grin, Will ducked his head down so he could whisper in her ear. "So how about we go and resurrect a cockerel together?"

Chapter Twenty-Four
It's Not the Fall that Kills You

As the *Warrior* flew north, it was buffeted by storms which hung like curtains over the Western Ocean. One after another after another rocked and battered the ship, forcing Kennedy to steer away from the heavy weather and fly closer to the Barsian coast than he'd intended. Closer to the obsidian ruin. He didn't know if the creature in the tower still wanted to hurt them, or exactly how far it could reach, but every mile nearer to that place made him more anxious.

It was about an hour before lunch, on another torrid day of wishing the storms to their west would dissipate, that the Soulbound burst into his cabin, holding a hand to her chest, her expression bordering on panic.

"Something's coming!" she shouted. "You need to get to the helm and call the crew to battle stations. NOW!"

"What is? What's wrong?" He leapt to his feet, almost tipping the table over in his haste. "Are you ok?"

She opened her fist to show blood coating her palm, and he watched in horror as the flow increased, quickly beginning to cascade to the floor.

"What happened? Did you cut yourself?" he asked, pulling a handkerchief from his pocket.

"No," she snapped. "Just LISTEN to me. I don't know what's going on, but I know we need to run. Use the storm for cover. If you don't order the course change, I will."

"But..." Kennedy tried to wrap the handkerchief around her hand.

She grabbed his wrist, blood oozing from under her grip. "There's no time! Philip, trust me, *please*."

Whether it was the desperate tone of her voice, her extremely uncharacteristic use of the word please, or something else that changed his mind, Kennedy didn't know. The moment he nodded in agreement, she let go of his arm and ran out of the cabin.

"HURRY!"

The instant Kennedy stepped outside, the hairs on the back of his neck stood up, and a gnawing pit seemed to open in his chest.

"BATTLESTATIONS! HARD TO PORT!"

As the ship's alarm bells sounded, he sprinted to help Urzish haul the wheel over in as tight a turn as the *Warrior* could manage.

"What's going on?" Urzish strained, her muscles bulging. "Why are we turning into the storm?"

"Can't you feel it?"

"Feel what? The way you're trying to break the wings off?"

He rammed the engine power levers to full as the bow finally started to point towards the swirling bank of grey clouds. "We need some cover, and that's our only option."

He was about to leap down to the main deck, when his eyes focused on the Soulbound who was standing by the cabins, her entire attention captured by something high in the sky behind them. Ruby and Kilar were at her side, trying to staunch the blood from her hand, but her position was fixed, almost as if her feet were welded to the planks.

"Captain!" Urzish called. "Sparkz wants to know what's going on."

Kennedy shaded his eyes and tried to make out what Arke was staring at, but the sun's glare made it impossible to see anything. However, the more he looked, the more uncomfortable he felt.

"Captain?"

The orc's voice broke through Kennedy's rising dread and he'd just turned to speak into the tube that led to the engine room when something hit the *Warrior's* stern.

The entire ship shuddered as a booming impact echoed around the deck. The engine started to sputter and black smoke poured from every hatch, spreading itself in a cloud behind them.

"SPARKZ!"

At first the only thing that came up the tube was smoke, and Kennedy quickly wafted it away as he shouted his brother's name again.

Finally he got an answer, choked and stifled, but the voice that spoke belonged to a terrified sounding Gabbi. "Direct hit to the engine room, sir!"

"Is everyone ok?"

"Sparkz said to land before we crash." Gabbi started to cough violently, barely finishing his sentence before the tube belched another cloud of smoke.

"Understood. Does he need help?"

"Not sure. I can't see him anymore... But he told me to stay here."

"I'll send back up." Kennedy nodded to Urzish. "Go find out how bad it is."

Forcing himself to think positively, he ignored the sweat that seemed to be breaking out all over his body. This time, he had an entire ocean to land in rather than a tiny canyon. Fear had no place in his mind. This was his ship, and he was going to bring her down safely.

Ellie appeared at his elbow. "Orders, captain?"

"Make smoke... well, more smoke. Prepare for crash landing in the water. Secure everything, close the portholes, prime the pumps."

"Got it!" The first mate hurried away, bellowing orders as she went.

It didn't take long before the sky around the *Warrior* was almost entirely obscured. Ruby and Irash created magical clouds of fog and smoke which Kilar populated with fleeting glimpses of the ship. Kennedy changed course as much as he dared, but they were slowing by the second, the fading energy from the stuttering engine clearly being channelled into their ability to stay in the air, not propel themselves through it.

As the *Warrior* dived towards the white-tipped waves, another shot from whatever was chasing them sliced through the smoke nearby with an audible crack. He changed course again, pushing the nose down even harder as he struggled against the oddly overwhelming sense of dread that kept threatening to overtake him.

※ ※ ※

DOWN IN THE engine room, Sparkz was wading through choking smoke and super-heated steam as he headed towards the main control panel. When the direct hit hadn't triggered a cataclysmic explosion, he'd let out a slow, relieved breath. The hours overhauling the damage control system after their crash landing at the Granveldt canyon had been well spent. However, now he was being both smothered and toasted, he wasn't sure if all that work had been a good idea. Being blasted into atoms without knowing a thing suddenly seemed preferable to getting choked and boiled before suffering the exact same fate.

Behind him, although hidden in the smoke, were Volk and Gabbi. He'd needed their help to get into the engine room, since the reinforced door was wedged tightly into its freshly warped frame. Once they'd levered it open enough to slip in, Sparkz identified two immediately life-threatening issues.

The first was the acrid mess of shorted cables that used to run from the aetheric crystal to the ship's propulsion and levitation systems. Quickly sorting through the melted wires, he found just one that was undamaged. He traced it to its connector with even more desperate speed. It wasn't in the group that led to the rune-covered plating that circled the hull. That meant they only had seconds before the buoyancy band failed and dropped them like a stone. Forwards was optional, lift was not.

Enacting a rapid manual reroute while murmuring prayers to any god that was strongly opposed to sudden terminal drops, he'd finally slapped the bare end directly against the metal and given Volk the job of holding it there until Kennedy landed or the residual energy in the crystal ran out.

The second issue was far more terrifying. Whatever had hit them had knocked out all the power. Every system was down, even the one so critical it was guarded by a three-stage redundancy. It was common knowledge that aetheric was the cleanest and most efficient source of energy that magic could obtain. It was less well known that it gave off magical radiation so strong that it could melt flesh. Sparkz had seen the aftereffects of an unshielded crystal, and as he struggled through the choking smoke, he knew he had to get the force field back online. Without its protection, the *Warrior* would turn into an irradiated BBQ pit in under ten minutes.

Clambering over the last of the destroyed pipework, Sparkz felt his way down to the control panel that spread from wall to wall at the rear of the engine room. He knew every inch of every section by touch, so he was confident that no matter what the damage, he could rig something which would restore power to the shield.

The smoke was so thick that the engineer could barely see his own arms, but he knew exactly where he was when his boot hit the edge of the giant console. He reached forwards carefully, mindful that he was likely to find a dangerously sharp and twisted heap of damaged metal. When he felt nothing, he enlarged his search area, but all his fingers found was empty air.

Crouching down, he double-checked that he was at the bottom of the casing before tracing it upwards for all of the four inches that were left standing. He shuffled one way and then another, trying to find even part of the control system, tension building in him as he realised his confidence had been horrifically misplaced. He could have worked with a mess of tangled and melted wires, but he was utterly helpless when there was a complete lack of anything. Sparkz had already figured out the engine room was less engine or room than mangled heap of angry, dangerous metal with a fizzing crystal at its heart, but he hadn't suspected just how bad things actually were.

He scrambled back to Gabbi as quickly as he could. "Listen carefully. Go to the freezer and bring me everything in there. EVERYTHING! Get the others to help. You understand?"

When the teenager coughed out a rough affirmative, Sparkz shoved him towards the door before grabbing the speaking tube. "I need Arke – right now!"

"She's not... ok." Kennedy's reply was strangely stilted.

"What the hell does that mean? Unless her head is severed from her shoulders, GET HER DOWN HERE!"

"What's going on?"

"The engine room is toast – controls are completely atomised. The shielding on the crystal is minutes away from failing," Sparkz explained. We abandon ship, or we buy time by making a giant purple ice cube. Your call."

"Will it work?" Kennedy asked.

"Yes! But not without Arke and her freezing spell."

⚹ ⚹ ⚹

Up on the main deck, Ibu had been struggling to bring the Soulbound back to herself. She was still immobile, staring up into the magical cloud bank, pupils blown, pulse bounding, and blood running down the fingers of her left hand.

"IBU! We need her NOW! Do whatever you have to!" Kennedy bellowed, his unusually hoarse tone conveying exactly how urgent his order was.

With the tense exhalation of breath at a tough decision made, Ibu reached for Stabbington's hilt.

"At last!" The voice that burst into her head was strangely accented and decidedly loud. "I have been shouting and shouting and cannot get her to hear me."

"What should I do?" Ibu asked, fighting the urge to yank her hand away from the sword.

"You need to break the connection. Knock her out!"

She opened her bag, unzipping a pouch and pulling out a square wooden case marked 'One Drop Stop'. A single measure of the earthy smelling tincture was usually enough to floor an orc, but Arke took four before she went down like a felled tree.

Ibu cringed as another long-range shot cut through the fog close to the ship but forced herself to contain her panic and concentrate on her patient. Moving quickly, she placed the Soulbound into the recovery position and started to check her vitals. However, as she pressed her fingers to Arke's wrist, the medic frowned. Her pulse should be slow and stable, not plummeting faster than the *Warrior* – past normal, past unconscious, and towards something disastrous.

"Don't you bloody dare!" Ibu grabbed a vial of *Jumpstart a Heart,* the emergency anti-death potion as the Soulbound's breathing started to rattle.

Striding across the deck, Ellie took in the scene with a single glance. "If she's dead, you'd better be a closet necromancer. She's needed in the engine room so get her up – I don't care how."

Ibu poured the entire *Jumpstart* into Arke's eye socket in one go. With a sudden gasp of air, her eyes shot open, and flickers of multi-coloured lightning erupted all over her body. The medic was just trying to check her over when the first mate shouldered her aside.

"No time for that. Help me lift her."

It took the crew mere seconds to manhandle a confused and groggy Arke to the engine room. Ellie hauled her to the top of the main hatch before shoving her down the stairs to land in Krugg's waiting arms. The ogre slung her over his shoulder and ran down the corridor, only stopping when he reached the crystal. However, the instant he set her down, her legs gave way, and she collapsed to the floor. Smashed with anaesthetic and then brought back round with a *Jumpstart*, it was obvious the Soulbound wasn't so much in a world of trouble, as having trouble working out what a world even was.

"What's wrong with her?" Sparkz looked up from where he was piling frozen goods around the crystal.

"Does it matter?" Ellie hauled Arke to a sitting position before slapping her with enough force to bloody her nose. "Wake up and do your magic shit before we all die!"

Ibu shoved the first mate aside and quickly dumped a bottle of *Just Say Go* into the Soulbound's mouth. "This should help." She waited a few frustrating seconds before grabbing a handful of ice and dropping it on her patient's head. "COME ON!"

"Uh?" Finally roused from her eclectic selection of crises, Arke peered at the smoke-filled room and the desperate people around her. "What's going on?"

Memory's Claws

Sparkz's voice was calm and clear as he moved to her side. "Freeze the crystal. Keep doing it until I say stop."

※ ※ ※

THE STORM THEY'D been running towards was finally upon them, sheets of rain pelting the deck and reducing visibility to a few hundred feet. Only Irash and Ruby remained at the helm with Kennedy, ready to use their magic to cushion the ship's last few metres of descent.

"They've stopped firing!" yelled Ruby.

"Probably think we're as good as dead!" Irash replied.

Kennedy glared at him. "Or they've run from the storm."

As the Ornithol grabbed Irash's arm and hauled him towards the bow, Gabbi's reedy voice echoed up the speaking tube from the engine room.

"Sparkz says he's performed his miracle. Now it's your turn."

"Good work! Tell everyone to hold on tight!" Kennedy replied.

With the enemy gone and the threat of being melted into a gooey mess averted, there was only one danger left to deal with. He took a deep breath and focused on the controls, adjusting the angles of the stabilising wings in the hope of finding even the tiniest bit of lift.

Ruby started praying to Chromatia as she lay down on the deck looking directly into the blackness of the ocean ahead. Irash fastened a rope around her waist and tied it to the railings before doing the same for himself. Gods were fickle creatures, but you could always rely on a good knot. He knelt by the railing and prepared to throw all his energy into one massive spell.

Below them, the waves with their frothy white tops were clearly visible.

"WHATEVER YOU HAVE, I NEED IT NOW!" Kennedy bellowed.

Ruby's magic burst into life as a rainbow-coloured glow that covered the front of the ship while Irash threw a cloud of writhing darkness below them. For a few precious seconds, the *Warrior's* nose came up and Kennedy felt her fly once more. It couldn't last, but it had to be enough. They needed to land on the water, not crash into it.

"HOLD ON!"

With a bone-jarring, spar-snapping, plank-rending impact, the ship slammed through the top of a wave before plunging down into the trough beyond. As she reached the bottom, momentum carried her deeper. Water cascaded over the decks in what seemed like an eternity of freezing cold, salty death, but suddenly the front of the *Warrior* began to rise, and she threw herself back to the surface.

Moments later, the crew rushed up to stow what was left of the wings and set a storm sail at the mast. Kennedy braced his arms against the heavy kick of the wheel, knowing he didn't have to yell instructions. They'd run this drill so many times he knew his sky ship would be transformed into a water-going vessel in seconds. It had to be quick as he needed to be able to hold her bows facing straight into the waves or face being capsized.

Above them, lighting crackled, and thunder started to rumble, but when Ruby scoured the clouds for their attacker, she saw nothing.

"You were right, I guess they didn't fancy the storm," she commented.

"Not sure I do either," Kennedy shrugged, "but it's better than the alternative."

※ ※ ※

THE NEXT THREE days were exhausting. Angry skies blew the seas into a frenzy, and the *Warrior* faced waves so enormous some of them towered far above her. Everyone worked around the clock, plugging leaks in the hull, or taking turns on the pumps while their ship was either clawing its way up a wall of water or hurtling into a trough. The wind's strength meant that they could barely keep even the strongest sail to the mast and Kennedy and Urzish split their watches, so one or the other was always at the wheel.

The fourth dawn broke to quieter weather, and by what should have been lunchtime, the winds had died away, the sea quickly becoming choppy rather than tempestuous.

As the sky cleared, the sun began to shine, and clouds of steam rose from both the *Warrior's* timbers and the crew who were lying exhausted on her deck. Kennedy left the wheel to Ellie and started working out their position while Volk lit the galley stove and prepared the quickest meal he knew.

"Still nothing?" Ruby carried a bowl of pasta up to the Soulbound, who stood on top of the cabins, telescope pressed to her eye. She'd scrambled up there as soon as the storm had abated and hadn't stopped scanning the skies since. "Food... It's hot... Arke."

The Soulbound snapped the glass shut. "Have you had some?"

"Yes, we all had a bit to keep us going while they make more. This is yours."

One by one, the crew crowded onto the roof, bringing up a huge vat of pasta, pots of coffee, and a variety of things they'd grabbed from the stores. They'd survived the attack, the crystal, the crash, and the storm. Everyone was exhausted and starving, but they were alive, and the sun was hot enough to dry the clothes on their backs. They'd take the win with bellies full of carbonara, peaches in syrup, flapjack, condensed milk, and some fizzy cola bottles.

They were still up there, chatting and dozing in the sunshine, when Kennedy headed off to look for Arke, who'd slipped away once the roof became too crowded. He found her standing at the bow, gazing towards the horizon.

"In your element?" He leant on the railing and looked out over the waves. "Forgot how much you like the sea."

"Like?" She shrugged. "It's more of an old habit. Once you've done a few years on the water, I don't think it ever really lets you go." She turned to look at him. "Anyway, how far did the storm push us off course?"

"We're a bit further west than I'd planned but we did make some good headway to the north as well." He yawned and rubbed a hand across his face. "Did you spot what was attacking us?"

"Whatever it was came out of the sun, so it was hard to see anything. Maybe I caught a glimpse but my memory's hazy. Probably all Ibu's potions."

"I did hear about her panicked *Jumpstart*, oh and of course Ellie really enjoyed slapping you," he grinned.

"By tomorrow she'll be telling the story of how she saved your life."

"She's losing her touch if she waits that long." Arke smoothed her hands over the railing, brows knitted together in a frown. "You don't have to skirt the subject, Philip, you should be asking what the hell happened to me."

"I assumed you'd have told me if you knew."

She nodded.

"So here's what happened – we had your back and it all worked out." He put a hand on her shoulder and squeezed gently. "We're all ok and we keep moving forwards. We're going to need your experience out here."

"It's simple," Arke replied. "Point bows. Set sail. Avoid trouble."

Chapter Twenty-Five
Task Failed Successfully

After the storm, the weather gave the *Warrior* some welcome respite. The skies stayed clear and the sun warmed the ship from dawn till dusk.

However happy this made the rest of the crew, it was obvious the Soulbound felt quite differently about the brightness and complete lack of cloud cover. When she wasn't converting energy to magical ice to keep the aetheric crystal safe, she was scanning the horizon and pacing the decks with a taut expression, never catching sight of anything but clearly anxious about the possibility.

It took until dawn on the fifth day for Arke to reach the point that she couldn't hide her exhaustion. She finished her final coating of ice and staggered backwards.

"Looks like you're tapped out." Sparkz grabbed her by the collar before she crashed into a cluster of twisted metal. "Sit down before you fall down. Or just fall down away from bits of broken pipe."

"I was a bit lightheaded, that's all."

He shrugged and started to wrap the giant ice cube with heavy blankets. "Do I have to walk you to the galley to make sure you remember to eat?"

"And have people think you care?"

"I do." He checked the sawdust at the base of the crystal was thick enough before tucking the insulation around it. "You're the only thing keeping this from turning us into lumps of badly seasoned meat... and I always keep my tools in good condition."

"He says the nicest things." Kennedy appeared at the doorway to the engine room. "I'm on breakfast duty, any requests?"

"If her answer is 'tea and toast', ignore her," Sparkz replied. "We need to force feed her like a goose in a crate. Gotta keep her output at max."

"*She's* right here, and you can piss off with that bullshit." Arke scowled as she headed to the door. "I'll make my own bloody tea and toast."

"Like you did yesterday? You fell asleep on your plate. Probably still got jam in your hair." Sparkz finished his last checks on the crystal and joined them.

"Icing the beast every four hours has to be exhausting," Kennedy soothed. "We can't help with that, but we can do other things for you – if you'll let us. For example – there are some fresh eggs left. Just enough for an omelette." He gently squeezed Arke's shoulder, a hopeful look on his face. "A cheese omelette?"

There was a pregnant pause as she swung her gaze up to meet his. "The good cheese?"

"The very best," he grinned. "I'll even keep my fingers out of the grater this time."

She nodded slowly. Exhaustion and irritation be damned, the darkness within her was a complete pushover for cheese.

"How about you get some fresh air while I cook? Sun's just rising."

A few minutes later, Kennedy trotted up the stairs carrying a perfectly cooked omelette and a steaming pot of tea, expecting to find Arke enjoying the morning sunshine. However, as he looked around, the only people in sight were Krugg and Urzish. They were supposed to be on watch, and he guessed they were, if that duty included hanging over the gunwales while giving wildly contradictory advice about climbing the boarding net to whoever was below them.

He hardly needed to guess who that was, he just had no idea why.

"What's going on?" he called, setting the tray down and striding towards the side of the ship.

"Arke's been fishing," Urzish replied.

"Fishing?" Kennedy echoed, confusion etching lines on his face. "But she doesn't like…"

Clearly tiring of watching the slow progress below, Krugg flexed his shoulders and began to haul on the netting. Kennedy's eyes widened in surprise as he saw the Soulbound and the results of her 'fishing' dumped onto the deck.

A wind-blasted, sunburnt, dry-lipped child with a rucksack strapped firmly to his back wobbled upright and launched at Arke before she'd even finished cursing the instigator of their rapid ascent. By the intense look on his face as he clung to her arm like a particularly emotional limpet, the boy believed she was the only safe haven in all the world. Suddenly realising she was now some sort of silver-haired support blanket, she levelled an expressive gaze towards Kennedy.

"She certainly doesn't," the Soulbound began, "… but Dozer has an allergy to small, sobbing things. He wouldn't tow the bloody boat over here unless I went with him."

"I see." Kennedy chuckled, looking down to where a battered pinnace bobbed alongside his ship before turning to smile at the boy. "Looks like you're a master mariner, young man – you sailed the ocean AND found your way to us. Welcome aboard the *Warrior*."

When the child just stepped even closer to Arke instead of speaking, she swallowed an exasperated sigh and patted him on the head. "This is Lewis."

Kennedy stuck out a hand expectantly. "Hi Lewis, I'm Captain Kennedy. Are you hungry? I've got a galley full of all sorts of food."

The boy kept his eyes on the deck while clutching the Soulbound's arm even harder.

"The big dog lives in her cabin. Are you sure you don't want to come with me?"

When there was no answer, Arke shrugged.

"Guess I'm sharing my breakfast."

⚔ ⚔ ⚔

Two hours later, Dozer's tail thudded softly against the rug while he sat next to Lewis. To the untrained eye, the Rottweiler would appear to be begging for scraps, but to those in the know, he was more of a thief than a beggar.

The hellhound had quickly forgotten his dislike of children when food had appeared, and the dog's hopeful clowning had overcome the boy's canine-related fears to such an extent that the Soulbound had to keep shoving Dozer's snout away from its preferred resting place of 'very nearly on the child's plate'.

"Are you sleepy yet?" Arke asked hopefully.

"Not really," Lewis replied, the dark circles under his eyes telling their own truth.

She pursed her lips, biting back an inappropriately sharp rejoinder to his obvious lie. "A rest then? How about you settle down in bed and I'll read you a story. Dozer can go with you, he's a very good teddy bear."

"I could sit here and listen." Lewis blinked owlishly.

Arke took a sip of her tea before forcing out the exact reply that her demon had suggested. "I promise I'll be here when you wake up."

Her only answer was a yawning boy heading over to the bed and getting under the covers with a deep sigh of contentment. Easing in a calming breath, the Soulbound tried to ignore Stabbington's smug satisfaction. He was insufferably pleased with his intuition and let her know in every possible way he could.

To drown him out, Arke started telling the timeless Barsian tale of a young halfling who became lost in the woods. After a brief moment of contemplation, she left out the less appropriate parts she'd used when suppressing Irash with that very same story. Mutant bears with opposable thumbs skinning children alive and using their intestines as balloon animals seemed a little inappropriate given the circumstances. So, she just made Gingerfrocks an adult instead.

Three rather grim stories later, the boy was finally asleep. It hadn't been as easy as she'd thought. He'd been sad when Gill's compound fracture had stuck out through her skin and slit Zack's throat as he tried to stop her rolling down the hill; but he'd disapproved of the earl who had marched his entire army to their deaths by his unwillingness to ask for directions. The Soulbound had scrambled a bit for her last story, realising that a more calming tone was needed, and improvised the tale of a giant egg monster that couldn't manage to get to sleep. Eventually, it grew too tired and fell off a wall, killing a family of pigs and creating an excellent breakfast for a woman with far too many children.

Padding softly across to her cabin door, Arke stepped outside and was almost immediately greeted by a plate of cookies held by an expectant Ruby. "Chocolate chip! How are things going?"

"Odd choice for a pet name." Sparkz was sitting on a nearby barrel, nursing a mug of coffee. "I'd have gone with 'Salty Tart', but I suppose it lacks a little nuance."

Arke simply retreated into her cabin, ignoring his comment that she had half an hour before she was due back in the engine room. The Ornithol followed her, nodding with full understanding as her friend indicated the sleeping child.

"Don't hate me, but that was quite funny," Ruby whispered, setting the biscuits down on the table.

"Stabbington seems to think so too," the Soulbound replied with a heavy eye roll as her head was still resonating with the sound of his amusement. "Shame there's no-one else for him to torture."

The demon's laughter stopped abruptly, and there was more than a hint of icy tension in his voice. "I must have my payback for all that cupboard time."

"You wanted to go in there," Arke reminded him, calmly munching her way through a freshly baked chocolate chip cookie.

"What was the alternative?" he asked.

She kept on eating, ignoring his loaded question. Whatever she said would be wrong anyway. She'd been experiencing a distinct internal chill ever since she'd re-acquainted with Will, definitely worse than the one there had been thirty years ago. Arke wanted Stabbington to get over himself and for his part, Stabbington made it obvious that he wanted her to get over Kromm. For two entities who'd shared so much for so long, they were still incredibly bad at dealing with any serious personal issues.

Ruby eased the plate of biscuits closer to her friend. "Did you find out what happened to the child?"

"Yeah, he said he was a delivery boy working on a packet ship called the *Albatross*. They were heading north to Levenbrandt when they were attacked by pirates. The captain put him in the pinnace, and he managed to slip away during the battle." The Soulbound picked up another cookie with a weary smile. "These are amazing, Rubes."

"And all he's got in the world is that bag?" The Ornithol gestured to the rucksack that lay on the bottom of the bed. "Looks pretty empty."

"Probably didn't have time to grab too much. He was lucky to get away at all." Arke tapped the top of Dozer's head as he tried to steal a biscuit. "Hey, you're not having any."

"Is chocolate as bad for hellhounds as it is for dogs?"

"No, but I will be if he steals my food." She pointed to the bed. "Go and be a good teddy bear."

Huffing a melodramatic sigh, the Rottweiler slunk across to Lewis. He was just about to hop up beside the boy when his hackles rose, and he sniffed warily at the rucksack. The Soulbound stood up, fingers suddenly crackling with arcane energy.

"Be careful!" Ruby urged. "It might be dangerous! Should I burn it?"

"Not when it's on my bed next to a sleeping child!" Arke snapped, before concentrating her attention on the bag. "Dozer's right, there's something magical in there. I must be tired, I didn't even notice the stench."

"What if it's another capstone?" Ruby's voice was suddenly hushed and reverent. "Maybe the gods are helping us!"

The Soulbound turned to her, trying to form a reply which took into account her friend's belief system. Then she gave up. "Rubes, the gods don't give a shit about us, and if you think any bag carried by a random stranger might contain a capstone, I'm never taking you shopping."

The Ornithol cocked her head to one side. "You're going to take me shopping?"

"That was all you heard?"

Ruby shrugged. "Look, I know you don't believe, even though a literal god intervened when you died. It just seemed like a strange coincidence, as if things are being put in our path to help us. Who else could do that but a god?"

"Any number of demons? The Firm? A powerful mage?" Arke slipped a hand inside the rucksack. "Not that it matters anyway, as this isn't a magic bag and what's in it isn't a capstone."

"Oh." Ruby sat down and picked up a biscuit, eating it in one bite. "That's disappointing."

"Hardly unexpected. The three we're looking for could be anywhere and I doubt we're going to be finding another for quite some time. So far no-one has ever heard of them, not us, not Crimbles, not Wi..." she quickly corrected herself, "...the Lord Commander."

"Really? Just call him by his name, Arke." The Ornithol's yellow eyes skewered her friend with a long, hard stare. "Everyone knows what you were doing down there for three days."

The Soulbound shrugged. "Yes, I was trying to find more information on the capstones."

"And the rest. The soldiers bringing up the stores were *very* chatty," Ruby tilted her head to one side.

"You can't believe scuttlebutt."

"Arke!"

"Does it really matter?"

The Ornithol's beak dropped wide open for a moment and then slammed shut with an audible snap. "YES! Of course it matters! You were... *personal* with a military commander who just happens to be a Barsian noble. *For three days*! Was it some sort of cry for help?" She grabbed another cookie and swallowed it whole.

"Shhhh, don't wake the kid!"

"Sorry, but what the HELL, Arke? You hate arrogant men. You hate Barsians. You hate nobles. And you really, really hate arrogant Barsian nobles."

"Friends close. Enemies closer."

Ruby sat back in her chair, shaking her head slowly. "If that's your new mantra, I'm never taking you to a fight again."

Snorting with sudden, uncontrollable laughter, the Soulbound had to hurry outside so she didn't wake Lewis up. Tears rolled down her cheeks as she leant against the wall, trying to breathe around the waves of mirth.

"What was in those cookies?" Sparkz watched her curiously. "Or are you having a breakdown?"

Arke was still chuckling as she replied. "Ruby's fault."

"What is?" Kennedy stuck his head out of his cabin door.

"This." Sparkz gestured to the Soulbound. "Never seen the ice queen laugh so hard. I wonder what could have happened recently to make her *so* happy..."

Ruby stepped onto the deck just before the barrel that the engineer was sitting on was 'accidentally' obliterated with a bright blue energy dart. She was carrying a wax-sealed wooden box about the size of a pencil case. The sight of it immediately wiped the smile from Arke's face and she all but snatched it from her friend's hands.

"What's that?" Kennedy asked.

"The kid had it with him. There's a note in the bag, says to deliver it to some address in Levenbrandt," Ruby explained. "I guess the captain took his courier business seriously."

"You would too if you were dealing with the Clockmakers," Arke growled, pointing at the insignia on the box's lid.

"The Chronomancers?" Sparkz scrambled to his feet. "I thought they were just a myth."

"If only." The Soulbound's expression bordered on disgust as she examined the box. "Time magic stinks like burnt hair, but the Clockmakers are full of so much shit sometimes it's hard to know what smells worse."

"If it was that important, then it's got to be worth something." Kennedy reached out a hand.

She shook her head. "We're in enough trouble as it is. So, you're all going to forget about this, whatever it is. We keep the box shut and we steer clear – nothing good ever comes from the Clockmakers."

Chapter Twenty-Six
Task Failed Spectacularly

BEFORE THEIR ENFORCED sea voyage, the crew had probably never contemplated why sky ships had become the standard method of transportation. After all, they had better things to do than muse on matters so far removed from the necessities of their own lives. However, those on board who were old enough to remember the days before flying vessels existed knew exactly why travelling above the clouds had been an overnight success. Everyone else on the *Warrior* had to learn the hard way.

The honest truth was that sea travel was slow. Slower than slow. Painfully, tediously, slow. The kind of slow that makes you lethargic, wearier when you woke up than when you went to sleep. Everything around them, the endless rolling waves, the birds, the clouds, the fish, seemed to be moving faster than the *Warrior* whose course crawled up the chart of the Western Ocean with all the get up and go of a depressed snail.

It was just after two o'clock on another boring and increasingly chilly day at sea when Sparkz walked into Kennedy's cabin and ruined both his afternoon nap and the rest of his week.

"She's cooked."

Kennedy slowly opened an eye. "Without context, that could be anything from 'Ruby fell in the oven' to 'Ellie's been in the potion cupboard'."

"If it was the latter I'd say baked." The engineer sat down at the table. "I'm referring to the silver haired aetheric tamer. She's running on empty. Less Ice Queen and more Exhausted Penguin. So we need to get the crystal off the ship sooner rather than later."

"We shouldn't be discussing this without her," Kennedy frowned.

"You think this is a discussion?" Sparkz shook his head. "Magic looks like it's easy, just wave a hand, shit spews forth, happy days – but it's not. The bigger the spell, the more energy it takes to cast. Arke's icy blast packs a massive punch and she's using it every four hours, day and night. She'll say she's fine but she's not and I do *not* want to get deep fried because she doesn't freeze the thing hard enough."

"Ok." Kennedy yawned as he padded across to his chart table. "So, we either drop the crystal over the side and accept the loss – or we try and leave it somewhere salvageable."

"A deep water bay would be ideal." Sparkz ran a finger over the well-worn map of the Western Ocean. "Are you sure you haven't got any newer charts? This one looks older than time."

"Lucky we have it at all." Kennedy shrugged. "This part of the world is a dry zone for sky pirates, and if you add into that the Levenbrandt avoidance stance that Arke insisted on..."

"For *obvious* reasons..."

"Whatever. We haven't needed any maps that cover this region." Kennedy spent a long moment peering at the chart before reaching for his dividers. "Reckon she can do... four more days?"

"What does that say?" Sparkz squinted at the name written near a chain of isolated islands by Kennedy's finger. "Really? Someone called them the Spits of Spite?"

"They sound idyllic. Anyway, according to this, there's a deep bay right here by the easternmost one. Can Arke hang on long enough?"

The engineer grinned and patted Kennedy on the shoulder. "To avoid having to abandon our aetheric ice cube? Hell yeah, I'll get her over the line."

"What does that mean? Don't do anything stupid!"

"Of course not."

Chuckling to himself, Sparkz stuck his hands in his pockets and sauntered out of the cabin.

It was a great exit. Or would have been, if it hadn't been followed by the sudden cessation of his laughter and a diabolical roar from the crystal jaguar. Kennedy dropped his pencil and scrambled outside to see the engineer on the deck, Kevan's multi-faceted form on top of him and the Ornithol straining on the cat's leash with zero effect.

"Get this psychotic feline off me before I turn it into kitty litter!" Sparkz yelled, his voice slightly muffled by the weight of the world's worst example of a ship's cat.

"You startled him!" Ruby protested, before crouching down in front of the slavering creature and softening her tone. "Remember our talk about your anger issues, Kevan? Think of something calming. How about you try and picture a juicy steak, dripping with blood. That's your happy place, isn't it?"

The jaguar hissed, its multi-faceted teeth perilously close to Sparkz's face.

"Really?" he snapped. *"That's* the image you put into its head when it's contemplating filleting some exceptionally fresh, bloody meat."

"Maybe if you were a little less confrontational?" the Ornithol suggested.

"What do you want me to do, kiss it on the lips?"

"Absolutely." Arke was standing in the doorway of her cabin, hands in her pockets.

"Well, you always said that was how you wanted to go." Kennedy's attempt at keeping a straight face was doomed to failure as the Soulbound snorted with laughter and Ruby tilted her head to one side, looking up at him quizzically.

"Someone act like a grown up and get this creature off me!" Sparkz demanded, as Kevan started to growl at him again.

"When there are SO many more innuendos to make?" Kennedy tried to choke back his laughter while he watched the Ornithol's extremely ineffective cat-handling.

"Dozer, get your lazy arse out here!" Arke called and waited for a couple of seconds before turning to look into her cabin. "NOW!"

"Ruby, I'd let go of his lead if I were you," Kennedy warned, retreating into his room.

The giant Rottweiler erupted onto the scene, his curly tail starting to thrash in delight as he saw Kevan nearby. With a torrent of joyful barks, he bounced into a deliriously effervescent play bow in front of the crystal jaguar.

"This is your plan?" Sparkz wasn't sure whether to cover his face or his groin as the big cat readied itself to pounce, its entire body quivering and tail swishing. "For the record…"

He was cut off mid complaint as Kevan crouched so low that his words were lost in the creature's incredibly dense coat. Then, with an explosive leap, the crystal jaguar landed on top of the hellhound, who took off up the deck at a lumbering gallop before jamming the brakes on and catapulting his temporary jockey into the door of the lance controls. With a continued cascade of happy barks and lip curling snarls, the bad good boy and the bad bad boy began to tussle and tumble their way from one end of the ship to the other.

"They play so nicely," Ruby called from her safe seat atop the roof of the cabins.

"That's play?" Sparkz grimaced as he wiped jaguar drool from his neck.

"Oh yes. The boys have a big old bromance going on." Kennedy grinned as he watched the pair roll round the deck, legs kicking, teeth snapping. "We just have to make sure there's nothing breakable around when they kick off. Like barrels, crates, crew members…"

"And Kevan's always so much happier after their playdates," Ruby added.

"Playdates?" Sparkz grabbed a bottle of vodka from Kennedy's cupboard and sat down at the chart table. "I'd say you'd all lost your minds, but that implies prior ownership."

⚹ ⚹ ⚹

THE SPITS OF SPITE had clearly been named by a deeply disgruntled explorer who'd already used up their quota of synonyms for desolation as they mapped the Western Ocean. Each island in the small chain was a barren, basalt lump, covered in guano and echoing with the voices of several thousand gulls. There were no trees, no bushes and no easy landfall as every gritty black beach was guarded by a forest of rocky stacks that shone from the surf like rotten teeth.

"We need to make sure we stay well away from shore." Kennedy lowered his telescope. "If I'm going to be shipwrecked, I want it to be a tropical paradise, not this... whatever this is."

"It's an old volcano," Sparkz said as he focused on the conical island at the centre of the group. "Top's been blown off – must've been a significant eruption. A massive lava event would explain all this basalt too."

"On the plus side," added Ellie, with a distinctly feral tone, "fresh meat and eggs... I am SO done with fish."

"Can't see any sign of drinking water though. And we *really* need some," Kennedy sighed.

"Good chance there's some gathered in the caldera." Arke appeared at his elbow, her eyes bloodshot and her hands trembling. "So, let's deep six the purple peril and go foraging."

No-one commented on her appearance. She'd been like that since Sparkz had taken responsibility for keeping her energy levels high enough to keep icing the crystal. Repeated use of *Just Say Go* was incredibly stupid, it even said so on the bottle, but as Ibu didn't have the encyclopaedic herbal knowledge that Gurdi had, the *Go* juice had been their only choice. As a result, the Soulbound was running on heady magical fumes and a diet of as many cookies as Ruby could persuade her to eat. She hadn't slept properly for three days, and everyone knew not to provoke the disturbingly twitchy mix of volatility and sugar that was encased in an Arke-shaped body.

"Or you could always stay here and rest..." Kennedy rapidly found himself withering under a particularly intense stare and withdrew his foot from his mouth before she rammed it down his throat. *"But* now I think about it, seagull hunting sounds a lot more fun." He forced a smile to his lips and looked at Sparkz for some respite from her silent threat. "Ready to heave the thing overboard?"

"More than you could ever know. Oh, you're talking about the crystal."

Despite Kennedy's anxiety reaching buttock-clenching levels as they eased the lump of aetheric over the side of the gig, everything went perfectly. It sank to the bottom of the bay without a single concerning moment, let alone the explosions, irradiated fish, or territorial kraken that Sparkz had mentioned as possibilities. After securing its rope to a makeshift buoy, they headed back to the ship, only daring to comment on the successful operation once they were safely aboard.

"Good, because I'm bloody hungry!" Ellie was waiting, a huge bow slung over her shoulder. "We've got a few hours before it gets dark, loads of time to snag dinner."

Arke pushed past her and was in the gig before Sparkz had chance to cut the engine. "Head to the old volcano. Plenty of birds there and we can check for fresh water."

There was absolutely nothing positive to be gained from any comment on her peremptory tone, especially since they were all equally keen to get off the ship, even if their only choices of dry land were misshapen lumps of rock that had once been torrents of lava, or the mother lode itself. The gig was quickly back in the air and heading towards the largest island.

"So..." Kennedy began, as casually as he was able, "...either I'm having some sort of mental health crisis, or those seagulls are the size of small horses."

"What if they're Ornithols?" Ellie sounded despondent. "Dinner would be abso-bloody-lutely *ruined*."

"On the other hand, think about the drumsticks!" Sparkz grinned.

Kennedy cleared his throat. "Just to be clear, and not that I thought I would ever need to say this – we do NOT eat Ornithols."

"He once had a nightmare about his food starting to talk to him." Arke had her telescope to her eye as she watched Ruby flying towards the caldera. "But you're ok Ellie, I'm pretty sure dinner is still going to be roast sea-pigeon."

All heads turned to where their rainbow-coloured crewmate was attracting the attention of a large number of giant gulls. At first, she must have assumed it was curiosity, but as she drew closer to the top of the volcano, more and more took to the air, surrounding her in a cloud so thick she almost disappeared.

"They could just be friendly." Ellie's tone was still disconsolate.

"Or *they* could have no qualms about eating an Ornithol," the Soulbound replied. "That looks more like an angry mob than a polite hello."

Five minutes and an uncharacteristically expletive-ridden shout from Ruby later, the gig was hurtling towards a flattish patch of basalt at the base of the volcano. Plan D (for dinner) had been to lure any hostile birds down to an accessible area and despatch them when they were close enough to the ground that their meat wouldn't be prematurely tenderised.

Ellie was almost indecently excited, sitting with her supply of arrows laid out in front of her, one already nocked to her bow. She wasn't the best marksman, but with targets so unusually large, she was anticipating a good haul.

"We can't carry too many back to the ship, so let's not be greedy," Kennedy remarked, his eyes focused on their landing spot.

"Greedy? I'm hungry!" Ellie protested.

"And fish-flavoured chicken is still a step up from fish-flavoured fish," Sparkz added.

Arke was silent as she watched the chase above them. The rainbow-coloured Ornithol was faster than the gulls, but not by much.

The Soulbound leapt out of the gig before it had touched down, vaulting over the side and taking position by a rock as the cloud of birds tore towards them. The seagulls were obviously not Ornithol as they had no arms, nor any language other than their native screeching, but even if they had been, Kennedy knew Arke would still have peppered their ranks with her magical energy darts. It didn't matter who or what they were; they were attacking her friend.

That same mindset and the surfeit of *Go* juice in her system was also what scythed down two far less feathery assailants as they used the shrieking mob of gulls as cover to sneak up on the *Warrior* crew.

Kennedy had just added a particularly beady-eyed bird to the growing pile around him when an energy dart shot past his ear, almost giving him the piercing his shipmates had always wanted him to have. He was about to bellow a curse at the Soulbound when he heard a distinctly humanoid coughing fit directly behind him.

Spinning round, he wondered whether Arke actually had hit him in the head, because he thought he could see an extremely bald woman dressed in a beautiful velvet riding habit.

He rubbed his eyes, but she was still there, staggering backwards, one hand clutching the smoking lace at her chest, the other trying to catch the flowing black wig that was toppling into a puddle of seagull blood. Concluding that she was real, Kennedy briefly wondered if the gulls were changelings, before deciding it didn't really matter, since she was both armed and angry.

"You seem a little overdressed," he remarked, suddenly realising the others had stopped gull culling in order to face off against similarly lavishly apparelled enemies.

Sparkz was dropping some magic on a man who looked like he was dressed for the opera, while Ruby was introducing a purple jacketed gentleman to the end of her fists, and he almost couldn't see Arke for the voluminous cloak that whirled dramatically around her attacker. To his right, a blood and feather coated Ellie was finishing what Arke's other energy blast had started on the waistcoated man who had sought to stab her in the neck.

"You think to criticise *my* turnout when you are dirty, sweaty, and covered in bloody feathers?" The woman's unsettlingly nasal voice could probably strip the peel off an orange in under a minute.

Biting back a retort that would heavily reference the current location of her wig, Kennedy's gaze flicked to the needle-sharp rapier in her right hand. Whatever she looked like on the outside, its well-tooled blade told him the sword wasn't just an accessory.

"We're on a hunting trip."

"So are we." She clicked her fingers. "Get him."

Within seconds, one of the giant gulls dive-bombed Kennedy, knocking him to the ground, and the woman launched forwards, her blade flashing towards his throat in a killing thrust. However, her steel found nothing but basalt as he'd already sprung and merged with his alter, his own sword gleaming as it whipped through the air, neatly removing her head from her body. Shrieking, the gull whirled around and flew directly at Kennedy in an attack that was only ever going to be a one-way trip to a roasting tin.

"Next!"

He wiped his blade on the now lifeless lump of feathers and chunks of meat that would taste delicious with the right selection of herbs and spices.

"Ellie, you ok there?" He frowned as he saw his first mate crouching by her fallen adversary.

She held up a hand, glittering grains of what looked like salt running through her fingers and falling to the ground. "This guy... well. His body's gone. Just this stuff left."

"Don't lick it."

"That was your first thought?"

"No. Of course not."

He checked the others, seeing Sparkz's assailant wreathed in colourful flames, and Ruby executing a flying takedown on her already wobbling attacker. Those enemies still had bodies, unlike Ellie's opponent and the deflated riding habit at his feet.

A voice boomed out across the rocks, silencing even the raucous seabirds which circled overhead. "Who the devil are you and why you are trespassing on our island?"

With a sudden swoop of wings, a giant gull landed nearby and yet another immaculately dressed figure dismounted from it. The newcomer was tall and broad, with close cropped dark hair and a braided beard that reached almost to his belt.

As the stranger cast a disparaging eye over the scene, his dour expression left no doubt as to what he thought of the *Warrior's* crew.

"We come in peace," Kennedy replied, before gesturing to the chaos around them. "Unfortunately, your hospitality is somewhat lacking. We're not big fans of being ambushed."

The cloaked figure who had been duelling spells with Arke finally lost the battle and froze in place, ice coating every part of his body.

"At least this guy challenged me to a fight." The Soulbound stood beside the frozen mage, a livid burn on her right cheek. "Well... he hid behind a rock and threw a red-hot stone at my head. I assumed that was his way of asking to get his arse kicked."

The bearded man didn't even spare her a glance as he addressed Kennedy. "I'm Vice Admiral Oliver Cutler.

Tell your minions to respect the chain of command and not address me directly."

"Bold of you to assume he's the leader. What if I were?" Arke asked with a thin smile.

Kennedy recognised that particular expression as one which heralded a bucket load of trouble. Sometimes that look would give him serious anxiety, but today it made him want to chuckle. The vice admiral was as charmless as the rest of his people, and if the Soulbound wanted to use him to relieve a little tension, then that was absolutely fine.

"No-one puts a mage in charge," Cutler sneered. "They're far too easily squashed."

Arke stepped forwards, swinging Stabbington behind her and shattering her ice-cubed opponent with a single blow. "Then you need to pick better mages. Some of us are remarkably resilient."

"Do you have a point, or should I just pretend to be interested?" Cutler finally glanced over at her, his expression radiating sudden antipathy.

"I bet you hear that a lot," Sparkz remarked, ducking quickly as Ruby's fists encouraged his burning opponent to stop and drop. His foot initiated the 'roll' part of the manoeuvre, and they watched as the man's limp body accelerated down a slope before coming to rest against some pointy-looking rocks.

"I say, Cutler, they have quite the repartee." A blonde head suddenly popped out from the shelter of a nearby boulder. "The name's Vaughan. I'm perfectly harmless, more of an observer than a participant."

"I might have known you'd be doing an awful lot of nothing – as per usual," the vice admiral scowled.

Vaughan headed towards the *Warrior* crew, his expression warm and friendly. He wore a far less extravagant outfit than the others, a simple white shirt and yellow waistcoat above black trousers with legs that buttoned just below the knee.

"My apologies for the territorial nature of our avian friends," he began. "They are both excellent to eat and our local 'chariots of war'. It is important to make the best of what you have, after all."

"Vaughan!" Cutler's temper seemed to increase with every word that issued from his subordinate's mouth. "You useless streak of piss! You pathetic worm! Explain why you did not defend your fellow officers!"

"I was washing dishes, as per your orders, sir, when the others rushed out with great enthusiasm. I was far too terrified of not finishing the silverware and incurring your perfectly measured wrath to follow them immediately. Once I had completed my assigned task, I hurried out to find... this." He gestured around and finally slouched into something that might have been a salute. "Sir."

"Are you even armed?" Cutler snapped.

"Two of them, as per usual, sir."

The vice admiral drew his sword and levelled it at Vaughan. "How the mighty have fallen, once the first lieutenant aboard the flagship, and now a snivelling jester."

Standing well out of reach of the blade, the younger officer turned to look at Kennedy, his voice changing to a deliberately terrible attempt at a whisper. "And I only came out here to tell him that the reinforcements he's waiting for will be delayed."

"VAUGHAN!" Cutler's vocal cords hit a new high as he lunged forwards. "You bloody fool!"

The blonde-haired man side-stepped the sword with impeccable timing before turning to face the vice admiral. "Oh, were you buying time while the rest of your crew got here? And I just ruined that. I am SO sorry. I'm not having a good day today. *First*, I lost the key to the barracks door and *then* I gave away your really obvious plan. Bad Vaughan, bad, bad Vaughan." He darted off as his superior threw himself into a series of murderous attacks.

Kennedy looked at Arke with a tilt to his head as the situation grew stranger and stranger. "I kinda like the little guy."

"Maybe he reminds you of someone..." she suggested, tracking the mismatched fight and flight that was being enacted nearby.

The older man, beard braids clattering together like a tuneless wind chime, was slashing and stabbing while his far nimbler opponent was evading every attack with consummate athleticism.

"I don't think so," Kennedy replied with an innocent expression. "So do we kill one or both?"

"Common sense says both," Arke replied. "However, I can see you have that recruiting gleam in your eyes again."

Vaughan dived past them, sweat from his many exertions starting to bead on his brow. As he passed Arke, he hesitated, glancing at the ring on her left hand, before Cutler's blade whisked a smidgeon too close to his neck. He ducked quickly behind Kennedy, his voice suddenly quiet and briskly businesslike.

"His men are bonded to him. He dies, they die. The barracks door won't hold them for much longer."

"Point taken." Kennedy stepped forwards, silver sword gleaming. "May I cut in?"

"No! Let me deal with this pathetic insurrectionist and you can go free!" Cutler snarled.

With a sudden grunt, the vice admiral staggered, the points of two short swords sticking out from his perfectly tailored frock coat. As he dropped to his knees, Kennedy and Arke saw Sparkz standing behind him.

"I'm too hungry to piss about anymore. Are we killing the other prick or not?"

As Cutler gurgled and slumped to the ground, his body dissolved into tiny white grains. Moving almost indecently fast, Vaughan started to fill his pockets with the salt-like material.

"Not just yet. I'll admit I'm curious." Kennedy tapped the blonde man on the shoulder with the point of his sword. "Are you going to tell us what you are?" He pointed to the empty clothes. "Or what they were."

Vaughan grinned. "Happy to give you my entire life story over a full-bodied red, if you have one on board – I assume you have a ship?"

"No, we bloody well walked here." Sparkz picked up his swords and turned away. "Let's start loading the gig with dinner, Ellie. Plumpest breasted birds only. Yes, I know exactly what I said, no need to give me the look. What do you want me to say? Those with the meatiest pectorals?"

SEVERAL PLATEFULS OF the surfiest turf later, Vaughan stopped making pointed remarks about being handcuffed to a chair and began to tell his story. As after-dinner speakers went, he was the bomb. As after-dinner speeches went, it was... concerning.

Everyone was used to the concept of selling souls, so learning that Vaughan called himself a 'Depth' and was bound to a creature he referred to as the Mother of Salt hadn't worried them. Nor were they bothered when he admitted to being two hundred and sixty-six years old, able to breathe in water and rather partial to a slow waltz.

What actually turned everyone's stomachs was the information that Vaughan's admiral and the rest of the Depths were somewhere nearby in a ship that was eight or nine times the size of the *Warrior*. The fact that Admiral Von Lauken was described as someone whose grip on reality was greased by several lifetimes of infamous violence only added to the tension. If they'd been in the air, it would have been a non-issue. However, since they all knew that their current status was as the preyest prey that ever sailed the ocean, the evening ended on a distinctly unsettled note.

As the galley emptied, Arke stood up from her seat and walked over to Vaughan before lifting her left hand to show the Autarch's ring. "Why were you looking at this earlier?"

"I'm sleepy and drunk. Can we talk about this another time?" He yawned theatrically.

Moving behind him, the Soulbound ducked her head so her lips were level with his ear. "Whereas I'm awake and sober. So let me make this clear, you can answer my question, or you can be sleepy, drunk, and tied to a chair as it sinks below the waves."

He chuckled. "Darling, do remember I'm a Depth. My life and soul belong to the Mother of Salt, I subsist on her bounty, I bleed water and I cannot drown."

"I was listening." Arke patted him gently on the shoulder. "And by the way, I love that you gave yourselves a team name. But, in the event that you and your chair took a header over the side, it would take you a long, long, LONG time to shuffle back to dry land. Can't think it'd be at all enjoyable. So, just tell me what you know about this." She waved the ring in front of his face.

After a few seconds of contemplation, Vaughan began to speak. "I've lived long enough to learn to be open minded: you can do what you want to do, be who you want to be, wear whoever's jewellery you choose." He paused again, his eyes drawn to the obsidian band, his tone suddenly hardening. "But you reek of Cormydd, that disgusting excuse for an Autarch, and the admiral will smell you from a hundred metres."

He stopped, and the Soulbound shook her head. "You can't just stop there."

"Fine." He sighed. "Two hundred and whatever years ago, the Barsian navy was one of the greatest fighting forces in the world. Von Lauken was well on track to being Admiral of the Fleet until he disagreed with one of Cormydd's orders. Next thing we knew, his entire squadron was condemned to death. We fled, but the Autarch sent the rest of the fleet after us. They destroyed ship after ship, murdered crew after crew. Von Lauken lost his mind over it all, so when the Mother of Salt offered him a deal, he signed for everyone he had left. This ocean is her domain and out here, surrounded by her storms, that bastard Autarch cannot touch us."

"Cormydd died in the Night of Terrors." Arke shoved her hands in her pockets.

"So we heard. And yet here you are, branded like the finest steer." Vaughan watched as she strode towards the door. "We all need to stay away from Von Lauken, but your need is a must. He will think you're a spy and kill you on sight."

Chapter Twenty-Seven
Bang

A SMALL SHORE PARTY from the *Warrior* headed back to the largest island at dawn the next morning. The gig had been loaded with barrels, buckets, a series of airtight containers, and Krugg, as Vaughan had agreed to lead them to a source of freshwater deep inside the old volcano in return for collecting the salt from the Depths they'd killed the previous day.

"What's it good for?" Sparkz was working his way through a pocketful of gull sandwiches. "Weapons? Potions? Spells? Or is it just great with a boiled egg?"

"The Mother is savage." Vaughan made a quick warding gesture. "We eat and drink for pleasure, but it is her salt that sustains our lives. She bestows the minimum to assuage our needs, but if one of us dies then there is much... more."

Kennedy raised his eyebrows. "So how are you all still alive when there's free food around you, just waiting to be... harvested."

"Discipline." The lieutenant tugged at his shirt sleeves with a sardonic smile. "We're gentlemen, you see."

"You're telling me no Depth has ever killed another for the salt?" Kennedy asked.

"Never met a 'gentleman' who wouldn't chuck granny off a cliff if it suited him," Sparkz snorted.

"It has happened. After a hundred years or so, some of the chaps lost their grip on reality – there was a time where it was basically anarchy, but the admiral developed an unusual talent for..." Vaughan steepled his fingers together, brow furrowed, as if searching for the right term.

"Inspiring loyalty?" Kennedy suggested.

"I was going to say grisly acts of public torture, but it all amounts to the same thing in the end."

"See? Gentlemen my arse." Sparkz sank his teeth into another sandwich.

"Couldn't agree more," Vaughan replied. "The contract Von Lauken negotiated bestowed the Mother's gift on the officers only. The sailors' side of the bargain was... less advantageous. They grew old and died, yet they still work the ships, shambling hulks of pure obedience, their existence bound to their commander's."

"So, we have a literal cut the head off the snake situation," Kennedy mused, before quickly throwing an apologetic glance at the Soulbound. "Sorry, Stabbington."

"You're fine, he's sulking," Arke replied.

"Still?"

"Not surprised, poor bastard probably needs counselling after Theogenes," Sparkz muttered.

An abrupt and awkward silence suddenly fell over the gig as the Soulbound turned to look out to sea and Kennedy skewered the engineer with a warning glare. Krugg always tuned out of any conversations that didn't involve orders or food, but Vaughan, blue eyes gleaming with interest, was clearly both extremely interested and too smart to make an immediate comment.

The morning's work went smoothly, if not quite so silently. Krugg played the part of the pack mule with vigour since he was always keen to show off his strength and endurance. In fact, so keen that he had to be dissuaded from carrying four barrels of water, just to prove that he could.

"Only TWO," Kennedy ordered, having given up being polite. He was twitchy enough having to venture into the caves without the ogre arguing about how much weight he could carry. "If they get dropped, they'll break, and we don't have time to go back to the ship for more."

"But..." Krugg pouted, looking for all the world as if he was about to reiterate just how incredibly strong he was.

"MOVE!"

"This way, water bearer extraordinaire." Vaughan enacted a low bow complete with so many overly intricate hand gestures that the ogre completely lost his train of thought. "We shall away to the gig!"

In between Krugg wrangling and barrel filling, the group had very different priorities. Sparkz finished his sandwiches and took naps in a quiet corner of the giant cavern that was home to the lake of crystal-clear water. Arke explored the tunnels because she was too wired to rest, and Kennedy paced up and down, still worried about their proximity to Vaughan's admiral. He'd quizzed the lieutenant over breakfast and learnt nothing that gave him any more confidence about the *Warrior's* precarious situation.

The Spit of Spite was only one of the islands that the Depths used as a base for what Vaughan called 'living off the sea' rather than the piracy it really was. Cutler's vessel had limped its way to the Spit after a briskly fought battle and dropped anchor on the far side of the volcano for repairs. Neither the vice admiral nor his crew had been in a hurry to get everything fixed, as an eternity spent onboard a frigate was just as cramped and tedious as it sounded. As to the whereabouts of the flagship, Vaughan had shrugged, remarking that Von Lauken's motivations and plans were mercurial at best.

"He claims that being a Depth is a curse, as if he hadn't negotiated the deal himself, so he seeks a 'cure' with fanatical zeal. He searches for artefacts, mages, spells, documents, monsters – anything which might set him free."

"Set you all free," Kennedy noted.

"Yeah, that's what he says, and they all lap it up," Vaughan scowled.

"And you didn't."

"Why do you think I was given to Cutler with instructions to treat me like his bitch?"

※ ※ ※

THE MAIN CAVE system inside the volcano seemed to be well travelled, but completely devoid of anything particularly interesting. Arke wandered down a few corridors and located a kitchen, a dining hall, and a series of smaller areas with rudimentary beds in, but she didn't venture too far from the freshwater pool. She wasn't feeling terribly adventurous, as both her body and her state of mind could best be described as delicate.

The hangover from days of stimulants had yet to fade, and although Stabbington had been persuaded to give her some of his magical painkillers, he was terrible company. He'd been in the vilest mood since Theogenes, and two-way communication had dwindled to the bare minimum with every day that passed without her responding to his surly jibes or acidic remarks. She knew he was spoiling for a fight as much as she was stoically avoiding one. It wasn't like she didn't know what he'd say, didn't know why he was so furious, or didn't know he was right. She just didn't want to hear it, so she tuned out his needling, his arch comments, and his downright inflammatory exclamations.

However, no matter what personal issues they might have, Stabbington always had her back, and when his warning broke through her headache, she paid attention.

"Carefully increase your pace, do not turn round. There are two sets of footsteps coming up softly from the rear."

It was incredibly difficult not to peek at whoever was behind her, but she resisted the urge and lengthened her strides in careful increments, orange magic surging as adrenalin hit her system like a bolt of lightning. Hangover bypassed by imminent threat, her body was as quick to prepare itself as it had always been.

"There is a cave around this corner on your right. You may be able to slip in and let them pass." The demon's voice was calm but businesslike, as if he were suggesting a flavour of cheesecake, rather than describing a high-risk strategy.

The Soulbound slipped sideways into what looked like an officer's berth, and pressed her back against the wall, seeking to make the most of the darkness. She shut her mouth and breathed as slowly as she could through her nose as she heard the footsteps come closer. Suddenly aware that her orange magic was bubbling with a little more verve, she kept her left hand in her pocket in case it began to glow at exactly the wrong moment.

The faint light that came from the lanterns along the main passageways illuminated the forms of two men as they passed her hiding spot. One was wearing a short velvet cloak that rippled with his long strides, and the other a scarlet jacket so tightly fitted to his shoulders it looked as if it had been painted on.

Given their antiquated and flamboyant style of dress, Arke had no doubt that both of them were Depths.

"Be wary of your orange magic," Stabbington warned, "you are nowhere near your normal self after the last few days, and it is getting twitchy. The more I watch it, the more I worry. It is not a tool; it is more like a living thing."

"What an excellent time to start a discussion," she muttered.

"Whose fault is that?" he snapped.

At that particular moment, the Soulbound knew two things. The first was that her friends needed to be alerted to the fact they were not alone, and the second was that the over-use of *Go* juice was giving her serious rage issues. Stabbington had been wanting a showdown since Theogenes, but now was definitely not the time.

She stepped out into the corridor and cleared her throat. "Oh, thank goodness, I was quite lost in here!" Clueless maiden had always been one of her favourite impersonations.

Both Depths whirled around to face her, hands on their sword hilts.

The cloaked man affected a delicate bow in her direction. "Please, come with us. We will render you whatever aid you require."

"Thank you sir, but I would hate to be any bother. Perhaps you could point me towards the daylight, for I am quite lost in these tunnels."

Arke felt a hand on her shoulder just as Stabbington informed her that the red-jacketed man had teleported directly behind her.

"My colleagues must have left you unguarded, therefore you are fair game." The voice was silky smooth, even putting Vaughan's elegant tone to shame. "I call dibs. Finders keepers, after all."

"That's very disappointing." Arke spun around and Stabbington's sword burst into existence, spearing straight through the Depth as it materialised in her hand. The look of shock she'd seen so many times flashed across the man's face as he clutched at the blade and made an unintelligible gurgling noise. "I'm game. But never fair."

As he hit the ground, Stabbington shouted a warning, and she dived away from the sudden barrage of needle thin knives that the other Depth was hurling in her direction. The first missed by a hair's breadth, but as his eyes followed her duck and roll, the second and third carved their way into her left bicep.

"Ah, this one is accurate. He will not be easy." The demon almost sounded impressed, despite the fact that his host was trying to struggle to her feet with her dominant arm hanging uselessly at her side.

"Killing him was unwise." The Depth strode towards her, sword in hand. "The punishment for your actions will be worse if I allow the admiral to pass judgement."

She finally managed to stand up. "Sounds like an 'I'm doing this for your own good' speech."

He smiled, the lantern light reflecting off his perfectly white teeth. "I admire your spirit, my dear."

"It must've been bloody terrible to be a woman two hundred years ago," Arke snapped. "It's not great now, but at least the era of patronising manchildren is mostly over."

She backed away, watching his movements warily. She could fight right-handed, but for once she agreed with Stabbington – if she could avoid crossing blades with this particular manchild, she should. His aim had been perfection, his movement was lithe, and his calculating manner wasn't arrogance but more the result of a life lived at the hilt of a sword.

"Patronising what?" he asked, brow briefly furrowed. "No matter."

He sprang towards her, closing the distance far more rapidly than she expected, and the Soulbound had no option but to fight him. She had to wield Stabbington in her right hand as her left arm was a dead weight, so not only was her swordsmanship affected, her normal ability to dodge and weave was also severely disrupted. Her opponent proved to be exactly as skilled as she'd feared and if it hadn't been for Kennedy's alter sprinting silently up the tunnel, Arke would have risked using her magic six desperate parries ago.

"Do not wait any longer!" Stabbington insisted, as she staggered back, blood dripping from a deep cut to her leg. "You *must* push him away!"

Dropping her sword, she hammered two energy blasts into her enemy's chest, their impacts launching him down the tunnel.

Kennedy instantly merged with his altar and levelled his gaze at the swordsman as he landed nearby. "She's injured. Seems a little unsporting."

Leaping to his feet, the Depth's eyes ran over Kennedy with cold assessment. "She's a mage and now I'm outnumbered. Seems similarly unfair." With no further conversation, he bowed and disappeared in a rush of locomotive magic.

"You ok?" Kennedy looked over at the Soulbound as she leant against the wall, gritting her teeth as she eased the knives from her bicep.

"Been better. We need to go."

"I could not agree more." A deep voice, laden with icy nuance, echoed down the tunnel. For a second there was nothing to see, and then a giant figure teleported in front of Arke, arm outstretched and the muzzle of a pistol inches from her forehead.

※ ※ ※

KENNEDY'S EYES WIDENED in shock, but there was no time to react, no time to speak, no time to do anything but hear the deafening blast from black powder igniting and watch Arke crumple to the floor.

"I am Admiral Roland Von Lauken, you are on my island, and I do not tolerate Barsian spies." The tall man crouched briefly, placing his pistols on the ground as he looked towards Kennedy. "But you, you are not. I offer parley while we have a conversation." He began to walk down the tunnel, every step, every expression that of someone accustomed to command. He was dressed in a long sharkskin coat dripping with silver braid and trimmed with iron grey velvet that bore a distinct similarity to the colour of his close-cropped hair and angular beard. "I am curious as to what orders you have, what plans you made. How did she lead you here? Let us talk, man to man."

"I don't parley with filthy murderers!" Kennedy's voice came back to him with a rush, emotion clawing at his throat amid the thunder of anger that shook his body to action.

"Are you going to lie and tell me she doesn't belong to the Autarch? She reeks of his power." The admiral drew his cutlass, the polished blade sliding smoothly from its well-used scabbard.

Kennedy's reply was barely intelligible, a vicious barrage of primal words spat into life. He was lost to fury as his muscles scorched and pulsed, throwing him recklessly at his opponent, each breath ragged with the iron-tinged urge for brutal vengeance. His sword gleamed as he swung it with power that would have cleaved lesser blades in two and staggered enemies to their knees.

However, Von Lauken's massive frame barely acknowledged the blows that sought to shatter his defence. He pushed back, countering with explosive skill, the pair of them bound together by the chains of their duel. Kennedy dived further into instinct, his sword an extension of his arm, his body its anchor, its lever, and its strength. Experience, determination and the vision of Von Lauken as a pile of salt on the ground drove him to exploit every loophole, every trick, every tactic.

Their battle ebbed and flowed, the tunnel reverberating with the sound of steel against steel. Kennedy retreated slowly, baiting his opponent into the nearest cave. The older man was heavier and slower, which would be a disadvantage in an open space. Once there was more room to move, he launched into a chain of attacks, shifting direction and balance with blistering speed. With a feint and a slash, the gleaming silver blade sliced deep into the admiral's hand, but as Kennedy parried a vicious return, he saw only water dripping from the wound.

"I wield the power of the Mother of Salt, the queen of the ocean. You may as well try to fight the sea itself."

Von Lauken drew a dagger with his offhand and surged forwards, forcing Kennedy to throw himself to one side to avoid his charge.

"STAND STILL ALREADY!"

Kennedy was just leaping back to his feet when he heard the shout and stumbled as he turned towards the sound. He blinked in confusion as he saw Arke, blood streaming from her forehead, pointing a pistol at the admiral. She looked alive. She sounded alive. Unexpectedly and wonderfully, amazingly and furiously alive.

"You...!" Von Lauken sputtered, the essence of command that suffused his entire body suddenly faltering.

"No. You!" The Soulbound strode into the cave. *"You web-footed, moist-skinned, water-bleeding WANKER!"*

Kennedy sprinted over to her. She might be alive, but she was badly injured, and an orange haze was clearly building around her left arm. The entrance was behind them, they had a chance to get away, he needed to get her out quickly. "Arke..."

She fired. Von Lauken took half a step backwards before steadying himself. Then he looked down at the water trickling from a hole in his chest, coughed, and watched the deformed projectile fly out to land in a puddle at his feet.

"I didn't expect Cormydd to send me a foul-mouthed whore, but it's been a long while, perhaps he has new ideas. It matters not, I will slice you into ribbons and post you back to him, inch by inch."

"ARKE..." Kennedy insisted, grabbing her arm. They needed to run, teleport – leave – however that could be accomplished the quickest.

Ignoring him, she yanked herself free and stepped forwards slowly as she spoke, the orange glow now covering her entire torso. "*You* sold yourself to the Mother of Salt – you bent right over and begged! And you sold your friends. Your men. People who relied on you. Me? I fought him. I'm still fighting him, and I'm not going to give up! So if anyone's the whore – it's *you*!"

"Do NOT talk to me in that manner!"

"I can see how the truth would upset your gigantic ego. But I don't give a shit what you think. Look what happened to me because of you..." She held up both hands, the right now bearing an identical obsidian ring to the left. "I only used to have one until you shot me, but he doubled them up just to remind me how much I owe him for saving me. That bastard won't even let me DIE because he says he's the only one with power of life and death over me."

Orange light began to flare from her body like flames, and sparks jumped from her boots to the ground as she continued. "How would you feel after taking a bullet to the forehead, only to wake up with his voice in your head? He told me how happy he is to teach me this lesson. How he's *delighted* I needed his help. How he's thrilled to know exactly – where – I – am."

Feral magic rolled down her legs and bubbled across the rock in ripples that expanded with her every word. "I keep saying no. Not that it works. But it's all I have. No. No. No. No..."

She shouted her defiance over and over, her voice rapidly becoming lost in ominous rumbles that shook the cavern. Orange magic flowed from her like a river, diving into cracks in the rocks and disappearing.

Kennedy lunged forwards, but the admiral reached her first, grabbing her by the arms and shaking her.

"Arke, you have to stop this!" Kennedy tried to wrestle her away. "LET HER GO!"

The rumbling intensified, and a jet of steam blasted from a fissure in the wall. Chunks of rock were launched into the air as lava erupted from the floor, and seconds later, the entire mountain started to shake.

Suddenly Von Lauken released his grip, fingers probing the wound on his hand which had been covered in the blood from the Soulbound's left arm. After a strangely intense look at her face, he slammed a heavy fist into her temple.

The instant she lost consciousness, the orange magic stopped cascading from her body, but the cavern kept shaking, and the lava kept pouring. He threw her over his shoulder and started to run to the exit.

"Give her to me!" Kennedy tried to block the way.
"Move or die."
"Then I'm coming with you."

There was no time for either to argue as rocks exploded from every surface and lava covered more than half of the cavern's floor. Kennedy sprinted after Von Lauken as he carried Arke through the tunnels, dodging spurts of steam and leaping fissures as they raced the power of the rapidly waking volcano until they emerged on a beach on the east side of the island.

KENNEDY CLUTCHED THE Soulbound's unconscious body tightly to his chest as a crew of grey-skinned sailors heaved on the oars of the admiral's longboat. Behind them, the volcano was erupting with incredible force, its summit now wreathed in clouds of smoke that were only broken by spears of molten rock shooting high into the sky.

He forced himself to turn away, to slow his breathing, and try to corral his thoughts into a cohesive pattern. The others had had plenty of time to escape and his orders had been clear. They'd have had the gig in the air waiting for he and Arke to appear, and when that didn't happen, Sparkz was smart enough not to hang around an angry volcano.

Setting those worries aside, Kennedy looked down at the Soulbound's bloody face with a renewed sense of purpose. He needed to concentrate on keeping her safe. He had no idea what Von Lauken was intending to do, given the man had made no secret of the fact that he wanted her dead, but even if his change of heart was temporary, it might provide an opportunity to escape.

Chapter Twenty-Eight
Bringing Smexy Back

"You're finally awake."

It was a struggle for Arke to force herself back to consciousness. Her head was pounding, her tongue was dry and all she could smell or taste was sulphur. She tried to distract herself by checking in with every part of her body and quickly wished she hadn't, as there wasn't anywhere that didn't hurt. Memories were trickling through her mind like cloudy snippets of confusion, and she blinked slowly, trying to clear her vision while waiting for her demon to consider her ready to debrief. He always preferred to wait until she'd fully returned to reality – allegedly so he didn't need to keep repeating himself, but also, she suspected, because he loved a good dramatic pause.

"Arke, try to be calm and not overreact," Stabbington began, almost perfectly on cue. "You are unrestrained – at the moment. If you remain compliant, it may allow more opportunities for escape." His tone was soothing, even if his message was not. "You are aboard the Depth's flagship, and Kennedy has negotiated a truce. I do not know where he is, but your location is the admiral's cabin, so you must consider all of your actions and words carefully."

There wasn't much to say in response to that dispiriting news, so Arke concentrated on activating each of her muscle groups, forcing them to respond despite their continued painful feedback. It took a while to motivate her body to move, but finally she was able to persuade herself into a sitting position, even if she had to do it with her eyes tightly shut against gut-wrenching room spin.

"Good evening."

The sound of the admiral's voice drove her eyelids back up in an instant. Hatred always had priority, and although her memory was patchy, she hadn't forgotten her overriding loathing of the man.

She didn't have to clear her vision to see his towering figure at the foot of the bed, but as her focus returned, she noticed he was holding a glass containing a murky-looking liquid.

"There is a truce in place, your friend Kennedy is unharmed. However, understand this – I have no need for him to remain in possession of his life. Keep your claws, your sword, and your magic to yourself and he will continue as my guest. Whatever happens to him is *your* choice. Is that clear?"

It was obvious his hospitality was purely transactional – she had something he wanted, something that Kennedy did not possess. The implications made her skin crawl.

"Compliance should bring more opportunities to escape." Stabbington was a well-practiced voice of reason. "I know you will not act like a helpless damsel, but at least try to pretend you do not want to rip his tongue out through his spine."

Arke nodded, deliberately avoiding eye contact with Von Lauken as she replied. "If there is an agreement then I'll abide by it. But I need to see Kennedy."

"He'll be at dinner. Drink this." He moved closer, offering the glass. "It will help you feel better."

"So would a bottle of rum."

"No amount of alcohol could get you on your feet in time for dinner, but I promise this can. We have no use for medicine on board, so I cannot offer anything for your wounds bar bandages and rest, but this draught will increase your energy."

Glaring up at him, Arke took the glass and sniffed its contents suspiciously before tasting a little, surprised to find the ditchwater-coloured liquid had no flavour at all. Downing it in a single gulp, she sank back against the pillows as the admiral walked away.

Looking curiously around the huge room, she saw that one corner contained another bed, but the rest of the floor-space was taken up with tables and cupboards. Tracking her gaze from unit to unit, she listened to Stabbington remarking on the sheer amount of hide bound journals and the oddly eclectic range of items. Ancient statuettes and strange artefacts rubbed shoulders with rolls of parchment, amulets, and modern tools.

"Were you expecting my quarters to be full of women and wine?" Von Lauken was seated at a desk but had clearly been watching her. "I have better things to do with my time."

"This truce means nothing to you, it's just a method to control me. Why?" Whatever he'd given her to drink wasn't in the same league as *Go* juice, but it was clearing her head and energising her body. She eased herself off the bed, the sword slash on her leg burning under the sudden load, but she ignored it and limped towards the admiral.

He stood up and gestured to his chair. "Sit down and I will explain."

"I'll stand."

His hand shot out, his fingers fastening around her injured arm, and a moment of excruciating pain later, she was involuntarily seated, and he released her from his iron grip.

"A good officer picks their battles – that was not one you could win. And now your wounds need re-bandaging."

"A good officer? Is that what you think you are?" She forced her words out through gritted teeth as he peeled away the bandage from her bicep. The deep punctures from the knives had been painful on their own, but after his giant hand had squeezed them, it felt like her entire arm was on fire.

"Be silent and watch this."

He picked up a blade from his desk and sliced it across his palm, water springing instantly from the cut. Then, with the dull side of the knife, he scraped some blood from around her wounds and spread it over the incision. The red liquid hissed and bubbled on contact, but when he wiped it away, his skin was perfectly healed.

"I have been searching for over a hundred years for something that could free me from my curse." He leant over her, a hand on each armrest, his expression so intense it bordered on fanatical. "My crews have collected countless items, books, creatures, ingredients, *anything* that held a suggestion of hope. We have found nothing. Not a single thing that even hinted at a cure. Until you. Whatever you are, whatever you have – I *will* know it. That bitch said that only her salt could heal and sustain us. But if a little of your blood can do this, then what else might it be able to do?"

It took several slow breaths for the Soulbound to force both her temper and her bile back down after Von Lauken's speech. The presence of the medical style bed she'd been lying on and all the unusual implements and artefacts around the room had suddenly become far more alarming.

She was still trying to fashion some sort of reply that wouldn't end in violence when he started to re-bandage her arm, his touch brusquely businesslike as he continued to speak.

"Be assured that you have no choice, I will take what I require regardless of your opposition. That being said, I would much prefer you to be compliant, so let me make my case. You will want for nothing. Food, drink, clothes, jewellery, servants, anything you desire, with Kennedy safe and well at your side."

"Jazz it up all you like, you're still telling me I'm your science experiment."

"I have offered excellent terms for your willing participation."

Pushing herself to her feet, Arke kept her tone steady as she spoke. "Firstly, I'm going to need a proper bed and not that glorified torture table. There is no way you can convince me you haven't dissected hundreds of poor souls on that thing."

"And secondly?"

"Kennedy must never know the terms of our agreement."

※ ※ ※

"Arke!"

Kennedy's face lit up with a bright smile and he leapt up from the table so fast that his chair shot backwards. Striding across to the Soulbound, he wrapped his arms around her, smooshing her to his chest without a millisecond of hesitation. He didn't care that everyone in the officer's mess was watching, or that the appetisers were in the process of being served by a mob of shambling sailors. He was so happy to see her that nothing else mattered. The fact that his hug was almost instantly returned pleased him even better, and the anxious knot in his stomach all but disappeared. Sure, they were on the largest warship he'd ever seen, surrounded by hundreds of enemies, in the middle of the ocean, heading who knew where, but as Kennedy embraced her, he also chose to embrace positivity. They were together, she was ok, everything would work out.

"You can let me go now."

Her voice was muffled, but the fingertip poked in his side spoke volumes, and he stepped away, looking her up and down with a wry smile.

"Nice threads. Bringing smexy back."

Despite her preference for simple, utilitarian clothes, Kennedy had seen Arke wear whatever was necessary to get a job done. However, he'd never seen her combine bandages, an evening dress, and a military style jacket. In fact, he'd never seen that particular combination on anyone, although as he took stock of her outfit, he couldn't help but admire the statement she'd clearly intended to make.

The Depths had been isolated from Barsia for over two hundred years, so life on their flagship was like taking a step backwards in time. If Kennedy was honest, he'd been fascinated by everything around him – the lavishly decorated rooms, the strict hierarchy, and the intricacies in social interactions. He'd even enjoyed dressing for dinner in the old-fashioned outfit they'd provided. However, the moment he'd seen two female officers, resplendent in their gowns, feathers, wigs and shimmering jewellery, the magic of the history lesson suddenly evaporated. He knew Arke, and he knew how she'd feel about being expected to dress like that.

"Apparently women don't wear trousers to dinner," she muttered.

"And it's bullshit," he agreed. "But you made the right choice, keeping the peace seems the most sensible move at the moment. Y..." He bit back another comment, unsure if it would inflame matters.

"What?"

"Ah. I was just going to say you looked great. Inspired fusion of pirate and formal."

"That's not why I did it. I couldn't let that prick have it all his own way." She flashed him a brief smile. "I grabbed the jacket as we left – after all it'd be dangerous for me to catch a chill."

From the other end of the room, the admiral cleared his throat expectantly, his eyes fixed on Arke. She turned to see that he was holding out one of the chairs at the head of the table before looking back at Kennedy, her lips pursed in a thin line.

"Nope," she muttered. "I'm not sitting up there."

"You know I'll always follow your lead, but..."

She frowned. "Are you about to tell me this isn't the hill we want to die on?"

"Actually, I was going to ask if your revolution can wait till after the main course? I'm really hungry and it smells delicious." Kennedy piled on the boyish charm and hoped Stabbington was busy backing him up. The 'truce' was just imprisonment with a twist, but while it was on offer, they needed to take full advantage.

"Fine."

Everyone remained standing as she limped her way to her seat at the end of the table, her figure dwarfed by Von Lauken's sheer bulk.

The admiral held out a hand. "Your jacket?"

"Isn't it lovely?" Arke replied, deliberately misunderstanding his words and sitting down before he had chance to strip it from her shoulders.

She didn't see the brief flash of fury cross Von Lauken's face as he eased her chair closer to the table, but Kennedy did, and it gave him instant heartburn. Something about the Soulbound always seemed to draw a certain sort of person into her orbit. He even remembered his mother joking about how Arke was catnip for arrogant arseholes. Occasionally it went in their favour, and she made friends in high places, but in general, it went to shit.

As the dinner continued, Kennedy watched the decidedly stilted interplay between the admiral and his 'guest'. There had never been any doubt what was going to be the issue between Arke and Von Lauken. He was a domineering prick who preferred obedient women in dresses. Whereas she preferred domineering pricks who expected women to be obedient, bleeding out at her feet.

Anxiety about potential jacket-gate repercussions kept Kennedy awake most of the night. He knew there was nothing he could do without causing a massive diplomatic incident, but that didn't stop him from worrying. During his negotiations with the admiral, Von Lauken had assured him they would be treated as honoured guests, but that was before the Soulbound had regained consciousness.

Concerned that he'd missed one of their standard safe words, Kennedy forced himself to remember every syllable of his conversation with Arke. The lack of any was scant comfort, as he knew their absence didn't mean she wasn't in trouble, but it did mean she didn't want him to do anything. With all that on his mind, peaceful sleep was never an option.

A tap on his door at seven the next morning heralded an unexpected visitor. Kennedy greeted Lieutenant Orville politely, keeping his tone as neutral and his posture as relaxed as he could make it. Although they'd been properly introduced at last night's dinner, Kennedy hadn't had the inclination to spend time with the swordsman who'd caused some of the Soulbound's injuries back at the volcano. He knew that was a 'him' problem, as Orville had shown nothing but friendly respect since their arrival on the flagship. However, he was also aware it was far easier to be magnanimous in victory.

"I brought you some coffee." Orville held out a steaming mug. "And thought I'd ask if you fancied a tour. The admiral's orders updated this morning – as long as you're escorted, you're free to roam."

"I'd like to go and see Arke first."

"Could be a bit of a wait. The boss told us she'd had a rough night, so we're all to keep the noise down around his cabin, let her sleep it off."

Kennedy blew on his drink and waited in case an awkward silence might persuade Orville to reveal any other information, but after a pregnant pause, it was clear nothing else was forthcoming.

"As soon as she wakes up then."

"Absolutely." The lieutenant gestured towards the corridor. "In the meantime, please let me show you around the most fearsome ship in the Western Ocean."

Despite his deepening concerns for the Soulbound's wellbeing, Kennedy decided knowledge was power and activity was better than fretting. He'd already experienced the opulent rooms on the officers' deck – polished oak walls hung with gold framed paintings and floors covered in the thickest of carpets. Orville's tour headed past those and into the heart of the flagship. The *Depthcharge* was fully five decks tall and carried an incredible number of cannon and crew. Kennedy had never seen such a gigantic vessel, nor so many guns in one place before. However, its sheer size and firepower was easier to get used to than the hundreds of shuffling sailors that manned the ship. Orville barely paid them any attention, bar barking orders at any in his way, but Kennedy was unnerved by the soulless dead eyes, the grotesque greying skin, and the absolute silence. Crews weren't silent. Even if they were trying to be quiet, they still made noise. They still breathed.

After the disturbing experience touring the gun decks, Kennedy was relieved to emerge topside, where more of the officers he'd met at dinner were engaging in some remarkably idle combat training. Their sloppy footwork and bored expressions showed exactly what they thought of their morning's exercises, but in his opinion, absolutely anything they did was preferable to the gloomy silence below.

"Put a bit of bloody effort in! Just because the old man's not out here, doesn't give you an excuse to slack off!" Orville snapped as he led Kennedy towards the port side. "Clement's supposed to be supervising but he's sleeping off his hangover so the lazy bastards are taking advantage."

"Guess you have to have some sort of routine."

"The admiral is fanatical about keeping us sharp." Orville pointed over the gunwales. "Not that we're the reason the squadron is still going strong. The flagship is a monster but she's slow. The frigates are the secret to our success. There's three tethered each side, or should be – but we're missing the *Sorrel* – Cutler's ship. We found her anchored in the bay by the volcano, no-one aboard. Didn't happen to see any of the crew while you were there, did you?"

Kennedy shook his head. "No. Though to be honest we'd only just pulled in to find some fresh water."

"Guess it'll have to remain a mystery," Orville shrugged. "Now come on, what do you think of these beauties?"

Secured to the side of the *Depthcharge* in a perfect line were three frigates, all with crews of shambling sailors dotted around their decks. They were utterly dwarfed by the five decker, but Kennedy was more familiar with their type, and cast an appreciative eye over their fine lines. The old Barsian Empire had some terrible social expectations, but it certainly knew how to build an exceptional warship.

"Von Lauken calls them our hounds – they can take down smaller vessels or chase larger ones straight to us. There's nothing in this ocean we can't beat."

Kennedy made what he hoped were dutifully polite replies as an enthusiastic Orville continued to rattle on about tonnage, cannon, and tactics. His mind was elsewhere, busy worrying about the Soulbound as well as a new concern, that the *Warrior* would come after them and end up as matchsticks under the guns of the *Depthcharge* and her frigates.

THERE WAS NO news of Arke all day, despite Kennedy's repeated prompting. The officers were clearly in awe of their admiral, and not a single one would volunteer to disturb him when he'd given orders to the contrary. It was a singularly frustrating situation, and the only positive thing that came from it was the lessening of Kennedy's desire to exact revenge on Orville. The lieutenant appeared to be about as decent a person as could be expected. He was good company – surprisingly empathetic to his guest's worries, and an excellent purveyor of entertainment. After an afternoon of cards, billiards, chess, checkers and darts, Kennedy was almost surprised to hear the pre-dinner bell tolling.

"Time flies when you're winning many, many hands of poker," Orville chuckled, as Kennedy turned to look at the clock. "You're virtually a matchstick magnate, my friend."

"My riches know no bounds." Kennedy patted his mountain of winnings with a smile, then looked over to the wardroom doors as the other officers were hurrying out. "What's the rush?"

"They're heading to change for dinner. You'll have to forgive their excitement, it's not often we have guests to entertain." Orville stubbed out his cigar and stood up.

"Or to entertain you."

"Ahh... maybe." The lieutenant shifted awkwardly from foot to foot. "We've had no drama here since... well, ever." He turned back to look at Kennedy, expression suddenly animated. "You know her best, do you think she'll keep trying to push the old man's buttons?"

THE OFFICERS' MESS was a riot of expectation that was audible from the end of the corridor until the moment Kennedy walked in. As the door swung shut behind him, the room went silent and as he glanced around, barely anyone looked at him. He'd made awkward entrances before, but that had to rank as one of the most uncomfortable.

Orville stepped out from the crowd, carrying a bottle and two glasses. "Looking sharp, captain." As he handed a glass to Kennedy, he waved a hand towards his colleagues. "As you were, gentlemen."

It took mere seconds before the room began to buzz with renewed conversations and Kennedy downed his drink without even tasting it. He knew there was no scenario in which he was going to enjoy his meal – if Arke didn't appear, then he'd worry; if she appeared and did nothing provocative immediately, then he'd be on edge waiting for something to happen. And if, or more likely, when, she rocked up and started a fight, he'd be right at her side. No matter the situation, wherever she went, he'd always follow.

Downing a second shot, Kennedy closed his eyes briefly, letting the warmth of the alcohol burn a hefty dose of clarity into him. He'd leap into the flaming bowels of the deepest hell with her, but surely it wasn't wrong to wish that, just occasionally, she'd consider taking the stairs?

The officers' anticipation hit what felt like full volume when word came down that dinner should be served as the admiral and his guest were running a little late. Orville took the seat beside Kennedy, clearly endeavouring to find a line of conversation that would distract him from the theories about their tardiness that were being loudly debated up and down the table. His attempts would always have been in vain, especially when some of the bolder Depths kept asking Kennedy rather too personal questions about his absent friend. He ignored them all while trying to force himself to eat something instead of giving in to the urge to stare at the entrance.

The main course was about to be served when Von Lauken disappointed his entire staff. The doors swung open, causing perfect silence to fall over the room, but when the admiral stalked in, he was alone.

"Stay seated, gentlemen. My guest sends her apologies, she is still not feeling quite the thing and will not be attending dinner."

The disheartening news leeched energy from every officer at the table. Kennedy felt his emotions lurch from relief to worry and back again until he tasked himself to prepare the perfect phrases to persuade the admiral to allow him access to the Soulbound. Planning was the most soothing thing he could do, given the circumstances. He would wait until the man had a good meal and bottle or two of wine in him and then ask for an audience.

However, he needn't have wasted his time. The gravy had barely been poured when the doors opened again and Arke walked in. A ragged chorus of chairs being pushed backwards, and cutlery being abandoned on plates greeted her as the officers lurched to their feet.

"Are you ok?" Kennedy moved swiftly to her side, his gaze focused on her face. She looked paler than she had yesterday, with dark circles under her eyes and a pinched look to her cheeks.

"Wounds needed a bit of debriding, but these pricks lost their surgeon years ago. No matter, because all a woman needs for happiness is a beautiful dress." There wasn't so much of an edge to her whisper as a whisper to her edge.

"Arke," Kennedy hissed, "you don't always need to bash your head against a door until it opens."

Von Lauken's voice rang out across the room, his commanding tone instantly silencing whatever she might have said in return. "Come and sit down, my dear, you've had a long day."

"You should go..." Kennedy frowned.

"Don't worry." She flashed him the brightest of smiles. "I intend to."

If he was surprised by Arke's reaction to the admiral's thinly veiled order, as Kennedy watched her limp away, he realised several things in quick succession. Firstly, the gown she was wearing was... incredible. The style was far more modern than any he'd seen aboard, and he guessed it had been looted from one of the *Depthcharge's* recent victims. It clung where it should cling and flowed where it should flow. It was elegant, eye-catching, and exactly what every man in the room was staring at. Kennedy had zero doubt that the dress had not been the Soulbound's choice, which explained the self-satisfied look on Von Lauken's face.

His second observation was that her limp was far more pronounced and the bandages on her arm had increased in thickness and coverage.

The third thing was the boots. Definitely the boots. For all that was holy, unholy, or undecided, the boots.

With a wider smile that eased its charm over every officer at the table, Arke addressed the room with the most delicately earnest tone Kennedy had ever heard slide from her lips.

"My apologies for disrupting your dinner, gentlemen. You have no idea how long it took to get into this thing."

The admiral nodded his head approvingly, and Kennedy, who could barely take his eyes off her footwear, felt his heartburn ramp up at least two more notches. She wasn't so much playing with fire as covering herself with oil while smoking a cigar. It wasn't difficult to guess at the sequence of events that had led to this particular accident waiting to happen.

The incredible dress had probably been the reason Von Lauken was late – Kennedy couldn't imagine any world in which Arke would cheerfully acquiesce to wearing it, so he assumed there had been some sort of stalemate, which had resulted in the admiral coming to dinner alone.

It was hardly a leap of faith to surmise that once he was out of the way, she'd slipped into the burgundy satin gown... and the admiral's boots. They were about six sizes too large, and so long that the tops covered her knees. Everyone behind her had the perfect view of the terrible things since 'someone' had deliberately torn away part of the skirt at the back of the dress to showcase their act of defiance.

By the time Arke reached her seat, all the officers had taken the opportunity to marvel at her choice of footwear. Every gaze was focused on the admiral, and an expectant silence fell. As Kennedy watched, he was only vaguely aware that his hand was gripping the hilt of his sword with an intensity that left his fingers numb.

However, on this occasion, Von Lauken's expression didn't falter, his smile fixed in place as he slid Arke's chair closer to the table, his voice loud enough to be heard across the entire room. "It appears my lesson on etiquette must be repeated. Not to worry, my dear, we'll go over it *all* again after dinner."

Chapter Twenty-Nine
A Dress Too Far

Having realised the only way he was going to get any sleep after witnessing Von Lauken's honeyed creep mode was to drink himself into a stupor, Kennedy had done just that. He woke the next morning clutching a bucket and wishing the Depths had a healer on board. Alcohol had knocked him out and muddied the memories he had of the previous evening, but as always, there was a painful price to pay.

"You look rough."

The sound of an unexpected voice threw Kennedy into sudden panic, and he leapt to his feet, dropping the bucket, and swearing as it caught his little toe on its way to the floor.

"Are your entire crew this dramatic or is it just you and your tomboy friend?" Orville, steaming mug of coffee in hand, was sitting at the tiny table by the door.

"Are your entire crew outdated douchebags or is it just you and your admiral?" Kennedy sat back down on the bed, rubbing his foot as he waited for repercussions. He knew his reply hadn't merely crossed the line of acceptable replies, it had leapt it with both middle fingers raised while wearing a T-shirt with a picture of a baboon's buttocks on it.

"No, it's definitely all of us." The lieutenant chuckled as he turned back to the table and reached for a second mug. "Coffee?"

Kennedy was about to get dressed when he saw a bandage wrapped around his arm. Peering under it with a frown, a hazy memory leaked past his pounding headache. "Did we really duel in the dark? I thought it was a dream but..."

"Unfortunately not. It was a damned stupid idea – we're used to being saltily indestructible, but we could've got you killed."

"As I recall, it was your guys getting their arses kicked." Not even a hangover could smother Kennedy's chuckle as he remembered the previous night in a little more detail.

"The arrogance of alcohol," Orville shrugged. "Arm ok though?"

"Ask me later when everything else has stopped hurting. Any news about Arke?"

"Same as yesterday. Another day of rest – she didn't sleep well."

"What a surprise," Kennedy replied, with no attempt to disguise his accusatory tone. "I'm going back to bed, I'm sure you can see yourself out."

Orville nodded, slipping on his jacket before heading to the door. "I'll catch you later."

WHETHER IT WAS a sign that he'd been accepted after the midnight duelling session or simply indicative of the excitement among the officers, Kennedy wasn't certain, but as he strode into the mess that evening, the buzz barely faltered. A few of them greeted him by name, and Orville seemed to appear from nowhere with a shot of something heady, but Kennedy walked straight to his seat. He'd felt better around mid-afternoon, but the experience of physical peace had been fleeting as every tick of the clock brought dinnertime closer. Nursing a glass of water garnished with a feeling of impending doom, he tried to block out the excited chatter that bounced round the table as everyone waited for the admiral and his guest.

Sudden silence heralded their arrival and Kennedy stood, taking a deep breath before he turned. He didn't know what he was expecting, but what he saw wasn't it, or anywhere near it. Whatever had happened to the Soulbound had left her vacant-eyed and passive. It had also left her dressed in something which was both an affront to her style and her dignity. Kennedy was sure that back in the day, women probably didn't have to be coerced to flounce around in blush pink satin gowns with puffy sleeves and full skirts. But this was not two hundred odd years ago, and whatever had been done to Arke to make her wear the thing needed to be undone in a hurry.

"Good evening Von Lauken." Kennedy nodded curtly. "You and I need to talk."

"Captain Kennedy. I would love to stop, but as you can see, your friend isn't feeling quite herself." The admiral ushered the vacant-eyed Soulbound on, the air of a well-satisfied tiger emanating from his every pore. "Come along my dear, let's get you sitting down."

"Steady." Orville stepped in front of Kennedy as he went to follow. "You'll only make it worse."

"*Move!*" he growled.

"Think about it!" the lieutenant hissed. "This way he doesn't 'remind' her of her lack of manners after dinner."

Kennedy could barely drag his eyes from Arke's stilted movements as she walked to the top of the table with the admiral's hand pressed firmly to the middle of her back. Finally, he looked at Orville, the lieutenant's words having filtered through his anger. "Sounds like you and I need to have a conversation about what you haven't been telling me."

"Later," Orville whispered. "If you manage to keep your mouth shut."

※ ※ ※

When the last thing you remember is a quiet cabin and the overwhelming scent of roses, suddenly waking up in the middle of a room full of people is understandably disconcerting. Arke blinked rapidly, trying to dispel the rest of the flower-flavoured haze that hummed behind her eyes.

"Previously I have counselled you to remain calm and measured in your responses." Stabbington's voice was muffled, although his host clearly felt his venom spitting through her. "But not only has this egotistical, fanatical, arrogant piece of million-year-old jerky pissed all over the agreement by drugging you... his taste in dresses makes me want to rip his intestines out through his eye sockets."

Rubbing a hand across her face as she listened to her demon's rage, Arke finally took note of what she was wearing. The dress's low-cut front reminded her she wasn't built for topless waitressing. Its puffball sleeves were so large they could be used to teach children to swim, and the dusky pink ruched material looked like someone had seen a pig's arsehole and tried to recreate it in fabric.

With a deliberate turn, which was more to do with the way her body was taking its time to wake up than any attempt at intimidation, Arke settled her gaze on the admiral.

"Dinner is almost over, but I can assure you that you ate well, smiled beautifully and have been nothing but wonderfully appropriate all evening." Von Lauken looked down at her with the self-satisfied expression that had become painfully familiar every time he used her flesh to test his theories. He was winning – and loving it.

Keeping her eyes firmly on his, Arke slipped out of a pair of deeply uncomfortable heels and planted her aching soles on the hem of the incredibly unflattering gown. Then she explosively pushed herself to her feet.

With an audible rip, the dress fell apart, most of the fabric sliding to the floor, leaving only the puffball sleeves in place. Von Lauken launched himself upright, his chair clattering into the wall behind him. So Arke sat down, calmly availing herself of a new napkin and smoothing it over the petticoat, which was the only thing between her and a nakedness she was sure wasn't an accepted feature of any etiquette in history.

The admiral swept her entire dinner setting to the floor. "How dare you abuse my hospitality at my own table!"

"Where I come from, hospitality doesn't include drugging your guests to make them wear what you want them to!" She stood back up, ripping first one pink sleeve off and then the other before throwing them at Von Lauken's feet. "If you like this dress so much, *you* put it on!"

"Admiral." Kennedy was standing, hands raised in a placatory fashion. "I don't know what's going on here but honestly the best way to handle Arke is to let her be herself. If she wants to wear pyjamas and waders with a feather boa to dinner, so what? The more you restrict her the more she'll fight back. You don't control her, you just don't."

"I think you'll find that I absolutely do." Von Lauken's voice was suddenly as cold as the two steel blades that grazed Kennedy's neck. "Arke, we had an agreement, and I would remind you of it. Make your choice."

Kennedy froze. "Agreement?"

"She has something I want." The anger in the admiral's expression had been replaced with that self-same satisfied smile. "Arke, perhaps you should explain to Captain Kennedy how he is still, currently, alive."

"Arke?"

Dressed only in her petticoat, she limped slowly towards Kennedy. He had an officer standing on either side of him, each pressing a dagger to his neck. No-one bothered to stop her, and inside her head she could hear Stabbington revelling in their ridiculous arrogance. He knew what she was about to do, and the complacence of the Depths made it so much easier.

"What have you agreed...?" Kennedy asked, a deep furrow between his brows.

"I'm sorry, I should have said something..." she reached out, taking one of his hands in her own.

She saw the brief flash of anticipation cross his face just before she summoned Stabbington and slammed the tip of his blade to the floor. The explosive energy of her teleportation spell ignited around them, and in a split second, she and Kennedy were standing on one of the frigates lashed to the side of the flagship.

Reacting quickly, he dragged her into the shelter of the ship's gig. "What's going on? What is it he wants?"

"My blood. It's some sort of salt replacement – so he'll be able to exist without the Mother. He's doing experiments to find out what the active ingredient is and what exactly it can do, but honestly, he's just an amateur pissing in the dark."

"Experiments? Well, that's not happening anymore. We need to go – over the side, quickly." He tugged at her hand, but she pulled back, shaking her head.

"I have a better escape plan." She clicked her fingers and with a crackle of blue light, her Rottweiler-flavoured hellhound appeared on the deck beside them. Leaping up at her face, Dozer swiped a tongue from her chin to her eyebrow before Arke pushed him away. "This idiot will fly you back to the ship."

"What? I'm not going without you!"

"He can't take us both. Von Lauken won't kill me, but he'd happily dish you up for one of his stupid dinners. Head for Levenbrandt and tell Kromm everything. We both know the *Warrior* can't fight this beast alone – you need backup, and you can't get much better than him."

Voices started shouting on the deck of the *Depthcharge*, and all around the monstrous ship, lanterns were sputtering into life as the alert spread.

He hugged her quickly. "We'll be back for you."

"Not on your own. Promise me. Now get aboard the good dog Dozer."

Hearing his favourite words, the Rottweiler's tail started to wag, and his wings flared out with a creak of infernal leather. Kennedy tried to settle himself astride the hellhound, but his expression showed exactly how uncomfortable he felt.

"I'm really not sure about this! I can just about encourage a horse from A to B, but riding a flying dog...?"

"You'll be fine. Lean over his neck and hold on tight! Now go!" The Soulbound watched as Dozer galloped forwards and then launched himself into the air, powerful wings beating perfectly in sync with his happy tail.

As the hellhound and his passenger disappeared into darkness, Arke started to shiver. This part of the Western Ocean wasn't known for its temperate climate, and there was more than one reason petticoats weren't worn on their own. She'd been cold since Von Lauken had been using her blood for experiments, and her current situation was devastatingly frigid.

"And now it is time to go inside," Stabbington observed, his tone calmly factual. "You have done all you can, Kennedy is no longer at risk, and your teeth are chattering – which is wildly irritating."

"If I was a lady I'd apologise," Arke retorted, with a snort of laughter.

Her demon's reply was slow to come, but when it did, it was unexpectedly pointed. "Without that divorce, you are rather more than a Lady. What will happen when they find out?"

With a sudden burst of anger, she slammed his blade to the deck, initiating another teleport that shot her into the admiral's quarters with a reverberation that echoed through the entire Depth fleet.

"He is no good for you, Arke! He broke your heart! His mother wanted you dead! Are you so colour-blind that you cannot see all the red flags?"

"I'm not arguing with you." She limped across to the fire, adding a log and watching the embers flare into flame.

"Because you know I am right! It will happen again, and I will be the one to put all the pieces back together."

She stayed silent and let the warmth start to spread around her body as her demon continued his rant. It was going to get personal because it was personal. He'd been with her for all of her adult life. He'd been the voice no-one else could hear, the friend she would never be without. He'd been the difference between keeping going and giving up. He deserved to be heard. She listened until his storm blew itself out, his words exhausting themselves, his fury only weary sighs.

"So what do you want me to do?" she whispered, watching the fire dance in the grate.

"Not fall on his tongue like a postage stamp?"

"Ouch."

"The truth hurts, yes?"

There was silence, only broken by the sound of heavy footsteps striding towards the cabin door.

"Probably not as much as having pissed Von Lauken off again."

"Probably not. But two good things have come from this evening – Kennedy is safe, and I do not think you will be invited to dinner anymore."

Chapter Thirty
Smoke on the Water

KENNEDY'S RETURN TO the *Warrior* caused a storm of its own, the deck erupting with excitement and relief as he and his weary steed finally touched down. Questions were flung at him with volume and speed, but Sparkz took charge, ushering his brother into his cabin and shutting the doors firmly behind him.

"Let's give the big man chance to take a piss and change his clothes," Sparkz ordered before glancing at Lewis' anxious face. "Don't worry, kid. If Dozer's here, Arke's fine."

"Are you sure?"

"Yes. She's the only one who can summon that lump of gristle and slobber she calls a dog."

"He IS a dog!" Lewis scowled.

"Whatever you say, buddy." Sparkz looked around at the others. "While we wait, we'll fire up the toaster and get a brew going – THEN we can find out how that son of a bitch managed to outrun a volcano!"

The crew had never been known for their patience, although they did just about manage to listen to Kennedy's tale in silence. It was only when he finished that the cabin erupted with almost as much force as the volcano. Everyone had something to say, and in order to be heard, they had to shout louder than the person next to them. The air was thick with wrathful comments about Arke's situation, hilarity at her treatment of the hideous dress, and heaps of praise for the loyal hellhound.

Krugg poured Dozer a bucket of tea and Urzish massaged his shoulders while Lewis hand-fed him buttery toast until his burps had crumbs in. Finally, with a yawn and a lick of Kennedy's face, the Rottweiler waddled out of the door and created his own version of a monsoon against the nearest barrel before demanding to be let into Arke's room. Ibu quickly encouraged Lewis to accompany the dog and make sure he wasn't lonely in the absence of his mistress.

"Lonely? He'll be sprawled on her bed snoring within five minutes," Sparkz commented, adding more sugar to his own mug of tea.

"Exactly. I'm hoping Lewis does the same, the poor boy hasn't slept properly since the volcano – he's convinced he's some sort of bad luck charm," Ibu retorted.

"And I hope you told him he wasn't," Kennedy replied, eyeing the last piece of toast. It was only small, but he was very, very full.

"Of course. We told him crazy shit had been happening on the *Warrior* for months," Ellie added quickly.

"And that was fine – until you started telling him the stories in all their gory detail!" Ibu's expression made her disapproval very clear. "He's a child!"

"Annnyway..." Kennedy cleared his throat, placing the tiny square of toast back on his plate. "Now you're all up to speed, if no-one has any brighter ideas than Arke's, I'm setting a course for Levenbrandt."

"Sounds as if it's our only option." Ellie turned to the others. "Right, you lot – we need permanent eyes on the horizon. Double up the watches. Shout out at the first sign of anything that resembles a ship, even if it ends up being a seagull strapped to a whale's forehead."

"What she said." Kennedy yawned and stood up, heading to his chart table as everyone began to file out. "Lieutenant Vaughan, if you could spare me a little time. I want you to tell me about the Mother of Salt. Like, for example, how to let her know that Von Lauken is trying to wriggle out of his deal…"

⚹ ⚹ ⚹

Several torrid days after Kennedy's escape, Arke woke to the sound of Stabbington humming and the deliberately unsubtle attempts of Orville to rouse her from her slumbers.

"If you keep tapping the china together, it'll break," she growled.

"I am an artiste, and these are my instruments. The humble teapot, the delicate cup, and the wickedly indecent saucer."

After the night of Kennedy's escape, Von Lauken had assigned his second lieutenant to care for the Soulbound. Whether it was punishment for failing to secure the *Warrior's* captain or because Orville had offered, Arke wasn't sure. However, what she was certain of was that, despite a sterling effort on her part, she couldn't bring herself to hate him. He appeared to be unflappably affable, no matter what she said or did.

She pulled the covers over her head and growled out some phrases that would have definitely had her arrested, if not exorcised, in any city in Barsia.

"I bet you say that to all your devilishly handsome jailers." The blankets were peeled back, and Orville smiled down at her. "Your tea is brewing and your breakfast..." he pulled out his pocket watch, "brunch..." he peered at the hands, a deliberately quizzical expression on his face, "lunch is ready."

"Fine. But you're going to want to step outside while I use my luxury, state of the art bathroom."

"Not everyone gets a seat on their bucket," Orville replied with a chuckle. He was heading to the screens that separated Arke's area from the rest of the cabin when he turned to point in her direction. "Don't go back to sleep. Scrambled eggs never taste great when they're cold, and you know he'll make you eat them regardless."

She knew that all too well, and despite her exhaustion, a sudden flood of anger burnt its way down to the scar on her palm. As she'd expected, after Kennedy's escape, Von Lauken's mask had dropped, and she'd steeled herself for any number of violent reprisals. However, on finding her warming herself by the fire in his cabin, the admiral had elected to follow a different path.

"This room is now your prison, and know this – your behaviour will decide whether you are treated like a person or a beast. You will be kept healthy, you will eat and drink what we provide for you and rest when you are told; I will tolerate no attempts to avoid your part in my work. There is wondrous symmetry in the Autarch's property providing me what I need to escape the deal he forced me into." He'd paused and then leant down, his dark eyes drilling into her own. "But listen well, misbehave one more time and my ships will hunt your *Warrior* down. Our guns will send her and every soul on board to meet the Mother personally. I might even ask her to make them into crew for the *Depthcharge* so you can all be together again."

As those recent memories threw themselves into her head, Arke felt a sudden shiver pass through her before the pressure of her feral magic ceased. Her skin no longer prickled with energy but stretched with icy dullness over her bones. Things were slowing, her thoughts, her mind, herself, as dread cast its twisted cord across her chest. Stabbington was speaking, calling out something that might have been her name, but there wasn't enough of her to answer. She was cold and quiet and so very alone.

In what seemed like a blink of an eye, she realised she was on her feet, though she couldn't feel her legs, every connection to her body having dropped into the aching void. Orville was in front of her, his mouth opening and shutting, but she couldn't make out the words through the freezing stillness. He was lifting her arms and as her vision finally narrowed to one single, desperate point of focus, she saw her hand was running with blood.

Then she was all but lost, hearing only distantly the sharp clang of an alarm bell and the sound of a tremendous explosion that shook the entire *Depthcharge* to its beam ends.

✕ ✕ ✕

Kennedy was sipping coffee and writing in the ship's logbook when Ellie burst into his cabin.

"Captain, cannon fire from the southeast."

The familiar sound hit him the moment he stepped outside, a distant rumbling that echoed across the waves.

"It just keeps going," Ruby was standing at the rail, her head tilted to one side as she listened.

"That's a lot of guns," Kennedy noted. "A hell of a lot."

"Maybe it's the ship Arke's on?" The Ornithol's voice was almost squeaky with excitement.

"That's not necessarily a good thing," Ellie frowned. "Cap says it could sneeze and blow us to matchsticks."

"There's no harm looking." Kennedy grinned at Ruby. "Fancy taking a peek? Long-distance view only. Take no risks. Just find out what's fighting what."

As the Ornithol soared away from the ship, Kennedy strode to the helm and rang the bell for battle stations before bringing the *Warrior's* bow around to face the sounds of cannon fire.

"Ellie, I want every stitch of canvas we have on the yards. This baby might not be in the air, but she can still fly."

The Warrior was at full speed, launching itself across the waves as Ruby came in hotter than anyone had ever seen and skidded to a halt on the main deck. Kennedy strode over as she struggled to regain her breath after what had clearly been a breakneck flight. The closer they got to the sounds of battle, the more the hairs on the back of his neck prickled with the same sense of dread he'd felt before they were shot out of the sky. He needed to know what was happening before it was too late to change course.

"You ok, Rubes?"

She nodded, smoothing down her feathers in a distracted fashion. "Yeah. I... saw the... battle. It's moving this way."

"Good. And...?" Kennedy frowned as he watched her open and shut her beak several times. "Was there a giant ship there? Five decks? A load of frigates nearby?"

"Yes. The smoke is thick, but I saw enough."

"Who's she fighting?" he prompted as her voice tailed off.

"Three air ships. One of them is the... the... *Warrior*." Ruby looked around at the instant confusion her statement had created among most of the crew before focusing on Kennedy's back as he stared towards the sound of battle.

"It's probably a sister ship," Sparkz suggested.

Ellie put her hands on her hips. "It doesn't matter. Kennedy, we need to change course – there's no sneaking past airships – and we definitely can't fight them. Any of them."

The rumbling was growing louder with every minute, individual sounds becoming more distinct, the different notes of cannons, mortars and carronades followed by the familiar scorching crack of an aetheric crystal beam.

"Give the order, Kennedy!" the first mate urged.

"I can see the battle!" Gabbi called from his position at the top of the mast, a telescope pressed to his eye. "So much smoke! A massive ship being chased by airships! They're tearing into her something vicious!"

"Ellie, you're in charge. Try and stay parallel to the fight but whatever happens, keep your distance."

Kennedy swung a confident glance over his crewmates. "Whatever's attacking the *Depthcharge* is giving me the perfect distraction. I'm going back to find Arke and I'm going to bring her home."

Ruby's fingers were suddenly digging into his arm with a grip that transcended the description of 'firm' by at least five bruises. "Captain, I'm much faster than Dozer. Please let me come too."

"Bird means business. And she's right." Sparkz stepped forwards. "You're not going. WE are."

Chapter Thirty-One
Memory's Claws

THE AIR RUMBLED with the sound of cannon fire as Ruby and Sparkz flew low across the waves, carrying Kennedy and Vaughan towards the *Depthcharge*. As the acrid tang of cordite drifted into his nostrils, Kennedy struggled to control the oddest sense of dread. However, he was certain it wasn't the battle that was causing his chest to tighten and sweat to drip down the back of his neck, as he couldn't wait to see the mighty five decker and its admiral brought to heel.

In an attempt to combat the creeping doom, Kennedy forced himself into a logical dissection of its origin. Had he missed something vital from his hurried planning? After considering the options once again, he knew he'd made the right choice. Fly hot and low, head straight for the admiral's cabin and hope that the Soulbound was still there. He had an array of ideas for things that might happen if she wasn't, but none of them were worth worrying about before they were even onboard. It wasn't the plan that was the problem. Nor was it the mission itself, as this wasn't his first Arke-related rescue. Her resume probably listed her special interests as 'a passion for baiting the strongest enemy', 'getting in the way of sharp-edged weapons', 'a complete inability to back down despite overwhelming odds', and 'surviving'. It wasn't that trouble followed her, more that she rode it like a rodeo bull.

The only conclusion Kennedy could draw was the one that he couldn't understand. He'd felt similar anxiety just before the engine room had been destroyed by what had he suspected had been an aetheric blast. Then, not more than a few minutes ago, Ruby had reported a *Warrior*-type ship firing its lance at the *Depthcharge* and suddenly the feeling was back. It had to be linked, but he didn't know how or why.

As they neared the five decker, its guns fell silent, and their smoke began to drift clear. Everyone knew sea ships were vulnerable to air power, but it was still a shock to see such a gigantic vessel so defeated. The flagship was no longer sailing effortlessly, her previous easy movement now more of a drunken wallow. She was side on to the waves with her speed no more than a lazy meander. One of her mighty masts was gone, and enormous gouges from the aetheric lance had exposed sections of the lower decks. Three of the frigates were afloat, but all of them were mastless and beaten, sinking deeper in the water with every moment. Only one remained at all seaworthy and it was heading straight towards the *Depthcharge*. None of that caught Kennedy's attention as much as the sounds of hand-to-hand combat which rippled through the lingering smoke. The enemy must have boarded.

With a sudden burst of power, Ruby climbed hard. Their plan had been to smash through the wide windows at the back of the admiral's cabin. However, and with a brief sense of disappointment, the rescuers didn't have the chance to crash spectacularly through the panes of stained glass, for they were already shattered. The Ornithol landed in the centre of devastation so fresh it was still smoking. Shelves and tables were destroyed or overturned, the floor littered with broken jars, books, odd-looking artefacts and so much else that was no longer even identifiable. The front of the cabin was open to the sky, the smouldering slash clear evidence that the damage was courtesy of an aetheric lance.

"Over here." Ruby made her way through the wreckage to what seemed to be a shelter fashioned from desks, chairs, and tables.

Kennedy hurried over as Sparkz's jet-powered suit flew through the broken window and set both him and Vaughan safely down amid the debris.

"What the hell did this?" The lieutenant looked around in horror.

"Aetheric lance. More power than a broadside, all concentrated on one point," Sparkz explained.

The Ornithol crouched down, peering inside the rudimentary protective structure. "There's only a bit of blood here. That's good, right?"

"Absolutely." Kennedy pointed towards the main doors. "Get over there and use your super ears. See if you can hear Arke."

They all waited as Ruby listened intently, turning her head this way and that, before looking back at them. "Nothing. But whatever's going on out there – it all sounds wrong. Normally in a battle there's shouting and grunting and people crying out, but there's none of that. Just the sound of weapons and a really strange chanting."

"Pretty sure 'strange' is becoming our speciality," Kennedy remarked, sliding his sword free from its scabbard. "So, let's get going. Keep together, attack when attacked. Sing out if you spot the admiral, as he'll be easier to see, and I bet he's got Arke close by."

As Vaughan swung the door open, he hissed a curse-laden question that none of his new companions could answer. No-one moved for a long moment, taking their time to understand the scene in front of them. All across the main deck, the Depth sailors were fighting for their lives – or lack of lives. Cutlasses, pistols, muskets, pikes – every type of weapon was being wielded with furious desperation against... something that existed outside the visual spectrum.

"I would say that I've never seen so many invisible enemy, but..." Sparkz could never resist a dry comment.

With only half the combatants showing, it was easy to see the devastation that had been wrought on the previously picture-perfect vessel. The main mast was nothing but a shattered stump, the deck itself was rent and splintered, ropes hung down in burning loops. Sailors' clothes lay empty, the fabric ripped to shreds, while salt was thinly scattered over almost every surface.

Kennedy watched a small group standing back-to-back as they tried to hold the invisible enemy at bay. He saw them desperately fending off creatures they couldn't see and then he saw them fall, slashes appearing all over their bodies before they simply turned to salt. Whatever they were fighting was both incredibly efficient and astoundingly violent.

"There she is! Being carried up towards the bow!" Ruby exclaimed.

Dragging his attention away from the incomprehensible battle on the main deck, Kennedy noticed a group of sailors tearing down the ladders that gave access to the fo'c'sle. Then he looked to the foredeck itself, seeing a flash of Arke's silver hair as she was taken through the mass of Depths who were guarding what appeared to be the last stronghold aboard.

"And there's Von Lauken," Vaughan growled. "Looks like the rat is abandoning ship."

"Not with Arke he isn't." Ruby grabbed Kennedy and leapt forwards, wings exploding from her sides as they left the cabin.

Soaring over the main deck, the strangely synchronised chanting from the invisible attackers was finally clear. Grating voices on hoarse repeat carved their words with automaton accuracy: '*We serve the Autarch.*' However, there was no time to contemplate that particular implication, as a ripple of musket fire sounded from the foredeck and Ruby soared upwards.

"I think we've been spotted!"

Kennedy watched Sparkz accelerate past them and smash land among the horde of undead sailors. Vaughan was ejected at speed, his blades whirling as he carved his way into the dull-eyed crew.

"They've made us some room, let's get down there!"

Fighting a mob of mindless enemy was not as easy as it sounded. They pressed in tightly without form or sense, making it difficult to swing a weapon cleanly. Each step forwards was over yet another body that shuddered and twitched as it turned to salt. The *Warrior* crew held compass positions to cover every angle, keeping close together while hacking, punching, and kicking their way towards the prow. They heard Von Lauken's voice calling out to what they assumed was the only frigate still afloat, urging it to speed up.

Grim competence powered the foursome to the edge of the admiral's meat shield. There were only a few sailors left to kill before they could deal with the handful of Depth officers that stood between them and Arke. They could see her body slung over Orville's shoulder as he waited at the side rail, his gaze flitting between the approaching ship and the battle behind him.

With a deafening explosion, the fo'c'sle was suddenly deadly with grapeshot that sliced its way through not only the *Warrior's* crew but also what was left of the *Depthcharge's* rank and file. Kennedy was saved from injury by the unwitting sailor who attacked him the instant before the weapon was fired, but he heard Sparkz's armour take a series of hits, the rattling impacts quickly followed by a flurry of breathless curses.

Stepping out from behind his engineer-shaped shield, Vaughan launched his dagger into the eye of the officer who stood by the smoking swivel gun. "Randall, you were always a humongous penis."

"From fool to traitorous fool." Von Lauken's booming voice cut through the sudden exclamations from the officers around him.

"From admiral to desperate coward," Vaughan called back. "Run, Roland, run."

"Kennedy," Sparkz hissed. "Ruby's hit. It's bad."

He was right. As he turned away from Vaughan and Von Lauken's rapidly escalating confrontation, Kennedy saw the Ornithol lying unconscious on the deck, blood soaking through her feathers in countless places.

"Can you get her back to the *Warrior*?" he asked.

Sparkz nodded. "I've carried you before, and you're heavier. But..."

Kennedy interrupted before the engineer pointed out the obvious. Without Ruby or the jet pack, they had no easy way to escape. "Go before Vaughan runs out of steam."

"Ok, but I'm coming back for you."

With a sudden roar that silenced the flurry of increasingly ungentlemanly insults between admiral and lieutenant, Sparkz's jet ignited, and he shot away from the *Depthcharge*, Ruby in his arms.

"Look how your new 'friends' are leaving you to die!" Von Lauken crowed.

Kennedy straightened up slowly. "Heroic speech, dramatic pause, perfect line." He fastened his gaze on the admiral. "You're not worth wasting brain power over, so I just summarised. Let's get this finished."

"When Arke wakes up, do you want me to give her your ear or your tongue as a memento?" Von Lauken turned away as a rope was flung from the ship below. "Orville put her down and secure that line. The rest of you, kill them!"

Four officers, all their faces familiar to Kennedy, strode towards himself and Vaughan, while Orville quickly hauled up the thicker cable that would hold the ships together. Von Lauken stood over the Soulbound who was sitting against the gunwales, blood coating her left hand, her neck stiff, and eyes staring straight ahead.

"Arke!" Kennedy yelled. Despite his bravado, it was obvious that things weren't exactly going his way. Two against six wasn't a great ratio, especially if the six were well trained swordsmen with nothing to lose. He needed to get through to her before the Depths' numerical advantage became deadly. "Arke, wake up!"

It was at that precise moment that Kennedy's world stopped spinning.

A pair of new combatants suddenly appeared in front of Von Lauken. One was a tall man, dressed in a navy-blue frock coat, blonde hair tied back at the nape of his neck. The other was a woman all in black, a stiletto knife in each hand. She ducked and rolled away from the admiral's first strike, then seemed to shimmer into nothingness, before reappearing under his guard and driving a blade into his side.

Kennedy was frozen to the spot. He knew who they were, or who they'd been, or who they couldn't possibly be. They were dead. Arke had killed them. He'd seen their bodies. Yet they were there, in front of him. The tall man with the face so much like his own and a sword in each hand. The beautiful woman with her blonde hair coiled in a plait, who'd rocked him to sleep, who'd sung his favourite songs, who'd taught him to walk a high rope as if it were a road. The people in his dreams, in his memories, in the very heart of him.

All he could do was stare, wide-eyed and breathless, his guard dropping as his thoughts churned in stunned confusion. Three of the officers turned back to aid their admiral, but the last spotted his stupefaction and charged in for an easy win.

Shoving Kennedy to one side, Vaughan drove both his own blades straight into the torso of the other officer. "Sorry, old chap." As the Depth staggered backwards, the lieutenant gritted his teeth and quickly yanked the other officer's sword out of his own shoulder, wincing as water sprang from the wound. "A scar to remember you by, I suppose."

"Do you see that?" Kennedy's voice was hoarse as he watched the alter version of the tall man in the blue coat appear just in time to block a smashing blow from one of the officers.

"More people to kill? Yes. Let's do it."

He knew Vaughan didn't understand what he meant, but it didn't matter, he knew, and he finally understood the dread and Arke's bloody hand and the agonising tragedy of it all.

Then, almost as if the universe was hammering the point home, he heard the familiar crack of an aetheric beam. Looking up, Kennedy saw what Ruby had, not a sister ship, not a similar vessel, but another *Warrior*, one wrapped in wispy grey magic and bearing the flag of the Barsian Empire.

His eyes flicked back to the scene in front of him. He saw the admiral and his officers fighting for their lives. Fighting his parents, their bodies hissing with a haze that seemed to de-saturate the air around them as they moved. He remembered them working together before but never this well, never this fast, never this deadly. His father kept his alter in constant motion, springing and merging, attacking and defending. Kennedy had never seen him so powerfully in control, nor so attuned to his partner.

Joy's style had always been athletic, but now it was almost super-powered. She was in the air to avoid a blade from Orville a second after she'd somersaulted away from Von Lauken's cutlass, and then seemed to step through a veil, reappearing in another position to strike at the admiral whose white-hot reactions only stopped her knife by the tiniest of margins.

Where his parents were, so was the *Warrior*. But theirs bore the flag of the Autarch. It didn't make sense. None of it. It was just wrong, all wrong, and so unbearable that nausea rose in his throat and his eyes pricked with tears.

"KENNEDY! Get back in the game! Let them deal with the admiral," Vaughan yelled. "We'll never have a better chance to grab Arke."

The mention of her name dragged Kennedy back into the moment. The lieutenant was right, his parents' intervention had drawn the Depths away and left the Soulbound slumped against the railings. He sprinted towards her and crouched, waving a hand in front of her face, slapping her cheeks, and shaking her shoulders.

"Arke? Stabbington?" There was no reaction, no blue spark in her eyes, no sword at her hip to connect him to her demon. Kennedy hauled her to her feet and hugged her tightly, hoping the physical contact might do something to help. "Wake up, please. We need you."

She remained stiff in his arms, and he pulled back, desperately searching her blank expression. Suddenly, her eyes flickered to life, snapping to a point on his left side as she forced a single word to her lips.

"NO!"

Kennedy whirled just in time to block the deadly strike. The face he stared into was so familiar to him, the laughter lines, the dimples, and the furrow in between the brows which Philip senior always claimed was due to years of dealing with Joy. All of it.

All of it was his father, except the misty greyness that dulled the brightness of his hair and the blueness of his eyes.

"Dad. Please. Stop this."

All of it except the grey-tinged sword that Kennedy was struggling to keep from his own throat.

Glancing to his right, he saw Arke, Stabbington now in her hand, limping away from the fighting. He saw Orville, water dripping from a cut to his head, charge over to grab her. And he saw his father's alter materialise behind the lieutenant, blades raised.

Reacting with instant loathing, Kennedy sprang his own alter to block the blow on Orville's unprotected back even as he strained every muscle to hold his father at bay. "PHILIP KENNEDY NEVER FOUGHT LIKE A COWARD!"

He heard a sudden collision of steel centimetres away from his own neck and then Vaughan's voice, heavy with effort.

"Maybe he didn't, but this guy does."

✕ ✕ ✕

GRIPPING STABBINGTON'S HILT with both hands, Arke struggled to reacquaint herself with reality. She'd woken to a world gone crazy and the two rings on her fingers pulsing ominously. Yet the moment she'd seen Joy, everything had faded into the background.

All she saw, all she knew was Joy, even though she couldn't fully comprehend what she was seeing. Her feet stopped moving and warmth rolled through her at the sight of her friend. Despite Stabbington's voice urging her to focus on escaping, she couldn't look away.

"Joy..." she whispered, her eyes following her friend's every movement. "It's Joy."

"It is not!" the demon argued. "It cannot be! Arke, she is DEAD!"

It was Joy, and everything was going to be alright. Joy was back. Joy was here. Joy had come to help her. She didn't listen to Stabbington, for she could see her best friend.

And her best friend could see her.

Joy shimmered out of reach of the admiral's blades before reappearing next to the Soulbound, their eyes meeting for a long second.

"That is not Joy. THINK! You KNOW it is not her. Us me. USE ME!" Stabbington's shouts echoed in Arke's head, but instead of driving his blade through Joy's chest, her hand opened and dropped him.

Suddenly, Joy grabbed the Soulbound around the throat and another pair of hands gripped her arms from behind. Philip Kennedy senior leant close to her ear as his fingers dug deeply into her flesh.

"The Autarch will see you now."

An enormous wave smashed into the *Depthcharge* from the starboard side, scattering everyone across the fo'c'sle and soaking them in freezing water. It was followed by another and another as the sky darkened to a stormy blackness and the wind began to howl.

"The Mother!" Von Lauken roared, scrambling to his feet, and charging towards Joy, his energy seeming to increase with every wave that threw itself over the gunwales. "She comes to our aid!"

Whether it was the mention of the Autarch or the barrage of cold water that brought her out of her stupor, Arke wasn't sure, but what she did know was that reality sucked. Her body was weak and shivering, and everything round her was terrifyingly awful. She wasn't in any state to fight – she barely had enough energy to stand, let alone cast any spells. Recalling her demon blade to her hand more for Stabbington's companionship than an intent to wield him, she crawled towards the nearest railings. Looking around, she saw Joy was now fighting the admiral, while Philip senior and his alter were engaged with the surprise combination of Kennedy and Orville.

"Turns out the Mother of Salt *was* listening." Vaughan appeared and helped her up before standing protectively in front of her. "Kennedy thought we might need some help. Honestly, I wasn't expecting her to be so willing to pitch in, but I'm glad he made me ask."

"She sent the storm?" Arke shivered as the winds whipped across the deck and yet another wave showered them with water.

"Oh yeah," Vaughan grinned. "She's good at that sort of thing. And not so thrilled with the admiral trying to sneak out of his contract, but right now I'd guess her priority is to deal with the people killing her pledges."

As the tempest intensified, Kennedy and Orville were working hard to contain Philip senior despite sliding down the decks one moment and fighting their way back up them the next. However, their opponent seemed to be tireless. He whirled his swords with supreme confidence, his footwork fast and his alter immaculately timed.

Orville landed a heavy hit, but immediately afterwards, dropped to his knees, the alter's blade protruding from his chest. As the Depth crawled away, both Philip Kennedys fought on. Their alters sprung and merged continuously until their true bodies barely stayed in the same place for more than a second as they duelled from one side of the fo'c'sle to the other.

The storm grew wilder still as an air ship moved towards the *Depthcharge*. As it hovered almost directly overhead, Joy shimmered into position next to Vaughan and brought him to his knees with a knife to the chest.

"STOP!" Arke had to hold Stabbington's hilt with both hands as she smashed the killing blow aside. "JOY! Please – stop."

With a sudden series of strobing impacts that illuminated the entire scene, a barrage of lightning shot from the heavy clouds, each one smashing into the ship that loomed above them. Thunder rolled around as the rapid flashes pounded the vessel until it shattered like glass, its timbers crashing down onto the *Depthcharge*.

"Over the side!" Kennedy yelled, dragging Orville out of the path of a splintered and smoking piece of debris.

"Joy," the Soulbound whispered, her eyes and blade locked with her friend's. "Try. Try to remember."

A heavy hand clasped her shoulder from behind and she felt the pull of locomotive magic. "The Autarch will..."

Suddenly the admiral ploughed into her, the sheer force of his charge carrying them both over the top of the railings. As a white-tipped wave rose up to claim them, Arke's gaze clung to Joy. Or where Joy had been. An instant before the sea claimed her, she realised her friend had disappeared.

Chapter Thirty-Two
Safety is Relative

"Do not panic, I am the Mother of Salt. Your enemies cannot touch you here."

The voice did not belong to Stabbington, nor Von Lauken, nor anyone Arke knew. It was deep and melodic, with a calmness that sent waves of relaxation through her body. Freezing cold became perfectly warm, confusion became understanding, and wounds simply disappeared.

As she was eased back into consciousness, the Soulbound remembered Philip and Joy and the fight on the foc's'le. She remembered hitting the water and Von Lauken's triumphant expression suddenly turning to panic as a pair of pale blue eyes loomed out of the darkness below them. But she didn't remember seeing Kennedy escape the flagship.

"Philip! I need to find him! Could you take me to him? Please?"

"He is safe, as are my two servants who fought for you," the voice replied.

The Soulbound opened her eyes and immediately snapped them shut. Then, preparing herself with a slow, deep breath, she tried again. She'd assumed she was in the Mother of Salt's lair, and in a way, she saw she'd been right. As she looked around, she took in every feature of the cavernous mouth. The bioluminescence that lit the entire maw, the warm red tongue beneath her and the gigantic teeth – one of which had the admiral's body skewered on it.

"He got what he deserved in the end." Arke's lips pursed in a tight smile. "Thank you for not eating me."

"I will not eat him either, I do not consume flesh to survive."

"Nor did he. Though he did say my blood could replace your salt."

"Sometimes creatures find answers to questions they can never understand."

The Mother of Salt's tone never seemed to alter, no matter what she was saying, and every time she spoke, the Soulbound felt the oddest sense of peace wash over her.

"Is that your way of telling me not to ask?"

"It is not my place to explain."

Arke took another look at Von Lauken and rubbed a hand through her wet hair as she considered her next question. Vaughan and Orville had fought alongside them, and they deserved so much better than being skewered on a tooth in return.

"Now the admiral is dead, is his contract void? Your two servants risked their lives to help bring him to you. Could you release them from their obligations?"

"If you so desire."

"As they were the day the agreement was made?" The Soulbound knew enough about powerful entities to be aware that if she didn't specify exactly how they'd be released, it was possible the Mother of Salt would turn them into two-hundred-and-fifty-year-old mortals and shrug as they dissolved to dust.

"Naturally."

With a strange gulping sound, a pristine lifeboat bobbed towards Arke on the tiniest stream of water. "I must return you to the surface. My tempest will hide you from your enemies and usher you safely to shore."

THE STORM TOOK a day to blow itself out but was followed by good weather as the lifeboat sailed east. It took another day before they sighted the coast of Barsia, which, according to a smiling Kennedy, was exactly where he thought it would be.

After aiming the bow towards a short, stony cove in the lee of a granite cliff, four eager sets of hands ran their weather-worn vessel free of the surf, securing her well above the tidemark before they took a moment to ease their aching muscles. Surfing the storm in a tiny boat hadn't been the most pleasant experience, but they'd survived, and that was all that mattered.

"We need to find fresh water and see if there are any houses nearby." Kennedy pointed to the cliff and then to the Soulbound. "Up?"

"Up." She smiled, whistling so loudly for Dozer that Stabbington complained about the noise. "What, didn't you get enough sleep?"

As the Rottweiler sprang out of nowhere, barking in delight, Arke crouched down so that her over-excited hellhound could lick her face in relative safety. He often forgot to sheathe his extra teeth in the excitement of greetings, and she'd experienced plenty of bloodletting recently.

"Ah, I do not sleep. You sleep, and you snore. In the armpit of that lieutenant, indeed. Friendship can go too far," Stabbington retorted.

"I'll try to get shipwrecked with a boat load of nuns next time."

The demon snorted with laughter. "You have met Ruby, are you insane? They would eat you and pick their teeth with your bones. I suggest you climb onto your bat-winged idiot hound before you dig the hole any deeper."

By the time the others had taken their turn riding the best good boy to the top of the cliff, the Soulbound had climbed on a boulder to look north along the coast.

"See anything?" Kennedy called, shielding his eyes against the sun.

"You'd better come up."

Just visible around the headland, on her side in the surf of a huge stony beach, lay the unmistakable shape of the *Warrior*. Her battered sides were covered in sails in what had obviously been a last-ditch attempt to keep her afloat. Her masts were gone, her rudder was missing, and she was a pitiful sight.

Arke's voice was gentle as she sought to soften the blow. "She got them safely to shore. Look over by those rocks. They're ok."

As Kennedy dragged his gaze from the stricken ship to a cluster of makeshift shelters, she saw some of the tension leave his shoulders.

"Let's get down there, take stock and start moving north," she continued. "If the gig made it, it can tow the lifeboat. We'll stick close to the coast, camp at night. You'll flavour it as team bonding, and we'll get to Levenbrandt before you know it."

"You make it sound like a holiday." Kennedy put an arm round her shoulders and hugged her to him.

"Captain!" Vaughan's shout was staccato with tension. "Airship to the south."

They spun around to see the other *Warrior* approaching at full speed. Its silhouette was unmistakable as was the sudden flash of light cutting from its bows and slamming into the cliff face a hundred metres from them.

"We've got to warn the others!" Kennedy yelled. "Follow the treeline!"

The Autarch's *Warrior* was at maximum distance, but she was fast, and out in the open they were helpless against her. The four of them sprinted into the woods and crashed through the undergrowth. They vaulted over fallen branches and slid down muddy slopes, all weariness forgotten in the urgency of their task.

As Arke ran, she felt her palm start to bleed, and desperately tried to keep her focus in the face of what she knew would come next.

⚹ ⚹ ⚹

THE INSTANT HE spotted the Soulbound's bleeding hand, Kennedy ordered the lieutenants to pick her up and keep running under the cover of the trees. He assumed Ibu would be in the makeshift camp, and he knew she never went anywhere without her potion bag. Then he sprinted ahead, threading his way through the trees, desperately hoping he could alert the others before the enemy saw them.

Cresting the final rise, he skidded down the steep slope at the end of the bay where his ship lay lifeless in the surf. Her fate was sealed, but that of her crew still hung in the balance. His heaving chest flung out warning after warning as he ran along the treeline.

The other *Warrior* was flying towards them at full speed, the greyscale version of the one with her bottom ripped out on the rocky beach.

The one with the Autarch's troops aboard.

The one with his long dead parents in command.

The one with its aetheric lance ready to fire.

"RUN!"

He was out of breath, his feet scrambling for grip on the loose stones.

"RUN!"

He was hoarse with effort.

"RUN!"

Finally, they heard him.

He saw figures crawling out from the makeshift shelters and shading their eyes to look in his direction. Urzish took up the call, her voice bellowing across the camp as she threw a blanket-wrapped Lewis over her shoulder and hauled Gabbi to his feet. Ellie shoved Ibu ahead of her as the crew raced into the trees, Sparkz carrying his boots in one hand and toolkit in the other, Volk with his precious gun and Krugg with Giro in his arms like a baby.

Suddenly the hairs on the back of his neck stood on end, and Kennedy dived for cover as the hissing crack of the aetheric lance sounded behind him. He lay under a bush, covered in leaves, as he watched the first blast slam into his ship, slicing it almost completely in half.

He could not look away as the Autarch's vessel recharged and fired, time and time again, making an undeniable statement as it carved his beautiful *Warrior* into an impossible jigsaw.

"Captain," Ellie hissed from the shelter of a nearby tree, "we're all ok. Vaughan and his friend found us and Ibu's taking care of Arke." She waited a moment and then threw a pebble at his head. "Come on, we need you more than the ship does."

As the greyscale *Warrior* continued to vent its fury on the fully coloured version, Kennedy and his first mate made their way further into the woods, invisible from anyone flying over the close-knit green canopy. Understandably wary of ground-bound pursuit, they moved slowly, stopping to check behind them several times before they reached the glade where the rest of the crew were gathered.

The arrival of their captain immediately galvanised them into action, and he was hauled into the most overwhelmingly physical greeting he'd ever experienced. Once the initial wave of excitement had passed, Sparkz stepped forwards and pulled Kennedy in for a bruising hug. The engineer looked as exhausted as the others, but like them, he was smiling.

"Is there anything you can't survive? And not just survive... tell me how the bloody hell you managed to *hire* someone else in the middle of that shit show?"

"My incredible charm, obviously." Kennedy held the embrace for a long moment before stepping away, only to be enveloped in a tattered pair of feathery wings.

"So glad you're back!" Ruby tapped her beak gently on the top of his head.

"Pretty much had to lock her in sickbay to stop her heading off to find you," Sparkz added.

"And he's going to pretend he didn't try. Ask him how good he was at flying in a storm."

Memory's Claws

"Annnnyway..." Kennedy felt distinctly unprepared to take on his usual role as referee. A distraction, and hopefully, a quick exit, was required. "Where's Arke?"

Discussion immediately halted, Ruby pointed upstream. "She's..." She paused, head tilting to one side as she chose her words. "Remember that mind-bending potion Gurdi used on her when her knee was wrecked?"

"Oh!" He certainly did. "Did it work?"

"Yes?"

The question in the Ornithol's voice made Kennedy wonder if heading to see the Soulbound was a good idea. He needed time to think, to plan, counter plan, sub plan, bullet point, flow chart, pie chart, map, draw, outline and sign off. Dealing with Arke when she was in the grip of the strongest herbs he'd ever seen was not going to help any of his thought processes.

However, since he wasn't in the right headspace to act as referee, nor to tell his crew what had happened aboard the *Depthcharge*, Kennedy followed their directions to the nearby stream. After Dozer's sudden leap into his path nearly scared him into a new pair of trousers, he praised the hellhound's guard dog ability and walked into the clearing beyond. After smiling at the sight of Ibu curled up peacefully in a patch of bluebells, he looked over to where Orville and Vaughan sat against the base of a tree with a sleeping Arke draped over both of their laps.

"Is she ok?" he whispered.

"Apparently, she's never felt better. Oh, and the leaves are singing. The grass is communing with the soil. The trees are sighing. And the rocks are... rocking?" Orville chuckled.

Vaughan was quick to continue. "He's beautiful, I'm beautiful, she loves us, you, her, them. She wants to wrap everyone in a warm, soft blanket, but she can't promise to let us out for playtime – the world is a dangerous place."

"If that was all she said then you got off lightly." Kennedy chuckled.

"There was much – much more," Ibu yawned and stood up slowly. "But these gentlemen have promised to forget it all."

Gnomes were not usually known for their ability to intimidate, but as Kennedy looked over at Ibu's warning frown, he could quite understand why the two lieutenants were nodding as if their lives depended on it. Suddenly hit by the bittersweet realisation that Gurdi would wholeheartedly approve of her successor, he took a moment to compose himself before replying.

"Thank you, all of you, for looking after her."

Ibu patted her potion bag with a hand. "I'm glad the elixir worked better than my last idea – actually 'glad' just doesn't cut it. Healing a patient by nearly killing them isn't exactly what I'm comfortable with."

"Nothing wrong with a little professional pride," Kennedy smiled. "However, we're not fussy, as long as they end up alive, it's all good. Let me know when she's lucid."

A FEW HOURS after the aetheric lance ceased firing, Ellie shimmied up a tall tree and scanned the sky before reporting no sign of the Autarch's *Warrior*.

Bracing themselves, the crew headed back to the beach. It was just as sorry a sight as they had expected.

Their ship was barely more than chunks of wood bobbing in the shallows. Squaring his shoulders, Kennedy stood in front of everyone and cleared his throat. He was the captain, and he needed to set the tone.

"She might be done, but we're not. So, let's grab our stuff and head north to Levenbrandt. We need to salvage everything useful — weapons, personal items, clothes, food. Sparkz, my miracle working brother, please make us something to help carry what we find. Kilar and Irash, check every bit of timber and copy down all the protective runes you can. Then start drawing one of each onto everyone, starting with Arke." He looked from person to person, his eyes bright, his confidence visible. "We are the *Warrior*, and we get shit done."

※ ※ ※

"Drink." Ibu's bedside manner hadn't altered a bit despite their change in circumstances, and a bleary-eyed Soulbound took the water bottle without a murmur.

As she drank, she noticed that the back of her hands were covered in runes, and looking at the healer, she saw the same marks on her skin.

"Get this down you." Ibu handed her a bowl. "Cold noodles are all the rage when you can't have a fire."

"If you say so. What's up with the ink?"

"Protective wards, the same as were on the ship. Captain's hoping that'll keep the other *Warrior* from finding us."

With a slow nod, Arke started to eat and Ibu went to refill the water bottle. By the time she returned, the bowl was empty, and the Soulbound was standing up, stretching her back carefully.

"How are you feeling?"

Arke grimaced. "Very hungover. What did you use this time?"

"Drink some more water." Ibu grinned. "It worked and I didn't nearly kill you, so obviously it's a win."

With an ominously slow movement, Arke looked down at her, eyebrows raised. "What – did – you – use?"

"You were so high. So, so, so high." Vaughan wandered over holding two cups of coffee and gave one to the Soulbound. "We must do it again sometime."

"It's medication, not recreation," Ibu retorted, hands on her hips.

Her reply was an unapologetic bow from the lieutenant. "But how else will I know how the story ends? Arke fell asleep without finishing it."

Before the Soulbound could marshal her many, many thoughts into emphatic phrases complete with copious expletives, Kennedy strode across the clearing.

"For me?" He whisked the other coffee from Vaughan's hands. "Outstanding." Then he looked at Arke. "Are you feeling ok now?" When his only reply was a shrug, he dropped his arm over her shoulders. "Let's take a little stroll."

Walking slowly, and in silence, Kennedy led her a short distance away from the others before sitting down on a fallen tree and starting to sip his drink.

"We'll be ready to move in an hour, if we head northeast I bet we'll find a road soon enough." He patted the trunk next to him. "But first, I need to know everything you never told me about my parents. I need to understand."

"Yeah." Arke downed her coffee in one.

"Maybe start from the beginning?" he prompted. "You always said they signed a contract, but you didn't say what they got out of the deal."

There was a long moment of silence, Kennedy sipping his drink while the Soulbound paced up and down, frowning as she tried to organise her thoughts.

"They'd gone to ground at end of Joy's pregnancy while they waited for you to make your grand entrance. I was still on the *Warrior*, keeping the business going until they were ready to come back."

For obvious reasons, Arke didn't tell him that she'd been the reason he hadn't been born on board the ship. Seeing her friends so excited to meet their baby had reminded her of the son she'd had to give away. Guilt, pain and loss had hit her hard, and knowing how much she was hurting, Stabbington had taken it upon himself to talk to the Kennedys. Joy had understood immediately and made plans to take maternity leave in High Haven, buying a house there and settling into a briefly landlocked existence while the *Warrior* kept working.

"Then you arrived," she continued. "Apparently, you pretty much threw yourself out of your mother, ready to solo the world, and were the noisiest baby ever to exist if she didn't feed you constantly."

He chuckled. "Good to know I haven't changed."

She tried to smile, but the next part was the worst, especially now she knew what had happened to the Kennedys. Memories flashed through her mind, everything so painfully, awfully vivid that the words stuck in her throat.

"Do you wish for me to tell him?" Stabbington whispered. "I can do this so you do not have to."

She took a deep breath and looked straight at Kennedy. It needed to come from her.

"You were a few weeks old when you stopped crying, you stopped pretty much everything. They rushed you to a healer and he told them you were dying. They tried every doctor, mage, savant, and medic they could find, but they all said the same thing. A rare syndrome so fundamental that nothing could be done."

She saw the horror wash across his face as she spoke.

"But they wouldn't give up. They asked around and finally heard of somewhere that something very powerful visited. Apparently it could grant incredible boons if you were willing to pay the price. They didn't hesitate. It was obvious that whatever they were dealing with was bad news, but you were their son, and they'd have done anything to save you."

"So they sold their souls to the Autarch for me?" His voice was hollow, his expression broken.

"No! Well... obviously yes, but they didn't know who it was back then. No-one did. I didn't realise until I saw them on the *Depthcharge*. They assumed it was a demon or a god of some sort. The contract said at some point in the future they would be called upon to perform a task. That was it. And what was a job in exchange for the life of their son? Deal done."

"That's why she lectured me about demons," Kennedy sighed. "I always thought it was about Stabbington."

Arke nodded slowly. "They came back to the *Warrior* when you were about six months old. They'd agreed never to tell me, but your mother and I, we had no secrets." She shrugged, sitting down on the tree trunk beside Kennedy. "Anyway, we just carried on doing our thing and forgot about the deal. You were fifteen when they were contacted – they never told me what the job was, but they did say that it was so terrible they would never do it. We tried running, we tried hiding, but there was no escape. When your parents finally confronted the messenger, it showed them the part of the contract that stated if they didn't do what was asked, not only their lives were forfeit – but also yours."

"And STILL they didn't think to check the rest of the small print? Like the bloody line about their bloody souls!" He lurched to his feet. "You, of all people, should know how those deals go, Arke! Why didn't you make them read it? Why?"

She could barely even whisper her reply. The one which had eaten at her for the longest time. "Because they didn't want to know."

Chapter Thirty-Three
The Dangers of Exercise

"Ellie, I'm heading upstream to scout for a campsite." Kennedy tried to speak normally, even though his head was burning with emotion. "As soon as Sparkz has finished making carts, load up and follow me. Leave nothing and no-one behind."

He left before she had time to argue. He needed to be alone while he processed everything he'd just learnt. Walking wasn't enough, so he began to jog, and then to run, his footsteps pounding the earth, trampling the fallen leaves, and leaving their marks in the damp soil. When the forest gave way to grassland, he sprinted to the top of a rise before slowing to a stop as the landscape suddenly opened up before him.

Meadows of waving grasses spread in every direction, the endless green dotted with bright patches of flowers. Over to his right lay a lake, its smooth surface surrounded by swathes of bullrushes and the brisk conversations of birds. An island sat at its centre, the remains of a cabin just visible among the undergrowth.

Further off to his left, he saw buildings, but after using his telescope, he realised they were only the remnants of what looked like a once magnificent estate. Most of the settlement was nothing but ruins, and the grand mansion's defences had been breached by neglect, the holes in the roof and broken windows evidence of its slow decline.

However, where there was a big house there would be a road, and Kennedy sighed with relief. They could camp at the edge of the woods and gather their strength before pushing on. Exercise had helped pummel his feelings into submission, but while he was done running, he wasn't yet done thinking.

Away from the shelter of the trees, the sun beat down in full force and Kennedy realised just how hot and sweaty he was after his run. He spent a few minutes checking the sky for ships before heading down to the lake, stripping his outer garments and stepping in.

Curious waterfowl watched him push through the weeds and shoals of tiny fish darted in front of him as he waded deeper. Then he turned onto his back and began to float. Listening to the birdsong and feeling the gentle ripples around his body, Kennedy unwound his tangled thoughts and emotions. He couldn't fight the past, but he could use it to frame the future. None of them should bear the blame. Not him, not Arke, and not the parents who'd died all those years ago. Whatever game the creature in the obsidian tower was playing, it was using them as pawns. But Kennedy knew pawns could still win.

Personal peace restored, he headed to the island, curious to explore the tumbledown cabin he'd spotted nestled amid a tangle of vines. Peering through the crumbling walls, he saw both adult and child sized furniture, a tumble of faded crockery and a bucket filled with old-fashioned toys. The ruin was surrounded by peppermint gone wild and Kennedy picked some leaves, crushing them in his hand to accentuate their fresh scent.

"Parley." The word was recognisable, though the delivery was more of a hiss than a voice.

He spun round, wishing he hadn't left his sword on the shore, but couldn't see anyone.

"Par-ley." Whatever it was repeated itself more deliberately, as if it was unsure he'd understood.

"Who are you?"

"We wish to parley."

Shimmering into view in front of him, no more than twenty feet away, was a small misshapen creature. Black tentacles ranged in random positions over its gelatinous form. Behind it stood Philip and Joy Kennedy, expressions void, eyelids unblinking, gazes so clearly abandoned they seemed to pass right through their son's body.

"Then we parley." He forced himself to remain calm, to focus on the mutant as it floated towards him. "What do you want?"

"My master requires His servant return to Him to renew her vows of service."

"Arke?"

The creature hissed, blackness rippling through its form at the sound of her name. "She must be reminded of her obligations, but will rejoin your ship once her retraining is complete."

Kennedy fought back his immediate desire to tell the tentacled servant that there was no way he would ever let her return to the vile creature that called itself the Autarch. Anger flared within him, and it took every ounce of self-control to keep his expression neutral.

"If you release her to my care," it continued, "you and your crew can leave this place alive."

"Why does that sound more like a threat?" Kennedy clasped his hands behind his back so the urge to form them into fists would not give him away.

"My master has no need to threaten. I state His facts, which are absolute. Arke will be returned to Him. The only choice you must make is whether the rest of you will live or die."

"And this 'retraining', does it mean she ends up the same as them?" He glanced towards his parents, neither of whom had moved since they arrived.

Some of the mutant's tentacles turned in response to the movement of Kennedy's eyes, almost as if they were also looking at Joy and Philip. "No. As before, the only harm that will befall her is that of her own making."

Instead of releasing the torrent of fury that burnt ribbons of fire through his chest, Kennedy concentrated on the blank faces of his parents. His gaze lingered on his mother for longer, the pallor of her skin failing to disguise the achingly familiar features of her face. He saw the scar on her cheek that looked like the number nine, the ear that was missing its lobe, and the way the corners of her mouth turned slightly up on the left and the smallest bit down on the right.

"So what did he do to them?"

The creature gibbered to itself, the tentacles clasping and unclasping almost as if they were hands. Finally, it steadied the movements and hissed its response. "Their contract consigned their souls to His service. My master's beneficence recreated their bodies and blessed them with powers beyond their mortal forms, but they remain who they were."

"They do not," Kennedy retorted.

"I am Philip Kennedy." His father walked over to his mother, his hollow eyes looking directly at Kennedy before sweeping a bow towards him. Joy raised a hand, twisting it briefly as she did so, in empty mockery of the overly embellished wave he remembered so well from his childhood. "This is Joy Kennedy."

"Why doesn't she speak?"

"They have received His salvation. They are blessed with eternal life because of our Master, and they will forever return to Him to be remade."

"Why doesn't she speak?" Kennedy repeated. "She never stopped when she was alive."

He walked straight up to his parents, taking in every facet of their appearance. Everything was the same as it ever was, right down to his father's well-worn belt and the filigreed initials on his mother's locket. A sudden pang of loss hit him like a blow to the head and he was about to turn away when he caught sight of something round and black almost hidden behind the pendant.

"It was her choice," the mutant hissed. "You have twenty-four hours to make your decision."

Then they were gone, leaving Kennedy alone on the island, only the sweet smell of bruised mint lingering in the air around him. He strode back into the water, swimming with harsh, long strokes, kicking his legs as hard as he could and forcing the tension from his muscles in his demand for pure speed. He wanted to scream, he wanted to rage against the skies themselves, and he wanted to damn every useless, pointless, careless god that had allowed this to happen. And when his fury drained away, he began to make a plan.

Memory's Claws

Dusk was closing in by the time he heard his crew making their way through the thinning trees. He waved as they spotted him and jogged over, a smile springing to his lips as he fully appreciated the ingenious contraptions Sparkz had made to carry all their kit.

"Nice work on the carts!" he called. "Take five, have a drink, sit down for a bit."

"Philip," Arke hurried towards him, an anxious look on her face. "Are you ok? You left so suddenly."

Hugely relieved she didn't hate him for storming away after hearing the truth about his parents, Kennedy hauled her into the warmest hug he knew how to give.

"I'm sorry, it was a lot. I needed time to get my head straight."

She sighed and wrapped her arms around him. "I should've told you before."

"No, I wouldn't have been ready to hear it then. I kinda wasn't now... but I had to know."

Kennedy kept the hug going as he started to address his crew as they sat wearily against their carts. He'd been rehearsing his speech for an hour, trying to find the right tone to get his point across without being wordy or overly emotional.

"So listen up, folks, I have a couple of things to say. One – I'm the idiot who went swimming and forgot about the extremely *non*-waterproof protective runes Kilar so carefully inked on me. Take my stupidity as your warning not to do the same. Two – which is clearly a result of One, so here's a recap for anyone who missed it – I'm an absolute tool." He took a deep breath and made sure he had an adequate grip on the Soulbound before he continued. He didn't want her interrupting him before he'd finished. "A messenger from the obsidian tower came to see me. He's been ordered to take Arke back with him for some 'retraining'." He felt her try to pull away, but kept his arms firmly around her. "We have twenty-four, well now about twenty-two and a half hours to choose – we give her up, or she'll be taken by force. I'll be honest, having seen the Autarch's forces in action, it's obvious we'll be outnumbered – but that's our ace in the hole. They'll expect to roll right over us in seconds – they'll be so confident of victory, they'll walk straight into defeat." He paused briefly. "You should all make your own individual decisions – any of you can leave, take your share of whatever we have and go. It's not going to be a surprise that I'm staying with Arke, because the *only* way that thing gets its hands on her again is over my cold, dead body."

Then he released his hold and, as expected, the Soulbound stepped back and glared at him before turning and extending that same angry look to the rest of the crew.

"Walk away!" She heaved in a breath, her expression changing to one of stubborn defiance. "I'm *not* having your deaths on my conscience."

"Now you've told us that, we know you can't argue with our choice to fight." Vaughan tapped a finger to his temple with a cheeky grin. "Said it yourself."

"That's not what I meant!" Arke shouted. "You'll die if you stay! How are we going to beat airships and invisible troops?"

Kennedy had been waiting for his moment and stepped alongside her, his hand on her shoulder. "They want you in one piece, so blasting us with an aetheric lance or good old-fashioned cannon would be far too risky. That thing might have been able to stop a simple bullet to the head, but I doubt anything could put you back together if your body is scattered over the landscape in bite-sized nuggets."

"Attractive as that sounds, he's right," Sparkz agreed. "So, assuming we 'only' have his soldiers to deal with, we need to find a defensible position or we'll be overrun in seconds."

"How does a mansion sound? Old and built of solid stone," Kennedy grinned. "There's one about a mile away."

The engineer's face lit up. "If we control the battlefield, we have a chance. You have *no* idea how many plans I have for making traps from scraps and weapons from..." He thought for a moment. "Weapons from something that rhymes with weapons. We salvaged plenty of things that can be persuaded to go boom after a little preparation from the hands of a master engineer."

Ruby limped over and bumped her beak gently on top of Arke's head. "I'm not leaving you."

"I couldn't help you the first time, but I can now." Irash stood up and grabbed the handles of his cart. "Which way's the mansion?"

Ellie looked over with a scowl. "Nice try, but I'm not spending the rest of my life feeling guilty about abandoning you." Then she grinned. "Bitches stand together."

Arke was clearly winding up to argue when Ruby placed a hand on Stabbington's hilt. "He says to ask you one simple question. If the roles were reversed, would you leave us?"

There was a long, expectant silence before the Soulbound shook her head. "No."

"So buckle up, buttercup." Sparkz got to his feet. "Wagons roll!"

Kennedy kept an arm around Arke as he led the others to the top of the rise. Then he eased her aside and they stood together, watching as the crew hauled their carts towards the mansion.

"This isn't the first time today I've called myself an idiot." Kennedy flashed a wry smile before his voice softened. "But I am, because I bought into your woman of steel act and forgotten how you used to be. Whatever the source of these dreams, I'm glad I've had them. It's helped me remember what it was like when I was a kid, and each day was an adventure. One baby pirate and his four parents – mum and dad, you and Stabbington. I couldn't have asked for a better childhood. And if I was sent back to the past and given the choice, even knowing what I know now, I'd choose to be Philip Kennedy junior every – single – time."

Arke looked away, eyes squeezing shut, jaw muscles straining to control what was so clearly a massive emotional reaction. He squeezed her shoulder before continuing. He'd seen her helpless in his mother's presence and he'd heard the guilt in her voice when she'd told him about the contract. She was drowning in the pain of the past, and he needed to give her something to cling to.

"I lost one of my sets of parents to that thing in the tower and I'm *not* losing the other. So, we're going to that mansion, we're going to dig in, we're going to set traps and when the time comes, we are going to fight."

Kennedy's voice resonated with unshakeable resolve. "And we're going to make it right for mum and dad."

"How?" she snapped. "What can we do?"

"Back at the lake, I looked at them, trying to find a flaw, or evidence it wasn't really them. I didn't see anything until I saw mum's locket. That's the same as I remember – but behind it there's something I know isn't hers... this is going to sound weird, but it looks like the head of a nail."

"A – nail?" She frowned. "Are you sure?"

"An obsidian nail. I couldn't see past dad's cravat, but he might have one too."

Her expression was already becoming more animated. "Maybe the nails are some sort of binding mechanism. We could free them!"

"Yes..." he agreed.

"And they could come back." She pulled away from him and hurried after the others. "Come on, Philip! We've got work to do!"

"Arke, I... I don't think that's an option." Kennedy realised she wasn't listening, her walk turning into a jog as she headed towards the mansion. He sighed, knowing he was only talking to himself. "They're dead. But they'd want us to release whatever's left of them from his service, and that's what we're going to do."

⚹ ⚹ ⚹

THE ARBITER STEEPLED his fingers together, trying to concentrate on the scene below while the other denizens of the Gateway assembled for the emergency meeting. He didn't need to look around the table to know who was speaking, for even if their voices hadn't been easily identifiable, their comments were always on brand.

"Are you sure they're ready? He brought the parents into play much earlier than we thought he would. This is far too dangerous a game." Chromatia was curt and to the point, as was her style.

"Kennedy has the measure of them, but Arke does not. Can she hold?" The woman that responded first sounded worried, as well the god of love and family might.

"I doubt it. She was useless on the ship. She..." Booming voice, negative attitude – Thum, the god of order, had never liked the Soulbound.

Endraza interrupted him, her commanding tone a thinly veiled warning to her colleague. *"She will have to. This is a direct challenge, we cannot back down, we must not blink first."*

"It's playing out too close to his base of power, and far too close to the past. Leaving it to them is a dangerous course of action." No matter how Thum phrased it, his meaning was still obvious.

"If we intervene, he will know we are behind this and our plan will fail. I do not need to remind you of the consequences. They must do this alone." Endraza's voice was calm and her order clear.

"So they dangle on a thread while he snips away?"

"We have done our best to prepare them. I believe he will see defeat today."

There was a snort of derision from Thum, and mutterings from the other gods, but Endraza's pointed reply silenced them all.

"Are we not experts in the power of belief?"

Chapter Thirty-Four
Stand

It was dark by the time the crew reached the mansion. They hauled their gear through a huge, overgrown courtyard and into what had once been the grand entrance hall before stopping to rest. Unable to sit still for long, Kennedy headed into the stone building on the far side of the cobbled yard while Sparkz took inventory and Arke explored the interior of the main house, leaving dots of magical light for the others to navigate by.

Everywhere she went she saw doors slumping limply on broken hinges, and paper dangling from mould-covered walls. Decades of emptiness had destroyed what had clearly once been magnificent. Many of the rooms had been stripped bare, but some still contained remnants of the past. Occasionally, a dusty carving or a misted canvas prompted unwelcome memories of the obsidian tower, but she pushed them aside. This was not that place. This had been a home, and even empty and abandoned by its family, it was welcoming.

She stepped through a pair of heavy oak doors into a room that echoed with the sound of her footsteps and began to explore, dropping bubbles of light around her as she went.

Above her, chandeliers hung from rusted chains, and below her feet, the tiles still held a remnant of their original colour. Having crossed the vast floor, Arke finally reached the far wall where what must have been a colourful mural had been smothered by time itself.

"This has to have been the ballroom," she mused. "How many people could they fit in here? A hundred?"

"At least. This was a grand and beautiful house in its day," Stabbington commented, his voice almost respectfully soft in her head.

"I wonder who it belonged to."

She headed towards the side of the room where a set of double doors clung tenaciously to their frames, if not to the glass that once decorated them. Inching one open, she stepped out into a large orangery. An end wall was completely missing, the floor was covered in grasping vines, and the fruit trees that the building once nurtured were no more than empty pots smothered in weeds. A family of pheasants burst from cover as she walked through the darkness, but their grating alarm calls only disturbed themselves.

Just as she was about to head outside, she heard Kennedy call her name and turned back. It would take a lot of work to turn the mansion into a stronghold, but it was the best chance they had. The *only* chance they had.

※ ※ ※

"Captain!" It was barely past noon when Lewis scurried into the drawing room to find Kennedy helping Arke to board up a window. "Pair of sky ships, approaching slowly from the east!"

"Is there one with a big pointy lance on the front?" Kennedy asked. He hadn't renewed the runes on his arms, as he wanted the mutant creature to know exactly where they were.

"Not that I can see, sir."

"Well go and watch them. Come and find me if they start doing anything interesting."

As Lewis headed back to his post, Arke hammered a nail into the fragile window frame with such energy that it almost shot clean through.

"So the other *Warrior's* not there. Your parents had better be coming," she growled.

"They will. You got the knockout drops on you?"

She patted her inner pocket. "Yup. And the *Jumpstart*. Everyone knows what to do if they see my hand start to bleed."

JUST BEFORE THE twenty-four hours were up, the two vessels circled lower, the wispy grey magic that clung around their hulls now visible with the naked eye. Then they set down, in perfect formation, on what must once have been a beautiful grove of orange trees.

"The ships have landed!" Lewis ran into the ballroom, spots of colour on each cheek evidence of his breakneck run. "Soldiers are coming up on deck!"

"You saw them? How many?" Kennedy asked.

"Yessir, they were wearing blue uniforms. But everything got covered in smoke really quick."

Kennedy nodded slowly before putting two fingers to his mouth and whistling, the sharp note silencing the crew's chatter immediately. "Ok folks, huddle up." He waited as they gathered around him, their faces set and serious. "Looks like we're in business. This is going to be hard – but we've always done our best work when our backs are to the wall. Follow the plan, take care of each other and I'll see you on the other side." He squared his shoulders. "Gabbi, if you wouldn't mind giving them our answer."

The young man nodded and slipped out through the orangery to light the line of black powder that led to the letters N and O they'd written in gunpowder on the front lawn.

Kennedy and Arke were the last to leave the ballroom. They walked shoulder to shoulder through the wide hallways before climbing the rickety stairs to the servants' quarters. Time had removed all the interior walls on the top floor of the building, so all that remained was a long, open space with perfectly positioned windows for anyone who might wish to wreak havoc on the courtyard below.

As Kennedy settled himself at his station, he checked down the line. The upstairs contingent was in position, some holding rifles, others with fire bottles or canisters of explosives. The rest of the crew were elsewhere, each having tasks tailored to their personal strengths. He picked up his pistols and looked down at Lewis with a smile. The boy had pluck for days – he'd refused to be left safely outside the battleground, and volunteered to reload for Kennedy just as Gabbi did for Volk. He might be scared, but he was ready.

"I'm all set up, captain." Lewis gestured to the neatly stacked ammunition and powder in front of him.

"Good lad." Kennedy jerked his head to the window to their right. "Maybe Arke would like a quick hug before things get noisy."

Hearing her name, the Soulbound turned in time to brace herself against the sudden grip of a frightened boy. She stood silently, one hand stroking Lewis's hair as he clung to her, the other resting on the hilt of her sword. Kennedy caught her eye, and he was just about to say something when she snapped her gaze to the courtyard.

Smoke was everywhere. It had appeared in the space of a second, covering the bushes and grasses that grew around the old cobblestones and billowing higher, climbing the sides of the buildings. Lewis scrambled back to his position as Kennedy peered out of the window, barely able to see the tops of the double doors which led into their building. That was where they expected the main attack would be, especially since they'd loaded the deck by barricading all other the entry points on the ground floor.

Kennedy's strategy relied heavily on the assumption that their opponents were arrogant enough to assume strength of numbers would hand them the win. The arrival of the two big ships had given him confidence in his plan – the Autarch had clearly sent plenty of soldiers. Then the smoke had told him they were doing what he wanted – heading straight for the front door – and that Lewis had been right. These troops weren't invisible. So far, things were going their way, and Kennedy chose to believe they would continue to do so. After all, the only thing that lay between them and victory was a small army.

A small army of men marching in perfect step.

He listened to the rhythmic tramp of feet crossing the stone threshold and striding into the courtyard. The sound came and kept coming until not even the smothering smoke could keep it from echoing off the walls of the buildings.

"Steady!" Kennedy hissed. "Ruby – it's easier to hit an enemy we can see. Clear the air."

With a nod, the Ornithol started to cast a spell, her wings beating, slowly at first and then faster, twin rainbows channelling the power of the wind and starting to push the smoke back out of the gates. Kennedy glanced at the two-storey building opposite. It was exactly the sort of place he expected enemy mages to congregate in order to wield their magic from a safe distance. He'd been so certain that Vaughan, Orville, Dozer and Klaus were hidden inside, ready to wreak havoc once battle was joined.

Then he looked down at the smoke-free courtyard. Kennedy had guessed there was going to be a large number of enemies, but knowing hadn't prepared him for how he'd feel when they finally came into view. Trying to unsee the way they'd filled the entire space and were still queuing beyond, he concentrated his gaze on their antiquated weapons and uniforms. Each wore a silver cuirass over a blue tunic and red trousers, while on their heads were what must originally have been vibrantly plumed helmets. And all were covered in wisps of grey-tinged magic.

"That's the Autarch's Elite Guard!" Volk exclaimed and then shrugged as every face turned towards him with a frown. "What? Can't help enjoying a bit of military history."

After one final stamp from the soldiers' feet, silence fell. The troops stood like statues as the defenders at the windows looked to Kennedy. He held up a hand, palm outwards and mouthed the word 'Wait'. They needed to stick to the plan. No-one was to fire until the enemy hit the traps. At that point they'd be within range of Kilar, Irash and Arke, all of whom were ready to use their crowd control spells on the area directly in front of the doors.

The courtyard was still and silent as he turned to check on the Soulbound. She nodded at him, her lips pressed in a thin line, her glowing left hand clenched so tightly around Stabbington's grip that crackles of orange magic were bouncing off his blade.

Suddenly, something from behind her caught his attention, something shimmering in the shadows. Kennedy's eyes widened in horror as the mutant messenger came into view, tentacles reaching towards her. He fired his pistols just as it draped a single, pulsing tendril over the side of Arke's face. Rippling in reaction as the bullets struck its gelatinous form, the creature disappeared, and the Soulbound collapsed to the floor, Stabbington falling from her unconscious grip.

Kennedy dropped his weapons to Lewis and crouched next to her, checking her hand but finding no blood, and then trying ever more desperately to rouse her. Below them the Elite Guard surged forwards, triggering traps with every step – Sparkz had not been joking about the variety of anti-personnel devices he could put together. The courtyard shook with sound and fury as explosions flung earth, stone, and bodies high in the air, fire bottles ignited, and makeshift grenades launched nails and broken glass into the solid mass of enemy troops.

The Autarch's mages appeared at the windows of the opposite building, but were met with gunfire from the defenders. Soldiers were predictable, but spellcasters could cause havoc in seconds, and the plan had always been to deal with them as soon as possible. Now that battle had been joined, the *Warrior* strike team should be getting to work, but in the meantime, flying lead was the best magic suppression system they had.

The soldiers kept pushing forwards, ignoring the devastating countermeasures which ripped into their ranks. Irash and Kilar threw illusions and confusion into their centre, then had to dive for cover as a cluster of specialist troops started to pepper their positions with grenades.

As explosions rattled the walls, Ruby dived for the defenders' pile of homemade canister shot and began to light their fuses. Hurling one after the other into the mass of enemy below, she made sure to target the grenadiers first. Ancient crockery filled with gunpowder and shards of broken slate was exactly as effective at shredding enemies as Sparkz had said it would be. However, like all the other victims of the engineer's traps, the dead fell to the ground without a speck of blood or the smallest sound from their lips. As their life force disappeared, so did the soldiers and all their weapons, leaving only their footprints as evidence they'd ever been there.

At this stage of the battle, the defenders had expected the courtyard to be almost impassable for the sheer numbers of fallen and wounded, yet it was perfectly clear. The Autarch's silent troops continued marching towards the doors, their grey-tinged faces expressionless, their purpose all-consuming. Shattered limbs were ignored, torn flesh hung limply as whatever controlled them drove them onwards.

Memory's Claws

Having tried and failed to wake the Soulbound, Kennedy grabbed for the hilt of her demon blade. "Stabbington – what's wrong with her?"

The reply he received was in no way reassuring. "I do not know. She is here but I cannot find her. I will keep looking while you kill the enemy. What are you waiting for? GO!"

Spitting a heartfelt curse, he turned away and reached for his pistols. Losing Arke before she'd even had chance to join the fight was devastating, but the demon was right, he needed to pull himself together and start helping the others.

Kennedy straightened up and took stock of the battlefield. The building opposite was billowing smoke, and flames were visible in many of the rooms themselves. The *Warrior's* strike team had been busy, and a grin lit his face as he heard Arke's hellhound barking just before a burning mage tumbled out of a window. As the grey-robed figure magically slowed their descent and landed neatly in the courtyard, Kennedy fired one pistol and then the other.

"Gotcha." He handed his weapons to Lewis for reloading. "Remind me to tell Dozer he's a very, very, good boy."

Suddenly, a massive ball of flame slammed into the window next to him, its impact quickly followed by another and another until every defensive position had been hit by the rolling broadside of cataclysmic fire. Everyone threw themselves to the floor, pulling up their shirts to cover their faces as the window frames started to burn. Ruby was already in action, beating her wings to push the choking smoke away from the crew, as another thunderous barrage targeted the roof of their building. Kennedy peered out, in an effort to locate the mage who was creating such havoc but was driven back by the scorching heat of the magical flames.

"BALLROOM!" he yelled. The fire was spreading rapidly amid the ancient timbers and chunks of ceiling were already beginning to fall. "MOVE!"

The crew grabbed their remaining ammunition and started to withdraw. Kennedy saw Ellie slammed to the floor by a lump of burning plaster, but she quickly kicked it away and scrambled back to her feet.

"Lewis, go!" He shoved the boy towards the others, and turned, putting Arke's sword on her chest before picking her up.

Ellie was waiting for him at the top of the stairs. "We did good work here. There's a lot less of the buggers now."

He nodded, following her down. "Once they get past the explosive runes, they'll breach the main doors – and then it's Sparkz's turn to thin the herd."

"Never seen him so excited. Making death machines from gunpowder and rubbish is clearly what he was born to do." She turned to look at the Soulbound. "What happened to her? Can't see her hand bleeding."

"It's not. This is something new."

※ ※ ※

ARKE WAS A statue, her marble body encased in obsidian as she stood helplessly in front of the bright darkness. Her face was ripped in half, her limbs shattered, her torso torn, yet there was no pain. Only cold immobility.

Unable to turn away, unable to close her eyes, she watched the highest platform, where the mutant appeared, a pair of flickering orbs imprisoned among his twisted tentacles. As he released them, they expanded to form the ghostly likenesses of two people, expressions of pure terror on their faces as they looked at the scene around them.

Arke remembered this statue.

She knew where she was.

She knew who she saw.

She knew what she was seeing.

And she knew why.

The tentacled mutant bowed its head towards the bright darkness. "Philip Kennedy and Joy Kennedy – this is our Master. We serve the Autarch."

"No!" Joy's denial was suddenly silenced, her eyes bulging in agony as a monstrous hand appeared, wrapped itself around her, and began to squeeze.

"This is our Master. We serve the Autarch," the mutant repeated.

"Please stop hurting her!" Philip cried, reaching out for his wife, but unable to touch her.

"Pledge yourself and it will end. Kneel to our Master and you will receive His gifts."

He didn't hesitate. "I pledge, I pledge. Please don't hurt her anymore."

Philip was lowered to the platform and his ghostlike form dropped quickly to its knees, his words rushing out in sudden obedience. "I serve the Autarch."

A pinprick of blackness shot from the bright darkness and hovered in front of him.

"This is your salvation. Your promise of eternal life. Your gift from our Master. Take it."

Philip reached out a hand, clasping it around the obsidian nail that hissed with wisps of grey.

"Place it in your chest."

The instant he pushed it into his ghostlike body, he shuddered, his mouth dropping open in a silent scream as the magic exploded inside him, pouring itself into his outline with overwhelming intensity.

Arke watched helplessly as he was changed, renewed, and darkly optimised. And when it was over, a reforged Philip Kennedy stood on the platform, his vision locked on the figure beyond the veil, his bearing rigid, and his eyes dull.

As the giant hand withdrew from Joy, she started to shout. "What have you done to him? What is this place? Let us go!"

"Be silent or face the consequences." The ominous command came from Philip's mouth.

"NO! I will not yield to a monster. I will not go quietly, I will not..."

Arke watched her best friend fight with every power she did not possess in that room where the Autarch held every soul in his thrall, held every atom in his grasp, held every outcome in his will.

She watched Philip curl his hand around a second nail and thrust it into his wife's chest.

She heard the last word her friend would ever utter strangle itself within her.

She watched as the tide of grey magic swept through Joy's body.

She watched her fight to the very last moment, to the very last second, until she was nothing but obedience.

"She serves the Autarch."

Arke was a statue, her marble form encased in obsidian as she stood helplessly in front of the bright darkness. Her face was ripped in half, her limbs shattered, her torso torn, unable to move, unable to shut her eyes.

She could not see Stabbington as he battered his fists against the invisible wall that surrounded her.

Chapter Thirty-Five
Withstand

"They're coming!" Kilar leapt down the last few steps and slid under a barrier, taking position in a sheltered doorway to Sparkz's right. "They've got a..."

With an eardrum-bursting boom, the front doors crashed open, and a grey-tinged elven battlemage wound threads of fire around his hand before releasing a plume of flame down the corridor. Traps fired prematurely, explosions launched chunks of wall into the empty passageway, and canister shot exploded. Then the soldiers marched past their mage, forming a solid mass fully four abreast as they strode towards the defenders. Sparkz concentrated hard, his magical tattoo of a thermometer flashing brighter than ever before as he targeted the first wave of attackers, his spell making their armour glow red hot.

Krugg's hand hovered over a lever until the enemy hit a line on the floor. Then he roared a challenge and pressed down. With a hissing thud, a flurry of wooden stakes shot out from the odd-looking contraption Sparkz had created from rope, pulleys, and the sharpened balustrades from the mansion's staircases.

The guardsmen staggered back, their heated cuirasses failing under the impact. As they fell, Urzish sprang out from behind a set of secondary doors halfway up the corridor, swinging them shut before sliding a heavy bar in place to hold them closed while the others rushed to reload.

Twenty feet beyond the defenders lay the entrance to the cavernous ballroom. What had been a dance floor was now a maze of barricades made with clusters of ancient furniture. Kennedy's plan had needed a base, and this was it. When the strike teams and collapsing perimeters had thinned out the enemy, this was where they'd come together. This was their fallback position, their final battleground.

Kennedy followed the first mate to the back of the room and slid Arke behind the cover of some ancient tables. As he straightened up, his eyes were suddenly drawn to a door in the end wall and the unmistakable figure of his father's alter.

"Is that him?" Ellie hissed.

"His alter. So he's close." Kennedy handed her his pistols. "I shan't be needing these for a while. I've got... family business to take care of."

She frowned. "You know he's not your real family, right?"

"Oh yes. That thing's charade ends today." He looked to where a pale-faced Lewis was sitting with the Soulbound's head in his lap, his shaking hand gently stroking her hair. "Arke..."

"Is just waiting for her big entrance." Ellie reached out and squeezed his arm. "We'll watch over her. Go."

Kennedy slid his swords from their scabbards and settled their grips firmly in his palms. The thing that pretended to be his father wielded dual blades, so it seemed only fair that he did as well. With a last glance behind him, he headed towards the open door.

※ ※ ※

Stabbington had shouted, screamed, and thrown everything he had against the invisible wall that trapped Arke in the endless replay. Nothing had worked. He was helpless against whatever magic the Autarch's creature had used. Finally, he slid to the ground, breathless and exhausted from his efforts.

A spark of orange caught his eye, a bubble thrown into the air from one of the strange streams that flowed inside the Soulbound. He'd always tried to avoid them, for the way they flared and churned with her emotions terrified him. It wasn't magic as it should be, for it wasn't a tool and it wasn't an instinct.

A second orb spat upwards, then a third, and Stabbington watched as the flying drops multiplied so many times they became an orange fountain.

"Is it almost as if you are trying to get my attention. Well ok, you have it." He scrambled to his feet and strode towards the stream. "I know you have helped her before. So please do not bite me, I wish to try something."

Thrusting his fingers into the current of strange magic, Stabbington realised that although it looked like lava, it wasn't burning hot. Instead of the pain he'd been expecting, a welcoming warmth flooded up his arm while crackles and fizzes of energy sparked all over his skin.

His plan had been to grab a fistful to hurl against the invisible wall and see if this strangest of powers could do what he could not, but as he withdrew his hand, he found that what he'd gripped was the shaft of a bright orange javelin.

A sudden smile lit his face. "Perhaps I phrased that wrong. Maybe you can use me." He launched the weapon towards Arke and the terrible scene that replayed and replayed in front of her.

As it hit the transparent barrier, the spear exploded back into liquid. Droplets spat and sizzled against the Soulbound's prison, bouncing against the surface like angry amber hail. Stabbington watched with growing excitement as visible cracks began to form under the assault.

"It's going to take a lot more of those, but I am prepared if you are."

Energised, he reached back into the flow, expecting another javelin, but when he straightened, he looked in brief confusion at the orange shovel in his hand. Laughter burst from his throat as he waved the tool in the air.

"Yes!" he bellowed. "Why throw pieces when you can bring EVERYTHING?"

As Arke stood immobile, encased in the outline of a statue, forced to watch the endless loop of her friends' suffering at the hands of the Autarch, her demon started digging.

※ ※ ※

"Steady," Sparkz ordered, sweeping a gaze over the defenders in the corridor.

They'd just finished reloading his homemade crossbow when they heard a rumbling sound begin on the other side of the doors Urzish had barricaded shut. The noise grew louder and louder, the hinges straining against the magical assault, the wood shaking and cracking until the barrier finally ruptured, chunks of door hitting the walls and sliding to the floor. Silence settled for a moment before the elven battle mage floated towards the defenders, grey-tinged magic circling him like mist. Sparkz pressed the lever, but with a wave of the mage's hand, the sharpened stakes were blown aside, and he kept coming, fire starting to wreath his form as he prepared another spell.

Suddenly, Irash dropped through a hole in the ceiling and landed on the battlemage's shoulders. Stabbing a finger into the elf's eye socket, he yelled something in a guttural language, and with a blinding flash of turquoise light that cauterised the air, they both disappeared.

Reacting quickly, Krugg and Urzish sprinted to try to re-block the corridor, but it was impossible, as even the largest piece from the shattered doors was only table sized. The Autarch's Elite guard were marching towards them. They needed time to reload.

"Hold up the biggest bit!" ordered Sparkz, as one of his magical tattoos began to glow.

The wood exploded in size, creaking and straining under his spell, taking only seconds to expand enough to fill the gap and halt the soldiers' approach. Krugg and Urzish braced themselves against it while the others reloaded the crossbow. This was their final load of ammunition, and as the grey-tinged enemy battered the barricade, Sparkz settled his fingers on the lever.

"ON THE COUNT OF THREE – EVERYONE FALL BACK TO THE BALLROOM!"

※ ※ ※

KENNEDY MARCHED THROUGH the open doorway where the alter had been standing and strode into a library. He couldn't see his fake father in the room, but he wasn't about to be tempted too far from his crew. The fight would be here or nowhere.

"The REAL Philip Kennedy never hid away from a challenge!" he shouted.

"I am the real Philip Kennedy," replied a hoarse and stilted voice.

"You aren't. *He* died to protect his son." Kennedy turned as the thing that looked so much like his father walked into the library from a door at the end of the long room. "You're just what the Autarch scraped off the floor. Not even a poor imitation."

The older version of Kennedy drew his swords, both covered with the same wisps of energy that surrounded his own body. He bowed stiffly and made a show of readying himself, but the younger Kennedy had seen that trick before. He somersaulted away as his father's alter appeared behind him before springing back to his feet.

"Cheap tricks for a cheap copy!" he yelled, pointing the tip of his silver blade towards the man who was not his father. "I know who I am AND I KNOW WHO YOU AREN'T!"

⚔ ⚔ ⚔

The trench that Stabbington had dug was only feet away from the invisible barrier when the swirling stream of magic behind him took charge. A wave slammed into the back of his legs, knocking him to the ground. With a sudden rush of bubbling warmth, he felt it surge over him, using his body as a bridge as it leapt at the wall that imprisoned their host.

"YES! BURN IT DOWN!"

He watched as the orange liquid poured across the barrier, sizzling and cracking around the scene of the throne room, the bright darkness, the Kennedys, the mutant, and the Soulbound immobilised inside the statue of a woman.

"HURRY!" he urged, as more surged over him and into battle. "ARKE, WE ARE COMING!"

Suddenly, with an audible rending of energy, the invisible wall shattered. However, the stream of magic wasn't done. It threw itself at the illusion that imprisoned its host, smothering everything in its path until the statue itself melted away and the Soulbound crumpled to the ground. In an instant the furious waves became a lake of gentle ripples that surrounded her as she lay sobbing silent tears.

Stabbington hauled her to her feet and used a hand to slick her hair back from her face. "There is no time to be nice. Your friends need you."

She looked at him, her eyes unfocused and her voice cracking as she spoke. "I gave them to him."

"Then you take them back!" he growled.

"It's all my fault."

"So you will let that bastard win, let him trample you to the ground with guilt and grief!" He shook her hard before glaring into her face. "We do NOT have time for this. He is trying to break you so you cannot help your friends." He shook her again. "LISTEN TO ME or I will slap the shit out of you. Yes, I am a demon and I can do these things."

She blinked at him, her eyes slowly focusing. "Stabbington…"

"I may just do it anyway!"

"I am listening…" Arke looked down as orange tendrils wrapped themselves around both of their ankles and crackles of light spread up their legs. "But I… I'm not ok."

"And here is your superpower. You have never been ok." He dropped a kiss on the top of her head. *"I believe that now it is not just you and me. It is you, me, and this strange, strange magic. And we can do this. Go. Get in the fight."*

Chapter Thirty-Six
Understand

THE ANCIENT OAK doors they'd spent hours reinforcing were being chipped away, piece by piece. There were so many holes in them that the defenders could see the soldiers as they readied to breach. Ellie looked down at Arke's unconscious body and the terrified boy who clung to her, one of Kennedy's pistols in his hand. She and the handful of others who had made it back to the ballroom were ready. They bore wounds and burns, their clothes and hair were singed, but their weapons were loaded, and their faces were etched with grim determination. However, there were pitifully few of them, and without Kennedy and the majority of their own mages, it was obvious the Elite Guard would wash over them like a tide of death.

An unexpected noise by the orangery doors drew the muzzle of every gun. A soot-covered Vaughan appeared and then ducked out of sight as he saw the welcome he was about to receive.

"If you could avoid wasting ammunition on us, I'm sure we'd be terribly grateful."

"Get in here already!" Ellie called, training her pistol back on the doorway.

Orville, similarly coated in soot, his hands blistered and burnt, carried Klaus's blackened body straight to Ibu while Vaughan limped over to lean on the nearest barricade. One of his legs was soaked in blood and his jacket was still smouldering around a circular scorch mark that exposed the charred skin beneath. Gabbi ran over to him with a medical kit and some water as the main doors continued to rattle and splinter.

"Where's the captain?" Orville's voice was contorted by the *Just Say Go* that was clenched in his teeth. He downed the potion and dropped the empty bottle to the floor as Volk started to bandage his hands. "Not too tight, my friend, I still need to hold my sword."

Any reply he might have received was silenced as a portal opened and Irash staggered through, his body coated in grey-tinged tar, his scalp sliced open almost to the skull, and one arm hanging uselessly at his side.

"You should see the other guy."

As the magical doorway slammed shut behind him, he dropped to his knees, retched a puddle of black liquid, and passed out.

With a thunderous crash, the Autarch's Elite Guard finally smashed their way through the doors and stormed into the room.

"NOW!" Sparkz bellowed.

Gunpowder ignited under the soldiers' feet, blowing the men upwards like rockets, and the *Warrior* crew followed up with a withering volley. As they reloaded, Ruby dropped from the ceiling and slammed through any left standing. However, as she tried to fly away, a sudden ripple of musket fire from the corridor caught her in the wing, and she crashed down in a tumble of rainbow-coloured feathers.

Krugg charged towards the fallen Ornithol just as a rank of guardsmen bearing ancient blunderbuss marched into the room and fired. The ballroom echoed to their volley, and the ogre staggered at the impacts, but still managed to grab Ruby and dive behind a barricade. The crew returned fire, dropping the grey-tinged soldiers to the floor. Urzish quickly shoved a table into the empty doorway and Sparkz's tattoo flared brightly as he used his magic to make it fill the gap.

"Switch it up, injured to the rear!" Ellie called.

As she turned, a bright smile lit her face as the Soulbound hauled herself to her feet, easing her neck first to the left and then the right.

Suddenly Lewis leapt up, levelling his pistol at a shimmering patch of air behind Arke.

"DON'T TOUCH HER!" he yelled, and pulled the trigger.

The Soulbound spun around and stood protectively in front of the boy as the tentacled mutant ejected the bullet from its form with a hiss and a pop.

"Back off. Whatever you did to me won't work anymore," she snarled.

"Perhaps the illusion will not," it replied. "But what about everything else? I serve the Autarch. It is His will that gives me the power to walk unseen among you, to seed your dreams, to spring rivers of blood from your palm, and to imprison you in your own mind. Did you think those things happened by chance? My touch delivered them all." It paused, tentacles twisting in the air. "It is His will that you return. If you defy Him, His servants will take you by force."

"She's not going anywhere!" Lewis shouted, grabbing her arm.

"The answer is still 'No'," she replied. "I agreed to find the capstones, that is all."

"You are His SERVANT! You will do what He commands or face the consequences for your disobedience."

At the instant the mutant shimmered and vanished, Lewis cried out, his grip on Arke's wrist tightening and then abruptly releasing. She turned to look at him, only to see Joy yanking her stilettos out of his back.

※ ※ ※

IN THE LIBRARY, the two Philip Kennedys were playing a dangerous game of alter swapping. To begin with, they'd fought one on one until the younger Kennedy's athleticism had started to shine. One mismatched parry had forced the Autarch's version into using his other self and three had immediately become four as Kennedy followed suit. The long, narrow room lined with shelves of ancient, dusty books became the site of a whirling battle of strength and guile as the Kennedys merged and split, slashed and counter slashed from every conceivable angle and position.

As before, during their fight on the *Depthcharge*, Philip Kennedy senior had the advantage when his alter was in play. He was not only quicker in deploying his other self, but it seemed more powerful than his son's. Kennedy found himself defending – reacting rather than acting, deflecting rather than attacking and relying far more on acrobatic evasions than was sustainable. Finally, amid the melee of copies and originals, a grey-tinged sword struck through his defences and cut a deep line across his bicep. He merged with his alter, then quickly sprung it again as a distraction before sliding underneath a questing thrust and leaping onto the back of a sunken leather couch. Feeling the injury beginning to weaken his grip, Kennedy dropped his second blade and drew his dagger. Then he looked down at his opponent, the man who was so like his parent, except in every way that mattered.

"Blood from my blood." The older man's lips twisted into a thin smile.

Kennedy felt sudden revulsion flood through him. "You aren't my father – you're nothing more than a terrible copy," he roared. "My real father stands with me. He's at my shoulder, he's in my heart and he's in everything I ever do. You are not my father because my father STANDS – WITH – ME!"

The true Philip Kennedy, resplendent in his righteous fury, leapt off the sofa and charged. He could do what the empty husk in front of him could not, for it wasn't only his father who stood with him. His mother did too. He made sure his charge looked reckless enough to fool the grey-tinged opponent into staying in place and sprung his alter at the side of the room. Three strides away, Kennedy merged with his other self and hurled his dagger. His mother had insisted he was able to hit a rat at twenty paces. The man who was not his father was a far easier target.

The distraction worked, and the force of the throw buried the knife up to its hilt in the older man's stomach. As he took an involuntary step backwards, both Kennedy and his alter swept an arm along the library shelves and peppered the grey-tinged figure with a barrage of ancient books before he could summon his other self. Every tome was aimed directly at his head, and as a cloud of dust erupted around the man who was not his father, Kennedy charged again.

This time he didn't switch away at the last moment. Their blades crashed together in a whirlwind of sparks as he forced his not-father backwards with a series of devastating blows. The silver sword in his hands glowed brighter with every impact until, with a final mighty effort, Kennedy cleaved his blade through both of his not-father's in a single strike.

"Those are not your swords!"

Anticipating his opponent's attempt to escape, he summoned his alter in the doorway the split second before the older man's. As his not-father shimmered into flesh, Kennedy was already there, ready to thrust the silver sword deep into his chest.

"This is not your body!"

Ignoring the dagger in his enemy's hand, Kennedy swung his blade with every ounce of fury he had.

"AND YOU ARE NOT MY FATHER!"

The instant the headless husk hit the ground, Kennedy ripped open its shirt to reveal the jet black nail. The corpse was already flickering as if it was about to disappear like all the other dead soldiers when he thrust his fingers deep into the flesh. Gripping the icy obsidian, he yanked it free. The body jerked, shuddered and finally lay still.

"Fuck you, Cormydd."

Kennedy strode out of the room, tossing the nail on the couch as he passed.

※ ※ ※

ARKE WAS WAITING as the grey-tinged guardsmen forced their way back into the ballroom. Lewis had saved her from the mutant's magic, and though she hadn't been able to protect him from Joy, she could keep her away from the others. Her fingers were already coated with ice when the barrier fell, and she released her spell in an eruption of cold fury.

"JOY, DO YOU REMEMBER THIS?" she shouted, watching the frozen guardsmen splintering into glittering snow as their mindless fellows ploughed through them. "OR THIS?"

She hurled a barrage of magical energy darts at the doorway, demolishing both the wall and the ceiling above in a cascade of bricks, wood and plaster. With the massive pile of rubble blocking the entrance, the ballroom was now secure – at least until the soldiers found another route in.

Then the Soulbound strode towards the orangery, keen to draw Joy away from her crewmates before anyone else fell victim to her knives. "The Autarch wants to you to take me back to him." She stepped through the door and kept walking. "You want me? Here I am."

"LEFT!" Stabbington shouted.

She pivoted to avoid the stiletto strike and looked into Joy's face.

"It's just you and I here. Only us. Like that night we first met, in the stable of that inn. You were wearing that stupid mask. Do you remember? You tried to kill me, but I didn't want to hurt you."

"RIGHT!" Stabbington yelled.

Joy's knives hit empty air, and Arke's dive landed her among the shards of earthenware pots while her opponent's hollow eyes looked on impassively.

"I won't hurt you now. There must be some of you left. Some of my friend."

Appearing above her, Joy thrust downwards with her stilettos but the Soulbound rolled away and sprang back to her feet.

"LISTEN TO ME! Remember everything we did together! REMEMBER US!"

"Arke, I do not think she does," Stabbington warned.

"SHE HAS TO!"

The hilt of the demon blade lurched in her hands as Joy attacked from the right, the power of Stabbington's sudden defence hitting the knives so hard that one flew across the orangery.

Taking her opportunity, the Soulbound dropped her sword to tackle Joy, lifting her off her feet and slamming her into the mansion wall.

"Joy, listen to me. Please. You have to be in there!"

As quickly as Joy had vanished, she reappeared behind Arke, putting a leg between her legs and sending her crashing to the ground. The Soulbound grabbed Joy's knee to return the favour before grabbing her arm and twisting it, stopping only just before she dislocated the shoulder.

"Please, try to remember!"

That plea achieved nothing but another magical escape, and as Joy reappeared, she slammed a foot against the back of Arke's head, knocking her into the dirt before stamping on her right hand, the heel of her boot twisting and grinding with bone-breaking intensity.

※ ※ ※

THE WALL NEXT to the doorway of the ballroom was wobbling under the pressure of the soldiers behind it.

What was left of the *Warrior's* crew stood ready, even as the ceiling above them began to smoke, for the fire that had started by the courtyard was spreading across the entire building.

"We can finish this," Kennedy nodded, his mouth set in a grim line.

He strode into position opposite the impending breach with Ellie to his left and Urzish to his right. He'd been told Arke had led Joy into the orangery, but there was no time to worry about her now. He knew that behind the barricades were the walking wounded, crouching protectively around the seriously injured. He'd seen Irash coughing and choking on black bile, his body shuddering with magical exhaustion. He'd taken in the desperate sight of Ibu working frantically to save Lewis's life. He'd reassured a blood-soaked Krugg that he was certain the next *Just Say Go* could get him back on his feet. He'd stood silently by Klaus's corpse, and listened to Orville tell him how the Tiax, already badly hurt, had locked himself and Dozer in a room with three mages, defending the door so they could not escape the flames. The hellhound would reconstitute himself in his home plane, but Klaus was gone forever.

"Balls to the wall, captain." Ellie's eyes were narrowed in fury. "That's when we do our best work."

The barrier to the final battle collapsed in a rumbling flurry of dust and the Autarch's Elite Guard charged. Volk and Gabbi had been given all the guns and ammunition that remained, and they lay parallel to the breach, firing shot after shot. Blunderbuss followed pistol, followed musket, thinning them out, reducing the enemy's numerical advantage with every hit.

Memory's Claws

With the sudden whine of his jet engine at full power, Sparkz swooped over Kennedy's head and plunged through the mass of soldiers, toppling them like dominoes and continuing on out of sight.

"RUBY, LET HIM GO!"

Kevan, the crystal jaguar, had been a wild card, one they didn't want to use in case their meaty bodies tasted better to him than the enemy. But as Kennedy shouted, the Ornithol unleashed him and, with a feral snarl, he leapt at the enemies Sparkz had felled, ripping throats and gouging eyes as he charged down the corridor.

"COME ON!" Kennedy bellowed, striding forwards.

In the centre of the ballroom, Giro, the snail-like Vonti, could finally play an active part in the defence. Withdrawn into his shell, he was hurtling across the tiled floor and crashing into the enemy ranks. What didn't break under the impact of a gigantic carapace was knocked sideways or crushed under its weight.

Urzish charged towards the nearest guardsman, ripping the spear from his hands and shoving the blunt end into his throat before hurling herself further into the fray. To her left, Ellie had a dagger in each hand and was using her natural ability to stay low to its full advantage. She slid under heavy blows, slashed at legs to drop her enemies to the floor before driving her blades into them and rolling away before they grabbed her.

Still the enemy poured in, and, fully out of ammunition, Volk drew his sword as a cluster of them ran towards his position. Gabbi stood alongside him, cutlass in hand, the pair of them quickly obscured from view by the mass of guardsmen.

Giro cast another wind spell to launch himself across the room, but one of the soldiers saw him coming and lowered his spear, aiming the steel tip into the wide opening of the oncoming shell. Swinging the skewered Vonti around, his attacker launched him into Kennedy, who crashed to the floor, dropping his sword with the heavy impact.

As her captain fell, Ruby smashed her way through the melee towards him, her damaged wing bleeding and useless, but her yellow eyes snapping with rage. She was spinning, kicking, and activating her magical ring as she threw endless punches, the flames burning the soldier's faces and making them stagger sightlessly back.

Taking advantage of the distraction, Kennedy sprang his alter to where his sword had landed and merged with it before rejoining the fray.

"Sorry about disobeying orders, captain," Vaughan called as he yanked his blade from an enemy's chest. "One moment I was with the wounded, doing what I was told, and the next I was over here, stabbing some dull-eyed prick."

"I do so hate that when it happens." Orville grinned as he intercepted an axe that was swinging towards Vaughan before stepping inside the soldier's guard and burying his dagger in his throat.

Ruby continued her whirlwind charge across the battleground and finally burst through to where Volk and Gabbi had been fighting. The young man was standing over Volk's body, covered head to toe in blood, cutlass in one hand and the halfling's sword in the other, defending with a strength born of pure desperation. Two of the guardsmen attacking him turned to face her, but it was already too late. The Ornithol was spinning, and when she stopped, their bodies disappeared into nothingness.

Sparkz stumbled back through the breach, his armour battered and smoking, his helmet sliced open and blood dripping through the slash. "Courtyard's empty. They're done."

As Kennedy thrust his sword through the final blank-eyed soldier in his field of vision, he looked around in surprise. Sparkz was right, the Elite Guard were all gone.

"He's right!" Ellie panted, blood pouring down her neck from a slash to her cheek. "We did it!"

Kennedy turned slowly, checking on the rest of his crew. He saw an exhausted Kilar slump to the floor as Urzish wobbled over to a barricade, one hand pressed to her side. Ruby walked past carrying Volk's body over to Ibu, Gabbi following her like a lost sheep. Vaughan pulled out a hip flask and took a long swig before holding it to Orville's lips.

Still bleeding from his many wounds, Krugg hauled himself back to his feet. He limped slowly to the breach and peered through it in an almost comical fashion. "What? No more? I was feeling better – ready to hit things again."

The ogre turned to face Kennedy and suddenly stiffened, eyes springing wide open in shock as something sharp and invisible burst through his chest in a fountain of gore.

"We serve the Autarch."

The chanting echoed down the corridor.

"We serve the Autarch."

"EVERYONE FORM SQUARE AROUND THE WOUNDED!" Kennedy bellowed. "HURRY!"

⚔ ⚔ ⚔

IN THE ORANGERY, Arke scrambled to her feet, trying to ignore the pain from her broken hand as she waited for Joy's reappearance. After spinning away from the inevitable stiletto swipe, she fastened her gaze on her old friend's face before raising her hands.

"We had one rule, you and me. It was the first thing we agreed on. Do you remember? Respect the surrender." She knelt down, looking into Joy's empty eyes. "I surrender."

Lying in the weeds nearby, Stabbington's blade rattled furiously, but his host ignored the warning. This was Joy. When the Soulbound had been trapped in the statue, she had seen her fight the Autarch's power, she could do it again.

The reply was as unequivocal as it was instant. With a flick of Joy's wrist, a stiletto flew towards Arke's face. Her desperate grab halted it barely an inch away from her eyeball, the razor-sharp blade slicing deep into her skin.

Joy arrived behind her a second later, shoving a knee in her back while wrapping her own fingers around the handle to force it closer. The Soulbound tried to knock it aside with her shattered hand, but Joy was ready, catching it in a crushing grip and grinding the already broken bones together.

As that new agony weakened her resistance, the tip of the grey-tinged knife plunged into her eye.

Pain exploded in her head and her orange magic exploded in reaction. Power surged unbidden from her palm, firing the stiletto across the greenhouse to land with a clatter at the far end.

Joy grabbed her by the collar and threw her into an old planter, then followed, punching her in the temple before hauling her to her feet, swinging her stumbling form around and hurling her through a broken pane of glass.

Rolling to a stop in the grass outside the orangery, Arke struggled to her knees, one hand pressed over her eye and orange magic surging through her with boiling fury. The world was spinning with the agony in her head, and she could barely hold back the nausea that had gripped her after the knife had pierced her eyeball. Her first thought was for Stabbington, and she recalled him quickly, feeling a rush of warmth the instant he returned.

"Arke, please listen before she kills you, Joy is gone. This is not her." Stabbington's voice was unusually empathetic, his tone soft as he attended to the worst of her pain. "My magical morphine will not last long. You need to end her while you can still function."

From inside the ballroom, the sounds of desperate combat had barely ceased before chanting began to echo around the mansion.

Arke forced herself to her feet, using Stabbington as a lever to help her rise.

"The invisible soldiers," she hissed.

"If they are here, then maybe we are winning? LEFT!"

She spun away, but as she did, she almost lost her footing and instinctively flung out both arms to balance herself, leaving her injured eye uncovered.

Reeling with both horror and shock, Arke discovered the knife had not blinded her as she'd expected. Instead, she could see more than before. Way, way more. She could see past the Autarch's facsimile of Joy. She could see the truth behind the facade. And, more importantly to her survival, she could also see where the shell of her friend wove in and out of the ethereal plane.

"NOW we are winning!" Stabbington's voice was triumphant.

She steadied herself. "I still need to get that nail."

"You need to be CAREFUL," he warned. "You can see her, but you are injured and she is not."

"Not yet."

The Soulbound whirled and fired off a barrage of magical energy darts as not-Joy flicked into full reality, and watched with satisfaction as she retreated immediately. The same thing happened four times in a row and Stabbington commented that even the original Joy wouldn't have taken so long to work out that something had changed.

Finally, the Autarch's servant reappeared some twenty feet away and began to pace around Arke like a frustrated animal.

"You aren't Joy." The Soulbound chose not to attack immediately and just watched her opponent's movements. "You're a handful of cosmic vomit using her body to hide in."

The thing which, to a normal eye, looked like Joy, threw herself towards the Soulbound in a series of flips and tumbles. Just before she was in range of the demon sword, she ducked into a dive, aiming for Arke's legs. And stopped, her neck pinned to the ground by

Stabbington's blade. Her eyes were still open, and she was alive, but the Soulbound's perfectly timed strike had rendered her helpless.

"You didn't get all of her or you'd know I taught her that move."

Arke pulled her sword clear and flipped the body over, spotting the obsidian nail and using Stabbington's blade to lever it up. As soon as it began to rise, she eased it free with her fingers and launched it as far from her as she could.

The sound of chanting from the burning mansion ceased abruptly, and as she looked up, she saw the two grey-tinged sky ships accelerating away to the east.

Levering herself to her feet, the Soulbound heard boots pounding across the grass towards her and heaved a slow, tired breath as she gazed down at not-Joy. Kennedy stopped next to her, one hand reaching for her shoulder and squeezing it gently.

"Arke, she's not coming back."

"I know."

And if she looked through her left eye, she did know. She could see the past the perfect facade, through the grey-tinged magic, and into the void where Joy had once been.

If she shut that eye, she could see the expressionless face with its hollow eyes and sallow skin.

So she shut them both and saw Joy.

She saw how she laughed. How she hugged. How she cursed and shouted and cried and teased and punched and pouted and threw all of herself – wildly, excitedly, and wilfully, into every single breath she took.

Arke knew the Autarch had made her dream of her friends in order to control her, but in the end, all he'd done was release her from the guilt that had locked their memories away for so long. She was free, and now they were too.

She opened her eyes and thrust her sword through the core of the creature that was not Joy until its tip lodged into the ground beneath.

"Thanks for the memories."

Memory's Claws

Glossary

Aetheric – a concentrated, crystalline form of magic which can be harnessed as a power source. Aetheric crystals are made in Nidea so are both expensive and illegal in Barsia.

Barsian Empire – commonly referred to as Barsia; covering a large landmass, hugely influential until the Night of Terrors where it lost both its capital and its ruler, the Autarch. Now ruled by a High Council of nobles and religious leaders who are focussed only on survival through laws and taxes.

Bonelords – an ancient tribe living in the Greyspine Mountains, known only for their unusual armour and ferocious opposition to outsiders.

Bior – a race of metal constructs who gained sentience during the Night of Terrors. They are all uniform in basic appearance and similar in overall outlook, being loyal and inclined to serve.

Flotilla – a floating anchorage over the north central part of Nidea, below the Barsian border.

Fullport – a small coastal town on the Azure Straits, the hub for Barsia's southern fishery fleet.

Greyspine Mountains – the greatest mountain range in Barsia. Hellish in every way, inhabited by savage tribespeople. No-one in their right, left or central minds would go there.

High Haven – a unique floating city anchored over the Azure Straits on the border between Barsia and Nidea. Free in every way and fiercely protective of its independent status. No laws, no taxes, no guarantees.

Jumpstart a Heart – a potion which does exactly what it says on the label.

Just Say Go – a magical healing/energising drink. It's fluorescent green and hits with the equivalent of twenty espressos. If you don't wake up with that, you aren't even trying.

Mage – a wielder of magic. Since the Night of Terrors, Barsia requires any mages to be sent to internment camps or officially licenced.

Nidean Empire – commonly referred to as Nidea, located to the south of Barsia. A loose collection of principalities, all united in their use of magic and their distrust of each other. Once a vassal state of Barsia, now fully independent, Nidea is only one charismatic ruler short of declaring war.

Night Of Terrors – the night when Great Barsia, the capital of the Barsian Empire, and everyone within a hundred miles were removed from existence by a huge magical explosion. The shockwave that surged outwards from the epicentre killed and created in equal measure. Two hundred years later, Barsia is still trying to recover, unsanctioned magic is now illegal and the area around Great Barsia still an irradiated swamp.

Levenbrandt – the Bastion City of northwest Barsia. A small and picturesque but ancient city isolated by geography, Levenbrandt's ruler is not considered powerful enough for a seat on the High Council.

Orbella – a truly ancient mountainside city, constantly vying with Tattenberg for capital status but always falling short due to its constrained size. This is a city of modern marvels, clean air and deep thinkers.

Orbiculum – a magical way to kick down doors

between planes. Very much banned in Barsia.

Ornithol – a race of birdlike people who came into existence after the Night of Terrors. There are as many types of Ornithol as breeds of bird in Barsia. They all look like giant versions of their parent bird, with the addition of humanoid arms and legs.

Soleya – the religious capital of Barsia. Situated to the southeast of the Empire, Soleya houses the most temples and cathedrals of any city anywhere. Soleya is strongly ruled and deeply conservative.

Soulbound – selling your soul to a powerful entity in return for wealth, power or other gains makes you a Soulbound. The contracts are usually long, detailed and absolutely binding.

Tattenberg – the capital of Barsia since the Night of Terrors. Tattenberg is 'where work is life'. A hive of industry, its skies are always grey with smog, its innovative might and productive factories second to none.

Theogenes – situated to the southwest of Barsia. A beautiful coastal city, bathed in perpetual sunlight. The main city is perfectly designed and heavily regulated.

Tiax – a race of fox-like people. They range from nearly hairless and very humanoid to almost feral looking. Yes, the Night of Terrors again.

Vonti – a race of sentient snails with vaguely humanoid characteristics. Night of Terrors, you say? You'd be right. Almost unnaturally attuned to the natural world, they're slow and deliberate, in general, they have found Barsian life far too fast moving for their tastes.

Warrior – the best ship ever.

Memory's Claws

Coming Soon
Loyalty's Chains
The Barsian Job: Part 3

"A*NYONE NEED A change of underwear?*" Kazhar looked around the table at the other gods before pouring himself a glassful of whisky. "That was tense."

"They won!" Nehru smiled, biting into a gargantuan chocolate chip muffin.

"They did well, given the circumstances," Chromatia stood up, tugging on the cuffs of her multi-coloured shirt.

"Really? Even you, Chromatia? You're calling that a victory?" Thum snarled.

"Yes. So pay up, buddy." Kazhar grinned. "Your grudge against Arke is making me rich."

"It's not a grudge. Look what just happened! She's an emotional wreck. Utterly unfit for purpose."

"That was always going to be hard for her," Nehru retorted. "They were her best friends, the nearest thing to family she remembers."

"Oh, here it comes! We ALL know what you really mean, Nehru!" snapped Thum. "Try whining about something other than Arke's bloody memories!"

Nehru lurched to her feet. "What you did was barbaric!"

"It was necessary." Endraza raised a calming hand. *"If she remembered our roles then Cormydd would have seen it the first time he looked in her mind."*

"Thum didn't have to take all of her childhood. All of who she was." Nehru slammed the cupcake back on her plate.

"We had to be thorough, to make sure there was no trace of us in her head." Endraza held Nehru's gaze for a long moment. *"Plus, who she was back then – it wasn't good enough."*

"It still isn't," Thum growled.

"She was a CHILD!" Nehru protested.

"And now she's an adult." Chromatia shrugged, slowly turning to focus her eyes on Thum. *"Her weaknesses are mitigated by our people, and no-one can deny their success."*

"I…" Thum began.

"No more arguments," Endraza interrupted. *"Thum, concentrate on your part. Your man is in play – she needs stability, and he will provide that."*

"He's not a miracle worker." Thum folded his arms and scowled.

"Shows how little you know about love!" Nehru snapped.

Endraza swept to her feet. *"She's learning and she's growing. We play the long game and everything is aligning exactly as it should."*

Acknowledgements

EVERYONE NEEDS THEIR very own version of Ruby, a one woman cheerleading squad, a purveyor of the finest snacks, a willing participant in every crazy idea, and the possessor of the most unexpectedly savage wit this side of Nidea. I know, because I have one – her name is Jamie and she's absolutely awesome. No, you can't have her; yes, she's as amazing as she sounds; and no, she's not an actual Ornithol, even though she would undoubtedly love to be able to fly. She's also a harsh taskmaster, nagging me to start getting her favourite book in the series, *Loyalty's Chains,* ready to publish. Don't worry, Jamie, it's up next!!!

ONCE AGAIN, I couldn't do this without my full back-up crew, the Hamsters of the Apocalypse. They are invaluable, incredible and in my office while I'm trying to work.

OTHER THANKS GO to my editor, Francesca Tyer, and my artist, Nataly Zhuk, both of whom go above and beyond to help me bring the books from draft to print.

LASTLY, A BIG thank you to my publishers, my beta readers and all my wonderful friends who have been so excited and supportive right from the start.

www.fjmitchell.co.uk

Memory's Claws